Bolan wasn't a man given to rage or petty revenge

But blood cried out for blood, and he was reminded of the origin of his crusade in the spirit of vengeance for his fallen family. He fought the anger, wrestled it under control, harnessing that fury and force into the power and precision he would need to carry off his penetration into the hell zone this night.

Avenge the dead and protect those yet untouched.

The first motto was allowed to run its course, because that activity inevitably would lead him to the second vow. Dead terrorists weren't nearly as good at killing innocents. Not when they were swept away by the cleansing flames of the Executioner.

Rage and vengeance, though, took the Executioner only so far. The rest came from a soldier's duty to protect those he was sworn to defend.

Don Pendleton's Mack Bolan®
Season of Slaughter

A GOLD EAGLE BOOK FROM
WORLDWIDE®

TORONTO • NEW YORK • LONDON
AMSTERDAM • PARIS • SYDNEY • HAMBURG
STOCKHOLM • ATHENS • TOKYO • MILAN
MADRID • WARSAW • BUDAPEST • AUCKLAND

To Bobbi, for making the dark shine

First edition July 2005

ISBN 0-373-61506-X

Special thanks and acknowledgment to
Douglas P. Wojtowicz for his contribution to this work.

SEASON OF SLAUGHTER

Of all the Causes which conspire to blind
Man's erring Judgment, and misguide the Mind,
What the weak Head with strongest bias rules,
Is Pride, the never-failing Vice of Fools.
> —Alexander Pope,
> *Essay on Criticism,* Part II

Terrorists are motivated by their pride and their
hatred, which blind them to the truth. And that is
their fatal mistake.
> —Mack Bolan

CHAPTER ONE

The two men had birth names, but long ago they'd decided to lose them. Now the tall men were known by the authorities of a dozen nations simply as Adonis and Dark. They were men for hire and had the reputation of being the world's finest.

Despite a forty-six-inch chest and twenty-four-inch biceps testing the strength of a red-and-gold gymnasium T-shirt, the long-haired, blond Adonis didn't draw more than a passing glance. His arms and hands were criss-crossed with scratches, cuts and furrows from bullets over the years, and one hand gripped the heavy nylon straps of two, five-foot-long duffel bags. Only the veins bulging on the back of his hand and forearm showed any sign of effort as he strode along the airport terminal.

"Your choice. Security or radar?" Adonis asked.

In comparison, Dark was just as tall as his six-foot-six partner, but where the blond giant had his head rising above the crowd, the other kept his long, black-tressed head nestled tightly between his shoulders, hunching as if against a chill in the air. It was fifty-five degrees, and the sun shone brightly, making Dark wince more tightly behind his wraparound shooting glasses. At the question of his partner, his face split into a grin.

"I'll take the fun job," he said, his tone as cold and grating as a shovel in grave dirt, a faint hint of a British accent to his voice.

Adonis chuckled and handed the dark man a smaller bag. "Sure, leave me with the heavy lifting."

"You know you love it, Captain Beefcake."

Adonis looked his friend up and down, then nodded. "Be careful."

Dark slung the smaller satchel over his shoulder and gave Adonis a conspiratorial wink. "Then how would I enjoy myself?"

WEARINESS DOGGED Carl Lyons as he arrived at the airport with the van full of blacksuits and trainees. The men with him were a mix of familiar faces and strangers. After training and a full indoctrination, they would all be made part of the guard force at one of the nation's most elite nerve centers in the fight against terrorism. Jack Grimaldi was waiting at a helipad at Dulles, ready to take them all back to Stony Man Farm to begin the training.

Closing in on the terminal, the Able Team warrior became more mindful of the heavy Colt Python in its shoulder holster. Soldiers at every terminal were armed with M-16s and Berettas. Washington police were also on hand, MP-5s on slings, .40-caliber Glock pistols in Sam Browne belts. He wondered briefly at the cause of the new national Orange Terror alert, but he didn't want to confuse the issue by being part of a heavily armed group of men heading through an airport.

At a glance, he realized five of the nine men he was with were armed with at least a handgun.

"Make sure your law-enforcement identification is visible as we're going through the airport," Lyons told the men. "We don't need Homeland Security jumping down our throats if they discover that we're carrying."

There was a chuckle among the familiar members of the group, but Lyons wasn't sharing in it. He'd been on the line with Able Team too often and forced into open conflict with members of the CIA or supposedly friendly foreign government agencies.

He glanced to a stocky little fireplug of a guy who was riding shotgun beside him. With a full face that lent him a cherubic demeanor and crystal-blue eyes that seemed alive with the thoughts swirling behind them, he seemed on automatic pilot. He was a veteran of the blacksuit program, and the Able Team leader remembered that this guy had actually accompanied Mack Bolan in the field in a desperate mission in Egypt.

"You all right?" Lyons asked.

David Kowalski gave his chest a rub, tracing a line across his torso. "Just thinking about getting back to work, sir."

"Don't call me sir. I work for a living."

Kowalski had his leather jacket in his lap and Lyons evaluated him with a glance. His arms were long and slender, giving the illusion of leanness despite the fact that the muscles under the skin shifted tightly. No, he wasn't a power-lifter as Lyons was, but there was strength in the corded ropes hiding under the skin. A more apparent gauge of his strength was the stretch of his T-shirt, showing off a chest that rivaled his own.

The whole effect reminded Lyons of a pit bull.

Kowalski withdrew a chain from under his T-shirt collar, then bent to sit upright and don his jacket, covering the shoulder holster.

"Southpaw?" Lyons asked.

"Despite every effort to cure me, sir."

"What did I say about calling me 'sir'?"

Kowalski smiled. "You never gave me anything else to call you."

"Call me Ironman."

"Ski."

Lyons nodded. "Okay, gang. Wait here. I'm going to drop off the van and then we'll be off to the Farm. Don't wander too far, and no more than fifty pounds of loot from the duty-free shop. Any more and we start dumping you out of the chopper."

This time Lyons shared in some of the mirth that rippled through the back of the van. Kowalski chuckled, but got lost again in thoughts of a future in conflict.

ADONIS PAUSED as he watched the group of men getting out of the van. They all had the look of hardened professionals—well-trained police or military men—and he didn't doubt that they were together for a reason. He knew that Washington, D.C., was the center of a lot of law enforcement and military training resources, both official and unofficial, and together they looked like students en route to one of their classes.

He had attended a couple local schools around the area, which had been part of how he'd continued to hone his deadly tradecraft. Most of it was from hands-on training, but there was something to be said for a controlled classroom environment.

Adonis continued along, carrying his gear, the only sign of anything out of the ordinary being the way his muscles rippled up and down his long arms as he gripped the heavy duffels. The new missile systems were supposed to be man-portable, but the launcher and its four rocket shells still strained against the 250-pound-test nylon on the duffel straps. He made his way through the terminal lobby, relatively invisible for the sheer fact that his T-shirt and bags sported the emblems of the Washington Redskins.

A few travelers whispered as he walked by, but they assumed him to be one of the giants who wore shoulder pads on the offensive or defensive lines of the football field, not a mercenary who had moved beyond being a pawn on a battlefield. A wave of revulsion washed over Adonis as he passed people.

He was glad that the RING had established most of these people as expendable in its crusade to make the world a better place.

"Can't make an omelet without breaking a few eggs," he mused under his breath.

A couple of green-and-brown camouflaged young men walked toward him and he smirked. Who could believe in a government that issued woodland camouflage to people patrolling an airport? It reminded him of the novelty T-shirt he once saw—the same patterned camou with big white letters reading Ha, Ha, I'm Wearing Camouflage. You Can't See Me."

If it was to make them more visible, he would have to think that a military uniform and an M-16 rifle were about as blatantly obvious a sign that they were armed forces personnel as was needed.

"Sir?" One of the young men spoke up.

Adonis kept walking, ignoring him.

The other one stepped in front of him.

Adonis smiled, continuing to walk, bumping the man aside. It was only then that he stopped and looked at the wide-eyed youngster. "I'm sorry. I didn't see you. It must have been the camouflage," Adonis quipped.

"Like we haven't heard that twenty times today," one of the National Guardsmen said almost soft enough not to be heard.

"We'd like to take a look inside your bags," the other guardsman said. He didn't seem so authoritative now.

Adonis shrugged and smiled. "Go right ahead."

He set both bags down, letting them clunk against the floor tiles with a resounding thump. The Guardsmen bent to pick up the bags and found themselves pulled off balance by the sheer weight. Adonis sighed at their relatively poor physical condition before he looked at his palms, rubbed red and raw by the nylon straps despite the heavy calluses put on them by his long career.

"What do you have in these things?" the first asked.

"Missile launchers," Adonis said coolly.

The guardsman paused while the other unzipped the other bag and choked back a horrified response.

The two looked at each other for an instant, but it might as well have been an eternity.

Adonis was in motion, one of his long legs sweeping up from the floor in a savage scythe of speed, the toe reaching up and crushing into the throat of the man kneeling over the open duffel. Blood erupted from the guardsman's lips, his head snapping up and back, body lifted from the ground by the savage force of the kick. The giant professional didn't need any more evaluation than the feel of crunching cartilage on his toes to know his first victim was dead.

Adonis spun on the other guardsman, who was frantically clawing for his rifle, mouth opening to scream. Instead one massive paw closed over his victim's face, his other hand chopping down hard on the guardsman's forearm. Bone snapped on impact, satisfying the big man as he yanked his victim off his feet. A pistoning fist flashed up and into the rib cage, again producing the crunching impact of destroyed bones. The young soldier spasmed, eyes staring pleadingly.

"I'll be merciful," Adonis whispered. He brought up his other hand, wrapped it around the dying man's head and gave a savage twist. The breaking neck sounded like a cracking tree branch and the body slumped to the ground.

Adonis evaluated how long the two kills took and realized that the crowd around him was still silent, trying to figure out what was going on. Barely a few seconds, he figured as he closed his duffel and calmly picked up both bags, continuing on to his date with the tarmac.

It was up to Dark to provide the distraction he'd need to get out there.

DARK WALKED with purpose now, dangling the satchel at his side with playful glee. His head had risen from between his shoulders and he moved with a grace and smoothness belying his intent. Passing between the glass doors of the terminal, he paused and hung the strap of his bag around his neck.

"Ladies and gentlemen!"

The crowd slowed, looking at him. Out of the corner of one eye, the camouflaged shapes of National Guardsmen shifted, their attention drawn to him.

"May I have your undivided attention for a moment?" Dark called.

He plunged both his hands into his bag and withdrew two guns that looked as if they belonged in a science-fiction movie. They were Calico 950 submachine guns, sleek, angled weapons with long, helical magazines that could fit fifty or one-hundred rounds in a tube magazine across the back. Dark, naturally, had had his Calicos fitted with 100-round magazines, extras securely strapped down just past the mouth of the open bag.

He planned to make noise and cause carnage, both in vastly liberal amounts.

One National Guardsman, a young black woman, spotted the weapons first and started to go for the Beretta on her hip. He gave her a moment to cry, "Gun!" then leveled his left Calico at her, tapping off a burst.

Blood exploded from the woman's shoulder and face, her body spinning to the ground. Other National Guardsmen cried out in surprise and outrage as she fell. Dark pivoted in a half turn and, punching his right Calico toward them, swept the two men with a longer burst, fanning them down with a wind of 9 mm Parabellum death.

Screams exploded in the terminal and Dark leaped from his vantage point, his long coat flowing behind him like the leather wings of a devil. People were running, scrambling to get away from the figure in black that had just exploded into a fit of murder right before their eyes. He crouched deeply, to take advantage of running bodies as a shield against more oncoming soldiers and security people, then held down the triggers on both Calicos. Pivoting and firing, he swept the crowd for a good three seconds, sixty rounds flying uncontrollably in a wild storm of destruction. Bodies slammed into the ground, some struck by bullets, others thrown down by the panicking crowd that stampeded and trampled over them.

Dark never could get over his giddy surprise at how easy it was to turn a crowded, public venue into a charnel house simply by inciting a little panic. Bodies were strewed about. He figured there were twenty to thirty of them, all motionless, only a few of them people he'd actually slain with a bullet, the rest crushed underfoot by squealing, terrified, so-called "innocent bystanders."

He moved out of the center of the walkway, hitting a shoulder roll over a ticket counter.

A blond ticket woman went white-faced at the sight of him landing almost on top of her. Clear blue eyes regarded him with abject horror and she curled even tighter into a ball.

"Please! Please don't hurt me...."

"Hush," he admonished, putting down his gun.

She seemed to relax from a state of paralyzed panic, looking back into his face. She probably thought he was going to take her hostage. Dark instead stiffened his hand and sliced it hard into her exposed throat. She gave a small kick, her head striking the counter, throat folding and collapsing over his hand. Blood began to seep from the corner of her mouth and her nostrils, her gemlike eyes still staring at him. Dark closed them with a two-fingered caress, then dug into his bag with his free hand. He withdrew a canister and thumbed out a ringed pin.

The ruthless black-clad murderer casually flipped the canister out and over the counter and, opening his mouth, screamed to equalize the pressure inside and outside of his skull just as the grenade went off on the other side.

He scooped up the other Calico and rose swiftly. He felt the concussion rolling off the stun grenade's detonation. Looking over the counter, he saw a hallway full of staggered security officers and National Guardsmen. With a single bound, Dark reached the counter, his trench coat billowing around him, obscuring his body and making him that much harder of a target to hit. Bullets whipped at him, but missed, either by inches or altogether.

The blazing-muzzle flashes of the Calicos signaled more bodies jerking under multiple impacts as the long legs of the trench-coat-clad gunman drove him across the terminal's hallway, stopping just as he spotted a knot of frightened travelers.

Spinning, Dark fired the way he had come, then hit the ground, sliding on the slick tiles as return fire chased after him, bullets sweeping and punching into the crowd of civilians. People screamed, a chorus of pain and death cries that were a symphony to the man in black.

"Oh, God! Stop! Stop shooting!" he heard over the din of his enemies' gunfire.

Dark stuck his left Calico in his bag and pulled out another grenade. This one was a fragmentation bomb, which he armed and skidded along the floor. It bounced off a window overlooking the airfield, then exploded as it skittered toward the defenders of Dulles International.

Dark didn't need to see the effects of hundreds of segments of wire propelled at almost a thousand feet per second to realize he'd cut himself a little bit of breathing room.

He took a moment to savor the sight of the carnage. It wasn't every day you unleashed a taste of hell on a major international airport, after all.

DAVID KOWALSKI SPUN in surprise when he heard the distant rattle of submachine guns. He dropped the magazine he'd been perusing, hands instantly plunging under his jacket, his left clawing for the sleek Beretta 92-F in its shoulder holster, his right flipping out the reassuring weight of the neck wallet bearing his badge and U.S. Marshals identification. He spun, looking to

"Carl Stone," the alias used be Carl Lyons. The big blond guy was already out the front of the duty-free shop.

The clerk at the counter was torn between shouting at the rush of men scattering perilously perched shelf items to the floor and diving under the counter at the sight of firepower filling their hands.

"Get on the phone to security!" Kowalski shouted. "Tell them they've got a dozen ASLET conference attendees moving to help back them up!"

"Ass let?" the clerk asked.

"We're Feds going for special training! Call!"

He spun and was heading in the direction of the gunfire when he heard the first grenade rumble in the distance. His thick legs pistoned faster, and though he didn't have the typical trim, long legs of a classic runner, what he lacked in stride he made up for in thrust. Soon, he was past several of the blacksuits and hot on the heels of Carl Lyons.

"What took you so long?" Lyons asked.

"Got the clerk to call security." Kowalski was already starting to feel breathless from the effort of keeping up with Lyons. He figured that somewhere along the line, the big blond warrior was a semipro athlete, maybe college football. Kowalski always hated running after those types because they never seemed to run out of breath even after the longest chases. "Don't need the situation confused."

"Quick thinking," Lyons growled. He looked up to see a knot of airport security men suddenly blown off their feet by a billowing cloud accompanied by a thunderclap.

The injured filled the air with shrieks and screams.

"Ski, you help with first aid and triage," Lyons grunted.

Kowalski paused, looking out the window. "Someone's outside."

Lyons turned his head, spotting the figure walking across the tarmac toward the taxiing airplanes, carrying two massive duffel bags in his hands. Behind him lay the crumpled form of a single man in the blue-and-black uniform of an airport security officer. "He's going to fire missiles at the jets moving to take off. If he hits them in the right spot, that aviation fuel is going to light them up…"

"Fielding, Jacobs, you've got EMT training. Help these guys," Kowalski shouted. He'd summoned up from his depths the exact mimicry of his old drill sergeant's voice. The barks got the men automatically moving, clearing them of doubts of what needed to be done.

He looked back to Lyons, who nodded in grim approval. "All right. Ski, take Newport, Roberts and Pullman and stop that big bastard on the field. The rest of you, grab a long-arm and on me!"

Lyons scooped up an M-16 and a couple of magazines and tossed them to Kowalski.

The stocky blacksuit raced toward the window, aiming his M-16 ahead of him and blowing out the glass. With a running leap, he was through the broken window, legs pumping the air as he realized that bullets were shearing the space behind him. Roberts wasn't jumping from the second-story window to the tarmac, but instead tumbling in a shredded stump of gory flesh.

Newport and Pullman made the jump, Pullman landing hard and twisting his ankle.

Kowalski didn't fane much better, his knees aching from taking the impact of a twelve-foot drop with very little flex. The pain would really kick in later, when his adrenaline high wore off. He dumped the magazine on his rifle and fed a fresh one home.

"Freeze! Federal officer!" Kowalski bellowed. He didn't expect the mysterious giant with the duffel bags to stop, but he hoped at least to catch the guy's attention. His finger pulled through the two-stage trigger break in anticipation of a better torso shot. The big man moved, all right.

He danced effortlessly out of the path of Kowalski's first fusillade of autofire. The muscular monster moved with the grace of some giant cat, slipping back to tear open the first duffel bag and pull out a missile launcher. Before Ski could chase down with the rest of the magazine, the man ducked behind a refueling truck.

"Hold your fire!" Kowalski shouted.

Newport held his fire, and Ski looked back to Pullman. The injured blacksuit wasn't getting up from where he'd collapsed on his injured leg, but he was positioned in a classic "seated rifleman" pose, the sling of his M-16 wrapped tight around his off-hand forearm. Even in the face of personal injury, Kowalski wasn't giving up.

"Get prone, Pullman!" Ski ordered.

The stocky Pullman swung his legs beneath him and winced as his elbows scraped concrete. His mustached face was pressed close behind the sights of the M-16, and he presented a much smaller target now.

Kowalski and Newport raced to the rear of the refueling truck. The big blonde hadn't made a move, but nobody would dare take a shot. If the fuel inside the "little" tank was ignited, the fireball would kill everything for a hundred feet, including innocents inside the terminal.

Kowalski waved his hand to Newport, who apparently got the picture. Kowalski was using the standard

L.A.P.D. SWAT sign language, a nationally recognized system that allowed approaching officers to communicate without alerting a perpetrator.

He swung around the left of the truck. Newport took the right. It was a lightning-quick dash; no way the big blond could react to two people charging him all-out.

Kowalski rammed into what felt like a brick wall and tumbled backward.

CHAPTER TWO

Carl Lyons crouched against the corner as Parabellum rounds ripped and roared from the bottomless helical magazines of the madman's Calico SMGs. With a surge of his thick, powerful legs, the Able Team leader somersaulted out onto the floor, tracking up with his Colt Python .357 Magnum slugs slashing at the tall figure in black.

Whoever this guy was, he walked like a miniature version of Godzilla, wading through the boot-deep dead and injured as if they were rubble not worthy of a second glance.

Kowalski had given a loud police warning to the guy outside, issued with a bellowing set of lungs that would do any Marine proud. Lyons didn't waste time with a warning. Instead his first action against the murderer with the black, fluttering coat was to open fire.

The man in black leather seemed to ignore the two solid hits that Lyons placed on target and the Ironman knew it had to be body armor. He was shifting up, trying for a head shot, when a storm of 9 mm slugs ripped at the tile leading up to him. With a fraction of a heartbeat to spare, Lyons rolled, curling up in a ball as twin lines of detonations snarled past him, marble-colored ceramic erupting in countless volcanoes. A pair of slugs managed to knife across Lyons's forearm, wide strips torn from his heavily muscled limb.

"Tag, you're it," Dark said, chuckling, backing away as blacksuits poured around the corner to Lyons's defense.

"Play tag with this!" the blond commando growled. Aiming low and lunging to his feet, Lyons only managed to nick the thigh of the mass murderer with his third shot.

Dark took a half stumble, then spun, sweeping at chest height.

"Down!" Lyons bellowed, diving to the floor again. He felt a bullet pluck at his hair as he slammed into the floor. His Colt Python skittered loose from his hands, knocked free by the impact. He kept moving forward, hands clawing at floor, forcing himself not to look back at the men who were probably dead or injured from the madman's latest fusillade.

He'd have plenty of time to take care of the injured once he put a total stop to this madman.

Dark's twin Calicos, spitting out fireballs of deadly fury, were swiveling to track him. Lyons could hear shouting over the rat-tat-tat of the dual machine pistols.

"Adonis! Adonis! Get that missile up and away!" Dark shouted.

The Calicos ran empty just as their black muzzles stared Lyons in the eyes.

"One hundred shots only, creep," Lyons growled. He took Dark with his shoulder, ramming home with all the force of his two hundred pounds. It was like shoulder-blocking a child's blow-up punching bag.

Dark gave resistance for a moment, then disappeared, the trench coat snapping and slapping across Lyons's face.

A rapidly descending elbow hit Lyons in the small of his back, but the Able Team leader was moving so fast, the strike slipped off him. He skidded to a halt, looking back at the man who, gathering his leather trench coat tightly around him, smirked at the big, blond ex-cop.

"You're either lucky or you're good," Dark said.

"Being both never hurt," Lyons attested. This time his leap wasn't a football tackle but the savage pounce of a predatory cat, his arms lashing out. He didn't manage to grapple Dark, but he felt his hand go numb from where he punched the murderer in the collarbone. There was a loud grunt of pain, but the tall pillar of black leather and attitude spun, bringing a forearm up into Lyons's ribs.

Air exploded from his lungs and he slapped face-first into the ground.

Lyons pushed himself off his belly, curling up and rolling to one side as he heard the batlike rustle of the trench coat's tail flaps beat the air like wings. Any slower, the big ex-cop realized, and those two, steel-soled boots that shattered floor tile like eggshells would have crushed him into a pulpy red mess. Lyons lashed upward, snapping a kick into Dark's midsection, blowing him off his heels, making him scramble backward.

Lyons was up again in a moment, bringing up his forearms as Dark waded in with *shuto* palm strikes and *kenpo* knuckle punches. He blocked and deflected most of the strokes, cursing himself for being thrown onto the defensive. Usually his tactics were to attack, not pussy-foot around.

Doing just that left the Able Team leader reeling backward. If he survived this battle, his forearms would be blackened masses of bruises. With a sudden wriggle, Lyons was out of the path of the darting fists and suddenly inside the range of those long, looping arms. Dark had about an extra six inches of reach, but that was a weakness because arms that long usually belonged to fighters who would fight at maximum distance. Lyons had learned to fight with long kicks and punches, and close-range strikes and knees.

Leading with his left knee and following up with a pistoning right hand, Lyons felt Dark's torso thump loudly with his impacts. A head butt rebounded off the terrorist's nose and lips, sending a cascading spray of gore pouring down into the Able Team leader's eyes. Half blinded by the blood, he was encouraged and even inspired to inflict more damage. He was a wild animal, moving in for the kill. A quick alternating hammering of lefts and rights struck Dark in the ribs and abdominal muscles. The savage barbarian that Lyons had become reached around to try to smash the kidneys of his prey, but the tall target in black always kept half twisted away from the mauling clubs swinging at his vulnerable organs.

Pain exploded under Lyons's jaw, flipping his head back. A knee managed to snap through his defenses and catch him right under the navel. The rocket-like knee-stroke made him convulse. Hands clasped behind Lyons's skull and pulled him forward. In desperation, like a heavily muscled turtle, the big ex-cop tucked his head in tight, his shoulder muscles sheathing his spine and lower skull in thick, heavy sinews.

Dark tossed Lyons over his hip, dropping him to the ground. The floor was cold and harsh but he knew how to take a fall. Lyons wrapped his bullet-gouged arm around the black-denim-clad leg of his adversary and wrenched hard, sending the man stumbling off his feet and into a double kick that only through grace and agility didn't end in shattered ribs.

"Adonis!" Dark called.

Lyons glanced out the window as he saw something streak from the ground. He rolled to a combat crouch, pulling his backup Colt .45 from its holster. Maybe a .45-caliber slug would stop a missile in midflight toward its run against an airplane.

The missile was homing in on a jumbo jet hanging heavily in the sky, and Lyons opened fire, hoping against hope to hit the lazily climbing rocket, glass shattering as his first slugs burst through to chase the missile.

Then the damn thing swerved, looping crazily.

Lyons prayed for a second that his gunfire had cut off the missile, but horror stabbed deep into his heart as he realized that the missile had a lock.

It was tearing toward the radar tower down the airstrip.

"Dammit, no!" Lyons bellowed. Suddenly the gun was kicked from his hand.

The fight with Dark wasn't over yet.

ADONIS LET the empty launcher drop as he watched the radar tower disappear. It was painted a dull maroon red, but when the shaped-charge warhead struck it at 400 meters per second, it disappeared into a yellow-white flash of flame, blackened steel chunks tumbling through the air.

He turned back toward the pair of lawmen on the tarmac. He was torn between crushing them to bits and making for his extraction rendezvous. Decision made, he knelt at the second bag and flipped open a folded-down LCD screen. The second bag was actually the carrying case for a man-portable Satellite Communications System.

Fixx had put this piece together for just this occasion.

He picked up the radio mouthpiece, slipped a Desert Eagle from a side pocket in case anyone got antsy around him.

"This is Dulles International. We're sorry for that glitch," Adonis said. He made his voice an octave deeper to convey that air-traffic-control-professional flavor. "Everything should be all right now."

There were dozens of questions clambering over the lines as Adonis ran his big, blunt fingertips across the keyboard of the SCS box. He closed the lid and ripped the cord free.

Right now, the unit was transmitting false radar telemetry to every aircraft in the area. Simultaneously it was blanketing radio communications with sheets of white noise and static, preventing the real Dulles air traffic from doing anything in its power to stop the madness that was about to ensue. "I wonder if we'll get our own special date," Adonis said, walking away from the SCS.

One of the lawman was struggling up to his feet. Adonis remembered slugging the tall, lanky lawman. He hadn't quite gotten enough power behind the punch, just enough to flatten the guy for about thirty seconds. Adonis lifted the barrel of his Desert Eagle and stroked the trigger, a .50 Action Express round blasting from the huge, dark eye.

Thunder shook the air, but Adonis rode out the recoil and lowered the gun. Something hurtled explosively at him, accompanied by a deep-throated growl. It was David Kowalski, smashing against the giant. There was almost a foot of height difference between them, and perhaps fifty pounds of sheer muscle, but the man hit like a brick wall, knocking the big man off his feet.

Adonis didn't go down. He staggered back, got his feet under him and let Kowalski spill back off of him. With a swinging right hook, the butt of the Desert Eagle clipped the smaller man's jaw, spinning him like a top. The blond giant admired the squat little man.

The blow would have twisted the head off anyone else, but Kowalski turned back and brought up a left cross that carried every bit of muscle behind it. Adonis felt the punch crash into his jaw, lights flickering somewhere above his brow, then clubbed down hard with both his free fist and the Desert Eagle.

Kowalski collapsed, grunting from the double strike.

A roar built up in the air and Adonis looked up to see a 737 coming in too quick to the runway. Its instruments were being told that it was three hundred feet higher than it really was. He smirked as the plane hit the ground. Landing gear sheared off as it struck at twice the speed it was built to take.

Metal peeled away in sparks mixed with plumes of smoke; flames jetted outward.

In an instant the 737 became a four hundred-mile-per-hour flaming coffin for the people inside. The impact of the skipping airplane off the end of the Midfield Concourse terminal was just a technicality, spinning like a ninja-star into the grasslands just off of the runway. The airplane came apart in a shower of boiling flames and silver flakes, like a winter storm in hell.

Adonis sighed. "Beautiful."

Gunfire rattled from behind him, and the giant swerved, too late realizing that the gunfire wasn't directed at him. Divots of asphalt were being kicked up as an M-16 rattled. Adonis brought up his Desert Eagle, swinging around the front fender of the fuel truck, seeing a stocky, mustached man firing at the SCS bag.

The Desert Eagle thundered and Pullman screamed, his shoulder joint gouged out by a .50-caliber hollowpoint. Bone splintered and flesh spewed across the pavement.

Unfortunately it wasn't the arm with the trigger finger. Pullman kept firing, burning off the last of his clip. To his right, Adonis heard the impacts of M-16 slugs on the LCD metal casing, the crackle and sizzle of shorting electronics. Acrid smoke rose to meet his nostrils as Adonis fired off two more shots. Distracted by the destruction of the Satellite Communication System, his two rounds merely took Pullman in his right bicep, shattering the humerous bone completely. Pullman flopped onto his back, screaming in agony, arms reduced to useless spaghetti.

Adonis stood and pulled up his muscle shirt, revealing a belt full of grenade pouches hidden by the loose hang of the tank top. He plucked a grenade free and lobbed it atop the SCS. "Sorry, Fixx."

He turned and started away from the box when a pair of arms wrapped around his ankles. The giant tripped, hands flying out to catch himself just as the shock wave of the explosion washed over them.

Adonis twisted, prying his feet from the vise grip of the stocky Dave Kowalski. Arms clawed and groped, trying to keep the blond giant from crawling to freedom. Though blood poured from bashed lips and flames burned on his pants, the lawman was still fighting.

The blond mass murderer bent double, bringing down one massive, clubbing fist hard into the side of Kowalski's head, making it roll on its shoulders. Again, the pit bull of a human being wouldn't let go, despite the laceration down his temple. As blood flowed, more fight seemed to invade him, like a shark smelling blood on the water.

Adonis again brought down his fist.

This time the arms went loose and the golden-haired titan scrambled free. He looked around for his Desert Eagle to finish off the little freak when he spotted the sleek, bug-like form of the Black Hawk skimming across the airfield.

Adonis bent and gave the bloodied face of David Kowalski a gentle, almost grandmotherly squeeze.

"Don't forget me, little man. We're still going to have fun."

JACK GRIMALDI WAS apoplectic. Gunfire was raging at the Main Terminal "M" gates and there was someone popping off a missile from near Midfield Concourse B. A passenger jet had just come screaming out of the sky, turning into a fiery phoenix from which no creature would rise.

"Stony Man! Stony Man! Do you read me?"

"This is an open line, G-Force!" Barbara Price admonished on the other end.

"Too freakin' bad! Dulles is being turned into a hell zone!" Grimaldi snapped back. "Someone took out air traffic control here. We already have a passenger jet full of casualties!"

The Stony Man mission controller went from angry to business in a moment.

"We're running a fast diagnostic through Dulles right

now!" Price responded. "Keep under control. What do *Dragon Slayer*'s systems say?"

"Radar just went from haywire to a semblance of normal. There might have been on-the-ground jamming causing…"

Grimaldi looked up through the bubble windshield of the high-tech helicopter. Two planes, not quite overhead, clipped each other. One wobbled and managed to keep on a straight path.

The other wasn't so lucky. Chunks were torn from the tail.

"Dammit!"

"Jack! Get it together, man."

"I'm fast-dumping the readout from my systems," Grimaldi replied.

"Flight recorder data being received," Price answered.

Grimaldi could hear her, distant and muffled, shouting for members of the Farm's cyber team to get on the case. The pilot, however, was watching the damaged airplane trying to hold itself straight. His forearm muscles flexed in sympathy, fighting against the movements of the plane with an imaginary joystick. "Come on, come on."

His throat went tight and constricted. One of the wings suddenly disintegrated, not in a flash of spraying volcanic jet fuel, but in a shower of metallic flakes tumbling off the side of the jet.

"No!" Grimaldi wheezed, watching helplessly as the aircraft suddenly did a savage flip, nose diving into a clot of trees beyond the second runway.

He wanted to look away, but he watched the blossoming of a new flower, dying inside as he watched the death of hundreds.

CARL LYONS GAVE a vicious back fist across Dark's jaw, flesh bruising and tearing on his knuckles and the terrorist's face. The two men were engaged in savage combat, the Stony Man warrior and the mass murderer given in to unbridled homicide. Again and again, the Able Team commander was bringing his ham-size fists flashing and darting, impacting against the deadly agent.

Lyons, if he was paying attention, didn't care that most of his blows were being deflected with effortless speed. A forearm against a wrist would blunt a chop. A fist would slam into bicep muscle instead of ribs.

Dark was weaving and dodging, blocking and blunting the lightning-fast *shotokan* strikes Lyons was firing out, realizing the pattern. In a moment he danced lazily backward, like a ballerina exiting the stage, rebounding off one of the metal ribs holding the angled windows of the M terminal in place. Lyons kept the chase.

Dark leaped forward, charging as he was charged, bringing a steel-toed boot into contact with Lyons's upper chest. Bones snapped and the blond ex-cop spit up blood. It didn't slow him. Lyons pivoted and spun, bringing the lithe, tall murderer to the ground with a spine-jarring impact. Had not Dark flattened out, tucking his chin to his throat, his skull and spine would have been smashed to pieces.

Dark snapped his heel up and into Lyons's face. The Able Team leader staggered backward, brain jolted by the sudden impact. Rivulets of blood flowed from his nose and the corner of his mouth. Dark noticed that the feral rage in the cold blue eyes of the lawman was glazing over, losing its focus.

If pressed, this dumb bastard would fight to the point

of brain death, and keep going, like something out of a George Romero zombie movie.

A savage punch lashed out and Dark grabbed the wrist, swinging his elbow up and over, bringing it down hard on the joint. Bones cracked and Lyons roared in mindless, animal fury. Dark felt himself lifted up as if he weighed less than a feather, tossed nearly twenty feet down the hall.

The terrorist landed, rolling with the impact before he skidded hard against a service counter. The cheap plywood and plaster cratered with the collision, his body forming a pocket where he struck. The big blond guy was tearing down the hallway like a freight train.

Dark pulled his pistol, a high-capacity Caspian .45, and opened fire on the lunging form, bullets slamming into his attacker in a seemingly endless stream. But he kept coming and coming, even though his legs and shoulders sprouted streams of blood. As the last shot left the barrel of the custom-combat pistol, Dark realized that he was firing at center of mass, and probably only impacting a set of concealed body armor, similar to the armor that had stopped this crazy bastard's two .357 Magnum rounds.

Lyons leaped across the last few yards between him and the prone Dark. The tall, thin man in the trench coat surged out of the way at the last heartbeat, leaping from the path of the muscular jungle cat in human form, bringing the Caspian's frame down hard against him.

Lyons smashed the counter to pieces and Dark whirled, stamping his steel boot down hard on both his ankles. Bones cracked and snapped as the onslaught caught Lyons off guard. Dark straddled the downed Able Team commando and used his empty pistol as a hammer, bringing it down and down again, savagely pummeling until his own hands were drenched with blood.

An angry shout filled the air and Dark looked up just as he was about to bring the bent frame of his .45 down one more time. There were a dozen armed men racing up the hall and he was fresh out of ammo or guns. Scooping up Lyons, he used the half-conscious Stony Man warrior as a shield, gunfire cutting wildly across the distance when a strangled cry told them to stop, but not before a few more slugs chopped into unarmored arms and legs, as well as his Kevlar-protected torso. The body jerked against him and Dark managed to drag the limp figure of Carl Lyons to the hole someone had made to go after Adonis.

"Get down here!" Adonis bellowed.

Dark gave his adversary a hard shove to the side. The man was still breathing and, in a way, Dark was glad for that as he spun and dropped from the window, landing with knees bent to absorb the impact.

That man of iron had given him a damn good fight.

Someday they'd have to finish the war that started today.

Dark looked around, plumes of choking smoke and flame rising from the multiple plane crashes. Circling jets were sweeping away, and their helicopter was racing in, right off the deck.

"I love it when a plan comes together," Dark said with a mirthless grin.

CHAPTER THREE

The trail had not grown cold.

Even if it had only been the carnage and destruction caused at Dulles, Mack Bolan would still be stalking through the shadows of the warehouse district, laden with weapons and dressed to kill.

If it merely had been the wounding of one of the few close friends he had in the world, Carl Lyons, Mack Bolan would still be on the prowl of the midnight alleys of Washington, D.C., stalking the savages he had labeled Animal Man.

The combination of hundreds of innocent lives *and* a fellow soldier from across all his bloody miles set the Executioner to seething. He wasn't a man given to rage or petty revenge, but blood cried out for blood, and Bolan was reminded of the origin of his crusade in the spirit of vengeance for his fallen family. He fought the anger, wrestled it under control like a writhing, savage crocodile, harnessing that reptilian fury and force into the power and precision he would need to carry off his penetration into the hell zone this night.

Avenge the dead. Protect those yet untouched.

The first motto was allowed to run its course, because that activity inevitably would lead him to the second vow. Dead terrorists weren't nearly as good at killing innocents. Not when they were swept away by the cleansing flames of the Executioner.

Rage and vengeance, though, only took the Executioner so far. The rest came from a soldier's duty to protect those he was sworn to defend.

Perched on the corner of a warehouse rooftop, Bolan put the pair of night-vision binoculars to his eyes, fighting off the memories swarming unbidden to him like moths from the shadows.

BOLAN HEADED the vanguard through the hospital halls, his face drawn with the news of that afternoon's mayhem. Trailing behind like the swept-back wings of a Tomcat, Hermann Schwarz and Rosario Blancanales kept the pace, keeping in tight formation, their shorter legs pumping faster to handle the breakneck speed of the tall soldier's looping strides.

Schwarz and Blancanales—Gadgets and Pol to most who knew them—were the partners of the man lying helpless in a hospital bed.

Bolan spotted Hal Brognola at the entrance to the ICU, standing over a familiar form sitting in a chair, head swathed in a bandage, cold packs lashed fast to his skull. The young man looked up, eyes swimming for a moment and then focusing on the Executioner.

"Colonel?" David Kowalski asked. He sounded dazed, unfocused, but only for a moment. The slouch suddenly left his spine and he squared off his shoulders. "Sir…"

"Just Mack, not sir," Bolan told Kowalski. "What happened?"

"Monsters. They weren't human, sir."

Bolan felt a chill, remembering a rampaging serial killer in Denver, sent by an enemy to specifically call him out. It was a nightmare the likes of which the soldier never wanted to encounter again. "Were they specifically targeting anyone?"

"Mostly people who were fighting back," Brognola stated. "But the one guy who took down Stone, he was using armor-piercing ammunition. At least, he was firing AP ammo as far as the submachine guns went. For every fatal hit, there were three people down the line or behind cover injured by stray bullets."

Bolan looked at Brognola and he remembered the tally of dead and injured. Nearly a thousand were injured and over five hundred dead from the Dulles massacre. Uneasy anger fought his outrage at the treatment of his friend. Bolan took the nearest distraction he could. "Are you okay, Kowalski?"

"I've got a concussion, but I'll be okay in a few hours," the U.S. Marshall answered.

"The doctors told him he should be in bed for the next 48 hours," Brognola corrected. "He wouldn't stay in bed."

Bolan looked at the doors to Lyons's ICU room. All he could see was a bulky figure on the bed. "Carl?"

"Eight broken ribs. Both ankles are broken. His left elbow is dislocated. Ten bullets removed from his thighs and arms. He has a collapsed lung. He has nine skull lacerations, but only one skull fracture," Brognola explained. "It's a miracle he doesn't have brain damage."

Schwarz managed a half chuckle. "I always knew that thick skull of his was good for something."

Bolan felt a token of relief. "Can we see him?"

"Sure," Brognola said. "But only for a moment. He's under heavy sedation."

Bolan led the others, somehow having picked up Kowalski as one of the flock, into the ICU room. Carl Lyons lay, stretched out, eyes heavy lidded, one arm wrapped in heavy plaster, IV tubes everywhere.

The Executioner was stunned, pausing at the foot of the bed. "Carl?"

"…dammit…"

"I don't want to hear that out of you," Bolan ordered.

Angry blue eyes stared back from under a thick, contorted brow. "Failed…"

"You fought them off. The whole airport could have been destroyed. Dozens more killed and scores more injured," Bolan replied.

"Pullman stopped that computer thing they had," Kowalski spoke up. "And he might never be able to use his arms again."

Bolan could see Kowalski's face redden at the realization of what he'd said. Lyons was feeling a world of guilt and wasn't physically much better off than Pullman with his shattered arms.

"Computer thing?" Schwarz asked, diverting the subject from horrific injury back to business.

"About this wide? Tiny flip-up screen?" Blancanales demonstrated, spreading his hands apart.

"Yeah. It also had a radio handset. At first I thought it was just a SATCOM, then the airplane came in too steep and tore itself apart," Kowalski mentioned.

Bolan could hear the strain in the younger man's voice. He lowered his voice, putting a hand on the man's rock-tense shoulder. "You did what you could."

"What I could. Look at Mr. Stone… He's wrapped up like a fucking mummy and has more tubes and wires sticking out of him than my fucking DVD player!"

"Take it easy, kid." Blancanales cut him off. "Just because you didn't get as banged up as Ironman doesn't mean you didn't try. You're supposed to be in a hospital bed yourself."

"I can walk," Kowalski grunted.

"I like this guy. He's like Ironman, only smaller and cuddlier," Schwarz cut in.

Kowalski looked between Blancanales and Schwarz, then to Bolan.

"Sorry," he said with a half smile.

"I'd feel just like you do," Bolan admitted. "You weren't prepared for what happened. Nobody was."

"We did receive some warning," Brognola advised. "'The sky will fall when we cut down the radome.'"

"What was that?" Bolan asked.

"A message received at both CIA and FBI headquarters a half hour before the assault began," Brognola said. "It was signed the Righteous International Nihilism Group."

"The RING." Bolan put together. A bitter taste filled his mouth. Bolan had been briefed, as well as Schwarz and Blancanales, about the madmen who called themselves the RING.

"Who're they?" Kowalski asked.

Bolan glanced over to Brognola. The head Fed nodded approval at Kowalski being informed of top-level security information.

"The RING has been showing up in intelligence captured from terrorist groups lately. I've found a couple references to them in Egypt, and these three—" Bolan waved his thumb at the men of Able Team "—picked up a reference to them when they raided a violent militia group a few weeks back."

"Terry Nichols and Timothy McVeigh did hire out their

expertise to instruct the Abu Sayyaf Group in the construction of explosive devices," Blancanales spoke up.

"And the Abu Sayyaf Group receives much of its funding and organization from al Qaeda," Bolan finished.

"Christian identity nut bags and Islamic jihad crazies in bed together to attack the U.S. government?" Schwarz added.

"Killumall," Lyons murmured through his wired clenched jaw.

"Carl's getting jealous," Schwarz said.

With almost Herculean effort, the Able Team leader managed to turn his hand around and raise a middle finger to the team's electronics genius.

"And he's getting healthier," Brognola said. The big Fed leaned over Lyons to emphasize his point. "But you'll be benched for a while."

Lyons pointed to Kowalski. "Him."

Everyone looked over to the U.S. Marshall.

"Not under strength," Lyons growled. Bolan knew that Ironman wasn't going to let Able Team enter the fray without its full compliment of three warriors. The blond ex-cop also knew that Bolan couldn't fill that role because his part of the investigation might go elsewhere.

"I…" Kowalski began.

A low rumble escaped Lyons's chest. "Watch my partners."

With that, Lyons's eyelids drooped down, the fallen warrior slipping into half consciousness.

FINALLY DISMISSING the memory, Bolan adjusted his position. He counted four men, trying to look like winos, but they were unconvincing. Not with clothes that didn't show any fading. They were torn and frayed, but the colors were too fresh for them to be anything but quick camouflage. Even without getting close, the Executioner could also tell that the clothes were unsoiled by nature's effects on alcohol-soaked bowels and bladders.

He adjusted the Accuracy International AWC rifle and swept its scope across two of the four men he could see. The other two were walking lazily, trying to imitate a drunken stumble, most likely, toward the far end of the warehouse.

Through the magic of optics, Bolan could make out the boxy frame of a MAC-10 or an Uzi under the folds of one of the many layers of abused shirts on the fake winos. Bolan swept up the scope and looked over the man's face. It was too clean-shaven and not wrinkled enough to have been that of a man condemned to the streets. The eyes, though, were the biggest giveaway.

The winos Bolan had seen, had eyes that looked around in terror at a world that had proved too big, too terrible, for them to deal with.

The man whose eyes Bolan looked into from a distance had a look that was sharp and alert. There was fire going on inside the brain controlling the raptor-like stare. This wasn't some human version of a rabbit twitching in response for threats, but a stationary predator. He lay in wait, a harmless log to trip over, just a piece of human driftwood until you stumbled too close, and then the strike came.

Bolan slung the AWC over his shoulder and reached down for his crossbow. He wasn't going to start shooting. Not yet.

Getting close to the enemy, finding out his plans, was what was needed.

The Barnett crossbow gave a soft, almost musical thrum as it launched its grapnel bolt, loops of nylon rope hissing from a puddle at Bolan's foot until the fiberglass-and-steel shaft snagged the other roof. The force of the bolt launch primed a mechanism inside the grapnel so that as soon as the device struck the subtly curved rooftop, it sprang open.

Bolan gave a sharp tug, pulling the black-and-silver grapnel back against a piece of off-white painted steel support ribbing. There was a dull clank in the distance and the nylon rope resisted his pull. Bolan gave another sharp tug, putting his back into it. He didn't want the grapnel coming loose while he was sixty feet above the ground, dangling over a pair of men with submachine guns.

Satisfied that the grapnel and the rope would hold his weight, Bolan turned and tied off the end, making sure there was no slack. He spent one last moment checking his gear. He decided to leave behind the sniper rifle. It would be too long and ungainly in the close quarters of the warehouse. Instead he gave his Heckler & Koch MP-5-K machine pistol, a deadly little weapon in its own right, a check. With two magazines clamped together, and the sling looped over his head and under his right arm, he had swift access to the gun, and excellent recoil control with a sharp push against the shoulder strap and a tight grip on both pistol grips. Bolan let the little subgun dangle, withdrew a leather strop and wrapped the nylon cord with it, kicking off from the roof edge.

THE WAREHOUSE ROOF was a little treacherous, slick from evening mist, but the treaded black-rubber soles of Bolan's combat boots helped him find traction on the

curved surface while his hands were chewed on by
rusted-out metal and paint. He would grab for a hand-
hold, and come away with rust gouged into his cal-
loused fingers and palms. More than once, a sliver of
steel would make him jerk back his grip in midstep.

The slip would bring him to his knees, and he
clenched up, holding against a fatal drop. Finally he
reached the skylight in the center of the roof. He
crouched, peering through the window, keeping his face
back far enough to avoid lighting it up from below.
Amber light spilled in the center of the half-empty storage area.

There were three men inside and, out of the shadows,
like the enormous, droopy legs of a monstrous tarantula,
he could see two rotors of a helicopter in the spill of
light from hanging ceiling fixtures. From the angles of
the rotors, Bolan recognized a Black Hawk UH-60.
While there were plenty of places in Washington, D.C.,
where military equipment was kept, this wasn't on the
official rolls.

This wasn't even a part of the black operations rolls,
according to Aaron Kurtzman and the cybercrew back
at Stony Man Farm. A helicopter, seen picking up the
two murderers of the Dulles massacre, was spotted setting down in this area. Only by the grace of Hal Brognola's stalling and Kurtzman's lightning-fast research
abilities were the Stony Man warriors able to pin down
the helicopter's likely location. It had taken an hour of
searching the warehouse district to get the exact location, and another half hour of climbing and crawling,
but Bolan was now in striking distance.

He took a loop of duct tape and ran it along one of
the panes in the skylight, quickly fashioning a handle.
With his free hand, he pulled a glass-cutter from his bat-

tle harness and carved free a rough half circle, tall and wide enough for his six-foot-three, two-hundred-three pound frame. Slithering, Bolan braced himself on the window ledge with his thighs until his arms stretched to the catwalk below. Firmly grabbing the rail, he was able to pull himself forward, slinking down onto the catwalk gently and under control. One hand braced on the rail, the other gripping the catwalk's grille for support, his knee came down while his foot stayed hooked in the windowpane.

Finally he reached the end of the walkway, weight coming down slowly and silently. The men below didn't even notice.

Bolan fisted the little MP-5-K, crouching and keeping watch on the half-empty warehouse. The Black Hawk was in the process of being spray-painted, new stencils giving tail markings. There were no numbers identified on the black chopper at Dulles, and as far as Bolan could see on this setup, black numbers were being painted onto the now red-and-white helicopter. It took a few seconds for the Executioner to recognize the Coast Guard lookalike.

A short, lithe woman walked briskly out of an office. She had dark black hair and tanned skin, but from her aviator glasses, Bolan couldn't make out her nationality. Not at that distance.

The woman stopped about ten feet from the helicopter. "What's keeping you so long?"

"We ran out of paint, ma'am," one of the workmen said.

"Did you send someone for more paint? Bad enough I had to lay up here. At least no one would notice a Coast Guard chopper flying along the Potomac. Right away, that is."

"But…Harpy…"

"What but?" the woman snapped. She took a fistful of coveralls in her hand and Bolan could almost smell the fear coming off the poor guy.

"I'll get someone on it."

Harpy. Bolan couldn't place the name right off the top of his head, but it seemed familiar to him. He watched as she let the worker go and fished out a cell phone from her pocket, flipping it open.

Bolan quickly took an opportunity. He reached into his battle harness and pulled out an unformatted cell phone, set up by Gadgets and turned it on. A quick tap of a few keys and the phone began searching, its internal processor invisibly and silently humming to capture and clone the signal of Harpy's phone.

Bolan pocketed the phone and pulled out his ranged microphone, aiming it toward the pilot as she spoke. The minimike would only be able to pick up her half of the conversation, but it was better than nothing. Plus, he would be able to record that half of the conversation on the MP3 pod in his harness's belt pouch.

"What kind of operation did you leave me with here, DeeDee?" Harpy growled.

Bolan noted the name.

"These rotten-brained idiots don't even have enough paint for the helicopter. Did you not tell them I was coming?"

Harpy untensed, letting her head roll back. A sigh escaped her full lips and she turned, aviator glasses hiding her eyes behind ribbons of distorted reflection.

"I know these are just local help you got, but—" Harpy's voice cut off. Her head turned a moment and she slowly began to move in a circle.

Bolan felt a chill go through him. He checked the cell

phone from his pocket, shifting his gaze between the little phone and the black-haired pilot. The cell had completed the cloning process and he flipped it open, listening in.

"…someone has broken in on the line. Your signal's been cloned!" a woman's voice with an Irish lilt confirmed.

Harpy snapped her telephone shut and started for the office.

Bolan stuffed the microphone and the cell into his cargo pants' pocket and swept up the MP-5-K. He held his fire, presuming that he could avoid the firefight for a few minutes. He needed more hard intel.

"We've got an intruder! Forget the paint!" Harpy shouted.

Bolan cursed and started back toward the skylight. He reached for his throat mike to transmit to Able Team, but all he heard was the telltale sign of electronic countermeasures jamming. He checked back at Harpy's silhouette in the office door. She was holding a massive collection of cylinders.

"Take a good long look at our bird, asshole!" she shouted.

The Executioner recognized the brutal outline of an MM-1 grenade launcher and turned his MP-5-K toward Harpy. The pilot beat him to the shot, spraying the Black Hawk with a trio of 40 mm grenades before ducking back into the office, avoiding Bolan's Parabellum spray.

Metal bulged, puffed out and finally burst apart in a volcano of steel and ceramic. A rotor twisted upward, knifing through the catwalk that Bolan stood on, sheering through the steel before it exploded into a hundred shards. The soldier spun, trying to escape as the tail boom of the Black Hawk folded upward from the concussive force that smashed it apart. Again, the catwalk came under a hammering assault, metal tearing from the ceiling and walls.

The long steel grille walkway began to fall away from the ceiling.

Bolan tried to grab a section of railing, but it twisted and wrenched out of his hand.

Gravity took hold of the Executioner as he tumbled out of control to the flaming rubble-strewn floor below.

CHAPTER FOUR

Hermann "Gadgets" Schwarz's blood ran cold when he heard the first howl of electronic jamming across his communications setup. He pushed open the door of the van, diving out of the driver's seat. "Striker's in trouble!"

Rosario Blancanales was already drawing the micro-Uzi SMG from under his denim jacket, and the pair of them raced toward the warehouse. David Kowalski was slipping out of the van and hot on their heels when Schwarz held up a hand to him.

"Get behind the wheel! We're going to need a fast extraction!" Schwarz ordered.

The blacksuit stopped, the longing in his face to run and help out as evident as if someone had carved it into his flesh. He turned and piled behind the steering wheel, firing up the engine.

"Good man," Schwarz said, spinning to get back onto Blancanales's heels.

In the distance, the worst sound that Schwarz anticipated suddenly filled the air, the thunder of explosions ripping from the warehouse that Bolan had entered.

The Able Team electronics genius put down his head and dug in, legs kicking harder to launch himself to his friend's aid when Blancanales snapped out one hand to grab him aside.

A spray of gunfire filled the air just where Schwarz would have been, the guards disguised as winos opening fire on the two men rushing toward them.

Firing one-handed, Blancanales pumped out a trio of short bursts, doing nothing more than keeping their heads down, but giving himself and Schwarz the opportunity to dive for cover. More bullets sliced the air, punching out chunks of stone and brick above their heads.

"What the hell is going on in there?" Blancanales asked.

"I know Striker didn't start blowing up shit," Schwarz replied. "They must be going scorched earth on us."

"I hate it when they do that." Blancanales's voice grated as he fed a fresh magazine into his Uzi. "Low or high?"

"I'll go low. Your old knees can't take all this banging off the pavement," Schwarz decided.

"On three. Three!"

Blancanales swung up, Schwarz kicking out flat, both their machine pistols tracking the pair of disguised guards as they tried to flank the Able Team pair. Parabellum slugs flew in a furious storm, deadly leaden hail burning through chests, bellies and thighs in a wave of devastation that left no doubt the enemy gunmen were out of this fight.

Except, both enemy guards were crying out in agony, clutching shattered and torn thighs, machine pistols dropped and forgotten. Blancanales grimaced, then nodded to Schwarz.

These men were wearing body armor. Only by the fact that Schwarz had aimed for lower belly and upper leg shots had they managed to knock the fight out of their adversaries. Schwarz gave a sharp whistle and a wild wave of his arm toward the van.

"Prisoners," Blancanales said.

"You slap, tag and bag them, I'm going to check on Striker," Schwarz ordered, getting up off the concrete and moving toward the door of the warehouse. He reloaded on the run, letting his nearly emptied magazine go spinning away through momentum.

Reaching a doorway he spotted on the side of the warehouse, he was forced to drop down behind the trio of concrete steps as guards from the other side of the warehouse opened fire. Bullets sent chips of stone flying and raining into Schwarz's tousled hair, one slug bouncing and shrieking past his ear.

Survival reflex demanded that the Able Team warrior curl up and fall back, but experience told him otherwise. Reaching into one of his pockets, he pulled out a small black disk the size and shape of a high-tech hockey puck, except for some flat panel switches built into the rim. Digging his thumb in, he clicked the disk on and hung his arm back. The minute the initial storm of gunfire dissipated, Schwarz let loose with the disk.

The plastic flash-bang grenade sailed and landed between the two men, who didn't recognize it for what it was until it was too late. The thunderbolt of its detonation sent the pair tumbling to the ground. Bounding to his feet, Schwarz took aim at the pair and blasted out their knees in single-shot mode, burning off only five shots to keep them anchored and out of the fight.

Schwarz grabbed the door handle, but jerked his hand away when the searing heat bit at his nerve endings.

Dropping back down to the bottom of the steps, he swung up his MAC-10 and blasted the door handle. Chunks of metal spilled to the ground and he turned, firing at the thick hinges, blasting them apart with his second magazine, then stepped out of the way of the falling door.

The hot breath of a hellish inferno washed over Schwarz.

THE CATWALK SLICED its way toward the floor and Bolan knew that if he didn't fall just right, he'd be crushed under tangled steel. The flames and the bone-breaking force of dropping nearly forty-five feet were matters he'd come to later if he managed to survive being guillotined and mangled by a metric ton of mangled metal. With a powerful kick of his legs, the Executioner let go of the catwalk.

He threw his arms out ahead of him, like Superman taking to flight, hands flat as knives to cut down the resistance of his forward motion, while making himself as wide and glider-like as possible to catch the air beneath him. It was a trick he'd learned in parachute school, controlling a fall by making the surface of the body into a sail. It was negligible lift, but lift nonetheless, and he sailed at least fifteen feet from the catwalk when he tucked himself in tight and hit the ground shoulders first, rolling onto his back.

The impact with the concrete floor was body-jarring, shaking him to the core, and he could already feel the sheet of bruised skin and muscle swelling along his back. He was alive, though, and his spine was in one piece. Bolan could tell because he could feel the hot lick of flame burning at his cargo pants, and the wicked cut from a piece of twisted metal on his leg.

The Executioner hauled himself to his feet, looking at the office where Harpy had disappeared. She was busy cutting out through the opposite entrance. Bolan swung up his machine pistol and fired off a short burst through the window, smashing it apart before the weapon choked. Bolan looked down and saw that the magazine tube had been dented on impact with the floor. Ripping the magazine free, Bolan fed the other sidesaddle-clipped magazine into the well. He vaulted through the blasted-out window, and dropped to the ground as pistol fire cracked and bucked.

Flames roared behind him, breaking more glass. Bolan scanned around and saw that empty paint canisters and spilled paint were burning. He was glad there wasn't more flammable liquid in the warehouse when he caught something out of the corner of his eye.

A five-foot-tall, twelve-foot-long yellow cylinder to one side of the wreckage of the helicopter. The word "flammable" in foot-high letters on the side, Bolan realized that he was staring at hundreds of gallons of aviation fuel.

"Striker to Able! Striker to Able! Can you read me?" Bolan shouted into his throat mike.

The Executioner looked back and realized that there was a possibility that his Stony Man partners would come charging in at any moment to give him backup. If the jamming would only quit, he could dissuade his friends from coming inside.

A door suddenly opened across the way, a hot wind stirring up as the overheated air finally had someplace to escape. A shadow in the doorway had ducked free of the initial flaming release.

Bolan opened fire, stitching the doorjamb with precision, looking to make his allies in Able Team pull back. He knew, though, that the Stony Man warriors wouldn't be held at bay by mere gunfire for long. He wished he could get his message across in some way. He noticed the desktop. A pen and paper. And a rubber band.

As SCHWARZ was beginning to go through the doorway into the inferno, a blast of machine-gun fire chopped into the doorjamb. Reflex tugged him out of the way just in time as bullets hammered the steel frame of the entranceway. Ducking, he brought up his MAC-10 and glanced over his shoulder. The heat from the doorway was making his covered skin drenched and his exposed face prickle as it dried out.

He crouched in a half retreat, looking back as Blancanales hung off the side of the Able Team van, driven by Kowalski.

Schwarz held up one hand and the van rolled to a slow stop, twenty feet from the doorway.

"I'm taking fire from inside," Schwarz called.

"Fire, smoke, hot air, the whole works," Blancanales called back, dropping from the sliding panel door and rushing over to join his partner, SMG drawn.

Suddenly a curved chunk of metal clattered noisily through the opened doorway. Schwarz and Blancanales pulled back, ready to dive away from a grenade blast when they recognized the curved shape of an MP-5 magazine. A piece of paper had been wrapped around it with a rubber band and Blancanales quickly plucked it up, pulling the note free.

"'Aviation fuel set to blow. I'm out the other side. Striker,'" Blancanales read.

"Aw, hell," Schwarz cursed. "Into the van!"

Blancanales didn't have to be told twice, and the

two Able Team veterans raced for the side of the van. Kowalski had it in reverse, slowly coasting until the two men clambered on board.

He hit the gas hard, and wasn't afraid to bounce Able Team or their prisoners around as he gunned the engine, sending the van blistering like a bullet away from the warehouse, fighting the wheel with one hand and staring our the rear window.

Hitting the brakes, he didn't quite send the Able team commander slamming into the rear door of the passenger section. Still, Schwarz heard the crumple of fender metal as they smacked a brick wall, sheet metal screeching on stone and spitting sparks as Kowalski kept the van plunging into reverse.

In the distance, a tongue of flame snaked out the doorway, windows suddenly vaporizing as orange clouds of superheated air smashed them apart, raining in deadly fury down onto the access road alongside the warehouse. Had the van stayed there, everyone inside would have been incinerated.

But what about Bolan?

THE EXECUTIONER HIT the ground, skidding along the concrete until he was behind the huge tire and axle of an 18-wheeler's trailer, the massive disk forming a foot-and-a-half-thick shield as the shock wave of the exploding fuel tank crashed numbingly across him. The trailer itself groaned, and Bolan looked up in helpless horror as it appeared for a moment that the thing would flip over onto him.

Instead Bolan was engulfed by the outermost edge of a wave of superheated air. The glow of flash flared, casting him into midnight-deep shadow, then disappeared.

The fireball hadn't reached him, but Bolan's skin was red, raw and dried out where exposed and his clothes were drenched through and through with sweat. His heart hammering, the Executioner got up, scanning the area, but he saw only desolation. Deep in his heart, he knew the quiet self-loathing that Carl Lyons and David Kowalski were flogging themselves with. Bolan knew how easy it was to beat oneself up over a setback. Right now, his ego was nearly as bruised and battered as his flesh.

He'd lost Harpy, but he had the cell phone and the cloned line. It might not be much, but it was something.

He had clues. The jamming. The paint. The cell phone. And two names: Harpy and DeeDee.

"Gadgets? Pol?" Bolan asked, his parched throat crackling.

Static greeted him, changing in tune with a muted voice beneath it.

"Gadgets?"

"…scrambling's dissipating."

"I lost the targets," Bolan said. "But I got some names and identification."

"We have two prisoners," Schwarz answered. "You need medical assistance?"

Bolan looked at his bleeding leg. The cut from landing on the chunk of wreckage was now accompanied by knees skinned raw through torn pants. He did a quick check and his elbows matched his bloodied knees.

"A little," Bolan answered. "But let's wait until we get back to the Farm, unless you have someone worse off."

"Two prisoners with gunshot wounds in their legs. One's nearly bled out," Blancanales answered. "We're pulling around to pick you up, but I don't think we'll be doing more than one interrogation tonight."

Bolan sighed. "I'll be waiting by the 18-wheeler."

BURTON GROSS'S EYES opened gummily. His head felt like it was full of cotton wool and his legs were numb. He tried to wipe the crust from his eyes, but then stopped sharply and suddenly. He recognized the familiar grip of handcuffs and blinked away his grogginess.

The room was dark, so dark he could make out only vague details around him, such as the fact that there were four men standing around him, and another figure in a chair next to him. That's when Burton realized he was seated.

The back of a chair pressed against his forearms, providing the leverage to keep him sitting upright, his legs entwined around the legs of the same chair. He shuffled his shoulders, trying to get some slack, but the people who'd chained him had done a thorough job. Looking down into his lap, he saw that his legs were bound in silvered duct tape, red-soaked gauze poking out around the sides of improvised bandages. He realized why his head felt so full of cotton; he was under sedatives or painkillers. Were he without drugs, he'd be screaming in agony.

"You were shot in the legs," a voice said grimly.

Burton glanced up, seeing the tallest man he'd ever met. His lower face was obscured by a black scarf, nose and jaw completely hidden behind dark silk. The only features he could make out were dark hair and two icy-jewel eyes that stared through him with merciless regard.

"I'm a prisoner of war. I demand proper medical attention," Burton said through a dry mouth. Blood loss was making him slur his speech, and he fought to raise his indignation up to be strong enough.

The cold, icy eyes regarded him in silence.

"I said, I'm a pris—"

The chair was kicked out from under him.

"Shut the fuck up!" came an out-of-control bellow. "Fuck your medical attention!"

Burton twisted, seeing two other men, wearing similar scarves, wrestling a fourth man. It was a struggle.

"Not yet." The grim man spoke. Reaching down, he lifted up Burton effortlessly and sat him upright.

"You inhuman pricks...."

Iron fingers clamped around his throat, cutting off his words.

"Do I look like an official member of the government?" Bolan asked. "Those bandages are only in place long enough for you to spill whatever knowledge is in that hate-filled little skull of yours, Burton Gross."

Gross tried to take a breath, but the grip of the tall, grim man was irresistible, crushing down. He felt the blood vessels breaking in his skin and stars flashed in his vision as he struggled to wheeze down a lungful of oxygen. "No...wait..."

"You wait." Those icy eyes burned now with a hatred that Gross shrank from. His wrists strained against the handcuffs, blood pouring down his fingers as he fought to pry himself free. He wanted to find the nearest mountain and take shelter beneath its tons of stone, but he couldn't move.

Even his eyelids failed him, peeled wide open in abject horror.

"There are passengers and crews of two passenger jets who won't be breathing, who won't be getting medical attention. Ever again." The tall wraith's growl seemed to shake the room, shaking Gross's very soul. "You can wait a few moments for your next breath. And you can do without treatment for your legs."

The fingers released Gross's throat and he coughed, spasming and bending as far as his bound arms would let him. Sputum filled his throat and he spit it up into his own lap, not caring about the mess, only sucking in sweet fresh oxygen.

"I'm a true Christian soldier in the—"

Gross's head suddenly bounced and it was only a moment after he was in midfall that he realized something had struck him in the head with the force of a sledgehammer.

"Restrain yourself or leave the room!" Bolan admonished Kowalski.

"Just let me start cutting pieces off this sick, baby-murdering fuck!" the U.S. Marshall bellowed. Gross could see the strain on the other two men's faces. He couldn't be sure if it was a ploy, but they struggled to hold back the enraged man. Muscles bulged and veins rose on taut arms as they gripped him.

"The Army of the Hand of Christ, Our Lord, doesn't believe in abortion," Gross murmured, almost defensively.

Kowalski got one arm loose, popping free. Schwarz literally leaped to bring the fist back in line before it smashed Gross's face into a smeary pulp.

"Fourteen children died on those planes, and another three died in the airport, asshole!"

"That's enough. Pol, watch this man," Bolan growled. He moved over to Kowalski and Schwarz, and the three people disappeared through a doorway.

Blancanales stepped around to a table and poured a

glass of water for Gross, putting it to his trembling lips. A lot of the cold water splashed down his neck, chilling him, but he savored the long drags of cool liquid down his throat.

"You've got a break," Blancanales said sympathetically.

Gross sucked in frightened gasps. "I wasn't behind this. They only told me to watch over the warehouse."

"I know. But 'I was only following orders' doesn't satisfy some people," Blancanales answered. He pointed toward a shadow off to Burton's right. "We got as much as we could out of him."

Gross glanced over to see Jacob Kelly and winced, turning away to avoid looking at the horribly butchered corpse. "Jesus God!"

"God isn't here for you, Burton," Blancanales answered. "And the colonel, he hates men who take God's name in vain."

"But we don't…"

Blancanales shook his head. "You don't get it. You believe in your god. He believes in his god. Trouble is, he slaughters punks like you for breakfast, lunch, dinner and a late-night snack. You're with the Army of the Hand of Christ? He's the incarnation of the *Fist of God*," Blancanales growled. "And whatever made you think we have anything to do with the government? Do they do that?"

Gross swallowed, going pale as Blancanales forced him to look at Kelly. His eyes accustomed to the half light, he saw the man's lap strewed with messy, rubbery loops. "Please! Please!"

"I can try to make it merciful on you. A quick bullet to the head and it'll be over, no torture. No being thrown into the lye pit with Jacob…."

Burton shuddered, tears pushing out between his closed eyelids. "I'll tell you anything, make it quick. Not like Jacob...."

"Do you know the woman who was in the warehouse?"

"Only by the name Harpy," Burton whispered.

"She looked Asian. What were you doing with one of those people?"

"We couldn't really tell. The Army, we were just getting money from her people. She was flashing it around, and the bitch wasn't treating us much better than shit on her boots."

Blancanales nodded. "And what were you paid to do?"

"To paint a helicopter. Trouble is, I think Martin spent half the money for the paint."

"Martin Sellers?" Blancanales asked.

Gross looked up. "You...you know all of this?"

"Enough. We just want to confirm what Jacob told us before he died," Blancanales replied.

"He was a good man. He believed in God, and this country, not the way these politicians are tearing down our freedoms and liberties. You're a man outside...you know what I speak of," Gross murmured.

Blancanales shook his head. The guy had lost it.

"You didn't have to destroy him like that. He has a family. He has a mother and a sister and two beautiful nephews," Burton continued.

Nothing more of use was going to come out of Burton Gross. He turned Gross to look at Kelly, and thumbed the horrifically hollowed eye socket. Clay crumbled free.

"It was maroon-colored fuller's earth. The intestines are just sausage casings. Jacob bled to death on the way here, and we got most of our information about you from your fingerprints," Blancanales told Burton.

The captive militiaman looked over, tears flowing down his cheeks. "And me?"

"We're leaving you for the cops, and an ambulance. You're not worth the bullet it takes to kill a sellout like you," Blancanales told him. He pulled a syringe with 200 milligrams of Thorazine and injected it into Burton's pinned arm.

Sleep claimed him in moments.

CHAPTER FIVE

The flame blazed with almost blue heat before DeeDee Thunder pressed her cigarette into the lighter. Two puffs, and already the smoke burned good into her lungs. She flipped the little lighter shut, then stepped into the conference room, knowing already who would be there and who would be making a fashionably late appearance.

Mojo, with his weird little glasses strapped to his head, reminded her of her little brother, she thought with a wry grin. His rusty hair poked up like a brush, accentuating the thinness of his face and neck, which seemed almost like a continual twig. He looked up from a book as she entered, leaned over and flicked on an air filter sitting in front of him, then went back to reading.

"And a bloody happy good day to you, too, Mojo," Thunder told him as she strode past, exhaling an extra-long lungful of smoke over his head. She gave a grin as he gave a couple of wheezing coughs before his air purifier cleared the air.

Harpy was here, too, and she didn't look happy. Her

hair was in disarray, unlike the neat feathering that she normally had. It was badly chopped, and she clacked her claws on the tabletop, lips pursed tightly.

"Bad hair day, love?" Thunder asked, cigarette bobbing between her lips.

"You could say that," Harpy said with a half scowl.

Thunder nodded. "How did the cleanup go?"

"I blew up the helicopter. A couple of the AHC bastards piled into the SUV with me as we got away," Harpy said. She managed a serene smile, the tension leaving her. "I shot them both in the head and dumped their asses into the Potomac."

"Washington, D.C. police found a couple other bodies, and they have one of them in custody." Skyline spoke up. If Thunder knew what nationality Skyline was, it wasn't from his face. His dark-skinned features were craggy and could have been anything from sunburned Italian, Hispanic, Japanese or Arab and all points in between. When he spoke with the other members of the RING core group, it was in completely unaccented English, but he spoke other languages with such fluency that it made it impossible for anyone to figure out his true native language.

It didn't matter to Thunder if Skyline was human or Martian. He could read the pulse of a city, any city, with his own personal network of info scouts. He was also so quick and stealthy that he made Dark seem like a stumbling-drunk elephant, and was a chillingly precise and deadly sniper.

Everyone in the room was among the best in the world at what they did.

Harpy was a highly skilled pilot who was wanted by a dozen nations for drug, gun and fugitive smuggling. She was also fast on the draw and had gunned down more than a hundred thugs—police or criminal—who had tried to interfere with her.

Mojo was a biochemist who, before Operation Iraqi Freedom, had been doing research on the sly for Saddam Hussein. The man, despite his twiglike build, was a survivor. An Israeli assassination team sent to murder him got sent back to the prime minister in assorted small boxes.

Thunder awaited the arrival of Fixx, Dark and Adonis, knowing that tempers were on edge because of the warehouse debacle. She cursed inwardly as she spewed out a plume of smoke.

This should have been a time of celebration. The strike on Dulles had gone off flawlessly.

Or almost flawlessly.

Someone had caught the Black Hawk's arrival on radar.

There was resistance in the airport. Dark called it the best fight he'd ever had.

The conference room doors burst open in an explosion of black, twisting trench coat. Speak of the devil, Thunder thought. And literally, Dark was a devil by reputation. For years, he was one of the CIA's top black operations assassins, a cleaner without peer. After teaming up with the man now known as Adonis, the two of them ruthlessly eliminated threats to the free world, from the lowest protestor to the most deeply ingrained terrorist cell in the nation's capital. Then, one day, Dark and Adonis disappeared.

Thunder had managed to find them. She'd recruited them because she needed the best. Though, with his face covered in bruises, lip swollen to disrupt his speech, he didn't look like the best.

Despite the battered features he wore like a mask, his mood seemed good.

"Hello, ladies, gentleman…Mojo," Dark said out loud.

If Mojo looked up from his book, Thunder couldn't tell through his blood-red goggles.

Adonis and Fixx were both behind him, separating and going to their respective seats at the conference table, sitting down to relax.

"Have a seat, Dark," Thunder said.

"No, thanks, none of these match my decor," Dark returned.

Harpy sneered. "You're in a good mood for looking like that."

Dark grinned. "You should see the other guy."

He grabbed a chair, gave it a twirl and hopped into it, letting the spinning leather seat bring his battered combat boots to a gentle rest on the polished mahogany of the table. He folded his arms behind his head and reclined.

"This isn't a joke, Dark. The Feds have a live prisoner," Thunder told him. "The man's only a Christian Identity thug, but he does know about the RING forming an alliance of terrorist groups, especially among al Qaeda-allied groups and American militias."

Dark sighed. "But that was your plan all along, DeeDee. The Feds find out and don't have a clue as to our real plan."

Thunder flicked ashes in Dark's direction, prompting him to sit up and brush off his beloved trench coat. "They weren't supposed to find out yet."

"You did tell us to split up," Adonis said. "If Dark and I stayed at the warehouse, we could have taken care of the snoopers without starting a five-alarm fire."

Thunder grimaced. "I know. I screwed up, and nearly got Harpy cooked. We have to be careful. Just because we're the best of the best, it doesn't mean we can walk on water."

"Says you," Dark interrupted. "How goes the RING rumors?"

"The Righteous International Nihilism Group is only picking up attention at high levels. Nobody is even remotely interested in letting the world know about us through news agencies," Thunder said.

"I still say we should have called ourselves the Right Indignant Nasty Gobs. Posh ass Nihilism Group," Dark said, holding up the point of his nose, his voice coming out in honks.

Thunder stared from her seat, lighting another cigarette as Dark rose and paced the floor. "Dark, I know for a fact that you were born in Arizona. What the hell are you doing talking like a damn Londoner? And why don't you paint the logo of the Brotherhood of Evil Mutants on our headquarters while you're at it?"

Dark scowled. "First, I'm a mimic. I spent eight years doing cleaning for the government in England and posing as a limey. I like talking like that."

His lip came out in a mocking pout. "And secondly, the Brotherhood of Evil Mutants don't have a logo."

"Sit down and behave," Thunder ordered.

"You don't pay me enough to behave, love," Dark returned.

Thunder sighed. "Dark, it's been a long day, and rumors have it that we have a big scary on our tail."

"A big scary?" Dark asked. He leaned both hands into the table, eyes wide at the prospect. "Tell me more."

"There doesn't seem to be much intel on this agent, but I want to make sure that he's off our case. We don't need anyone messing with us, not this close to the O'Hare operation," Thunder stated.

Dark nodded. "He's as good as cold and on a slab, DeeDee."

Thunder smirked, blowing smoke rings into the air.

"THE PICTURE ISN'T PRETTY, folks," Hal Brognola explained as Bolan, Able Team, Barbara Price, Jack Grimaldi and David Kowalski sat around the War Room table back at Stony Man Farm.

"What could be uglier than hundreds of people murdered?" Kowalski asked, discomfort sitting on top of him like an elephant, crushing the breath from him. He was an alien to this part of the Farm. Usually, he either worked the fence line as a guard, or trained with other lawmen and soldiers skilled and lucky enough to be noticed by the staff. The blacksuits heard rumors, felt vibes that the Farm was something much more. Buck Greene had told them to put those thoughts at rest, but more than once the contingent of elite cops and special operations soldiers were drawn into the field, rallied against a crisis, and usually lead in that action by the black-haired man at the end of the table. Not until a desperate day in Egypt did Kowalski learn the true nature of the tall man who came and went from Stony Man Farm.

Barbara Price glared at the young man, but Bolan shook his head, cutting off any reproach for the newbie at the table. Kowalski settled back in. It was a desperate situation, and Bolan had conceded to having Kowalski present as Phoenix Force was otherwise occupied on their own search-and-destroy mission halfway around the globe. Price made a show of "vetting" him with Buck Greene and Bolan himself.

"It's part of my job to be paranoid," she explained to Kowalski.

Something told him that there was a deeper issue at stake, and he remembered a bit of craziness with a blacksuit named Jim Gordon.

"They have the technology to do this all over again," Brognola explained.

"What technology?" Schwarz asked.

"The missile they fired, it was experimental technology. Five disappeared from a shipment to the Developmental Naval Warfare Group," Brognola explained.

Bolan frowned. "And the missiles are designed to be man-portable radar seekers."

Brognola nodded. "Right. The idea is to send in a Special Forces team ahead of an air strike, and fire anti-radiation missiles to knock out the enemy's ability to see us coming. This way the team only has to get within the maximum range of the rocket motors and not have to deal with tight patrols. Indirect ground fire makes our teams able to stick to canyons and fire upward at an angle, and the radar detectors in the nosecone home in on anything hot."

"Push-button warfare," Schwarz said. "A nifty piece of kit."

"Considering what it did to an airport," Blancanales noted.

"It wasn't the missile that crashed those planes," Grimaldi corrected. "Ski mentioned that there was a SATCOM-style portable unit on the ground. It was transmitting deliberately falsified altitude and radar readings, resulting in a collision and a crash."

Kowalski could see the pilot's tortured features, and remembered the horror of the fireball slamming into the asphalt. He remembered it was called survivor's guilt. The only one who didn't seem softened by the spiritual drain of that guilt was Mack Bolan.

"Pullman took out the computer when he saw what was going on. I couldn't even think," the U.S. Marshall admitted.

"These people came prepared," Price started. She passed out several folders. "We got only blurry, grainy pictures off the main video security cameras, but Aaron and the team managed to work some of their magic with a video enhancement program."

Kowalski opened his folder, seeing the face of the blond giant as he stood over two murdered National Guardsmen. He knew him instantly. "Good cleanup job."

"We verified the other with Ironman," Price explained. "They're known as Adonis and Dark, a couple of supermen who have been bouncing around the covert operations world for the past couple decades. Their reputation is that they're the world's finest."

"So how come they're not working for us?" Blancanales asked, sarcasm cutting his voice.

"We have our standards," the Executioner answered. The grim timbre of his voice told Kowalski that this was far from their first atrocity. It also soothed some of the young man's fears of what he was getting into, learning even a tiny fraction of the inner secrets of this black bag operation.

Bolan locked glances with the young man. "You can relax. You've earned enough clearance with us."

"Thank you, sir," Kowalski said, feeling much younger and smaller for a moment.

Bolan's smile was welcoming and genuine. "You don't have to be so proper. I work for a living."

"Back to these two. They disappeared a couple years back. We thought that maybe someone caught up with them. There were some kills we could attribute to those two here and there, but nothing concrete," Price continued. She glanced over to Bolan. "And given the state of the world, it could have been anyone taking out these particular targets."

"What kind of targets?" Blancanales asked.

"What do you have in mind?" Price asked.

"Maybe rivals of certain Christian Identity militia groups?"

Price looked at her folder. "I'll have Aaron look into the affiliations. You could be right."

"He usually is," Schwarz chided. "And he doesn't use a computer, either."

"Still makes your job easier," Price quipped.

"Lady, gentleman, not in front of the rookie. We're supposed to be mature," Blancanales said.

"So much for that theory," Bolan said dryly. "Where did the missiles get ripped off?"

"It was a snatch-and-grab in California," Price said. "Not only were the MARS stolen—"

"MARS?" Bolan interrupted.

"Man-portable Anti-Radar System," Price told him. She didn't continue as she turned to watch something else.

Schwarz was looking over a list from one of the pages of Price's information packets. He scratched his temple with his middle finger for a moment.

"What's going on up there?" Price asked.

"There's some very specific technology listed here that was in the shipment. We're talking stuff that most of the firms in the Silicon Valley couldn't handle," Schwarz explained. "I think we can possibly narrow down who could do something with this hardware if we called in an old mark."

Blancanales grinned. "You mean, Jackie Sorenson?"

Schwarz nodded. "No offense, Ski."

"Mr. Stone asked me to keep you from being understrength. Frankly, I'm not sure how he meant for me to do that, but any more bodies, especially someone you know would be appreciated."

"All right," Schwarz answered. "But don't call me Frankly."

The old joke got a small grin out of Kowalski, and Schwarz was pleased with the result.

"All right. Gadgets, you hook up with Dr. Sorenson," Price said. "Rosario, you and Ski dig into the possibility of a Christian Identity militia being involved in the snatch. We don't have time to handle this nightmare one lead at a time."

"I'm going to be elsewhere," Bolan surmised. He was looking at some paperwork he'd pulled from his own folder. "Terintec, in suburban Chicago. Those are the people who developed the MARS?"

Price nodded. "I know you're not in the same league as Gadgets, but you do know your way around military applications of technology."

"Colonel Brandon Stone, U.S. Army Special Forces, retired this time. I've been sent by the Pentagon as an adviser to Terintec to evaluate progress on the MARS system in the absence of the stolen missiles."

"That's right," Price told Bolan. "We've arranged an appointment with a Dr. Sable Burton for you."

Bolan plucked the photograph from the file, studying it for a moment. His lips set firmly, then he returned the photo to the file.

"We're not going to have forever on this," Brognola said. "Get moving, otherwise the President will pull the plug on us, and do something reckless, like suspend Constitutional rights."

SABLE BURTON PUSHED her glasses up on her nose once more.

"Why don't you get contacts?" Gina Larkin asked, brushing her tangle of long, rusty curls from under the strap of her ID badge.

"Because they make my eyes hurt too much," Sable lied. In truth, she had a phobia about putting things into her eyes.

Larkin snorted derisively. "Well, you'd think after all the work you put into this project, you could try something like laser surgery."

"I work with lasers for a living, Gina. Lasers and radar and electronics. I don't want those things poking around in my eyes."

She ran her ID card through the scanner and the steel door in front of her gave an asthmatic hiss and shrugged out of the way. Larkin followed right on her heels, prompting a figure in a gray jumpsuit and a gun belt to stomp into their path.

"Ms. Larkin, you know the rules," the security guard said. As if to add weight to his words, he tapped his nightstick on the rail in front of Burton.

"And what about me? I'm going to be late," Burton said, screwing up enough courage to sound defiant.

The big, smug guard gave her a smirk. "You shouldn't have let her through on your keycard swipe."

"I didn't!"

"What's the problem?" a deep, resonant voice rumbled behind them. Burton turned and saw a man in a ribbed black commando sweater and matching cargo pants. It took a moment for her to take in the whole effect of the man, like the blast wave off a bomb finally reaching her after she saw the first spark of explosion. Except for his face and hands, he seemed carved by a classic Greek sculptor out of pure obsidian, his long, powerful body an example of a warrior's ideal.

Burton felt her heart skip at the sight of him, then turned away, back to the security guard, hoping no one noticed her. She felt as though everyone could see the tingle that ran through her at the sight of the man in black.

"And you are, sir?"

"Colonel Brandon Stone, U.S. Army, retired."

The guard looked at his clipboard. "Sorry for the delay."

"I swiped my access card. The woman ahead of me swiped her access card. And you obviously know this woman. What's the purpose of holding up this line with your weapon out?" Mack Bolan asked.

The security guard seemed to stiffen for a moment, as if he wanted to go head-to-head with the tall stranger. However, the air went out of the guard's sails. He slid his nightstick back in place.

"Ms. Larkin, just swipe your card and don't be so lazy," the guard said, his voice dropping to a murmur.

Burton caught Stone's cold stare and realized why a testosterone fit had been averted.

Those were the eyes of a man who was not to be trifled with. She tossed Larkin a quick glance and saw that her friend had already had sized him up and was grinning from ear to ear at the sight of him. Larkin moved back to the entrance, slowly, brushing against Bolan's body in the narrow hallway. She gave an unfelt apology for getting so intimate, but the man in black was unimpressed by her nearness.

Burton blushed with embarrassment. If Larkin, tall, willowy, with great breasts and barely concealing her sexuality underneath a thin, filmy spring dress, couldn't get a rise out of that stoic, broad-shouldered man, what chance did she have? She was shorter and still wearing a lumpy sweater and jeans under her lab coat, fending off the recently faded Chicago winter. She quickly dismissed the thought.

She had work to do today. If she wanted to meet someone, there was always online relationships, or even heading out with Larkin and picking up the guys who didn't score with her. Burton continued on to her office, too lost in her self-image issues to notice that she was being followed. She stopped at her door, then looked up, seeing the electric-blue eyes of the stranger looking down at her.

"I'm here to be briefed by a Dr. Burton," he said.

She looked at him, a long look for her as she was only a shade over five feet tall, with long brown tresses that hung a few inches past her shoulders. She pushed her glasses up on the bridge of her button nose again, and smiled.

"Pleasure to meet you, Colonel Stone," she said after giving her throat a quick clear. She offered up a hand and Bolan took it in his, surprised at how small it was in comparison.

"Same here, Doctor."

Professor Sable Burton was a woman who could help him understand, perhaps, just how the terrorists who'd hospitalized Carl Lyons and killed hundreds of innocents at Dulles International Airport could get their hands on top-secret weaponry.

"How much do you have to be briefed on, Colonel?" Burton asked, walking behind her desk.

Bolan scanned her office. It was little larger than an office cubicle, and bookshelves were stuffed with paperwork and reference materials. She barely had room for personal touches, the most prominent of them being a battered old, stuffed black dragon with a purple belly, its eyes droopy and crossed, head tilted.

"I just need a refresher," Bolan replied. "How much proprietary technology is needed to complete the radar-seeking warhead?"

"You mean, stuff only we could produce? That was the point. We were trying to make it fast and easy for the Army to keep in production. You'd still need our technicians to put it all together, but it's supposed to be a cheap and easy weapon," Burton answered. "It's basically just fire and forget. Set it off and the soldiers can move to a safer place even before the rocket exhaust clears."

"With a proper sample, someone could reproduce this," Bolan said thoughtfully.

The woman nodded, looking a little pale. "Was it our missile used in the Dulles incident, Colonel Stone? It's too much of a coincidence for someone like you to start poking around just after—"

"You're right," Bolan admitted. "Do you know any details about the stolen shipment?"

"I'm a physicist, not a salesclerk," Burton replied.

Bolan frowned. "Who would be in charge of getting the missiles out for field testing?"

"You'd have to talk to Hector Terin. He's the president and lead developer."

"Could you take me to meet him?"

"He went on an extended weekend. He'll be back tomorrow. Until then, would you want to look around the facility? To kill time?"

"That sounds like a good plan," Bolan admitted.

CHAPTER SIX

Wearing the darkness like an old friend, the Executioner paid a visit to Hector Terin's estate in Oak Park. He wasn't convinced that Terin was guilty of wrongdoing because he took a trip the same weekend that missiles developed by his company were used to commit mass slaughter. It wasn't guilt that the soldier smelled, though. Something was drawing his attention, instinct, based on past experience with countless similar situations.

Bolan stopped off at his hotel and changed to his blacksuit. He put on a pair of loose jeans and a jacket over the combination, making it look as though he was just walking around casually, the high-tech skintight garment just another tight black T-shirt under a leather jacket. The blacksuit had evolved over the years from a simple cat-burglar-style jumpsuit to an environmentally adapting suit that would keep him either cool or warm under the appropriate conditions, and was resistant to cuts and tears. The black coloration helped with blending into the shadows, but it was also a psychological weapon, too. Bolan's height and 200-odd-pound frame, with rippling muscle under black fabric and a

weapons harness, added to his ability to intimidate and
shock his enemies. Sometimes it granted him only a half
second, a heartbeat, but it had been a deciding factor in
enough shoot-or-die situations.

He remembered the videotape of Dark in action at the
airport. He was another person who had taken the idea
of clothing as a psychological weapon and run with it.
The addition of the long flowing coat also had the bonus
of altering Dark's center of mass, making people shooting at him hit the flapping tails of his trench coat when
they were looking for a chest hit. The trench-coat-wearing murderer wasn't just relying on a killer wardrobe to
carry his way through battle. Plain style wouldn't let
someone beat Carl Lyons so badly he was left in a hospital bed with a collapsed lung and a score of broken
bones.

If anything, Bolan recognized that Dark had no style
at all with his hand-to-hand combat. Men like that were
the most dangerous, because someone with a definitive
fighting form could be anticipated. The mass murderer,
however, combined maneuvers and improvised. That
was Bolan's approach to martial arts, despite the efforts
of others to try to pigeonhole him into whatever the latest "dance craze" was in the chop-socky circuit. Not
that Bolan didn't "taste" martial arts on his own time,
learning new katas and moves to add to his arsenal of
hand-to-hand combat.

Mack Bolan didn't fear entering any kind of personal
combat, either swords or knives, fists and kicks, or guns
and grenades. He'd done it all.

This night, however, he was hoping not to get into a
shooting match with Hector Terin's guard force. Judging by the kind of security in place at Terintec's headquarters, it would be a step above the usual collection

of rental cops, but without a determination of guilt, Bolan couldn't bring himself to kill a man doing his job for a simple paycheck. He had his Beretta 93-R in its shoulder holster, sound suppressor attached, but that would have been a weapon of absolute last resort. Stealth would have to get him past the guards if he was to get information.

He could have asked Stony Man Farm for a lowdown on Terin's personal holdings or any of his private dealings, but something told Bolan that someone with the pull to issue top-secret weaponry to the most highly specialized combat units in the U.S. military would have resources that could spot Stony Man's cybercrew a mile away. Besides, there was something about being on-site. Breathing the air.

Feeling the vibes.

Bolan pulled himself partway up the wall around the estate and paused to feel the top of it. No broken glass was embedded in concrete to make crawling over the brick ledge a bloody and painful undertaking. Pulling himself up some more, he looked left and right. He didn't see any inlays that suggested pressure sensors. A pocketful of dirt from the base of the wall poured from Bolan's fist, the dust kicking up. No laser light was blocked by the floating dust particles.

That didn't mean much, in an age of infrared and microwave motion detectors. Before his fingers began cramping, Bolan swung both arms onto the wall and pushed himself up, kicking himself to a perched position on the wall. With a tree behind him, he was safe from being backlit from the street. He pulled out a field detector designed by Gadgets Schwarz. The little detector would give Bolan a good idea of what kind of electronic security he was facing. There was nothing.

The Executioner's instincts went into overdrive as he looked at the lit household. There was always a chance that Terin's suburban home wasn't protected by state-of-the-art electronics. Still, his eyes were adjusted to the night and he could tell that nobody was moving around outside, not even a guard dog.

With a single step, Bolan dropped from the top of the ten-foot wall, landing in a crouch. He ate the distance to the closest window, crouching beneath it. The estate itself was a corner lot, with a small bit of land around it and a small security wall. The house itself was on a built-up hill, grass rolling down to disappear behind decorative stone-and-iron railings. The home was three stories, with castle-like turrets at each of the corners, and in the last dregs of daylight before he went to change into his infiltration gear, Bolan noticed that the brick was light gray and each conical roof on the turrets was of red tile. Two great balconies poked out from the second floor. Access to them had been from tall, arched-glass doorways. The front door was under the balconies and surrounded by the stone pillars that held them aloft. The third floor was under a sloped red-tiled rooftop, with tiny porthole-like windows giving Bolan the impression that it was more like an attic instead of a main living area.

Crouched in the shadow of a tree and under a windowsill, Bolan could hear through the partially cracked window the sound of playing music. Risking exposure, he peeked into the room and met gauze curtains obscuring his view. He didn't hear any movement and no shadows made their way in the room.

Taking a risk, Bolan pushed the window, a pivoting design instead of a usual sliding style, inward and hefted himself through the opening. His boots landed on carpeting and he sidestepped behind the heavier curtains, listening for any reaction.

There was none, and Bolan slid out from behind the curtain. On one wall, in an ornate oak cabinet, a CD player was playing, the speakers spread around the room to provide a surround-sound experience. He moved over to the player itself and discovered that it was playing on repeat. There was no telling how long it had been on, but coagulated droplets were sticking to the top of it.

It wasn't a failure of the maid service to clean up some spilled wine. The fifteen-thousand-dollar system had somehow been spattered with blood. He looked around the room. The dark carpeting had hidden the bloodstains from his notice until now.

Bolan filled his hand with the Beretta and continued to stalk the house. He didn't bother shutting off the CD player. The sudden lack of sound might alert anyone else in the home. He also didn't need the hassle of fingerprints all over a crime scene that Hal Brognola would have to cover up.

The soldier made a circuit of the first floor and found himself in the kitchen, spotting a couple of doors. He tested one, a pantry, then the other, a doorway to a cellar.

Bolan gave the stairwell down a cursory glance, then carefully closed the door without making more than a subtle click. The basement would be saved for last, in case there were people on the upper levels. For all he knew, the blood droplets could have been from a cut caused by a wineglass, but he hadn't seen any broken shards anywhere. Just to be safe, he looked in the sink and found only a couple intact mugs. He checked the trash. There was nothing broken there, either.

He checked the first-floor bathroom and it was there that he noticed a towel with blood on it. He checked it and saw the familiar knife-edged pattern, painting the handtowel with crimson streaks. Bolan set down the towel and looked for a knife. Whoever made the kill had made a relatively bloodless incision. He figured it was a stab wound either to the kidney, which caused instant renal shock, or a stab through the base of the skull into the medula oblongata, the place where the spine met the brain. The skull puncture would actually be the least bloody.

Exiting the bathroom, Bolan swung around and up the stairs, Beretta leading the way. He crouched deeper as he reached the top of the stairs and looked down the hallway in both directions of the T formed between the stairway and the hall. He took the right turn first, and found himself checking on the second-floor bath and shower, and a master bedroom. The drawers in the master bedroom had been tossed.

Sloppy work, Bolan figured. Downstairs was fairly pristine, while up here was a shambles. The closet was thrown open and entire racks of men's and women's clothing had been tossed across the carpet. Boxes were dumped.

Then it came to him. The trashing of the master bedroom was supposed to make it look like a robbery. Maybe a robbery-homicide.

Someone else was stalking Hector Terin.

Bolan moved back down the other turn from the stairs and found a pair of smaller bedrooms, both disturbed halfheartedly, and the half-open door of a den or office. Pushing the door open with the suppressor of his Beretta, he saw the office was messy and lived-in, but didn't look at all as though it had been ransacked. Whoever the thief was, he was making it look like this wasn't his goal. Still, a spot of redness on the armrest of the leather executive's chair, still sticky, showed where a droplet of blood had come free from the killer. The chair was pushed back and away from the computer terminal, as if someone had just risen from it and was off and running.

Bolan took out a small, credit-card-size-and-shape compact disk from a small protective casing and inserted it into the CD-ROM drive. He checked the front of the computer and found four USB ports under a panel on the face of the tower. This helped the Executioner out immensely, as he plucked a pair of tear-drop-shaped devices from his harness. "Thumb drives" they were called. Using Compact Flash technology, each of the little devices, when hooked up to a computer, could upload or download over a quarter of a gigabyte of information.

The thumb drives were empty, and in Bolan's opinion, they were amazingly useful in collecting information. More durable than a compact diskette, or even a traditional diskette, they hooked up to the fast USB ports that transferred data at lightning speed, working faster than any rewritable diskette drive. In moments, the diskette was taking over the hard drive and grabbing document, spreadsheet and picture files from deep within the hard drive. Most of the other programs would be useless for providing information to Stony Man Farm. At the prompting that the two thumb drives were full, Bolan inserted a second pair until he ended up with five of the tiny thumb drives full of information. He collected his disk from the drive and, using a cloth, wiped down the computer to hide his fingerprints.

Making a choice, he decided to check the attic before heading down to the cellar. If he went down there, he'd be boxed in and blind to anyone approaching. A narrow set of stairs gave him access up and into the new area.

The attic was lighted only from spills from streetlamps that painted various surfaces in blue highlights. Bolan pulled a pocket flash from his harness and snapped a red lens cap over the light. The crimson wavelengths wouldn't travel as far or be as noticeable as white light, especially from the street, yet at crossroom ranges, it gave the Executioner plenty of light to see by. He could smell no trace of a corpse, nor hear of anyone in hiding. There was only old furniture covered by dropcloths, and wardrobes full of plastic-bagged clothing abounded, as well as assorted stored collectables.

Every instinct told him that there was a dead body on the premises, and a killer getting farther away by the moment. Bolan turned and left the attic, knowing he didn't have the time to toss the attic for clues or hidden files stored in any of the covered furniture. Time was of the essence.

Heading back, he went back to the cellar entrance and moved slowly down the stairs. The stench in the cellar was unmistakable. He found the body and his earlier assessment was correct. It was lying on a clear plastic tarpaulin, coagulated blood dripping onto it from the fatal wound.

The body was lying facedown, with a brutal puncture at the base of its skull. It was a man, a big guy, easily as tall as Bolan, with about twenty-five extra pounds of muscle. Unfortunately, muscle wasn't what made a good security guard. Brains, alertness and reflexes counted for more weight than just big, powerful fists.

He knelt and felt the body, testing one of the arms. Rigor mortis had set in, and the part of the hand that was resting on the floor was darkened with pooled blood. He'd been here awhile, though there was no obvious insect activity. Given how clean the house was, he didn't expect bugs at this time of year, so an indication of when the man died would be made more difficult.

Bolan shook his head and checked the man's face. It wasn't Terin. He pulled out a palm-size digital camera and took a couple of pictures of the victim to send back to Stony Man Farm for a possible ID. The killer had taken pains to inflict some damage on the guy before killing him. A couple teeth were missing and the nose was broken, nearly folded over onto one cheek.

There was nothing more he could do, and Bolan's gut churned at the murder of an innocent man. He turned and went back up toward the kitchen when he paused.

There was movement up above.

The Executioner was bottled in the basement and, from the sounds of things, whoever was coming in was heading right toward the basement.

STEPHEN CAUL HATED his job these days, especially being stuck with the goons he was working with. Still, they were devoted to the same cause he was: the destruction of the United States' government, a corrupt and squalid mess taken over by the Zionist Occupation Government. He never thought that he'd be able to stomach working with Arabs, but their hatred of the U.S. and Zionists was equal in every way to his own.

He wouldn't spend time with them. They reeked of garlic and were truly filthy creatures, despite their friendliness and noble intentions. He could also tell they barely tolerated him.

Tough shit.

Both the Army of the Hand of Christ and the Fist of God were giving Caul and his partners orders to work together. United, they could accomplish what neither group could ever hope to do on its own.

Caul, Davison and the two Arabs got out of the SUV and walked through the front door. His gloved hands kept him from leaving fingerprints on the keys or the doorknobs, and he looked back to make sure none of his allies were without their own gloves. One of the camel jockeys showed his leather-clad palms and wiggled them with a smile.

Caul thanked Christ for small favors and was the first through the door. The music was still playing, and though that didn't mean anything, it was reassuring. It meant that no amateurs were in the house. Of course, if a professional were present, he would have left things as he'd found them, especially the music.

Caul pulled his Colt .45 from its holster and led the way, stalking the house softly and silently. As if in a Conga line behind him, the others followed, their own guns drawn. Davison was scanning the staircase to the second floor for activity while the Arabs watched their back trail, making sure the front door was closed.

Caul paused for a moment at the central security keypad for the building. He'd disabled it after getting the code out of the stiff in the basement. It was still disabled, and he felt a wave of relief until he noticed the door to the cellar. It was cracked ajar.

He had left it firmly closed when he'd left.

His eyes narrowed and he closed his fist. Davison knew the signal to tighten up in formation. The Arabs also tightened in their place in the human snakeline. Caul pointed to his eyes and to the door.

Things had gone south fast.

He slid a sound suppressor from his coat pocket and threaded it onto his weapon. The others followed suit. A raging gun battle in a mansion would attract the Oak Park police, and while they were a smaller department than the neighboring Chicago police, they were still well-armed and organized. They'd also be able to call on Chicago's SWAT team for help if the situation got too loud and violent.

The group had their pistols muffled now and Caul led them to the cellar door.

For a moment a gut-squeezing silence endured, Caul and Davison on the left of the door, the Arabs at the hinges. Caul let the door swing open, then spun, aiming down into the stairwell. Nobody was there, and the light was still on. Taking the steps slowly, not letting his weight make any of them squeak, he edged sideways down into the basement, the muzzle of his sound-suppressed .45 sweeping ahead of him.

The stiff was still here, his head turned to one side. Caul finger-waved Davison down to him, then they separated, checking the improvised rec room in the cellar. There were few places anyone could hide, but the two AHC warriors checked them swiftly and silently.

In the meantime, the Arabs had made their way down and were moving to the next room. It was a laundry room, Caul remembered, and the two men were taking it with almost the same efficiency as the two ex-Rangers.

Nothing happened.

Davison wanted to say something, Caul could read it on his face, but the two maintained silence for operational security. Still, Caul waited for the Arabs to come back out. It was an uncomfortable minute before the Arabs returned.

"It could have just been a thief who was frightened off by the discovery of a dead body," Salih said softly. He still hadn't relaxed from his tensed posture, though, and his gun was still in a two-handed grip.

"Let's not count on it," Davison answered. He holstered his gun. "Someone give me a hand."

Caul nodded and motioned to the other Arab, Muqbil, and together the two men hefted the corpse and the plastic tarp it had been lying on, lugging their cargo up the stairs, leaving Salih and Caul alone in the basement.

There was a long silence between the two men. Caul glanced to a closet and Salih nodded, knowing that it was the one place not accounted for. The two men aimed their weapons at the door. Caul pointed to Salih, and then pointed toward the lower half of the door. Salih nodded and took a kneeling position.

Caul stepped to the closet door and touched the doorknob, keeping his gun away from the opening. There might have been a chance that whoever was hiding would try to dive out.

He threw open the door, and Salih, to his credit, held his fire.

The closet was empty. Caul hadn't checked this room before and he turned on the light, seeing a closed window at the other end of the tiny little storeroom. Shelving on either side was loaded with assorted supplies and spilling-over junk bulged from the drawers of a dresser at the other end. He stepped in and investigated more, but was satisfied there was no one hiding inside the few inches of shadow available in the room.

IT WAS A TIGHT SQUEEZE, getting through the window in the closet. Bolan's broad shoulders almost were his undoing, but once he was at the bottom of the window well, his boots scrunching on white stone, he saw that he was in a four-foot-deep pit that was at the back of the house. Grabbing the lips of the hole, he shoved hard, driving up and outward just as light spilled through the window he'd just closed.

He crawled forward quickly, turning to look back from the shadows to the little pit. A light went on in the closet and Bolan took that as his cue to back off and see what was going on around the front. Keeping low and to the shadows, he stalked around to where he could observe the driveway.

Two men were carrying the plastic-wrapped body and stuffing it into the back of the SUV. They'd be driving off and leaving the Executioner to twiddle his thumbs if he couldn't find a way to trace them. Bolan checked his harness and found one of Gadgets's little tracker bugs.

The only trouble was getting close enough to the vehicle without being seen by the two men outside. There was a call from the porch and one of the men moved back to the front door. The other was on the far side of the SUV. Bolan made a swift dash and was at the rear wheel of the vehicle, a big, dark green Bronco. He pulled a wad of adhesive and stuck it on the inside of the wheelwell, pushing the tracker hard against it. There was movement on the porch and Bolan dropped to the grass and rolled, slithering off into a thicket of ferns along the side of the driveway. The three-foot-tall plants covered him as he squeezed behind them.

The Ford Bronco gunned to life and started backward down the driveway. Bolan remained still. Fortunately the headlights were left off by the driver. The killer and his friends weren't trying to call attention to themselves, either. The Bronco paused at the gate, then backed onto the street after checking for traffic, only then turning on the lights.

Bolan was up and running for the gate, as well.

He had to get to his car before the Bronco was out of range.

CHAPTER SEVEN

"The body reeks." Ibrahim Salih spoke up as he sat in the back seat of the Bronco.

"That's what corpses do," Caul answered from the front. The other American, Davison, remained quiet except for a small grunt.

"We are merely asserting," Muqbil said, hands raised as if to fend off further anger, "that this is unclean."

"Fine. Have the U.S. government come slamming down onto us because we killed a man," Caul replied. "I'll even drop you off at FBI headquarters where you can wait till dawn with your thumbs up your asses."

Salih was tempted to put the barrel of his pistol against Caul's head and blast his brains out through the windshield, but Muqbil's eyes caught the rage in his own. A shake of the head calmed the reaction, though the hatred still smoldered.

Muqbil was a man of long patience, but not one to be crossed. Salih knew full well that when the time was right, the Americans would pay for being a constant pain to them, and the quiet Yemeni would be the first one to pull the trigger.

Silence once again reigned in the car, giving Salih time to ponder the death of Hector Terin's bodyguard. With his murder, any chance of a leak to their organization was plugged, at least for now. It wouldn't take long for someone to figure out, though, that Shephard, the bodyguard, wasn't missing work because of a simple cold. With the theft of the missiles from the SEAL shipment, and further appropriated technology missing from Terintec's ledgers, a savvy investigator would begin narrowing down leads in no time.

Salih knew those leads pointed directly to Caul, Davison and the Hand of Christ. Shephard was a former United States Army Ranger, like the two Americans, and had been swayed by literature appealing to the disenfranchised American white male. Trained to kill and expected to die for his country, and released from military service, there was a small, yet growing percentage of men who felt that they deserved better. They felt they deserved to live in a nation that didn't treat them or their religion as a second class.

Some simply were turning against blacks and other ethnicities, but men like Caul and Davison were "above" petty racism. Or so they said. Their war was with a government that had "abandoned" Christianity and replaced it with a kowtowing to the rich and the powerful, preferring to spill Christian American blood in defense of Israel.

For that, Salih could almost put aside his spite for the Americans, but they weren't forthcoming with their own courtesy. He knew they thought of him and Muqbil as just two more brown-skinned dogs from the Satanic races.

To be honest, Salih felt the same about the pale-skinned bastards. The less of them there were in the world, the better, and he was willing to start burning off the ammunition to do it. It was only the juicy prize of destroying the United States' government and their lap-dogs in Jordan, Yemen and Saudi Arabia. All that was needed was to push the men in power until they snapped and slammed the lid down on the freedoms these spoiled children didn't deserve, the lawlessness that condemned them before the eyes of God.

Then the reckoning would come.

"Yo! We're here." Caul spoke up, interrupting Salih's thoughts.

Salih looked at the restaurant and began getting out of the SUV. He paused, halfway out the door, seeing a Honda Accord drive by behind them. He caught only a glimpse of the big shadow behind the wheel, but the driver didn't pause or make eye contact. Instead, the Honda drove along and turned the corner, disappearing from view.

"You think we're being followed?" Caul asked, stepping beside him.

No, neither side wanted to end this partnership just yet. There was still work to do.

There'd be plenty of time for them to kill each other once their common, hated foe was destroyed.

MACK BOLAN AVOIDED eye contact except to make a pe-ripheral vision check on the SUV. He felt the attention of the first man out the back of the vehicle, but he fo-cused on the road ahead. The best way to avoid being noticed, he discovered, was not to pay attention to who you were evading. It worked in crowds better than it did in a forest at night, hiding among shrubbery, but the Ex-ecutioner had learned the tricks of urban stealth as well as jungle fighting.

After five blocks, Bolan couldn't find a parking space, none that wouldn't get ticketed or towed. With the car in registry to Colonel Brandon Stone, and a few thousand rounds of spare ammunition, grenades and a small arsenal of automatic weapons in the trunk, the Chicago police would begin asking uncomfortable questions about him should they begin snooping after hauling the car off.

Bolan found a good hideout after making a five-block circuit around the restaurant. It was a street with several cars parked along both curbs, reducing the drivable portion of the avenue to one lane. One house had a couple of lawn chairs and buckets on the street in front. Bolan moved in, clearing aside the chairs from the spot. If anyone was awake, they'd notice him fooling around with their stake on where to park their car in the limited area available, but it'd take a miracle for someone to get a tow truck in to haul him out, and he knew the police frowned on the practice of "staking."

Bolan edged the Honda to the curb. He spent the next several minutes rummaging through the trunk, deciding what he'd need if the soft probe went hard. He strapped on his Desert Eagle to balance out the silenced Beretta, and backed that up with a modified-for-silence Cobray submachine gun. The Cobray was a modernization of the old MAC-10, a simple, box-shaped autoweapon. With its rate of fire cut down to a controllable 800 rpm, a forward pistol grip, a new shoulder stock, tritium night-sights and a fat, sausage-shaped suppressor on the nose, the submachine gun was as good a choice as any for clearing a room or engaging a gunfight at the distance across a city street. If anything, the Cobray was more accurate than the gunfight-in-a-phone-booth MAC-10 because of the improved stocks, sights and rate of fire.

He slipped the submachine gun and several magazines into a smaller version of his war bag and clipped several smoke and concussion grenades to his harness. He contemplated something more lethal in the form of explosives, but knew that fragmentation grenades and the middle of a city were two things that didn't go well together. He was already risking innocent bystanders by upping the ante to automatic weapons.

He slipped the strap of the war bag over his shoulder and began heading back to the restaurant, preparations against a bloody conflict tormenting him each step of the way.

It didn't take Bolan long, and except for the occasional car driving past, its speakers cranked up to maximum, throbbing with an overamplified pulse, Chicago was on hushed tones in this neighborhood. Rustling trains, distant main-street traffic and barking dogs were a muted backdrop to Bolan's footsteps.

The restaurant itself was unlit, its windows revealing only an empty, hollow blackness like the other storefronts on the street. Painted on the glass were Arabic script that Bolan could make out as Arqad's Fine Eatery even without the translation in big, balloon-shaped English letters beneath. The menu was taped to the window and covered with similar cuneiform in the margins of an otherwise unremarkable sheet of paper. He made an effort to look as though he was studying the menu while his eyes adjusted to the darkness within the window. Deep in the shadows, a manlike shape was sitting at a table.

Bolan gave a shrug and, like a tourist, snugged his bag tighter over his shoulder and continued on down the street. The Arabic restaurant was surrounded on either side by a Middle Eastern grocery store and a combination storefront church and charity service.

He turned the corner and saw an alley that would provide him with a back entrance. His neck hairs tingled as he made the turn, seeing a dark shadow on the street now. It was in front of the restaurant where he'd been standing a moment earlier, and he cursed himself for acting like a tourist at midnight. He'd hoped the combination of a battered leather jacket, jeans and an old, well-used duffel bag would have labeled him as nothing more than a wanderer, at worst a "cleaned-up" hobo, at best, a student taking a new route through the city after night school.

It didn't work. Whoever had been in the restaurant was spooked by his presence, spooked enough to leave his guard post. Bolan didn't know what kind of communications his enemy had, and he wasn't going to risk getting out his own communicator to hear what was going on. Instead he kept going, heading to the alley. The bag was zipped open, and his hand was around the grip of the Cobray, ready to fire through the tough canvas in case the war started early.

The alley was all shadows and silence as he ducked into it. Out of the glow of the streetlamps it took the Executioner a moment to adjust to the new lighting, and once he did, he noticed back lots behind each of the separate storefronts. Rickety-looking old porches crawled up the backs of the brick monoliths, some painted, others left bare, none of them looking as though they could support the weight of a small child, let alone his own mass.

The most important thing was that no snipers were perched to rain a hail of lead down upon him. The SUV was still parked behind the restaurant, where he'd seen it from the street, however the headlights were doused. There wasn't even a lamp giving the alley a semblance of visibility. Bolan noted one pole with a lamp attached, but the bulb had been shot out.

Bolan took advantage of the low fences surrounding the small back lots, keeping himself in a crouch as he moved along. He glanced back. Nobody was following that he could tell. The SUV loomed ahead, and he reached the rear passenger side. The tracker bug was quickly retrieved and he pocketed it in its harness. Checking the back of the SUV, he noticed that the body was still there. He didn't disturb the scene, but instead headed up the short flight of steps to the back door of the restaurant. He pulled out the Cobray and tested the door, which was unlocked. There was a small spill of light coming from underneath, enough to give the Executioner a moment's pause. He wasn't sure what he was onto, but he didn't want to spend the next few days following armed murderers around the city of Chicago. They'd already killed once tonight, and they were linked to the RING, if they were involved in the theft of the missiles.

Bolan opened the door with one hand, aiming the Cobray with the other, scanning an empty kitchen. As he closed the door behind him softly, only allowing a muffled click, he heard the soft thumps of footsteps on the ceiling. He could see through the round portal windows that the dining area was still darkened, but light was spilling onto the floor. He stalked farther into the kitchen, looking left and right. The place reeked of garlic and other heavy spices as pots and pans were thrown in disarray in the sink.

Near the double doors was another stairwell, the door removed off its hinges long ago. The light spilled from there, and Bolan pointed the Cobray upward. He paused, remembering a conflict with a combined Iraqi-

Korean alliance of terrorists. One cell of Iraqi terrorists had set themselves up with their wives and children in the middle of New York City, in a restaurant. However, that building had been larger than this relatively cramped little eatery. He couldn't imagine more than four families being packed into the two floors above the main, but then, there was always the potential for even four sets of wives and kids to have been brought on hand to be used as human shields.

Bolan approached the steps slowly, steeling himself for the possibility of having to check his fire while his enemies cut loose. The potential for tragedy had increased tenfold. His crawl up the steps was arduous as he tested each stair to avoid a telltale squeak that would betray his approach.

Stealth was blown to hell, however, when a tall, gaunt man with rusty-red hair stepped onto the landing that Bolan had almost reached. The lanky redhead stopped cold at the sight of an intruder facing him down with a stubby, ugly automatic weapon in his hands. Even though his eyes were wide with fear, his hands moved swiftly with practiced speed toward a weapon tucked into a waist holster.

"Caul!" the man bellowed just as Bolan cut a burst of 9 mm Parabellum rounds through his belly and up into his lungs. The impact sent the gunman smashing against the wall, blood streaming from his mouth and nose. The crash of his body only added to the cacophony that turned the soft probe hard. Bolan rushed to the landing and crouched behind a doorjamb, spotting men dodging left and right from the entrance. They were in a living room of sorts, the center dominated by a circular table bearing assorted beverages and papers. He didn't have long to study the room as handguns with sound-suppressors attached popped and hissed, bullets chewing at the wall the Executioner had taken for cover. The soldiers squirted out a couple bursts into the melee, then stepped down a couple stairs.

His return fire had given the enemy some pause, and he took the opportunity to pull the pin on a concussion grenade and throw the bomb through the landing opening, letting it bounce once and detonate.

With no deadly shrapnel to slice flesh and cause horrific bleeding, the shock wave in the confined space served to make every man in the living room feel like he'd been swatted in the head with a baseball bat. Immediately after the blast, it took a will of iron to get back onto your feet and actually walk, let alone fight.

Bolan took the opportunity and charged up and out of the stairwell. He spun to the left, away from the living room, and saw a darkened dining room. Down the hall, two men stumbled out of second hallway just before the second floor's kitchen. They were armed, as well, and hadn't experienced the body-numbing shock of a stun grenade.

Raising their pistols, they took aim at Bolan, who dropped to the ground, landing on his chest and elbows, firing. Bullets ripped across the distance between him and his adversaries, chunks of flesh and bone blasted from thighs, knees and shins. The terrorists screamed in agony, tumbling to the ground. One still tried to shoot at the Executioner, his bullets tracking high, but getting closer with every squeeze of the trigger. Lining up the Cobray, Bolan ripped a burst into his face, the terrorist's skull exploding.

His partner screamed in terror at the sight of the decapitating blast, trying to claw himself away from the slaughter, but the Executioner spared another blast to swiftly put the crippled terrorist down and out of his misery. He couldn't leave an enemy behind him, not when he could recover from his pain and use the gun in his hand to shoot the soldier in the back. Bolan didn't like being so merciless, but it was a reality of combat.

The three men in the living room hadn't recovered from their painful encounter with his grenade, and Bolan disarmed each of them, tossing their handguns onto the table. One of the Arabs was holding his blood-ied arm and, after close inspection, he realized that even concussion grenades had a piece of shrapnel. The three-ounce cylindrical detonator had been launched by the blast right into the shoulder of the terrorist, smashing bone and pulping flesh. He remembered seeing tests where the detonators would have sufficient boost from their cardboard-bodied grenades to fly three-hundred feet and still dent concrete.

Bolan gave the wounded guy a hard right to the jaw, smashing the bone into the juncture of nerves just under the ear. Neurological overload sent the wounded man into unconsciousness and gave the Executioner one less headache. He got up and turned just in time to see the man he assumed was Caul rise and swat the Execu-tioner's Cobray into his ribs with jarring force. The breath knocked out of him, Bolan staggered back and found his head grabbed on both sides by clawing hands.

He released the weapon and brought his hands up and around Caul's wrists, pinning them against the sides of his head. Still, the man's nails dug hard into Bolan's scalp, and his powerful, lean body hauled the Execu-tioner's taller frame off balance. Losing the leverage fight, the soldier was flipped over the Hand of Christ man, landing hard on his back, rolled to all fours.

The Christian Identity soldier also got up quickly.

Despite his eardrums being hammered by the concussion grenade, the man maintained an incredible level of balance. That's when the Executioner noticed the crazed fury in the man's eyes. He had gone beyond brutal concussive trauma into madness.

Bolan surged forward, lacing both of his hands together into a hammer fist that he swung up under Caul's jaw. Bone cracked under the mighty swing and spit flew from the terrorist's mouth, but he stayed upright. A heavy combat boot shot toward the Executioner's groin and barely missed, striking his thigh and just above his gonads. The blow was enough to slow him, giving Caul a chance to reach out and try to grab Bolan again.

This time, the Executioner was ready.

He grabbed Caul's right wrist and spun, pulling the man's arm up tight under Bolan's armpit. He didn't stop his pivot, using every ounce of his weight to yank the arm out of its socket and flip the terrorist up and over. Agonized cries finally escaped Caul's lips as his shoulder dislocated, but that didn't last longer than his brutal contact with the floor.

A grunt escaped the man's throat and Bolan drove his elbow down hard into Caul's breastbone. He followed the hit with a hard punch to the temple.

His adversary finally went limp, and Bolan rose upright on rubbery legs. He glanced over to the last man in the room, an Arab who was holding his ears, looking up with big frightened eyes at the tall wraith in black.

Someone was stomping up the stairs and Bolan drew his Beretta in a fluid movement. Instinct told him it was the guy who had stepped out onto the street, coming up from his post to help deal with the raging battle.

As soon as he appeared in the doorway, Bolan punched two shots into him, then turned back to the stunned Arab, not even bothering to watch the lifeless guard go tumbling back down the stairs.

"Surrendering?" Bolan asked him, letting the Beretta drop to his side. He locked the man with the coldest gaze in his arsenal.

The Arab nodded emphatically, keeping his hands to his ears and away from his fallen pistol.

"Good," Bolan sighed with relief, holstering the Beretta. "For both of us."

THE VAN FULL of U.S. Marshals pulled up in front of the restaurant as the sky was turning gray, swarming into the building with guns drawn and grim resolve painting their faces.

Mack Bolan knew they wouldn't find resistance in the building. He'd crushed it with swift, violent action. He looked with worry at the information he had copied down.

Present on the table was a road atlas of the Chicagoland area. The document was big enough for there to be extensive views of all the parts of the city, but letting the book fall open, he found himself staring at a map of O'Hare airport. Nothing was marked down on the map itself, but he could see impressions of pen marks. A crumpled, marker-smeared piece of acetate next to it was wiped off too much to be useful as any indicator of what was being jotted down.

It didn't matter. After the past couple days, anything to do with an airport, especially the busiest airport in the country, set off the alarms in his brain. Another bit of mystery data was a map of Wisconsin, with a town off the beaten path noted with a pencil mark.

An assortment of handguns and improvised grenades was littered about the second floor of the building, and Bolan secured them away from the men he left bound. Now, with the arrival of the marshals, he felt free to head back to his rental car and get out of town. He'd make an effort to meet with Hector Terin back at Terintec, but once that was over with, he had a job to do, and his steps were being guided by a pencil-scratched Wisconsin road map.

CHAPTER EIGHT

Dr. Jackie Sorenson sensed the presence outside her door before she heard or saw it. The tingle she got from the new arrival wasn't one of hostility, though, and when she looked up at the sound of the knock on the doorjamb, she knew why she sensed him of all people.

"Did you hear me coming?" Hermann Schwarz asked, smiling.

"Gadgets!" Sorenson grinned and rose to her feet, wrapping her arms around the stocky Able Team electronics genius. "Still into your metaphysical studies?"

"Of course," Schwarz answered, returning the hug. He was holding back on the strength of his embrace, as if he were worried about hurting her willowy five-six frame.

Sorenson sighed and took a step back. "You're not in town for a social visit, are you?"

Schwarz shook his head, and the woman seemed emboldened by the admission. She walked back to her desk and heaved herself up to sit on its edge, pointing for Schwarz to take a seat in front of her.

"What's up?"

"We need some information from you, Jackie."

The woman nodded and leaned forward, cupping his cheek. "First of all, how is everyone?"

"Carl's laid out in a hospital bed."

"I told him not to play chicken with 18-wheelers."

Schwarz shook his head. "Someone put him down in hand-to-hand combat. And he took a bunch of bullets, but his body armor stopped most of them."

Sorenson was quiet. "This wouldn't happen to have involved Dulles Airport, would it?"

"Can't hide anything from you."

"I did some checking with some old contacts. They said only two men were involved."

"And only one man was responsible for Ironman being sent to the scrap heap for a while."

Sorenson raised an eyebrow. "And another man, on his own, managed to destroy the air-traffic control systems so completely?"

"He had an experimental antiradiation missile. And a computer."

Sorenson narrowed her eyes. "The software for air-traffic control is some of the most protected code in the world. It's not just anyone who can get their hands on it."

"That's why Barbara sent me to talk to you. You have any ideas who could have stolen it, or even just duplicated it themselves?" Schwarz asked.

Sorenson slid off the edge of the desk and walked toward her bookshelf. "You think I might have some fingers in watching out for cybercriminals, Gadgets?"

"You'd have to be listening in at the Farm to know about it just being two guys who wrecked Dulles," Schwarz replied.

He paused for a moment. "Does Aaron know?"

"He subcontracts out to me."

Schwarz nodded. "So what do you have for me?"

"Nothing off the top of my head, but we can look."

DAVID KOWALSKI LOOKED over to Rosario Blancanales. He could tell the veteran Able Team member wasn't pleased with the turn of events.

"No matter how good a role-player you are, you're not going to hide your Hispanic features," Kowalski told him. He pressed the throat mike, covered with a surgical adhesive to a spot just below his clavicle. "Testing testing."

"I read you," Blancanales answered. He handed over a dusty, sweaty-looking baseball cap. On the outside it looked as though it couldn't even be sold at a yard sale for a nickel. On the inside, however, the U.S. Marshall knew there were a couple thousand dollars of miniaturized electronics.

He accepted the hat, which bore a John Deere logo on the front. "No Chicago Cubs?"

"I wouldn't press your luck at being a Chicagoan around these chumps."

"South'n Illinois it is," Kowalski said. He spit out the window. "Ain't nearly so many spics and Jews around them parts."

Blancanales bounced a playful punch off the man's bicep. "You almost sounded like the real thing."

"God, just wash my mouth out with soap when this is over."

"Just don't get it washed out with lead," Blancanales admonished.

Kowalski nodded, then got out of the car.

According to Blancanales, Able Team had been working undercover, trying to root out the sources of automatic weapons and explosives that the Army of the Hand of Christ were employing in bank robberies and armored car thefts. So far, they'd managed a couple confrontations with splinter cells in three Northern California cities, but there was nothing that allowed them a definitive killshot against the organization. They'd managed to trace AHC activity to the combination gun shop and range.

Kowalski's jaws were grinding again. It was bad enough that these racist, homophobic pieces of crap were calling themselves followers of Christ and their actions the will of God. But law-abiding citizens of any religion were going to get tarnished by association because these thugs associated freedom from an "unfair government" with robbing banks, blowing up abortion clinics and fondling guns. Kowalski was a certified trainer in weapons handling, and he genuinely liked guns the same way people liked Corvettes or Mustangs. In his perfect world, though, all he'd ever have to do was put bullet holes in sheets of fancy paper, or maybe bagging a deer or moose to provide an alternative to store-bought meat for a winter.

He entered the shop and, as one, a dozen heads turned to look at him. There was a clerk at the counter, jawing with a couple "good ol' boys" and a couple tables full of men sitting and chatting up over assorted sporting magazines and mugs of beverages. He gave them all a smile and strolled over to the counter, looking at the handguns on display.

"What're you looking for?" the clerk asked. There was a hint of accusation in his voice, an unspoken request for him to find what he was looking for and get the hell out so that everyone could get back to what they were doing.

"I'm looking for a government that isn't standing on my neck, denying me the rights I fought in the Gulf to protect," he answered. He looked along the counter. "But for now, I'm looking for a nice American-built .45 with a lefty for southpaws."

He lifted his left hand for emphasis. "I'm a lefty."

The clerk smirked. "That's big talk."

"Why? You don't like left-handed people?"

"Talking trash against this nation's government. I can't believe you. What are you, ATF trying to see if I'm selling magazines that hold too many bullets?" the clerk pressed.

Kowalski sighed. "No. I want a .45. If you want me to get real specific, fine. I've been dying to pick up a Kimber Pro-Carry, but any four-inch-barreled .45 with an ambidexterous safety, Novak sights, a Wilson magazine and complete reliability will be fine."

"You know your guns."

"Told you, I'm a soldier. A Marine."

The men at the table spoke quietly among themselves. Kowalski looked over his shoulder, then passed them off.

"So you could go to any gun store around...."

"Yeah, but I'm moving into town," Kowalski countered. "I'll be here in a couple days, just enough for one of those stupid waiting periods to go by."

"Where are you moving from?"

"Southern Illinois. Metropolis."

"Metropolis?"

"Yeah. Home of truth, justice and the American way."

"There is such a town." One of the men at the table spoke up. "Took my kid to one of their Superman celebrations. They have them every summer, bring in guest stars, they have a Superman museum, too."

Kowalski grinned. "There's that. Trouble is, I just haven't been feeling the love back home. Wanted to look for someplace that appealed to me."

"Why California? It's more liberal here than Illinois," the clerk asked.

"It's closer to some old military contacts of mine. I was thinking of starting a security business."

"You look kind of young to be starting your own security firm."

"I'm a hands-on kind of man. I figure by the time I get tired of doing my own work, I'll be old enough to sit behind the desk and get attention from an intern like Blow Job Bill."

The room exploded into laughter.

"You don't want that right now?"

"I can chase tail on my own. When I get that old, I'll be glad to have it delivered."

"You're crazy," the shop clerk said. "Here. I did this myself. It's a classic Colt Commander and it's done up with all the Marine Expeditionary Unit, Special Operations customization. I presume that's what you were looking for."

Kowalski took the gun, checked that the chamber and mag well were clear by touch and sight, then checked the balance. "Got a mag full of dummy rounds? I really want to check the balance."

The clerk looked at him a moment, then nodded in approval, tossing him a magazine. Kowalski checked the top round on the clip, seeing the bright orange rubber bullet poking out. Even if he chambered the round, a pull of the trigger would only result in a dull click. He loaded the gun, chambered the top round and flicked on the thumb safety. He took aim at a section of wall covered with a Heckler & Koch products poster, thumbed off the safety and pulled the trigger with a resounding click. He handed the gun back to the clerk.

"I'll buy it. Trigger's just right—a bit heavy, but no mush on the pull."

"Not going to ask the price?"

"Fifteen hundred?"

"Thirteen, actually," the clerk answered. "Not as much demand for the middle-size .45s. Everybody either wants a short Officer's or a full-length Government model."

"Shame, too." Kowalski produced his credit card, or rather the one provided to him by Stony Man Farm under the name of Peter Steel. "Officer's models end up choking a lot, and the Government model is too big for warm weather. Besides, the Commander has the best balance of all three versions."

"Sign here," the clerk said. "You know what you want, kid."

Kowalski looked around the room, saw eyes still warily watching him, then smiled. "Seize the day."

He signed his receipt. The clerk put one copy in the register and handed him the customer copy. "Fifteen days. If you want, you can come by sooner to the range and target practice with it."

Kowalski pretended to think about it for a moment. "I don't have to head back for about four days. Maybe I'll be back around if business lets me."

The clerk eyed him for a moment, then shook his hand. "Come back anytime. We'll be waiting for you."

Kowalski returned the handshake, not voicing that he'd return, but they wouldn't be expecting him at all.

"YOU MADE FRIENDS and influenced people," Blancanales commented as they headed back to their hotel. "Not bad for your second day on the job."

Kowalski chuckled. "I'm not a rookie. Just more rookie than you."

Blancanales smirked. "Implying something, young whippersnapper?"

"Nothing a bottle of hair dye couldn't fix."

The Able Team veteran laughed and looked into the rearview mirror. "We're being followed."

"Oh, good. It's only been a whole three days since I shot at someone," Kowalski said, pulling a Beretta from the glove compartment. "Do you think they saw me get into the car with you driving? Did they get a good look at your face?"

"I kept from directly showing my full face. A tan and gray hair could belong to a caucasian man, too," Blancanales said. He checked the presence of his Kissinger-tuned Colt Government model, then continued to concentrate on driving. "I'm not going to make any effort to lose them. Keep the Beretta out of sight, in case any cops spot it."

"Right. We act like pros at spotting a tail, then they'll know we're bad news and any links we could get out of the shop..." Ski let his voice trail off as he studied the rearview and passenger mirrors. "Who's the tail?"

"A black Lincoln," Blancanales answered. "We could just as easily get information off dead bodies after they make the mistake of coming after us."

Blancanales quickly added, "Stay cool, kid."

"Draw them in and ambush them?"

"It's not going to be pretty, and it's going to be cold-blooded. If you want, I'll do all the work."

"I was a sniper-scout. With confirmed kills. And I don't even want to know how many terrorists I took down with Striker in Egypt. I can do the job."

Blancanales nodded grimly. "I didn't doubt your ability."

"Just whether I could live with myself. Where do we put the smack on these turds?"

"The hotel looks like our best bet. We'll set up our defense because these guys are going to watch where we went, maybe leave a lookout on the corner, and get ready to do some damage later," Blancanales told him.

"Sounds like you're used to having your hotel rooms shot up," Kowalski mentioned.

"Well, the running joke for us is that the other guys always got shot at when they got off the plane at the airport, and we always got ambushed in our hotels."

"Leave it to Mr. Stone to get taken down at an airport, then."

"I'll have to tell that to Gadgets. He'd get a kick out of that. Speaking of which… Ring him up."

Kowalski pulled his phone and dialed up Schwarz's phone. A voice popped up on the connection after the second ring.

"Able Group Investigations."

"Pol told me to call you. We've got a tail."

"You picked that up quick," Schwarz said. "So, bad news. I'll keep an eye out on my way to the hotel. You might get there first, so no blowing me off the doorstep with a limpet charge."

"We promise." The connection went dead and he put the phone away. He looked to Blancanales. "Well, he knows. What's the status on our shadow?"

"Still there. We're almost to the hotel, so hide your gun."

Kowalski lifted his shirt and stuffed the Beretta into his waistband, Mexican style, then let the folds of his jacket and sweatshirt fall over the handle of the big gun. It disappeared under the rumpled clothing that came down from his thick chest. "Done."

Blancanales parked and they both got out. "All right. Meet you in a couple minutes for a war council."

CHAPTER NINE

As much as the Executioner wanted to get on the road to Wisconsin, he still had work to do at Terintec, and a cover to maintain. He also would be lying to himself if he wasn't a bit curious as to Hector Terin's reaction the news about his missing bodyguard. He was also concerned about what else Terin might have on hand. The MARS missile was a dangerous tool by itself. But what if it were used to supplement something even more dangerous? On the itinerary for his review of Terintec's holdings was a demonstration of their variation on the U.S. Army's National Automotive Center's SmarTruck. The vehicle was a rolling war machine with every electronic warfare advantage and the added ability of having a combat laser and racks of grenades that ranged from high explosive to tear gas. It even had door handles that provided electrical shocks to anyone trying to gain unauthorized entry. The vehicle read like it came out of a James Bond movie.

Bolan, who had lived his fair share of James Bond-movie like experiences, reminisced wistfully about the War Wagon, his own old high-tech mobile home. It had been sacrificed at the end of his war against the Mafia, a blazing pyre to a body the world would believe was the Executioner as he died on that deadly, cold Saturday.

The SmarTruck reminded him, conceptually at least, of the vehicle that had been his home, his sick bay, his armory and his transportation for the first two bloody miles of his War Everlasting. This one even shared one feature—a missile launcher. Whereas Bolan's "firebirds" were intended for taking out mobbed-up mansions or armored limousines, the Terintec SmarTruck display was going to feature the SmarTruck/MARS combined platform. A synergy, as the public-relations people would say in corporate speak.

That was what got the Executioner concerned as he thought of the potential of a state-of-the-art urban warfare vehicle in the hands of a terrorist conspiracy like the RING. A few crashed airplanes and an airport massacre weren't going to be the be-all and end-all of terrorist attacks. Not with the RING's promises to pull down all the national governments around the globe. Bolan's instincts writhed like a nest of unsettled serpents, ready to pitch themselves in venomous, savage defense.

The press was waiting at the gates of the office complex and cameras flashed as a limousine began its crawl up the driveway. He'd gotten there an hour before and avoided the press thanks to Sable Burton leading him around to a side entrance.

"You don't like publicity, Colonel Stone?" she probed as the white limo came slowly past the mob of reporters.

"It'd be bad for my business to be seen on the evening news," Bolan admitted. "I don't like the spotlight."

Burton nodded. "I can understand that."

"Not really, but I appreciate the sentiment."

Burton sighed, giving him a lingering glance, then looking back as the limo finally cleared the crowd of reporters and cameramen.

"It's terrible about Shep."

"Shep?" Bolan asked. He didn't like lying about the fact that Aaron Kurtzman had identified the dead man thanks to digital photos taken from the crime scene. He also didn't have the heart to tell her that he was the one who had discovered him dead, not the way she talked about him. So he played dumb.

"Glen Shephard. He was one of Terin's top bodyguards. He was found early this morning near Greektown. Didn't you hear the news?"

"I didn't associate it with Terin," Bolan lied.

"He was stuffed in the back of an SUV. And the building the car was parked behind was filled with dead and wounded terrorists, according to reports," Burton continued. "Someone went in and performed like the wrath of God on them."

Terin's limousine finally pulled up in front of them.

Hector Terin was immaculately dressed, hair combed, nails manicured, seemingly none the worse for wear for having just gotten off a plane after a cross-country flight. Tall and lean, with a pencil-thin mustache, and black hair combed back to expose a widow's peak, he was a stark, severe man with piercing blue eyes. Bolan could meet the man's gaze evenly, and the two sized each other up.

Terin studied him as if Bolan were a bull who had wandered into his range. All that was left for him to do was to paw the ground and snort steam through his nostrils.

"Mr. Terin, this is Colonel Brandon Stone. He was sent to do some fact-finding—"

Terin cut Burton off. "The shipment to the Naval Special Warfare Development Group. I figured as much. Welcome, Colonel Stone."

He extended a hand and Bolan shook it. There was a great deal of strength in the handshake, but Bolan resisted the urge to turn it into a contest, even though he could feel Terin trying to squeeze a reaction out of him. "A pleasure to be here, sir."

Terin broke the grip and didn't take his eyes off Bolan. "Sable, I take it part of Colonel Stone's agenda is to accompany us out to the field to witness our latest testing?"

"Of course, Mr. Terin," Burton responded. She sounded uncertain and Bolan didn't blame her. While much more subtle than the battle of wills with an overzealous security guard the day before, there was still a war raging between the two men.

Whether Terin was sizing Bolan up as a corporate predator protecting his business interests, or was on edge thanks to his guilt in recent events, the Executioner didn't know.

"You know about the MAP-SmarTruck?" Terin told him.

Bolan tossed Burton a glance, but she shook her bewilderment at the silent struggle of wills.

"MARS Assault Platform Smart Truck," she explained.

"I've read the tech sheets on your modifications," Bolan replied. "If your theory works out, it will make things safer for air and ground forces."

"And you possess some doubts?" Terin asked.

"After Dulles…not anymore," Bolan said.

Terin stiffened, eyes flashing with a moment of indignant rage before he cast his gaze downward. "I was afraid of that."

Burton looked as though she'd been punched in the gut. "You mean, it was our missiles involved in the massacre?"

An uneasy silence settled over the three people. It was a minute before one of Terin's aids got up the courage to announce that they were behind schedule for the SmarTruck demonstration.

BURTON DECIDED to ride with Stone in his car when they were heading out to the test field. He offered, and she had some suspicions that he had a thousand unasked questions to lay on her. Something was going on behind the icy walls of his blue eyes, flames flickering in a brain that would not stop analyzing angles.

"Shephard, did you know him well?" Bolan asked.

Burton nodded. "He was a nice guy."

Bolan cast her a sideways glance. "Nice?"

"He was soft-spoken, quiet. Almost introverted, but polite to the point of knightly chivalry," she told him.

"Was he like this to everyone?"

"As far as I know. He got along with everyone at Terintec. It was only over the past couple months when he seemed to be in a dark mood."

"Depressed?"

"Sad and morose. He didn't want to talk with people as much. He wouldn't start a conversation, but it's not like he avoided people. Shep just got quiet."

"How close were you two?"

"Just friends. It was always the case that he was with someone, or I was with someone. We just ended up… we're…we were…friends and…"

Burton lowered her head, the weight of Shephard's loss finally hitting her.

She closed her eyes, trying to fight the burning behind the lids, trying to suck breath past the massive, crushing weight blocking her windpipe. It took a few moments for her to get her breathing back to normal. Her stomach still was twisted, nausea spinning in the core of her chest up from her navel, but stopping. She wasn't going to freak over this, not in front of a stranger.

"It's okay," Bolan said softly. His hand went to rest on her shoulder.

"No, it's not, but thanks," Burton answered.

"Was he a religious man?"

"He was, but he didn't try to push his beliefs onto other people."

"Christian?"

Burton nodded. "Catholic by birth, but he wasn't any denomination by the time we met."

"What kind of friends did he have?"

The woman's face flushed. "You already know what happened to Shep!"

Bolan frowned deeply. Burton felt her ears burning at the thought that he was playing dumb with her, and her nails dug into her palms.

"I knew," he admitted. "The men responsible for killing him are dead or in custody."

"What happened?"

"I don't know why Shep was murdered. Not yet." Bolan told her.

"The men who killed him?"

Bolan remained silent, but his eyes took on a pained look. He wasn't going to let her in on what he knew.

She pressed on. "Just who are you?"

"Someone trying to prevent more tragedies." His voice lost its authoritative edge.

Burton set her lips tight and looked out the window. "Shep wouldn't be involved in hurting anyone. I don't know what you believe…."

"Sometimes people can be bullied into following someone else's lead. A lot of times, when they fall in with the wrong crowd, they develop a conscience and start to do something, and end up getting killed for it."

They were getting closer to the field where Terin was putting on his display. The caravan of industry reporters and technology correspondents was turning in ahead of Bolan and Burton. Technicians were making last-minute adjustments to the testing ground even after weeks of work. Burton had been there very early that morning, taking care of finishing touches for the day's demonstration. She looked back to Bolan.

"You really think Shephard threw in with Arab terrorists?" the woman asked.

His icy-blue eyes widened in surprise. "Americans weren't mentioned?"

"What Americans?"

Bolan's jaw set hard. "There were two white men. Americans. From what I know, they were part of the Army of the Hand of Christ. AHC for short."

"The news said—"

"And I was there. One of them was called Caul."

Recognition burned across Burton's mind. "Caul? As in Stephen Caul?"

Bolan nodded. "That's what his driver's license read."

"Oh, God."

"You knew him, too?" Bolan asked.

"Just by name. I didn't like him. He just had

this…aura around him. I wanted to hit him with a two-by-four. Is he dead or alive?"

"Dead."

"Did he suffer?"

Momentary shock danced across Bolan's face. "He went down hard. I don't do torture."

MACK BOLAN FELT the cell phone vibrate in his breast pocket and answered it on the second throbbing pulse.

"This is Stone."

"Pol," came the terse response. Blancanales sounded a little tense.

"What's going on?"

"Just checking in with you. Our young new ally managed to get us a bite."

Bolan smiled. "I told you he was good."

"I should have never doubted you. We don't have much time, but figured we'd let you in on the situation."

"You let mother know?" Bolan was referring to Barbara Price, back at Stony Man Farm, the mission controller for the teams.

"Of course." Blancanales put on an air of mock shock.

Bolan grunted in approval. "Take care."

"That's what we do."

The link disconnected and Bolan put his phone away.

Things were building to a head again. He wanted this afternoon over with so he could contact Grimaldi and get him to Wisconsin.

"What's wrong?" Burton asked.

"Business as usual," Bolan answered. "Nothing for you to worry about."

A truck was being rolled onto the field, a lump of machinery in the back covered in a canvas tarpaulin that seemed to have the tech-press all a-flutter with anticipation and glee, like children on a Christmas morning. Bolan, being more direct, just turned to his companion.

"That's the SmarTruck under the tarp?"

"That's for me to know and you to find out," she said cryptically. Her irritation wasn't completely scrubbed free by the slight smile on her face, but Bolan was glad to see a change in her mood.

"Oh. Irony. I encounter that too much. Mostly it's snide arrogance and political double-talk. Last time I encountered irony, I think bell-bottoms were in style."

Burton took a deep breath. "You can be funny, Colonel Stone."

"Call me Brandon."

Bolan lowered his head. Something was in the distance. He could feel it, more than hear or see it, something that vibrated in his chest, though deeper to the core than the cell phone. He never fully believed in a sixth sense, the paranormal powers of the mind, but sometimes his gut feelings gave him a precognitive sense of danger. Gadgets Schwarz of Stony Man Farm was a strong believer in paranormal phenomena, even if they were explainable by an instantaneous subconscious assessment due to years of experience. Bolan could buy that explanation. His senses had learned every possible angle of ambush and threat in the world. He could memorize the license plates of every car in a parking lot or on a street around a building he went into with just a glance. He entered a room and would tally up every exit he could fit through in a heartbeat. It was no stretch for Bolan to imagine that ordinary senses actually did pick up subtler things than most people perceived.

Something had drawn his attention. It had raised the

hairs on the back of his neck and it was something he'd heard, something crawling under the sound of scripted podium speech and inquiries from the crowd. The vibration rose to his ears over the sound of people still talking and asking questions of Terin who had taken up a position next to the truck. As soon as it was audible at the lowest level, he knew what it was.

A helicopter of some kind.

He turned, scanning the sky, trying to focus on the incoming chopper with the help of his hearing.

"What's wrong?" Burton asked him.

Bolan frowned. "Incoming choppers."

"We have security."

"So did Dulles."

Burton paled, then put her hand to her mouth. "Are you armed?"

"Not with anything that could hold off a platoon coming off a helicopter. And nothing that could knock a chopper out of the sky. By the time I got anything out of the trunk, the assault would be under way, and even then, I start pulling out an M-16, Terin's security would start chopping me down."

"Oh, hell."

Bolan started toward Terin, with Burton was in pursuit. "What were you going to do in the demonstration today?"

"Show off the firepower of the SmarTruck."

Bolan knew the specifics of the vehicle. The heavy-shelled off-road vehicle had enough armor to ignore most battlefield threats and could return fire with a rack of specialized grenades and a turreted experimental laser. The Terintec version had, in addition to standard SATCOM communications, an electronic countermeasure suite that could choke an armored division. It could also umbrella an entire armored convoy against aerial strikes, denying enemy pilots radar or laser locks for their smart bombs. Plus it was designed with the MARS system in mind.

"Of course. The original SmarTruck wasn't our design, and we decided to go with a laser-guided 25 mm cannon and a shelf for MARS missiles. No live ammo or warheads, just blanks and guided drones," Burton quickly added.

"Doesn't matter, the people coming already have their own MARS missiles and perhaps everything they need to mass produce them," Bolan growled. He knifed through the crowd, reporters reluctantly moving aside until the first Black Hawk slashed overhead, rotorwash blowing like a hurricane among them. The crowd loosened, confused by the new arrivals, allowing Bolan and Burton to push through the throng to the end.

"Mass produced?" Burton asked, stunned by the comment.

Bolan reached Terin. "You have to get your people out of here. Those helicopters aren't part of your demonstration, and I think they're going to make a snatch."

The businessman darted a glance at Bolan, then followed the helicopters racing back in an orbit toward the field. Streaming canisters spewing smoke hissed out the sides of the low-slung aircrafts.

At this point, the reporters were taking off. Technicians were looking around in confusion, wondering whether to stay and hold their ground or to run. Tear gas added into the mix only broke their will to stand and fight, and they raced off toward the road or plunged into whatever cover they could find.

"Who would dare?" Terin asked, eyes wildly dancing across the mayhem around him.

"You tell me. I'm betting it's the people who had your bodyguard murdered last night," Bolan challenged.

There wasn't even a flinch from the businessman. Security guards were pushing the crowd aside. One of the bodyguards grabbed Terin by the arm and dragged him back to his limousine.

"Get the truck out of here!" Terin roared to Bolan. "Everybody else! Get out of here!"

Bolan turned and took out his car keys, tossing them to Burton. "Take my car and get out of here."

"Where are you going?" Sable called.

"With the SmarTruck."

"I thought you said you weren't armed!"

Bolan waved her off. "I'll improvise! *Go!*"

DARK HUNG in the door of the helicopter, the straps of his Calico 950 SMGs keeping them from bouncing around on his chest as the Black Hawk sliced through the sky under Harpy's skillful hands. Adonis was at his back, as were the handpicked and personally trained cream of the Army of the Hand of Christ and Fist of God organizations. He wasn't sure if they would be returning, and there were more such heavily trained troops back at the base, but it would be inconvenient to lose twenty men after weeks of indoctrination and teaching.

Dark wasn't getting sentimental, he was just tired of dealing with the racist sons of bitches every day. For the most part, he was able to keep them intimidated enough to make them bury their prejudices, but sometimes tempers did flare, and he'd had to kill one or two to send a message to the rest of the drones.

"Dark, check it out," Adonis said. "Someone just jumped onto the target truck. It looks like everybody's moving out."

Dark had to squint to see who Adonis was talking about. There were times when Dark could swear the big blond giant had binoculars for eyes. Everything about him was extra-muscled and strong. He noticed a tall, slender figure in black crawling into the back of the truck next to their target. "This must be the big scary that DeeDee was talking about."

Adonis frowned. "He moves well."

Dark pulled a pair of binoculars from his pocket and trained them on the truck when he saw something flash in the stranger's hand.

The helicopter jerked, Harpy's cursing filling his ears. A 9 mm bullet glanced off the stock of one of his Calicos, shattering the grip, and another round sparked near where his hand clutched the door frame.

"Dammit!" Dark spit. "He's shooting at us!"

"And here you thought there wasn't going to be any challenge today," Adonis cracked.

"Yeah, well you didn't just have a bullet bounce off your chest," Dark snarled.

Adonis pushed his partner easily aside, an M-79 grenade launcher held in one of his hands looking like a child's air rifle. He took aim at the truck and pulled the trigger, a strangling cloud of white smoke draping over the transport.

The man in black disappeared in the swirling mists.

"CS-CN tear gas. I doubt he's got the foresight to carry a gas mask with him," Adonis said. "I'd have used something stronger, but we want the truck in one piece."

"Harpy! Lay down some more of that old school cover!" Dark called.

"Please and thank you would be nice!" Harpy called back with only mock irritation.

"With sprinkles and a cherry on top, love!"

Harpy tossed him a kiss and the Black Hawk shook as a rack on the back of the sleek helicopter ejected a storm of projectiles onto the scattering assembly on the field.

Chaos took over and Dark was back in his element.

MACK BOLAN SCRAMBLED onto the back of the truck just as the Black Hawks burst over the tree line. He was impressed that the enemy, whoever it was, had some high-quality vehicles. He reached into his pocket and pulled out the little polymer-framed Beretta 9000. Since he was in polite company, he wouldn't be able to hide either his Desert Eagle or his Beretta 93-R, both massive in comparison to normal combat handguns. He wished he'd gone with the slight inconvenience of the Beretta 93-R right now, the extra length of the six-and-a-half-inch barrel would have given him better reach and accuracy against the incoming helicopters. Still, the snubby Beretta, capable of taking even the 20-shot magazines intended for his 93-R machine pistol, was accurate and reliable.

Bolan aimed at the lead aircraft and burned eleven shots, rewarded with sparks flying on the windshield of the helicopter.

He turned to the drivers of the transport who had their rear window open. "Those choppers are going to wreck anything in their way. Is the SmarTruck ready to move?"

"Yeah! It's gassed and ready to go."

"Are the fingerprint security systems set up?"

"Hell, no. This was a field demo. Be damn embarrassing if we couldn't get the damn truck working because Joey called in sick!" the driver yelled.

"Where's Joey?" Bolan asked.

"Right here," the guy in the passenger seat said. "What're you planning?"

"Driving the SmarTruck the hell out of here and limiting the potential for casualties. If I have to, I'll scuttle the damn thing," Bolan told him. "It can be rebuilt. People can't."

"I'll drive. You can handle the drones," Joey replied, slipping through the back window and into the transport bed. "Let's go."

Bolan weighed the consequences of letting the young Terintec driver accompany him, then realized he would need help. He ripped the tarpaulin free from the body of the SmarTruck and was taken aback by the so-called updates. The vehicle looked like it was straight out of a science-fiction novel, its nose a black Kevlar square that swooped into a windshield like a pilot pulling out of a dive. The whole vehicle was nearly one uniform shade of black, so much that he didn't even believe the windshield was made of glass.

Joey tore open his door and Bolan crawled in the other side.

"There's the controls for the missile launcher and the 25 mm cannon. There's only dummy ammo in it, so it won't tear through solid steel, but it's not blanks, it's plastic-tipped. If we're close enough…"

Bolan's smile apparently told Joey that he didn't have to finish the thought. The soldier knew that the plastic shells would still impact on a human body with enough force to break bone, even if they didn't penetrate flesh.

An eruption of white smoke burst to one side, a choking tendril being sucked into the cabin of the SmarTruck, and Bolan was caught off guard by the sudden rush of tear gas. He gasped, eyes burning. Joey was screeching and clawing at his face as his mucus membranes were put under savage assault. Bolan reached across him and yanked the door shut.

"Into the back!" Bolan ordered Joey. He gave the driver a good push to help him along, and settled behind the wheel, setting the truck into gear. Through the windows he saw that the ground around the truck was erupting with flashes and more bursts of smoke. The testing field was under assault, and crowds were being forced back by flares and columns of tear gas.

It was an efficient sweep, good enough to keep the security force busy helping civilians out of harm's way while the SmarTruck was attacked.

Stomping the gas, Bolan launched the SUV off the back of the transport. He counted four hammering heartbeats before the wheels struck the ground, digging into the grass as the SmarTruck slewed in a semicircle. His eyes were burning, but not to the degree that Joey's were. He hadn't breathed enough, and over years of hands-on experience and training, he'd inured himself to CS-CN exposure. His nostrils were dripping salty streams onto his lips as his mucus membranes swelled in response to the savage gas.

If this was the most that he experienced, then he wouldn't have to worry.

But life never went that easy for the Executioner.

One of the Black Hawks swung over the path of the SmarTruck, and the big blond giant from the Dulles massacre, Adonis, was in the door, aiming an M-79 grenade launcher at the windshield.

Bolan stomped on the gas, cranking the wheel to get out of the way.

That's when it felt like something more powerful than a locomotive smashed the SmarTruck.

CHAPTER TEN

Dark yanked on Adonis's arm, trying to keep him from blasting the SmarTruck to pieces with the grenade launcher. Instead the rippling, hard-muscled arm was immobile, despite Dark's best efforts to sway it. "Thunder wants that fucking truck in one piece!"

Adonis glared at him with hard blue eyes. "I used a flash-bang grenade. It'd feel like I hit them with a LAW rocket, but except for a broken windshield, our precious prize is intact!"

Adonis looked down at the hand that was gripping his forearm. "Remove your hand from my person, or I'll remove your hand from your person."

Dark let go, then thrust his finger into Adonis's face. "One of these days..."

The Black Hawk suddenly lurched as thunder sounded from below, Dark and Adonis stumbling into their troops in a tangle of limbs.

"Quit arguing, you old ladies!" Harpy snapped. "We're taking fire!"

Dark was up, hauling himself toward the doorway, seeing that the SmarTruck was tearing away from them, the cannon on its roof swiveling and popping off rounds. "They said that thing was going to be loaded with practice ammo!"

"A hunk of plastic moving at Mach 3 is still going to snap our rotors, simpleton!" Harpy returned. The Black Hawk lurched again, swinging around. Dark saw sky as his fingers dug into the flooring. Gravity yanked the other way and he felt his nails crack, his fingertips ripped raw by the g-forces.

"You're going to get us killed anyway!" Dark bellowed.

"I wish," Harpy muttered as she kept working the controls. "Shut up, hold on and get ready to unass!"

"In any particular order?" Adonis asked. He was standing on the helicopter floor, surfing against the turbulence, keeping level and steady. He'd traded his M-79 for a Calico, which he held in one beefy paw.

The Black Hawk went into a screaming dive toward the SmarTruck and Dark brought up his weapon, opening fire on the black Kevlar shell of the speeding war wagon.

MACK BOLAN'S EARS still rang from the concussive shock that left the windshield with a silver-dollar-sized hole in it. That gave him some hope, as it meant the hijackers still wanted the SmarTruck in one piece. He glanced in the back to Joey, the test driver, who had finally managed to stop choking and gagging. Bolan couldn't take the time to trade places with the wheelman, and even now, the Executioner didn't quite trust Joey's capacity for combat driving. His eyes were still raw and red as he gave Bolan a thumbs-up. The soldier let go of the joystick from where he was firing blindly into the sky.

Normally the Executioner would have made more certain of his backstop when firing off any weapon, but in this case, with ammunition that was designed to flutter harmlessly to the ground after a certain distance, he grabbed the stick, held down the firing stud and threw panic at his enemies. It wasn't much, but it was enough to give him breathing room. He was tromping the gas and blazing toward the tree line, where the Black Hawks would be forced to work for their prey. He glanced back. "When we get to the forest, get out of the truck and run for cover."

Joey nodded, mopping his tear-stained cheeks with his sleeve, wincing at each touch to his tenderized eyes. "I don't want to stick around for another round of what these guys can put out. I'm no hero."

"You're hero enough, Joey," Bolan replied.

He swerved as the ground erupted in front of him. Another concussion grenade landed and the roof of the SmarTruck rippled and thumped with the rain of slugs hammering into it. From the sound of it, the gunners were firing 9 mm submachine guns, and the whole effect wasn't to stop the SUV with any damaging hits, but to steer the vehicle by panicking the driver. Unfortunately for them, Bolan knew he was driving a tank, and wasn't going to be fooled. He plowed onward, pedal to the metal. He shot a glance at the driver's-side mirror. Sable Burton wasn't taking Bolan's advice and was plowing the rental car through the grass, keeping pace, but staying away from close proximity of the SmarTruck.

The soldier's brow furrowed. Burton dealt herself into this battle after he'd specifically told her to get the hell out of the way. Still, he tallied the arsenal in his war bag, resting in the trunk of the rental car. Anything would be better than plastic 25 mm shells and his short-barreled Beretta pocket gun against terrorists with grenade launchers.

The Executioner hit the parking brake and the SmarTruck swerved hard, performing a 180-degree turn, mud and grass flying in rooster tails from the spinning rear wheels. The Black Hawk was lunging up on him, and Bolan flipped the controls for the SUV's dazzle lights. Even in bright day, the headlights of the SmarTruck were designed to produce a blinding, painful burst that could stun and disorient enemy troops. The lamps flared and the first Black Hawk swerved hard again, spiraling higher while the second Black Hawk swerved wildly toward a copse of trees to one side.

The second helicopter wasn't recovering from its terrifying plummet and it crumpled into the ground. Armor plate and ceramic rotors bent, twisted and shattered apart in a lethal impact. Trees were shredded by the tons of aircraft plowing through them and a burst fuel tank suddenly sent a blossom of fiery orange spewing into the sky before it blackened into a dark cloud of smoke.

One down.

He looked around for Burton and saw that she was still driving the rental toward the tree line. She may have chosen to get in over her head, but she wasn't stupid about it. She was sticking with Bolan's original plan, and he wouldn't mind having the option of a smaller set of wheels than the bulky SmarTruck to drive out of the forest.

The first Black Hawk flew back over him, and gunfire scythed out of the side of the helicopter, slashing at the back fender and tires of the Honda. Burton managed to swing the nimble little car between two trees and get out of sight. Bullets chased, and bark burst from multiple impacts, but Bolan was confident she wasn't hurt. He reached for the stick again, but Joey cut across him and slipped into the shotgun seat.

"Nail them?" Joey asked as he settled in, swinging the coaxial camera to focus on the Black Hawk.

"Cut loose," Bolan ordered. "I'm going to be rolling for the trees again."

"Once I get the camera lock, you can flip this thing upside down and the cannon wouldn't miss!" Joey boasted.

"Let's not test that," Bolan growled, tromping the gas again. The 25 mm cannon thundered above, the entire SmarTruck shaking with the recoil of the heavy charges spitting plastic shells skyward. The Black Hawk took a torrent of hits and literally leaped out of the way before too many impacts skewed it out of the sky. The pilot impressed Bolan, though. He thought about the woman from the warehouse back in Washington. Harpy. She was a top pilot, and again, it was another Black Hawk helicopter, heavily equipped and charging after Terintec technology. If the skilled pilot wasn't the predatory witch who nearly blew him into flaming hamburger only a couple days before, then Bolan would eat his Desert Eagle.

Another salvo of 9 mm slugs crashed across the roof of the SmarTruck and Bolan jerked in conditioned reflex. He heard Joey curse and looked over to see if anything had hit him.

"They knocked out the coaxial targeting camera," he told Bolan. "I can't see the chopper to hit it."

"What about the MARS?" Bolan asked as he aimed for where Burton had plowed the Honda into the forest. "The chips are live, right?"

"Yeah. We set up a dummy radar target. The drones would be launched, home in on it and pow!"

"You think that Black Hawk's operating with radar systems?" Bolan asked.

Joey glanced into the mirror. "They have the radome on the nose."

"Fire at will," Bolan ordered, again spinning the SmarTruck out to run down the Black Hawk.

Joey flipped the missile controls and the SmarTruck gave a hydraulic grunt, two square launchers pumping themselves loose from the sides of the vehicle. The helicopter swerved, gunners pumping out rounds and sweeping the truck in merciless bursts of autofire.

Bolan swung the SmarTruck around, keeping the missile launchers pointed in the general direction of the Black Hawk. "Locked?"

"Got it!" Joey shouted.

The SUV shook, reminding Bolan of his original war wagon, when it would unleash a firebird missile on a target. He mused about having the Farm acquire a SmarTruck for him in his stateside missions in the heartbeats it took for the first MARS missile to barely miss the enemy Black Hawk. The pilot was exceedingly good, and the unarmed drone slashed into the sky, curving around and seeking out the radar pulses from the nose dome like a hungry shark seeking blood. Even without enough explosives in the tip to blow a radar installation to smithereens, the rocketing drone would hit a flying helicopter fast enough to shred steel and knock it out of the sky.

The Black Hawk poured on the speed toward the SmarTruck, the MARS channeling in full throttle behind it. The helicopter was moving at mere feet off the ground, and if the pilot didn't move, Bolan would have to hit the brakes or swerve hard to avoid smashing both vehicles into tons of flaming wreckage.

Suddenly the helicopter popped up, gaining a hundred feet in a single bound.

But the MARS was still on its original course, right down Bolan's throat.

SABLE BURTON GOT OUT of the Accord and looked back into the field where the SmarTruck and the Black Hawk were staging their desperate battle. She didn't dare step closer to the tree line, as the rattle and hammer of automatic fire was almost deafening. She glanced toward the rear of the car. The fender was chewed to ribbons by what looked like thousands of gunshots, and the trunk was half popped open, its lock mechanism destroyed. The license plate was long lost, but Burton was certain she'd knocked that loose bouncing the Honda over fallen branches and ruts.

She glanced back at the SmarTruck, then reached for the trunk, wrestling to pull it open the rest of the way. It took two tugs, but she was strong enough to pop the broken mechanism. Colonel Brandon Stone had mentioned that he didn't have anything on him, but she knew a man like him wouldn't be too far from the tools of his trade.

Burton was betting on the fact that there would be something in the trunk that would help out. She wasn't a trained rifleman, but she was an engineer. The workings of an automatic rifle wouldn't be that hard to figure! The lid swung up and a canvas bag lay in the middle. She quickly checked the sides—no holes were punched in it. The zipper ripped loudly back as she tugged it open, seeing a neatly arranged selection of handguns and rifles inside. Her heart skipped a beat at the sight of such imposing firepower.

She grabbed one weapon, the largest she could find, and studied it. It was an M-16, she knew that much. She'd seen it used by guards at Terintec and its use in countless movies. Her hand searched for the cocking knob and located it, but she stopped herself, checking to see if there was even a magazine in place. She found a big curved box that looked as though it would fit and she slammed it in, driving it into the feed well. There was a reassuring click and she reached for the bolt on the black rifle. The T-shaped prong slid back along the butt of the rifle, and when she couldn't pull it farther, she pushed it back into place, unsure if letting it go would damage the mechanism. She remembered from a cable television program that the mechanisms were damaged by rough handling in Vietnam.

She swung the rifle around and took aim at the helicopter, pulling the trigger.

Nothing.

Panic filled her, then she looked along the side of the rifle. Above the trigger was a lever pointing to the word Safe in raised metal letters. It didn't take a rocket scientist to figure out what happened if she moved the lever, but being one helped in looking for what to do on the rifle. Safety lever slid into play, she shouldered the rifle again and saw the Black Hawk diving at the SmarTruck.

Burton pulled the trigger and the M-16 erupted. The sound was deafening and she was shocked off balance. She wasn't sure if she hit anything, but something big and explosive smashed into the ground just off to the side of the hard-swerving SmarTruck, vomiting sod and grass into the air.

The contrail of a jet engine spewed from the impact site and Sable trembled with shock. It had to have been a one-in-a-million shot. She'd downed a missile in flight!

She almost let the rifle drop, but held on to it, turning back to the Honda to get another magazine out of the bag. She probably couldn't hit another moving target in her life. Still, what did Einstein say about God playing dice?

She stopped.

The SmarTruck was barreling through the trees, the front fender taking dents that quickly popped out, leaving nothing more than scuffs on the flexible, resilient nose. She recognized Joey Lambert coming out the driver's-side door, his face red and swollen, but otherwise none the worse for wear. Colonel Brandon Stone was coming out the other side, and a wave of relief came over her. A momentary smile on his face told her he had the same sentiments.

"You got the trunk open?" Bolan asked.

"Enough to get one of the rifles out. But I closed it again in all the excitement."

Bolan frowned, then lifted one boot, stomping the jammed lock mechanism. The trunk flipped open and he reached in for his war bag. "I don't have much time. Joey, Sable, I'll need your help."

He looked up, face growing grimmer as the sounds of rotors thundered closer overhead.

DARK HUNG ON, glaring out the side of the Black Hawk. Mr. Big and Scary had to have thought that the trees would provide some protection. He sneered and aimed into the canopy and tapped off a long burst with his Calico to let the mystery man know that he wasn't in the clear yet.

"Stop wasting ammo," Adonis called.

"It's not wasting ammunition to lay down suppressive fire," he answered. "Who knows what he's doing down there?"

Dark glanced over. "That Skycrane near yet?"

"I don't know, and I'm not bloody well turning on the radar again!" Harpy snapped. "Not when he has more of those missiles, warhead or not!"

Dark shook his head. "You're going to have to switch to decaf, Harp."

The woman was too busy keeping the aircraft in a steady orbit to flip him the finger, but she was right. In the hands of someone who could improvise on the spot, even dummy weapons were as lethal as the real thing. He only had to look over at the flaming wreckage of the second Black Hawk to be reminded of that grim fact. Hard trained men, and one of Harpy's own black-leather clad lady sky-pirates were roasting their way to hell down there.

The militiamen and the terrorists could go rot, but a fine piece of ass like one of Harpy's shiny black air-witches was a damn shame. The man their informant had identified as Colonel Brandon Stone was going to need to pay a little extra for that. Dark knew that Harpy already despised the mysterious soldier for nearly getting caught in the backwash of her own inferno.

Sparks danced along the side of the Black Hawk and Dark ducked, Adonis only moments behind. Bullets sliced into the cabin of the speeding helicopter. Harpy unleashed a new round of cursing and men behind him screamed in agony as they were riddled with bullets. Dark looked back, seeing one man trying to hold his eyeball into his face, shrieking for someone to help him stop the pain.

Dark ended the pain with a point-blank bullet to the

forehead, then dumped the corpse out the side of the chopper. The mission was a first-class goat screw anyhow, and one more corpse wouldn't make any difference. He looked back to see a figure standing at the tree line, nestled against the trunk of a sturdy cedar, the muzzle of a rifle blazing as bullets filled the air.

Another wave of sparks rang along the tail boom, but Harpy was already out of the path.

"We have these things called machine guns!" she called back. "Machine gun that asshole to death!"

"I love it when she talks dirty," Dark quipped, poking his Calicos out and opening fire with both machine pistols. Adonis, at his back, merely grunted and lunged to the grips of the door-mounted M-60. They originally weren't going to use the M-60 on the SmarTruck itself, only on anyone too stupid to try to get between them and it. The crowd, to Dark's disappointment, had stayed out of the way.

But now, it was time to watch the big guy go to work with the monstrous cannon. Thick fingers curled around the twin D-shaped handles and the M-60D erupted and roared with a thunderstorm of flying lead. Blazing tracers mixed with the regular load flashed in the air like laser beams, hitting the ground and bouncing while the heavier slugs chewed into dirt and wood.

Bolan beat a retreat from the tree line, but Adonis's stream of relentless autofire was still whipping through the forest, chopping through slender saplings and tearing chunks out of older, thicker barks. Brass tumbled from the side of the snarling machine gun and the blond giant kept up the heat, his long hair whipping in the wind.

To Dark, it was like watching the Thunder God raining that old time religion down on the primitive screw-heads. Lit by the lightning of the flickering muzzle-flash, Adonis milked the paddle trigger for another long burst, his arms bulging and rippling. Veins rose on his forearms as his muscles flexed and fought to control the relentless recoil of 800 rounds per minute of unbridled fury. The Norse gods hadn't disappeared with the rise of Christianity, they'd merely gone to sleep until one of them woke up in the form of this titan Dark was watching today.

But Adonis's chiseled, clean-shaved, perfect features broke into an angry rictus, teeth bared in fury.

"He's gone! I missed him!" he roared.

The M-60 ripped out more bursts, sweeping the forest.

"How can you miss?" Dark asked.

"He disappeared. He's gone!" Adonis repeated. He shook the M-60 on its mounting, trying to squeeze even more death and destruction from its barrel, empty bullet casings flying everywhere with the savage throttling. "Dammit!"

When the belt ran dry, Adonis finally lost it, and with one heart-stopping roar, twisted the weapon off its mount. Metal screamed and tore. Wild-eyed, the Nordic titan glared at Dark.

"Well, it's empty," Dark said, trying to diffuse his old friend's rage.

A snarl rose to a screech and Adonis hefted the M-60 in one hand and sent it flying.

MACK BOLAN HAD TO ADMIT that whoever the M-60 gunner was up there, he was skilled and determined. If he hadn't been running in a serpentine pattern, using every single bit of cover between himself and the squat, black helicopter above, he'd have been sliced into so much sandwich meat by hungry bullets. Instead he was making his way back toward the SmarTruck and the Accord, hopping over downed saplings as he looped back to where he'd started his run, expecting the aerial gunner not to hose down an area he'd targeted before.

That's when the M-60 slammed into the ground, barrel first, like a spear from heaven. Metal warped under the collision with the ground, but the barrel kept the thing sticking straight up. It landed only ten feet away from him, and in a rare moment of shock, he wondered if the thrown machine gun had actually been aimed at him. Keeping to the canopy of a tree, he looked up, and the Black Hawk passed by, sweeping the edge of the forest.

In the air, another ugly buglike craft was zipping along, this one far more spindly and dragonfly-shaped. It only took a moment for Bolan to recognize the workhorse Sikorsky C-64 Skycrane. The helicopter had been in operation, constantly evolving over the past forty years, performing amazing feats of cargo transportation, rescue and firefighting. Only the UH-1 "Huey" utility helicopter had proved more enduring and versatile over the decades.

Its presence here meant that the RING's lapdogs were on a schedule. He couldn't imagine that the Black Hawks believed that they were anywhere close to being able to snatch the truck. Not yet.

Bolan turned and continued his dash back to the Accord and the SmarTruck. Sable Burton and Joey Lambert had finished planting the cakes of C-4 against the trunks of the trees around the truck.

"I didn't sign on to wreck this baby on one of its first trips out," Lambert said. Ache in his face showed a real affection for the amazing set of wheels.

"This won't damage it too much, and it can be recovered later," Bolan told him. "But they're here with the hardware to take this baby."

Lambert only had to listen carefully for a moment to hear the second set of rotors. "Skycrane?"

"Good ears."

"Nah. I just figured that's the only thing that could lift this heap," Lambert answered.

"Even better brain. Into the Accord. We're going to cut through the woods as much as we can until we reach the road," Bolan answered.

"We're running?" Burton asked.

"I'm pulling you two out of the way of a war. If it was just me, I'd do my best to wear these guys by attrition. I don't have the freedom to do that with two civilians in tow. In now!" Bolan ordered.

Lambert took the wheel almost on autopilot. He started up the Accord, Bolan piling himself into the back seat and Burton taking shotgun position. The Executioner took the stock of his M-4 and smashed out the rear window, cubes of plastic-sheet-covered safety glass dropping with the first two impacts like diamonds raining from the sky. The third impact from the steel stock lifted the whole thing in one pliant, spiderwebbed mass, and Bolan swept it off the trunk.

"Go!" Bolan ordered as he flipped open the safety cover on his radio detonator. His thumb pushed the switch and the shock wave of a half dozen cakes of C-4 going off at once swept through the forest in a concentric circle.

Burton looked back, eyes wide in surprise. "There goes my Sierra Club membership."

Bolan looked back at her. "Human lives or trees, Sable?"

"That's if those trees crashing slowed them down," she answered.

Bolan looked back; he hoped so, too.

"Stop the car. Joey, get this thing out of here," Bolan ordered. "Don't stop until you get back to Terintec."

He grabbed the straps of the war bag and bailed out of the rental.

"I'm not going to leave you—" Lambert began.

"It's an order. This isn't up for vote," Bolan growled. He slung the duffel's straps over his shoulders, fisted the rifle in both hands and disappeared into the forest.

He wasn't going to leave anything to chance.

CHAPTER ELEVEN

Bolan traversed the woods, stalking closer to the perimeter of blasted trees. Lambert and Burton did well, planting the explosives on trunks just right so that the detonations would snap trees in two, dropping them atop the SmarTruck or against the fenders, branches like claws keeping the vehicle entangled. He crouched and undid his war bag, pulling the holsters for his Beretta 93-R and his .44 Magnum Desert Eagle, strapping them on and loading the handguns and spare magazines into place. The little Beretta 9000 still rode in his pocket, and in his shoulder and belt harness he had two knives, garrotes and a knuckle-duster to supplement his war load.

He shrugged the straps back over his shoulders and took care not to trap the Beretta machine pistol in its holster. Having to rely on the pistol for a fast draw and getting it snagged on the nylon handles of the duffel would be the surest way for the Executioner to end his career. He peered through the small GC scope atop his M-4, trying to get a better view of the forest through the trees.

Figures were around the SmarTruck, two last hardmen fast-roping down from the Black Hawk. An angry voice was calling out orders, and Bolan swept, looking for the source, keeping as low and out of sight as he could while still allowing himself a view of the scene. The shouldered M-4 would put him on equal footing if someone spotted him, even though the scope on the rifle had its lenses well shaded to prevent a reflective flash giving away his presence.

He saw the boss on the scene—tall, lean but powerful, with a mane of flowing black hair that ran over the collar of his BDUs, twin Calico submachine guns hanging crisscrossed across his chest.

Dark.

The sight of the man who nearly beat Carl Lyons to death set every nerve in the Executioner's body on edge. One tap of the trigger and the murderer would be flushed off the planet in spectacular fashion. He looked around and spotted his partner, Adonis, even more huge and impressive than he'd appeared on the security footage from Dulles International Airport and David Kowalski's descriptions. He was dressed in identical black BDUs, except for the sleeves being cut off to reveal a set of arms that made a professional wrestler look emaciated.

Bolan tensed, knowing that he could end their careers in murder, but he couldn't bring himself to do it. They were the first link to the high command of the RING, his best chance to work his way up the ladder to take out the shadow organization. He took his finger off the trigger, letting his breath out. Watch and wait, for now, he told himself. The time for cleansing flame would come later.

He distracted himself, thinking of the angles. His cell

phone was in his pocket, but he'd have to wait until the enemy got some distance away before he could use it. He didn't want to risk their picking up on his signal. The moment they started to move, he'd call Jack Grimaldi and have Stony Man Farm try to track the Black Hawks through local radar. If he did get a lock on them, and Grimaldi did manage to pick him up in time for a pursuit, the margin would be by the skin of his teeth.

He looked at the cell phone again and made a decision. The civilians were out of the area, there was no need to worry about Sable Burton and Joey Lambert. If the enemy detected him, then he was the only one at risk, and he was decked out in one-man army mode. If they came for him, it would make life that much easier.

Life always got simple when the Bolan blitz was on.

He flipped open the phone and dialed furiously. "This is Striker. I have bad news," he said after the connection cycled through several cutout numbers.

Barbara Price's voice was on the line instantly. "We picked up a hint of it when the local 911 dispatch suddenly got hit with forty calls."

"Three helicopters, now two, are making a grab for Terintec's update on the SmarTruck," Bolan explained. "I dropped a couple trees on it to make it hard for them. I'd like Jack on the scene with something big, fast and preferably heavily armed."

"I'm getting him on the hot link right now. We can't get an armed chopper up in anything less than an hour. He has an Air National Guard Kiowa, but there's only a locker full of supplies for you on it."

"All right. Striker out."

He flipped the tiny cell phone closed and stuffed it back into his pocket. There was no indication from above that the Black Hawk had picked up anything on its electronics. The men on the ground were cursing and wrestling with trees instead of looking for a mysterious phone caller.

All the better.

Except the Honda Accord was pulling into the field, and Dark and Adonis were going to meet it.

Bolan cursed under his breath and started for the clearing.

SABLE BURTON LOOKED OUT the back window as Joey Lambert wove the Honda Accord through the trees. The fender bashed against a bark here and there, but the Terintec driver didn't go slower than twenty-five miles per hour, and he wasn't being stopped by any trunks. Within minutes, they reached the blacktop. She looked to the right, anticipating the turn, when suddenly the Honda veered to the left.

"Where are you going?" Burton asked. "We're supposed to…"

She stopped, then looked down at the ugly, black little handgun in Lambert's right hand. Burton took a deep breath and looked out the window. "How many of you got jobs at Terintec?"

Lambert smirked. "If I told you, I'd have to kill you, Professor Burton."

The woman frowned, biting off her response. She wasn't going to provoke the man with a gun aimed at her belly. She'd sit and bide her time.

Lambert deftly handled the car with one hand on the wheel and one aiming the pistol at her, steering them back toward the proving ground. "I was supposed to deliver the truck to them. But I figure you'd be a nice bonus."

Burton kept her mouth shut. She wasn't going to let

Lambert give the enemy anything more to manipulate her with.

"Then there's the fact that your friend Stone is running around with a bag full of guns and a hard-on to go it some more against these guys. That'd be worth even more brownie points, don't you think, four-eyes?"

For emphasis, he tapped the muzzle of the gun against her glasses, knocking them askew. Burton wrestled down the temptation to grab his arm to try to chew off his hand. Instead she resettled the glasses on her nose, tucked them tighter behind her ears and kept looking ahead.

"You're a nice, cold little bitch, aren't you?" Lambert asked as he stopped the car. "Too bad I won't have the time to warm you up some. I bet—"

A fist pounded on the window, interrupting the traitorous driver. Lambert rolled down the window.

"What's this, Lambert?" Dark asked him.

"This is one of the chief technicians involved with the project. Figured maybe you could get something out of her," Lambert replied.

"And what was the deal with not putting a bullet into that madman you were hanging out with?" Dark asked. Lambert tensed up, as if the man's very words were a death sentence.

"He was behind the wheel. I shoot him, the truck would have gone out of control."

Dark shrugged. "And this lady... Oh, yeah. Professor Sable Burton. Physicist. Applied Laser Dynamics."

Lambert seemed to relax. "Pretty good catch? And you have the SmarTruck, too."

Dark smiled at Lambert. "Yup. No thanks to you."

Lambert's relief evaporated and he tried to swing the little pistol around. Burton didn't see anything more than a bright flash of yellow before her glasses were smeared with blood and gore, sticky, salty fluid stinging into her eyes.

The gunshot in the enclosed space left her head throbbing, ears ringing, and it felt as if she'd lost control of her hands for a moment. She didn't know what to do, and all she could really hear was a high-pitched squeal emanating from nowhere. It took a heartbeat to realize that she was the one emitting the squeal, and some part of her consciousness wasn't blaming the rest of her. One moment she'd felt as though she was controlling the situation, the next, she was wearing the brains of the man who just kidnapped her.

"Could you please stop that noise?" Dark's voice cut through the haze.

Burton swallowed hard, breaking the cry, and she fought with her glasses, trying to wipe the dripping blood from her eyes. A sixteen-ton weight parked on her chest, and blocked her breathing, but other than that, she realized she was all right.

Just in the hands of a man who casually blew the brains out of another human being.

"Thank you. That could have gotten annoying," Dark told her. His eyes flashed a brilliant blue. "You wouldn't like me when I'm annoyed."

"I don't think so," Burton agreed, keeping her voice low. She finally cleared her eyes, but her glasses were caked with gore. All she saw was the blurry features of Dark.

"Need help with your glasses, ma'am?"

Burton was stunned by the question. "Yes."

She turned and looked at the mass that produced the sound. It filled the entire window. Her eyes focused as well as they could, and at nose-to-nose range, she was looking at the chiseled, beautiful features of a man with flowing golden hair.

"My name's Adonis," he said. He reached in and plucked the glasses from her fingers.

Burton lowered her head, then touched her hair. Her ponytail had come loose in her earlier struggle to open the trunk. Now her hair was wet and sticking to her neck. She reached up and ran her fingers through it, but she touched chunks of bone and squishy flesh. She shivered all the way down her spine and squeezed her eyes even tighter.

"Maybe it's better I don't see, right now," she said.

"Too late, miss," Adonis told her.

"All right, you big Boy Scout," Dark called. "We better get moving."

Burton was pulled from the car, the big hand rough on her forearm, but gentle as she could feel muscles strong enough to yank her arm from its socket tugged her to her feet. A hand went over her eyes and she flinched for a moment, then her vision cleared somewhat, her smeared glasses back on her face. Streaks still made her vision blurry in spots, but at least she had the ability to see farther than a foot in front of her nose.

"Not going to say anything?" Adonis asked.

"Thank you," she answered.

Dark appeared as sudden as a heart attack and twice as jolting. "No righteous struggle? No indignation?"

Burton shook her head. "I'm not going to provoke you."

"So you'll tell us everything we need to know?" Adonis pressed.

She looked up at the blond titan, her lips pressed tight. She glanced back at the Accord, Lambert's cored skull visible through the open window.

"Maybe I'll be provoking you a little."

Dark gave her a gentle tap on her cheek. "That's my girl."

"I'm not your girl."

Burton felt her chin and cheeks squeezed between strong, merciless fingers. "You are now. And you will be for the rest of your life. But that won't be too long, darling."

And then, the air detonated around her.

MACK BOLAN SAW Lambert drive right up to Dark and Adonis, and after a brief exchange, the driver was dead and Sable Burton was in the hands of the two murderers. They were too close to her for him to be able to do anything with the M-4. Not when he had another group at his side.

He took a precious moment, doomsday numbers tumbling, fingers working in the side pocket of his duffel. By touch, he recognized the stun-shock grenade and pulled it free of its anchor straps. Bolan didn't even bring his hands together to yank the pin, his thumb finding the pull-ring and snapping it out with one hard yank. The grenade continued on, a perfect side-arm pitch right toward the rental car where Dark, Adonis and Burton were standing.

The blast was deafening and all three went to the ground. The Executioner didn't miss a beat, long legs snapping straight, propelling him along in vast, ground-eating strides. Cries of anger sounded to his right around the SmarTruck, but Bolan was a wraith, slicing through the forest too fast for them to see.

M-4 out front, he rushed toward the Accord. The car would be his way out of here, with Burton in tow.

A gunshot sounded behind him, dirt kicking up over his heels.

Bolan reached down and grabbed up Burton by her arm when something sliced around, ramming into the back of one of his knees. The Executioner stumbled, M-4 knocked from his grasp. He'd concentrated too much on making sure that she got to safety that he hadn't taken the chance to immobilize Adonis or Dark. Bolan stumbled against the side of the Honda, grabbing the roof for balance.

"I hate those things!" Dark groaned. His eyes were unfocused, and he had one hand over his ear, but he was still getting up. Adonis lurched, and in a heartbeat, he was standing straight, but disoriented still by the concussion grenade.

Bolan swung Burton out of the way and lashed out with his combat boot, striking Adonis right below the navel and folding him up. A hard elbow-strike against Adonis's head punctuated that exchange, the big man tumbling to the ground dazed. The soldier's elbow was screaming in pain from having been forced to hammer something harder than a bowling ball.

He didn't have time for that and turned back to Dark. It was too late to get in a preemptive strike on the man in black, as the murderer grabbed Bolan by the straps on his shoulders and swung him over in a hip toss. Landing on the crush-proof compartments for his arsenal, Bolan grunted. Fresh bruises and pain swam across his back, driving the wind from his lungs. He couldn't stop, though, bringing up his leg hard into Dark's midsection. The knee lifted the black-haired killer and a pistoning fist caught him in the face while he was still off balance.

Bolan rolled out from under Dark, who was coughing and trying to gather his wits. Two big hands suddenly lunged out, grabbing for his arms, pinning them down before he could go for either of his handguns. Adonis's crushing grip stopped the Executioner cold. He was being lifted off the ground by the golden-haired giant, and all Bolan could do was lash out with his legs.

The soldier took a quick glance at what he could aim for, and saw the side of the car. He stomped hard on the roof with both feet and pushed hard, going up and over behind Adonis. The backward flip brought him to the ground, deep in a crouch. The big man was half-turned, already reacting to the Executioner's maneuver, when Bolan snapped his legs straight, rocketing himself hard into Adonis's waist and lifting him off the ground. Hundreds of pounds of struggling human flesh rebounded off the side of the rental, and Bolan swung a flurry of punches into the mass murderer's back, kidney and stomach. It was like punching a statue, Adonis's muscles were packed as hard as marble.

Still, Bolan's earlier assessment was right. He was big, he was strong, but he was no man of steel. He felt pain like any other man, and could succumb to injury just as quick.

Adonis roared and pushed Bolan away, fist coming down but only glancing off his shoulder. The Executioner hooked his foot behind the titan's ankle and punched hard, directly into his enemy's solar plexus. Breath exploded from parted lips, froth breaking from Adonis's nose, before he completed his backward tumble, head bouncing off the fender of the Honda, leaving a dent in it.

Dark was up again, dazed, blood trickling over his chin. A Calico machine pistol was leveled right at Bolan's gut.

"You're good, but not that good," Dark taunted.

The whistle of metal slashing first air, then cloth and

flesh, broke the gunman's speech, his muzzle rising as his body twisted away from a sudden burst of agony. Burton, her nose bleeding from her encounter with the concussion grenade and rough handling, her clothes caked with the contents of Joey Lambert's skull, stood sneering, holding the broken antenna of the rental car. She held it in one hand, like a fencer's foil, and she lunged again, slicing the wicked length of metal across Dark's forearm.

Bolan took the opportunity to swing up his boot and kick Dark hard across the gut. The man went down from the combined assault and the Executioner's hand went for the Desert Eagle in its holster.

The only link to the RING be damned. He would find another way to get the heart of the organization.

The .44 Magnum leveled at Dark's head when gunfire crackled from the tree line. The Black Hawk was swinging around overhead.

"We have to get out of here!" Burton yelled.

Bolan returned fire on the gunners in the distance, engaging the worst threat first. "Get the body out of the car! Hurry!"

As the Executioner laid down cover fire with the .44 Magnum pistol, Burton opened the car door and dumped the half-decapitated turncoat out of the driver's seat. Her initial panic over his death had gone, as had the queasiness over being coated with skull, blood and brains. Now her survival instincts were kicking in, and Bolan noticed she was made of some strong stuff.

The Accord started. Bolan lowered the empty Desert Eagle and was firing his Beretta 93-R from his off hand. With a single bound, he was across the hood of the Honda and in the shotgun seat. Burton was slamming the car in reverse before Bolan's feet even left the ground. Bullets dinged and clanged against the fender and grille from the distance, but the Executioner's main worry was the helicopter overhead and the quickly recovering Dark and Adonis.

The two men were firing at the car from a closer range, and only Burton's instinct to keep low prevented her from getting cored through the head by a .50 caliber handgun round. Bolan swept the pair with his Beretta, 3-round bursts chasing after them, but the killers were quicker than Bolan could aim, and across the testfield the Accord was bouncing too much for anything resembling precision marksmanship. He pulled back into the car and stuffed the barrels of both guns between his thighs.

Fresh magazines were ripped from their positions on his belt and shoulder harness, replacing the empties with the speed that came with experience and training. Another blast of gunfire riddled the windshield, but Burton cranked on the emergency brake, spinning the Honda into a 180 degree turn. Bolan felt himself crush against the door of the car, but held on to his guns, watching the world spin around him. The engine ground noisily. The spunky little engineer got the car in drive, cut the emergency brake and tore off toward the road.

But as long as the enemy had the Black Hawk, there was no escape for the two of them.

THE CUTS ON HIS BACK and arm stung deeply, but they were nothing that couldn't be fixed with a few sutures and a good hearty meal to replace the blood loss. Still, they were annoying, reminders that a little female scientist could take him by surprise and prevent him from getting his kill. Dark shielded his face from the winds whipped up by the helicopter's whirling rotors as it descended. "Pardon me, driver, but does this helicopter go to the Loop?"

"Get in! They're getting away!" Harpy snapped with a scowl. "You two are supposed to be the hardest bad-asses on the planet!"

"We are when we're not getting over being hit with a concussion grenade!" Adonis shouted back.

The Black Hawk rose, and Dark hung on to the back of Harpy's seat, looking out the windshield. He couldn't believe it, then, when he saw them turning away from the road.

"What are you doing?" Dark demanded.

"He's running for cover. Skyline just told me that half the police in three counties are on their way here. He also told me a military chopper just took off like a bat out of hell from O'Hare, and guess which direction it's headed?" Harpy mentioned.

Dark hit the wall of the cabin, grimacing as metal overcame flesh. "Damnation."

"The crew got the SmarTruck hooked up to the Sky-crane anyway," Harpy explained. "We don't have to hang around this hole."

"Not with a whole bunch of guys with rifles on their way here," Dark snarled.

"I liked Kharisma," Harpy hissed, looking over at the still-burning wreckage of the other Black Hawk. "She was a good pilot."

Adonis frowned. "We'll avenge her. That Stone guy isn't going to live out the end of this week."

Harpy settled the Black Hawk near the tree line. Of the men they'd brought with them, only four were able to walk their way to the chopper as it waited for them.

"This is a total blow-off," Adonis said with a frown. "Less than a fifth of the force we started out with."

Dark glared at the walking wounded. He could see fresh bodies fallen beside trees where they had been burned down. "You know, it really doesn't matter to me. They're a bunch of worthless bigots. Cannon fodder, really."

They looked to Harpy.

"What the hell. DeeDee said that they were all expendable," Harpy conceded.

Adonis pulled his second Desert Eagle, reloaded his first one and nodded to Dark.

Dark only grinned as he leveled the black, unstaring eyes of his twin Calicos at the unsuspecting militiamen.

SABLE BURTON PULLED OFF the road as the fleet of wailing and flashing sheriff's and police vehicles ripped up the road. She was shaking, head pounding. Dizziness threatened her sense of balance and it felt as if she were going to flip over, even though she was buckled in and clenching the wheel as if it were her lifeline to reality.

A hand rested on her shoulder. The contact made her jerk, but she didn't pull away. Instead, through blood-smeared glasses, she saw the face of Colonel Brandon Stone watching her, concern replacing the hardness that had been in those ice-blue eyes only moments earlier. She folded her lip under her teeth, biting hard, trying to use the pain to clear her mind, but it wasn't working. The only thing that came out was the stinging flush of her tears in her eyes.

"Oh, my God. What the hell was that?" she asked.

"It's something I try to protect people from with every waking breath. I'm sorry you got caught in it. I tried to—"

"I couldn't leave you behind."

"You helped me more than you could know," Bolan stated.

"But they got the truck, they killed Joey and they almost killed me. They would have killed you all because they caught me and—"

"It's okay," Bolan told her, knowing the torrent of words was the result of adrenaline and survivor's guilt.

"They still have the truck."

She was shaking, but the aftershocks of terror were fading now.

"That was some good fencing," he commented.

"No. It was sloppy, and it was with a worthless piece of metal."

"It stopped Dark, and it saved my life. And then there was that 180 you pulled. Where'd you learn that?"

"A misspent childhood. Before I went to the Illinois Institute of Technology, I earned a little cash on the midnight circuit, drag racing and stuff."

"That didn't show up in your file."

"Because I didn't get caught. I didn't even shoot the missile that was aimed at you."

"What?"

She felt her face reddening. "For a moment, when I opened fire with the rifle, the helicopter was passing by. Then I saw the MARS drone smash the ground."

"I don't know. I was too busy trying to get out of the way to see if you actually hit it. Stranger things have happened in combat," Bolan told her.

"You're just saying that."

Bolan rubbed some dried, flaking blood off her cheek, his intense blue eyes meeting hers. "I guess it didn't take a rocket scientist to figure that out."

Burton managed a chuckle through her tears. "Gina's the rocket scientist. I'm the laser specialist."

Bolan's phone vibrated, and he dug for it. "Stone."

"Striker, are you okay?" Barbara Price's voice was on the other end.

"I'll live. Just a few bruises. Nothing major," he answered. "Professor Burton is okay, too, just shaken up."

"Who is that?" Burton asked.

"You know how James Bond has M?" Bolan asked. "That's your M?"

Price chuckled on the phone in his ear. "More like your Moneypenny."

"I'm going to need some background info on a Joey Lambert, driver for Terintec," Bolan said into the mouthpiece.

"Any reason you suspect him?" Price asked.

"If she's asking why," Burton rumbled, "tell her it's because I'm wearing Joey's brains. Dark blew them out after he didn't do the exact right job for him."

"She sounds angry," Price noted to Bolan.

"You want me to put you two on the phone together?" the Executioner asked.

"No, thanks," Price said.

"Jack's on his way to you. We're triangulating your position."

"What about the Black Hawk and the Skycrane?" Bolan asked.

"They've been operating under radar. We lost them," she told him. "Sorry."

"I'll find those two again," Bolan told her.

"Those two… Dark and Adonis?"

"And maybe Harpy."

Price stepped away from the phone for a moment. Bolan held on.

"The police are reporting that there are ten dead bodies left all over the testing field," she said as soon as she came back. "They must have cut their losses, because everyone looked shot to hell."

Bolan frowned. "I hate to sound like it was a school-yard brawl, but they started it."

"No one's blaming you for starting this, Striker."

Bolan sighed. "No, but you know who to blame if this doesn't get finished."

The frustrated Executioner hung up the phone, just in time for Grimaldi's Kiowa to come thundering into view.

CHAPTER TWELVE

The door crashing open caught David Kowalski by surprise. He sized up the three burly men who rushed in, deciding that if they had been let through this far, then it was time for him to play along with the game Able Team had planned after Rosario Blancanales dropped him off at his hotel room. Had the three intruders been openly armed, Blancanales let him know that those men wouldn't have lasted three steps. So instead of trying to kill him, they were here to take him captive, or to at least bully him into a position where he could be convinced to join their cause. In that case, Blancanales and Schwarz agreed that it was best for him to follow along and learn what he could.

The trio paused as they saw him, clad in a soaking towel, hair damp and matted to his head. Kowalski wasn't going to let their intrusion continue without a reaction. He was a Marine, and a born warrior, and being attacked was met with a swift, uncompromising return strike. A growl erupted into a bellow as he lunged at them, snapping one fist hard like a battering ram, hitting the lead guy in his breastbone. The impact sounded like a drum being struck, and he went back hard, feet leaving the ground. The other two were knocked off balance and Kowalski decided that if they wanted to take him, they might as well get a look at all the goods.

He grabbed his towel and with a twist of his wrist, whipped it hard at the face of the man on his left, wet cloth cracking on flesh. A scream burbled from the AHC kidnapper's lips as his hands went up to the wicked welt. Kowalski spun and brought both fists together across the jaw of the third man, launching him backward across an easy chair by the window. He didn't stop atop the tumbling divan, instead continuing on, headfirst through the coffee table next to it.

Splintering wood echoed through the room as Kowalski grabbed the towel-whipped fool and drove him face-first into the wall. The knobby, jagged stucco turned from cream to crimson as skin and muscle tore on the guy's face. Kowalski wasn't done with him, as he followed up with a pistoning knee that blew into the AHC man's belly. With a savage roar, he sent the would-be kidnapper sailing across the room, landing atop his friend in the pile of shattered furniture.

The first guy came up swinging, but by now Kowalski was in the state of mind neuropsychologists called tache psyche. It was where his perceptions were bumped up so that the world seemed to move in slow motion, but his peripheral vision disappeared in a black tunnel of focus. Brain racing faster than a supercomputer, he ducked the first two wild fists, then responded with two direct right jabs to the chest. The big man was caught off guard by the sudden strikes, and tried to curl up, his arms going to protect his ribs when Kowalski came around with his strong left hook. The guy tumbled and crashed to the floor, neck taking the full brunt of his hit.

Kowalski looked at the unconscious tangle of men around him. He had turned and was reaching for his clothes when a shadow fell across the door.

"Just your pants," a voice ordered sharply.

Kowalski froze.

"Put your pants on. Do you think I want to see that ass all day?" the speaker demanded.

He glanced back to see a gunman. He was lighter in build than his three friends, and the way he conducted himself hinted to Kowalski that this was the brains of the operation.

He complied, pulling himself into a pair of pleated, khaki slacks.

"Can I wear shoes, too? A lot of places won't let me in with no shoes and no shirt, but I think in California, they're a little easier on the whole shirtless look," Kowalski quipped.

The man stepped closer and he recognized him from the gun shop.

"No. I don't think you're BATF. And you sure as hell didn't react to my pals here like anyone in law enforcement."

"I hope they only got the job because they're your friends. Because if you hired them to be your muscle on talent, you got a nickel's worth."

The gunman smirked and slipped his pistol into his waistband. "If they're worth a nickel, you're the whole dollar."

"I said at the gunstore that I'm a Marine."

"What division?"

"Fifth Marine."

"Unit?"

"Twenty-Sixth Expeditionary Force."

"That's only a six-month assignment."

"I'm…I was, I mean…command element. Full-time," Kowalski admitted.

"Name's Jeremiah Watson," the man said. He took a step forward. "You got discharged?"

"Quiet-like. Our leadership would rather let the blood of Marines spill than have the flow of oil disrupted," Kowalski said with a grimace. "Any official trial would have brought to light the fact that a leader I thought I could trust was just another lying politician, compromising every freedom away so that those… those animals could have free run of what I fought and bled for!"

"He was not the man of Christ he said he was. We could have told you that," Watson explained quietly. "And you…"

"While my brothers were dying, and I was bleeding, I kept fighting. But I hurt too many civilians," Kowalski continued. His forearms swelled, rippling down to his wrists, knuckles cracking and turning white. "That's what they said. I opened fire on a crowd of noncombatants, but they're all the same."

Watson placed his hand on Kowalski's shoulder. "God is on our side, son."

"Your side?"

"The Army of the Hand of Jesus Christ, Our Lord and Savior."

Kowalski didn't relax his anger. He'd gotten through the front door. He'd impressed a hate group and ended up hating himself.

"HE'S GOOD. He stuck with the script," Dr. Jackie Sorenson said, sliding the headphones down past her silken blond hair. She regarded Schwarz and Blancanales, filled with happy memories of the time or two they'd worked together. She breathed out, then looked to the second monitor in the back of Able Team's van.

"The transponder's good. A ten-mile tracking radius. We don't even have to move to keep track of them," Sorenson added.

Schwarz smirked. "We've been working on our hardware between blowing shit up."

"I presume you mean the Royal we," Sorenson said, winking at Blancanales.

He managed a smile. "Hey, someone has to be the Ironman whisperer. Lift this, Carl, hold up that transponder, don't let go of sparkly cord."

Blancanales put the van in gear and pulled out after giving the AHC men a head start. A ten-mile radius was one thing, since the radio waves sent out could bounce off the atmosphere. In reality, line of sight, two miles to the horizon, was far more reliable, but the processing software made for less guesswork. They had a cushion in case of unexpected circumstances such as a train delay.

The transponder was built into bandage on the back of Kowalski's heel, right where blisters would form. Full of transistorized wiring, it was the only way for them to disguise the fact that it was a signaling device. A cell phone or a pager, by its very nature, would be confiscated and even powered off or thrown away to keep the user from communicating with the outside world. The bandage, however, wouldn't be assumed to be anything more than it was. The technology inside the flat little transceiver taking every advantage of advanced miniaturized electronics to stack the circuit boards for transmission processes into the transponder.

Sorenson had been briefed on the tracker tag, as was David Kowalski when it was adhered to his heel. As a sacrificial lamb, he was relying on the members of Able Team to cover his back. Before Kowalski was brought out, Schwarz had curled into the shadows behind a garbage Dumpster, a silenced Colt M-4 Commando trained on the doorway. Blancanales had been in another position, on a rooftop, his own silenced rifle ready to chop down anyone intent on harming the young blacksuit.

The silence was brittle enough that when the phone rang, Schwarz nearly leaped on it.

"We hear you," Schwarz said matter-of-factly, the humor drained from his voice. Relief seemed to sweep over him in the next moment.

"Striker's okay," he announced.

Sorenson looked surprised. "What happened?"

"Adonis and Dark stole the SmarTruck. Striker did his magic, though, limiting civilian casualties to zilch, and killing almost everyone on the other team."

"Except the helicopter crews, and I presume Adonis and Dark." Blancanales spoke up.

Sorenson sighed. "Nobody's perfect."

"That's the thing. Usually he walks right over the opposition. To be that close..." Schwarz began.

"Gadgets, these are the guys who put Ironman in the hospital," Blancanales stated. "It could have been Striker laying dead when they got through."

"But he's not," Sorenson stated. "He's alive, and he's still fighting."

The Able Team van sped along, keeping pace with the young man who was in their charge, holding a little more hope than they did moments earlier.

SABLE BURTON FELT the water slosh down over her and she prayed for it to sweep away the caked mess that was on her body. She ran her fingers through her hair, try-

ing to separate strands that were glued together by dried
blood, leaving it with the consistency of straw even
while under the assault of the shower nozzle. She pulled
hard, feeling the strands pull free from her scalp, and
she whimpered, but after an eternity of lather and hot
water, she started feeling free of the hardened muck in
her hair.

She didn't want to look at the drain, her stomach
twisting at the mere thought.

Instead, she threw open the shower curtain and
grabbed for a towel. She blotted her eyes, then saw
Bolan, cleaning out the scratches on his face with io-
dine.

"Oh…"

"Your virtue is safe with me," he told her.

Burton tucked the towel under her armpits, covering
her nudity as best she could. "I'm sorry."

"For what? Needing to wash up?" Bolan asked. He
shot her a glance and she could tell that she wasn't anything special that he hadn't seen before. She looked
and felt exactly like a drowned rat, her hair tumbling in
tangles around her face. "This is a rare opportunity for
me. I usually don't get much time for a shower after a
bad skirmish."

"The drain's all filled with bloody hair," Burton mentioned. Queasiness swept her again and she didn't even
dare look back at the tub.

"I'll clean the drain."

Burton rushed past him and out into the next room.
The locker room was part of the Illinois Air National
Guard, O'Hare International Airport Air Reserve Station. Once home of the 126th Air Refuelling Wing, the
facilities had been emptied out in 1999 as part of the
shutdowns implemented by the Base Realignment and

Closure Commission. However, that didn't mean that Colonel Brandon Stone couldn't arrange for having a little activity on the premises. The facilities were capable of providing residence for one hundred men. Most of the time, the station was used by DEA and Border Patrol agents for the sake of interdicting smugglers trying to bring in narcotics across Lake Michigan, but for now, the place was empty, except for her, Stone and his mysterious pilot, Jack.

She saw a packet resting on one of the benches. Jack Grimaldi was off to one side, trying to look everywhere but at the short, half-naked woman in front of him. His face was reddened and he had to clear his throat before he could speak.

"Fresh clothes for you," he said. He ran his fingers through his short hair and turned away.

"I was showering long enough for you to go shopping?" Burton asked. She opened the package and saw a Chicago White Sox sweat suit, black with white silkscreen lettering. "The souvenir shop."

"Yeah. Got your size off the clothes you were throwing away," Grimaldi answered. He turned his back to her, granting her some privacy. "Hope you don't mind."

"I don't," Sable told him. She noticed a sports bra and shorts were part of the package, as well. "No panties."

"What?" Grimaldi asked.

"You didn't buy any panties," Burton told him.

Grimaldi blushed. "Well, they looked clean enough…"

"Clean enough?" Burton asked. "Women are not like men. They just can't step out of the shower and put on the same underwear they were wearing before!"

"It'll only be for a little while, until I get you home," Grimaldi said.

"You found a bra. Go get me some panties."

"We don't have time for that," Grimaldi told her. She could tell he wasn't thrilled with giving her the news.

Burton's shoes, only slightly spattered with droplets of blood, were resting on the floor under the bench. She quickly got into the clothes and sat to put on her shoes.

"You all right with me coming out now?" Bolan asked from the bathroom.

"Yeah," Burton announced. "I'm as clean as I can feel wearing yesterday's panties."

"Excuse me?" He came out, face covered with a couple puffy new scratches, but otherwise still looking as rugged and handsome as the first day she'd seen him. She tried to dismiss her attraction to him.

It wasn't working.

Burton blushed and looked away. "Never mind, Colonel."

"You're sure you didn't get hurt?" Bolan asked her. He touched her chin softly, looking at her face. "You got bruised."

"Dark was toying with me," Burton answered. "Those are his fingerprints."

She was ashamed at letting herself get touched by that madman. She would have given anything to crawl under a rock, when Bolan's hand rested gently on her shoulder.

"I wouldn't worry about it. He won't harm you," Bolan told her.

"Want me to get an irregular to pick her up and take her back home?" Grimaldi asked.

"That'd be fine," Bolan said.

"But—"

"But nothing," the Executioner cut her off. "I have

my job to do, and I can't do that with a civilian in tow, even if she is a damn good street racer and knows a few things about fencing."

Burton chewed her lower lip, the reproach as stinging as any slap across her cheek ever was. She could see that Bolan immediately regretted being hard, but he wasn't backing down.

"I'm sorry. People who are around me tend to end up dead," Bolan continued.

She nodded. "You're right."

His big hand gently cupped her cheek. "You did well. You helped me as much as anyone I know ever could. I just can't bear the thought of seeing an innocent hurt."

Burton met his steely blue eyes, seeing them full of warmth. "I'll never see you again."

Bolan smiled slightly. "No."

The woman stepped back from him, a bittersweet smile straining her face. She walked over to a small table at the other end of the locker room. Grimaldi was on his cell, calling for the ride. She looked at a thermos of coffee next to a pile of papers. She bent to get herself a cup, when she saw the map of Wisconsin. The town of Sparta had been circled in pencil. She froze as if she were looking at a viper.

"Sable, is there something wrong?"

"You're going to Sparta?" she asked.

Bolan stepped up to the table. "Yeah. You know something about that?"

"Fifteen miles out of Sparta, we acquired an old lumber mill," Sable answered. "It's where I worked on perfecting the SmarTruck's offensive laser."

"But the truck only had a 25 mm cannon," Bolan stated.

"The laser's perfected, but we're not showing the U.S. Army until we get more money. Terin's dangling the MARS before them as bait for us to get the contracts for improving the vehicle, and then we'll take the job for the laser to insure renewal of development on the truck. In any case, the laser is ready. And we even field tested it."

"In Wisconsin?" Bolan probed.

Burton shrugged. "There were tons of logs, the weather conditions were crap and we tested year-round. The summers were as dry as most deserts, the winters were wet, soggy and foggy. We were able to make sure the laser worked in every condition. I personally poured bags of imported Arabian sand into the electronics to make sure it wouldn't clog up."

"Were the MARS tested there, too?" Bolan asked.

"At a quarry, two miles up the road," Sable said. "It's an active quarry, but Terin paid the owner to let us use high explosives on the site."

Bolan looked at the map, grim determination etching his features. "I'm still not bringing you with me."

"Do you know what to look for?" Burton asked.

Bolan narrowed his eyes. "I know how to scout a hardsite."

"But you wouldn't know what, if any, high-tech weaponry they had on site. I know the laser, divided up into its primary components, looks like the leftovers of a microwave oven or a VCR."

Bolan looked at Grimaldi.

"So do I put the irregular on hold?" Grimaldi asked.

"You're supposed to back me up in keeping bystanders out of my fights," Bolan said.

Grimaldi shrugged. "She's the rocket scientist, Sarge."

"I thought you were a colonel," Burton said.

"He got promoted when he started kicking terrorist ass on a regular basis," Grimaldi explained.

"Ah."

"That's the point. She's a rocket scientist, not a commando," Bolan told Grimaldi.

"I only dabble in rocket science. I am a professor of quantum electronics and laser physics. And I'm not asking to be given an M-16 and go blazing into action. But I do know what the MARS components look like."

"Radar is emitted electromagnetic energy," Grimaldi said, matter-of-factly. "The MARS is sensitive to those emissions, right Professor?"

"Then it reinforces that lock with a standard laser targeting system, like on the Maverick and Paveway II Air to Ground missiles," Burton said. "Redundant systems."

Bolan took a deep breath. "You do what I say."

She raised her hand. "Girl Scout's honor."

Bolan narrowed his eyes. "I read your file. You were no Girl Scout."

Burton lowered her hand. "That's kind of creepy that you know about me, and I know nothing about you."

"I'm Dark's flipside. The only difference is, I don't believe there are acceptable civilian casualties," the Executioner told her.

"In other words, you're going to remind me every step I take that I am in danger, and I have to follow your lead."

"Precisely."

Burton folded her arms. "So when are we flying out to Sparta?"

"Let's at least get you a jumpsuit," Bolan said. "Jack…"

"Already calling for an irregular to get some proper

clothing. We'll be off the ground in an hour," Grimaldi called back. He grumbled under his breath as he put the phone to his ear. "Looks like I'm going shopping for panties anyhow."

CHAPTER THIRTEEN

"Here," Watson said to Kowalski. They sat in the back of the Chevy Suburban as it wound along the road. Sunset was quickly approaching, the skies splashed crimson.

Kowalski found himself wondering if it were a portent of blood yet to be spilled.

He looked down and saw the butt of a handgun being offered to him. "A gun?"

"You bought and paid for it," Watson explained.

The U.S. Marshall accepted the pistol, the exact one he'd picked out at the gunshop. He felt the balance of it, then smirked, stuffing it into his waistband. He let his shirt drape over it.

"It's not loaded," Watson informed him.

"No kidding?"

"Well, you—"

"I put it away so nobody looking in the car window would see me waving a gun around," Ski growled. "Want to pull over at the nearest AT&T store so I can buy you a fucking clue phone?"

Watson glowered. "I don't appreciate that language."

"And I don't appreciate amateur hour. Pull this heap over!"

"You think we're going to let you go like that?" Watson asked.

Kowalski leaned forward and grabbed the chin of the man sitting across from him. It was the guy who'd had his face ground across the wall. He screamed as tender, torn flesh was squeezed hard, blood still soaking a handkerchief he was pressing to the slashed wounds. "Want a reminder of what I'm capable of? You think you can stop me with this penny-ante bullshit? They're chump change, and I'm a solid-gold, twenty-dollar piece."

He slapped the man on his ravaged cheek and leaned back, stuffing his finger into Watson's face. "You got something that impresses me, show it. Up until now, though, I haven't seen anything other than a bunch of jerk-offs who probably masterbate to shooting at pictures of racial stereotypes."

"I will not be taunted in this—"

Watson stopped talking, unable to speak. An iron grip was on his throat, and the hate in his eyes was replaced by terror as he saw his reflection in the shiny metallic box magazines Kowalski withdrew from the militiaman's pocket. With one hand, the ex-Marine fed one of the magazines into the butt of the .45, while the other still held its cruel mastery over Watson's windpipe.

Kowalski's pistol came up, and only then did the stranglehold disappear. The sound of the slide snapping back and forth resounded through the SUV and everyone looked back at him.

"Now, if anyone starts shooting, everyone dies," Kowalski said, glowering. He leveled the barrel at Watson's nose, so he could see right down into its depths at the round tip of the 230-grain hardball round. Only the sound of the safety clicking on brought even a shiver of a reaction to the militiaman.

"Pathetic," Kowalski continued. He stuffed the .45 back into his waistband. Reclining, he let his eyes close. "Let me know when we get where we're going, or someone wants to explain something to me, whichever comes first."

Watson began to reach for the weapon under his jacket. A rustle of motion, then pain exploded. His lips were smashed and shredded across broken teeth by the impact of stainless-steel pistol across flesh. He screamed, hands clutching the torrent of blood pouring down his chin.

"From now on, if you dream about pulling a gun on me, you better wake up and apologize to me," Kowalski told him, eyes still closed, his body, save for his gun hand, relaxed and slouched.

The rest of the SUV ride went quietly for Kowalski.

AFTER JACK GRIMALDI BROUGHT Mack Bolan and Sable Burton into Sparta Municipal Airport, the soldier wasted no time getting him and his companion a rental car.

Burton looked at the vehicle, a Chevy Impala, her face covered in doubt.

"What's wrong?" Bolan asked.

"Another rental car?" she asked him.

He shrugged. "I can't carry one in my pockets, at least not big enough to drive around with."

"I do have a question about the people you work for. Nothing that could threaten national security, but something that's been eating at me," she said, getting into the passenger seat.

"What's that?" Bolan asked from behind the wheel as they pulled out to the airport's exit.

"You get shot at a lot, right?" Burton asked.

Bolan nodded.

"And your rental cars, they really take a beating, don't they?"

"More than I'd like to admit," Bolan answered.

"How can you keep renting cars? I mean, the insurance alone on wrecked cars must run into thousands," Sable continued.

Bolan turned onto the road, looking at the map. His cheek tugged involuntarily into a smile. "It's pretty high. I don't keep track."

"Millions?"

Bolan wiped his mouth. "Maybe."

"And the insurance companies don't think anything of all these wrecked cars charged to Colonel Brandon Stone?" Sable asked.

"My people are good at erasing computer records."

"There's still people at the counter," Sable returned.

Bolan sighed. "So some information gets around. I handle everything through some very special authority, and I have some good people to clean up my messes."

"Like witnesses?" Sable asked.

Bolan shook his head. "I would have never started an operation like that."

Burton watched as Bolan opened his windbreaker, the extended magazine of his pistol poking out like an ugly metallic tumor under his armpit. She noticed his eyes glancing between the driver's-side mirror and the rearview mirror.

"Is there trouble?" she asked, not bothering to turn.

"We're being followed," Bolan explained.

Burton slouched deeper in her seat, unsettled. "What are we going to do?"

"Continue to drive. Can you take the wheel?" Bolan asked.

BUSINESS REPLY MAIL

FIRST-CLASS MAIL   PERMIT NO. 717-003   BUFFALO, NY

POSTAGE WILL BE PAID BY ADDRESSEE

GOLD EAGLE READER SERVICE
3010 WALDEN AVE
PO BOX 1867
BUFFALO NY 14240-9952

Get FREE BOOKS and a FREE GIFT when you play the...

LAS VEGAS

GAME

Just scratch off the gold box with a coin. Then check below to see the gifts you get!

YES! I have scratched off the gold box. Please send me my **2 FREE BOOKS** and **gift for which I qualify**. I understand that I am under no obligation to purchase any books as explained on the back of this card.

▼ DETACH AND MAIL CARD TODAY! ▼

366 ADL D749

166 ADL D747
(MB-05R)

FIRST NAME	LAST NAME

ADDRESS

APT.#   CITY

STATE/PROV.   ZIP/POSTAL CODE

7	7	7	Worth TWO FREE BOOKS plus a BONUS Mystery Gift!
🍒	🍒	🍒	Worth TWO FREE BOOKS!
🔔	🔔	🍀	TRY AGAIN!

Offer limited to one per household and not valid to current Gold Eagle® subscribers. All orders subject to approval.

The woman nodded. "What will you be doing?"

"I might end up going EVA."

"EVA?"

"Extra Vehicular Activity."

"There's going to be more shooting," Burton stated numbly. "Any idea who they are?"

Bolan was to the point. "Army of the Hand of Christ. Fist of God. Possibly a combined group."

"Fist of God. I remember a security alert at Terintec. They're a Middle Eastern terror group," Burton said. "Let's switch. I'll climb into your lap, then you slide to the shotgun seat."

"You can handle it?" Bolan asked.

"I'm not the rail I was when I was a teenager, but we can do the switch," she told him, crawling across the parking brake. Bolan scooted out from under her, keeping his foot on the accelerator while she steered until she situated herself.

Burton hit the steering tilt on the go, setting it up so she could handle the car better, then yanked the driver's seat forward so she didn't have to manipulate the clutch, brake and gas by tiptoe. She gave Bolan a nod and he looked back over her shoulder.

"I could pick up some speed and get us to the quarry. I know a way around the old lumber mill," she said.

"They'd probably have fewer people at the quarry than at the mill, if any," Bolan agreed.

"Want me to take it easy, or do you want me to give them a show?" Burton asked.

Bolan looked back. "Give them a show."

The woman grinned, popped the clutch and threw the gearshift into fourth, the Impala's engine snarling to livid fury.

HARPY WIPED her sweaty brow on her bare forearm, looking back at the others as they spent time dragging the chassis of the SmarTruck onto a rolling pallet. The truck was far too tangled into the trees to get out easily, so Adonis laid some charges. The tires and axles were wrecked, but the trees were cleared. It hardly looked like anything worth stealing anymore, but the Kevlar shell and the wheels, even the engine, were all superfluous to the electronics built into the vehicle.

She returned her attention to the helicopter. Dents from gunfire covered it and she could see where the strain of evasive action made a hydraulic line loose, but nothing a little bit of work couldn't fix. It was flyable; they wouldn't have been able to dash up to the Spartan Lumber Company Mill otherwise. The windshield was starred with 9 mm bullet impacts, and the machine-gun pintle was as useless as an erection on a castrated bull after Adonis threw his fit.

The machine-gun mount wasn't as important as the hydraulic line, though, and she and her crew were busy working on it and replacing the starred and pocked windshields. It was all she could do to take her mind off the loss of one of her best pilots.

"Harpy," someone said.

She turned away from her work on the Black Hawk, seething indignance at the interruption. "What?"

"We got news from Sparta Municipal. Two passengers and a pilot came in with a Learjet about twenty minutes ago and rented an Impala," the man said.

Harpy regarded him, her full lips disappearing into a thin line. "Two people? A man and a woman, by any chance?"

"The man was tall. Over six feet. Dark hair and complexion, and wore black clothing. The woman was about a foot shorter, long dark hair."

Harpy's eyes glinted as she stared at him. "Are they headed here?"

"No. They spotted their tail and took off down a side road, driving like a bat out of hell. They're heading toward the quarry."

Harpy looked over her shoulder at Dark and Adonis, then back to him. "How many people do we have up there?"

"Five on guard duty," he told her. "And another two carloads on their tail."

"How many?"

"Six men total."

Harpy nodded. "Get me a couple more guys and pull some serious hardware from the lockers. We're heading out to the quarry to break big Stones into little stones."

SABLE BURTON THROTTLED DOWN through the turn, taking it tight and on the inside. It was risky pulling this kind of speed at night, but the back roads were notorious for being empty and she'd learned as a teenager how to gauge oncoming traffic. In the passenger seat beside her, her companion was relaxed as far as the reliability of his driver allowed him to be. He was concerned that a second car had joined pursuit of them, and that could only mean one thing.

Their tail had cell phones and weren't shy about calling in for help. That didn't bode well for the Executioner and his companion considering that they were heading toward a rock quarry that could be a nest full of enemies. Bolan was only anticipating a soft probe this night, so only the Beretta 93-R and the Desert

Eagle, along with various knives and other close-quarters implements of death were with him. Anything heavier was back at the plane with Grimaldi.

No matter. The Executioner was a man of improvisation.

"If I can get some distance," Burton said, "I think I know a turnoff where we can lose these guys."

"A little distraction?" Bolan asked.

"Sounds good to me."

Bolan leaned out the window, unleathering his .44 Magnum Desert Eagle. The massive hand cannon would do some damage to one of the pursuing cars, but the Executioner's main goal was to give Burton her moment's lead. Triggering the Magnum pistol, he laid a fusillade of fire across the two cars trying to keep pace with her.

Brakes squealed behind them and Burton hit the gas, the engine's growl starting the moment the cars behind them swerved and fought to slow down. The woman hit the next curve and cut their speed, swerving along the shoulder. Bolan glanced forward, seeing that they were aiming down a bike trail.

She killed the headlights, stamped the brakes, then let the car drift as soon as the Impala got to a manageable speed. She was busy negotiating subtle curves along the course of the ribbon of asphalt they were on when they finally came to a speed where she could put on the emergency brake without gouging the mechanism to ruins. Bolan, watching behind, saw the two pursuit cars thunder past.

"I know this bike path," Burton explained. "I used to ride down it when I started feeling claustrophobic at the mill."

"Good thinking."

"Now we chase them?" Burton asked.

"They're heading full-tilt toward the quarry," Bolan said. "Does this path come close to the quarry?"

"In fact, it does. About two miles up, you'll be able to climb a fence and be on the quarry grounds. The cars have about eight miles of road to loop around to the main entrance," she said.

"Drive."

Burton put the Impala in gear.

THE EXECUTIONER STRIPPED out of his windbreaker and his jeans. Underneath was a blacksuit. It took only a few moments for him to insure everything was well situated, even in the dark and by touch.

Burton looked at him, her big green eyes wide, reflecting the distant lamps of the quarry. Awe covered her face as he underwent his transformation to battle mode, streaks of black greasepaint covering his hands, cheeks and forehead to help him blend into the shadows.

"Stay here," the Executioner whispered. "Keep with the car and if there's shooting, get down. If I'm not back fifteen minutes after you hear the first gunshot, hit reverse, get down the road and get back to Sparta and my pilot."

"You'll be dead, is what you're saying."

"Dead, or in no condition to continue the fight. Maybe Jack can call in someone who can finish it. Or I'll be on the run and going back to Sparta under my own power. It's a backup plan. I don't want you getting shot."

"But don't you have a cell phone?"

Bolan paused. "Yes, I do."

"Well, put mine on your speed-dial," Burton told him. She produced her own little pocket phone.

Bolan shook his head. The damn thing was small enough to have fit in the professor's pocket, and yet he barely noticed the bulge, not connecting it with a piece of vital communications technology.

"You ring me, but don't say anything, that means I hot-tail it out of here. All you have to do is just push the Send button. If you have something to say, I'll hear it anyway," Burton told him.

"I might not be able to reach the cell. Good plan, though. But still—"

"I know. Stay the hell out of the way."

With that, Bolan threw his windbreaker over the coil of barbed wire atop the fence and vaulted over it. He came down on a five-foot ledge overlooking a deep precipice. Despite the lights across the quarry, on the landing, shadows still wrapped around him, and taking long, loping strides, he made his way toward the collection of trailers and sheds that made up an improvised work area. The trailers were still on wheels, and orange plastic fencing surrounded small, one-man Bobcat bulldozers in a temporary corral. The whole setup looked flexible enough to crawl up, down or laterally along the quarry, keeping up with the milling and blasting of stone. There was just one thing that disturbed the soldier's senses.

He'd been to enough mobbed-up construction areas and quarries to realize that shotgun-toting guards didn't stroll around well-lit quarries in the middle of the night if it was a legitimate business. It was a little something that struck the Executioner as highly suspicious.

The two cars rolled in quick and Bolan sprinted the last fifty feet to take cover against a bank of portable toilets. He looked for the next closest cover and saw that there was a trailer, seven yards away, behind piles of cast-off sandstone and other unusable rock. Shuffling noiselessly on hands and feet, he got closer to the trailer, and darted under the bottom of the trailer before anyone could notice his blacksuited form flickering in the shadows just outside the spill of the lamps.

He eased his Beretta 93-R from its place in his shoulder holster, the sound-suppressed weapon probing the darkness ahead of him as he continued along in the deep shadow of the trailer. Men were getting out of the two pursuit cars, and someone was heading up to greet them.

"What the hell's going on?" one of the chasers asked.

The quarry crewman shrugged. "Harpy just called us and told us to expect her. Where did those two go?"

"They must have pulled off, but I can't tell you where," the driver said. "How long until she gets here?"

"She said to give it ten minutes. She's driving. But that was five minutes ago," the quarry man said.

That was about all the Executioner needed to hear. Harpy was on her way, and there was a chance that she could be bringing a full-size army. The soldier had to start evening the odds now.

He burst from his hiding space, Beretta spitting 3-round bursts.

CHAPTER FOURTEEN

The Executioner's first target was the driver of the lead car, who was still busy trying to figure out what was going on with the guy in charge of the quarry. From his vantage point in the space between the trailer and the sharp slope that formed a wall of mossy soil around the edge of the quarry, he was all but invisible until he moved. He looked right at Bolan rising from the shadows, and his eyes bugged out like hard-boiled eggs. The militiaman's mouth started to work as his hands clawed desperately at the pistol in his waistband. For all his speed, he wasn't quick enough as the 3-round burst from the Beretta caught him high in the chest, subsonic slugs chewing up through his breastbone until the last shot smashed through his windpipe.

The quarry boss jerked backward, shouting in surprise as the man in front of him detonated in a spray of crimson. He was still stepping back when Bolan's second burst smashed into the base of his skull. Black hair flew as the rounds slammed in. The impact of the trio of bullets spun him around, and Bolan watched the quarry boss's forehead flap like a flag where his burst blew an exit cavity through his brainpan.

Two down, too many to go, the Executioner reminded himself as he switched the Beretta to single shot and took the driver's shotgun rider through the heart with a single round. The man staggered, staying on his feet as his brain didn't quite process his cardiac pump being torn in two, so the Executioner punched another shot through the man's open mouth. Doubly dead, the AHC fighter tumbled backward to learn the final fate of his soul.

Even with a silenced weapon, the sudden dropping of three men in midconversation caught the attention of the two shotgunners at the front gate. At the boss's final shout, they suddenly burst into Bolan's line of sight from the mouth of the quarry, shotguns still aimed at the ground as they raced to investigate.

"Good God!" one of them cried out as he saw the gory head wounds on all three of Bolan's first targets.

That was the last prayer the gunner for the AHC ever spoke as Bolan stepped to within two yards of his head. From only a few feet away, the Executioner punched a single 9 mm hollowpoint right through the guy's temple, brains erupting in a volcano of gore on the other side. He gripped the dead man by the collar with his other hand, yanking him in tight as the second shotgunner screamed in shock from being sprayed with brains and blood.

He brought up his pumpgun, firing blindly and hammering out three rounds of buckshot. If it hadn't been for his human shield, Bolan would have been the final recipient of twenty-seven .36-caliber pellets. Instead, the buck lodged in dead flesh, only one pellet passing through soft viscera to clip Bolan just under his ribs, slicing skin before dancing off into the night. The Executioner pushed his Beretta through under the corpse's arm and ripped a 3-round burst into the blood-spattered gunner.

The shotgun-toting killer was struck just above his navel, bullets plowing through his intestines, one 9 mm slug crushing its way through a vertebra. He jerked and spun spastically to the ground, his legs suddenly deprived of signals from the brain. Bolan flicked the selector to single shot once more and pumped a solitary mercy round between the AHC gunner's eyes, ending his suffering and any threat he might pose.

The Executioner shoved aside the corpse he was using as a shield. He traded his Beretta for the Desert Eagle now that the silence had been broken by the thunder of shotguns. Men were racing from a trailer, including the pair who had been in the second car. They had congregated with the gunners at the far trailer, presumably to chew the fat while the men who were in charge held their last-minute powwow closer to Bolan.

Right now, they were busy scrambling for their own weaponry, caught flat-footed by the gun battle between Bolan and the shotgunner. None of them was even considering taking cover, or even bothering to aim. They stabbed the air ahead of them with pistols and shotguns and opened fire. The Executioner dived to the ground, his body slicing the night with panther-like grace. Landing in the gravel, he brought up the Desert Eagle.

The first 240-grain boattail hollowpoint collided with the driver of the second chase car, a man with his gut hanging out over his waistband and squeezing the trigger on a .45 as fast as he could. The .44 Magnum slug met him right above the bulbous belly, tearing up and through his heart and smashing out his spine. Heart torn in two, spine snipped like twine, the driver somersaulted face-first into the gravel and shuddered like a mountain of jelly before he was stilled forever.

Bolan rolled to his right, triggering the Desert Eagle while he was on his back, the second round plowing up under the bearded jaw of a second AHC charger. The hollowpoint round struck bone and spread wide open like a blossom of copper and lead. Velocity pushed it through flesh, creating a grisly tunnel of death out the top of the man's head. Death yanked the second guy on a short leash, hurling him backward and into the path of another gunman behind him.

An AHC warrior with a shotgun leaped to the side, tromboning the slide of his weapon to spray the ground with 12-gauge devastation.

Bolan was rolling in earnest now, ignoring the digs and stabs that the rocky ground was inflicting on him. He twisted hard, keeping ahead of the line of shotgun blasts. He hated wasting ammunition, but he triggered a salvo of slugs at the shotgunner. Bellows of rage and pain filled the air, the 12-gauge blasts stopping as the gunner tumbled to the ground with shattered knees and shins.

He looked up at Bolan, as the Executioner's form loomed over him.

"Cut me down, a thousand believers will take my place! Heaven shall be victorious!" the wounded man snarled.

Bolan shook his head, aiming the Desert Eagle at the man. "You're right. Heaven will be victorious. But you're not invited to the celebration."

The Magnum pistol thundered and the Executioner moved on. The doomsday numbers were tumbling hard and fast now as the countdown to Harpy's arrival loomed. Bolan didn't want to get caught between two hardforces, especially one containing Adonis and Dark.

The window in one trailer smashed out moments before a shotgun blast filled the air. The sound of breaking glass was the Executioner's cue to take cover, and he spun, racing back toward the dead shotgunners. Taking a moment to scoop up the two shotguns, he quickly darted left and skidded to a halt under the protection of one of the automobiles that had chased him and Burton. Bolan checked the two scatterguns and shouldered the one that contained the most ammunition. He'd reload the other from shells stored on a sidesaddle holder.

Buckshot hammered against the windows on the far side of the car, metal popping as double-caught pellets tore into it. Bolan swung around and sighted on the enemy gunner's vantage point. A wave of nine slugs erupted with a single tug of the trigger, and the Executioner was jacking the slide to feed another round into the breech, nine more missiles launched right on the heels of the first. Glass panes tinkled and aluminum rattled as the salvo struck the side of the trailer.

No return fire answered from that window anymore, but Bolan wasn't taking chances. He shifted position from the back of the sedan to the front hood. He kept low, his head barely visible, yet painfully vulnerable should the enemy sniper decide to rouse himself and begin to shoot again. With a clearer vantage point, though, Bolan noticed the head and arm of the shotgunner hanging over the windowsill.

He did a quick mental count of the dead.

Nine down.

No guarantee that there weren't others still in lurking, so the Executioner quickly stuffed fresh shells into his shotgun and emptied the second weapon completely.

He put replacement shotshells in the sidesaddle holder on his gun, and everything that was still loose was stuffed into a pocket of his blacksuit. In the dark, Bolan couldn't be sure, but he figured all he had was buckshot loaded in the weapons. He'd have preferred the option of rifled slugs to allow for distance combat.

He pulled his cell phone and hit the speed dial.

"Brandon?" she answered.

"Fight's about over here, but it'll get hectic again. Head back to the airport and wait with Jack. I'll do what I can here," Bolan told her.

"They're still coming for you," Burton countered.

Bolan sighed. "What else is new? Get moving."

The Executioner shut the phone, slung his shotgun and went to the explosives shack. He had an ambush to set up.

"STILL NO ANSWER from Cole and the boys," Lee told Harpy, folding his phone away in disgust.

Harpy sneered as she rode in the shotgun seat. Across her lap was a Heckler & Koch MP-5, and in a shoulder satchel resting against her hip was a collection of spare magazines. She also had her 9 mm USP pistol in a thigh holster. All in all, she figured she had three hundred rounds for her automatic weapon and another seventy-five for the pistol. If she couldn't put Stone to his eternal rest at the bottom of the granite quarry, she didn't deserve to be a part of the RING's core command.

By now, Adonis and Dark would have gotten the clue that something was wrong when Harpy disappeared with two cars, seven men and enough submachine guns and ammunition to start a small war. It wasn't that she didn't respect Adonis and Dark for their abilities, but each member of the RING's leadership was him- or herself one of the deadliest people on the planet. Each had survived countless attempts on their lives, and the average body count of the membership was in the high forties, low fifties. That didn't take into account operations they engaged in, or the people they directed to engage in slaughter.

Her two partners, even if they did guess what she was up to, would be smart enough to stay at the mill and prepare a defense against Stone in the event that she failed.

Not that Harpy intended to.

"Slow down," Harpy cautioned. "We'll stop about seventy-five yards from the front gate and take the rest of the way on foot."

She nodded to the guy with the cell phone and he quickly rang the other car. He gave her a thumbs-up that the message was conveyed. Harpy gave the grip of her MP-5 a solid squeeze and looked ahead through the windshield.

"Time to pay, Colonel."

DARK SHOOK HIS HEAD in disbelief as he realized the ramifications of Harpy's disappearance.

"Stone is in the area, and the silly bird's gone to get her piece," he announced.

Adonis was back to his old, unflappable self, the rage of battle long since passed. "Which means that whoever brought him is probably at Sparta Municipal. It's the only way to explain how he got here so quick."

Dark looked at Adonis. "Are you thinking what I'm thinking?"

"Yup, Brain. But if nobody cares, then why exactly *did* they write a song about Jimmy cracking corn?" Adonis asked deadpan.

Dark chuckled. "You're the better pilot. Take the

Black Hawk to Sparta and drop in to get a little insurance against our man in black."

Adonis gave Dark a half salute. "Up, up and—"

"Just get moving," Dark snapped.

The big blonde grinned and headed for the recently repaired helicopter.

Dark turned, plans for mobilizing against Stone whirling through his head.

STALKING THROUGH the darkness, Harpy kept her weapon up, sweeping the midnight forest. The lights were still on in the quarry, but it was quiet except for the rumbling of a running engine. She noted mentally to censure whoever was wasting gas that way when she realized that the driver could well be dead. Reaching the edge of the trees, she knelt, the rest of her crew following suit.

"Lord," one of them breathed as they surveyed the carnage spread across the terrain, bloodied bodies strewed and dumped in unnatural poses.

Harpy saw the car that was still running, its door half open. A man with his hand still wrapped around the stock of a shotgun sat in the front seat, his face caked with blood and gore.

So much for her disciplining the guy.

"Anyone else speaks out of turn, you'll catch a bullet in the head. The man we're going after is dangerous, stealthy and skilled," Harpy whispered. She got up, and Corbin, one of her AHC men, took the lead. He was a former Ranger, and a point man for when his unit took to the field. She let the man do his job since he had years of experience at it, from Ethiopia to the Gulf. She didn't have much respect for most of the people that the RING was uniting under its hate-binding banner of destroying world governments, but Corbin at least carried himself as a professional and did his job with efficiency. That scored big points with Harpy.

Corbin stopped, raising his fist. Harpy and the AHC militiamen all came to a halt at the signal. The ex-Ranger had spotted something. She kept her eye on him, knowing that he would tell her what threats lay ahead.

SLOUCHED IN THE FRONT SEAT of the Crown Victoria, Mack Bolan felt the blood congealing on his face. He kept his eyes open, mouth slacked, and he could taste droplets trickling down from his upper lip. Movement in the trees just to the side of the entrance to the quarry caught his peripheral vision, but he didn't move or react to it.

In his left hand, the stock of the shotgun he'd borrowed was gripped to the point that the stippling on the handle was grating into his palm. In his right hand, hidden by his thigh and the shadows of the dashboard, lay a radio detonator. It was a frantic few minutes, getting det cord and explosives from the shack. Industrial-grade C-4 wasn't the kind of stuff the Executioner usually used, but it was free, there was plenty of it, and he wanted to make some big impressions. He used his usual stash of quarter-pound cubes with radio-activated fuses to prime the stuff.

He wished that he knew exactly what kind of force Harpy had brought with her. If it was Dark and Adonis, the amount of explosives used wouldn't be overkill.

Even if not, Bolan was still targeting a member of the RING.

And it wasn't as if he was using up his own explosives anyway.

CORBIN ADVANCED SLOWLY as his two partners held open the chain link fence. Once he was on the other side, he reached back and held the flexible barrier at bay so the others could squeeze through. Once the trio was in, he continued down, the barrel of his Colt Commando leading the way.

The two soldiers of the Army of the Hand of Christ followed silently, betraying nothing with their movements. It was a good, tight formation. They were spread apart far enough that they wouldn't all get hit in a single burst of autofire, but close enough to be able to communicate by hand signals and to cover each other in the case of a firefight.

Corbin motioned for his men to stop and, pressing himself tight to the trailer, slowly rounded the corner. He peered through the Aimpoint Scope atop his rifle and focused in to its full four times magnification, looking at the running car. The last Corbin remembered, there were no men on duty at the quarry who were left-handed, and none of the men in the cars were armed with shotguns. It could have been a driver who grabbed a shotgun and tried to make a getaway, but if that was the case, how could he get such a gory head wound on the right side of his skull through an undamaged windshield?

The point man's instincts were jangling on full alert.

He spied the alleged corpse in the driver's seat and saw the face of the man sitting there. One eye moved, almost imperceptibly, staring right back at him through the scope.

"Gotcha," Corbin snarled.

A soft beep distracted him in the instant before he pulled the trigger on the Colt Commando. A fraction of a heartbeat later, Corbin and his two partners were atomized as the trailer evaporated in a ground-shaking explosion.

HARPY FELT THE EXPLOSION through the soles of her feet a moment before she saw the sky lit up by several pounds of high explosives.

"Corbin's down!" she shouted. Her group split into two teams and they raced to cover either side of the quarry entrance. The men racing across in the open received the benefit of a wave of automatic fire lead by Harpy herself as she pressed tight to the hillside.

The quarry itself was a massive cloud of backlit dust as the lamp poles spilled light through the raining debris. One set of lights was on the ground, sputtering as if striving to stay alive after being upended. She saw only the vague, hulking outline of an automobile still parked in the entrance, where Corbin had been suspicious of the body. With two-thirds of a 30-round magazine left in her weapon, she aimed and hosed the car.

Bullets sparked all over it as other gunmen took the cue. The rattle of autofire was deafening and the car visibly shook under waves of impacts. Harpy reloaded three times, emptying her gun into the parked vehicle. She didn't even bother to count the hail of lead thrown at the Crown Victoria by the other guys.

"All right! Enough!" she shouted.

By now, the fallen lamppost had died, its lights giving one last flicker. The cloud dimmed, lit by only one pole now. The frame of the automobile stood, but the windows were gone and it was resting on chewed-up rims, tires shredded to mere ribbons. The roof of the car was half caved in, as well.

If anyone had stuck around inside that deathtrap, he'd be the makings for stew meat.

Harpy took a tentative step forward, her men following suit. The MP-5 rested against her hip, ready to spring up to sweep the darkness.

"Wait. The cloud hasn't dissipated enough yet," she warned.

"You think he survived that?" one of her men asked.

"No. But you've seen those movies. 'Nobody could have survived that!' Ten seconds later, they're gagging as the nobody they just shot at gets up and is strangling them with their own intestines," Harpy snapped. "We wait until my signal."

"That is the guy who killed off the team that went with Adonis and Dark to get the truck," another spoke up.

Harpy smirked. "We're taking no chances."

"No, ma'am!" they said in unison.

The AHC men were as good as their word. They were quiet, eyes searching the spill of light for signs of movement as the dust cloud continued to settle to the point where they could see details through holes.

Glass shattered, bulbs popped and the quarry was suddenly thrown into complete darkness.

"Fuck!" Harpy growled, triggering a long burst from her weapon. The AHC gunners followed suit. Having no target this time, they simply swept, taking huge slices of terrain and pouring bullets out. Harpy stopped after one magazine, as did the others.

They were down to half the ammo they'd brought with them, and all they had to show for it were lots of casings on the ground, a wrecked Crown Victoria and empty, mocking shadows all about them. Harpy looked to her team.

"We're withdrawing. Enough of this bullshit," she snarled. "We're not taking the fight to him."

She waved her team back to her side of the entrance. They complied quickly, crouching low as they dashed across the road. No gunfire chased them, but that was probably because their enemy didn't have the kind of firepower necessary to engage her team.

Harpy kept telling herself that.

It was her and four men, and she hadn't been able to do shit against Stone. Now he was dictating the course of battle, and leaving her a choice of attacking a well-scouted, defended position, and possibly encountering more high explosives, or retreating.

She chose discretion over valor.

Adonis and Dark would handle this screwhead. That's what they got paid the big money for, and she would apologize for trying to take matters into her own hands.

Harpy turned and started forward when she glimpsed her group out of the corner of her eye. She remembered she had four men left.

So what were five bodies doing following her?

"Scatter!" Harpy shouted, bringing the MP-5 around, bullets spitting from the muzzle.

CHAPTER FIFTEEN

Harpy wasn't as good a soldier as she was a pilot, but Mack Bolan couldn't fault her on that. He was still off balance from the blast that had taken out her scouts. Only by a mad dash had he been able to disappear into the choking cloud of smoke and flying dust before she and her team rained a hell of a thousand bullets against him. His heart was still hammering from the near-death experience of setting off the trailer so close to ground zero, and then being chased by enemy fire, but when he realized that the AHC team was focusing on the only thing they could see, he clambered up the hill on the far side of the quarry entrance.

Crouching there, he took several deep breaths, resisting the urge to hack up the tickling dust cloying in his throat. They stopped shredding the Crown Vic about the time he finished wiping his eyes clear of the dust that had accumulated in them. Vision no longer irritated by grit, he could see that Harpy was left with four armed killers, and she seemed to have enough extra magazines to make life very difficult for him.

Five enemies.

Too bad, he thought, as he dropped the shotgun in the mad dash to get out of the way of enemy gunfire. The Executioner still had his handguns and plenty of ammunition for them, though. He heard some discussion.

He'd thoroughly unsettled the five people below him, and they were trying to figure out whether it was safe to go snooping around a half-lit quarry with a skilled killer and an unknown amount of explosives planted in their path. It reminded him of the old days when he'd walk brazenly among organized crime leaders and soldiers who were talking in wide-eyed disbelief about the unstoppable Bastard in Black, never realizing who was sitting just in earshot. It was an old thrill, Bolan regretfully admitted as he recovered his strength, but it was the simple things in life that kept him going.

He leveled the silenced Beretta at the remaining lamppost and with a 3-round burst, knocked the entire quarry into darkness.

Once more, the militiamen and their boss opened fire, but this time they controlled their ammunition expenditure to just one magazine. Bolan knew they wouldn't waste any more than they had to. They probably had used up half their war load on the Ford while the dust was still flying.

That was all right.

They were scared out of their wits.

Prey for the Executioner.

He slipped down behind the group as Harpy announced their retreat, and padded gently up to them, slipping among their numbers. Bolan was a shadow amongst shadows.

And once again, Harpy came aware of the Executioner's presence.

"Scatter!" the pilot screeched like her namesake. The weapon in her hand was barking, and the Executioner dodged behind one of the AHC soldiers. Bolan extended the barrel of his Beretta until it was a contact shot on one of the slower men, stroking the trigger to blast a combined mess of bullet and brains out the back of his skull. Cored, the militiaman died without a sound, but he didn't fall.

Bolan gripped the collar of the man's shirt, holding him up like a shield as he opened fire on the rest of the crew.

The militiamen paused, not wanting to gun down their own friend, and only Harpy's salvo of 9 mm slugs collided with the dead man. Bolan swung his Beretta at her and opened fire, but the woman had the reflexes of an eagle, power diving out of the way of his return fire. With a curse, the Executioner shifted his aim and took the man to her right, pumping a round into him at throat level. The guy's windpipe burst open and he vomited up blood, clawing at himself to suck in fresh air.

Bolan ignored the dying man as the others were getting their act together. One of them was armed with an M-16. The Executioner shoved his lifeless shield at the man, who screamed in shock and rage as his initial burst ripped into the corpse. The two AHC men, living and dead, collapsed into a tangled pile of limbs, the M-16 knocked out of the rifleman's hands.

Bolan chased the last guy with a couple shots, but he disappeared behind a tree just as the Beretta clicked on an empty chamber. With a curse, Bolan let the gun drop to his other hand, raising the Desert Eagle. The militiaman took courage from the sudden lull in the shooting and swung around with his autoweapon. Before he could even pull the trigger, the Executioner hammered him with a .44 Magnum hollowpoint, the heavy round goring through bone, gristle and flesh to tear into the gunner's rib cage. The AHC man spun into view, struggling to bring up his weapon to try to bring his killer to hell with him, but the Executioner finished the fight with a single round plowing between his eyes. The top of his head was shorn off and he flipped backward into the darkness.

Bolan spun, looking for Harpy, but the woods were silent. In the distance, a car started, and he took aim at the sound. No headlights or taillights presented themselves to give the Executioner a target to shoot at, though. The pilot was savvy enough to not call any more attention to herself.

She also wasn't sticking around to figure out who'd lived and who'd died. Bolan didn't blame her.

But the next time the two met, someone wasn't going to walk away.

THE CELL PHONE in Sable Burton's pocket warbled as she was almost back to Sparta Municipal Airport. She plucked the phone free and hit the button.

"Brandon?"

"Yeah, it's me." Bolan's voice came over the connection.

Relief flooded her, but only for a moment. "And Adonis and Dark?"

"Didn't come for the floorshow. But they'll have a message racing to them."

Burton looked back over her shoulder. "Who got away?"

"Harpy. I'm pretty sure she was by herself. Just stay at the airport with Jack. I'm on my way to you to pick up some supplies," Bolan explained. "Our friend was nice enough to leave me a car."

Burton was about to ask, when she realized what he meant. "Just be careful and get back soon."

"I will," Bolan said.

The woman hung up as she pulled into the airport entrance. She dropped the phone in her blouse's front pocket and left it there, pulling the rental car into a parking spot. Getting out, she admired the Impala's condition, nary a scratch on her first high-speed chase. She turned and walked toward the rental office, then reconsidered. Just because Stone had borrowed another vehicle didn't mean they wouldn't have use for a second set of wheels. She twirled the keys around her finger, caught them in her palm, then stuffed the lot into her pocket.

Jack Grimaldi was waiting in the lounge next to the rental office and looked up, concern on his face when he saw her. Burton did her best to look nonchalant, but she was still fighting a heartbeat that was racing a mile a minute. It had been more than fifteen years since she'd done anything remotely exciting. The past twenty-four hours had been an exercise in adventure that she thought only existed in movies and novels.

"Where's Brandon?" Grimaldi asked.

"He got another ride. He'll be back for some party favors."

Grimaldi grinned widely. "You pick up the crypto-speak very well, grasshoppah."

"Too many years of romance and adventure novels."

"And where exactly did you fit in the time to be a physicist?" Grimaldi asked.

"Evelyn Wood speed reading courses, and the fact I sleep four hours a night."

Grimaldi nodded knowingly and chuckled. "Want some coffee?"

"No, thanks."

The pilot shrugged and took a couple steps toward the coffee machine when outside, the darkness lit up under the effect of powerful strobes. Grimaldi paused in midstep, looking aghast out the window.

"What's wrong?" Sable asked, rushing to his side.

Grimaldi looked around the airport lounge. People were only now just realizing something was wrong as the big black military helicopter set down outside. His hand went momentarily for the Colt .45 in its waistband holster, but he thought better of it in a crowded area. "We got to get moving."

Burton nodded. Arguing was last on her list of priorities, and the two people raced to the front entrance of the terminal.

The woman glanced back to the airfield and saw that the squat, cockroach-like Black Hawk had swung closer, dropping off a towering figure from the side before it climbed and just missed a collision with the main building's roof. The giant that swooped down from the sky charged after her and Grimaldi.

"Jack!" she called, throat half strangled with terror at the sight of the man bearing down on him. He was an obscenity in full motion, enormous limbs propelling him with a speed that defied anything she thought of as natural. His clean-shaved, beautiful and boyish face robbed of its appeal by the cold, expressionless nature of a paralyzed mask. This wasn't a man chasing them, but an oversize Greek statue come to life, body surging in hot pursuit.

Grimaldi spun, seeing the same thing she did, and this time he did pull the Colt .45 from under his leather bomber jacket, snapping the gun up. The slide whipped back and forth, shell casings kicking from the breech, the thunder of the muzzle-blast pounding on Burton's ears like trip-hammers. Her eyes, though, still remained focused on Adonis as he continued to bear down on them. The Stony Man pilot couldn't be missed now that he was within ten feet, but he slowed to a walk. His chest rippled as slugs hammered into his chest, Grimaldi emptying the pistol until the slide locked back.

Adonis was upon them in two strides, but Grimaldi was swinging his pistol like a hammer now. The blond giant dodged the swing, avoiding contact between the steel pistol butt and his skull. Instead he wrapped a beefy paw around the pilot's wrist and gave a hard twist.

Grimaldi screamed and dropped to one knee. "Sable! Run!"

Adonis punched Grimaldi in the temple, then shoved his unconscious form away from him, hands reaching out for her. Burton spun and launched a spearing kick into the big man's groin. Her foot impacted on hard muscle, only eliciting a grin on the giant's face.

"You're only making me horny by doing that, Professor Burton," Adonis told her. "Will you come with me this time?"

"Go to hell!" the woman snarled. She launched herself at him, fingers slashing and raking air, seeking out soft flesh and eye sockets.

Adonis's massive hand wrapped around her throat and she gagged, feet suddenly dangling in empty space. She clutched his rock-solid forearm, trying to take the pressure off her windpipe when she felt Adonis shift his thumb slightly, pressing hard under her left ear.

Pressure suddenly roared within Burton's head and she tried to squeal for help, but blackness rushed in on her like a tidal wave, sweeping her into a sea of unconsciousness.

WATSON AND HIS battered men stood to David Kowalski's right as he waited at the empty desk in the bivoac. Checking his watch, Kowalski realized that it was nearly midnight.

"Does your boss keep late hours?" he asked Watson nonchalantly.

Before Watson could say anything, the door to the office opened and in strode two men. One of them was tall, with short-clipped, straw-colored hair, his face covered with freckles. He had craggy features, wrinkles on his face showing years of mileage. The other man was dark-skinned, his nose hooked over a bushy mustache and beard in sharp contrast to his companion. Both, however, were dressed in crisp woodland-camouflage BDUs.

"I am Colonel Logan. This is Colonel Sahleen. You are Peter Steel?"

Kowalski snapped to a salute of these men, not out of reflex, but he faked a good simulation of it. It had been years since he'd had the desire to salute any commanding officer. Actually, that wasn't true, he reminded himself. There was Striker, or Colonel Brandon Stone as he was being called these days. He put all the feeling into the salute as he would for Striker.

"Sir! Lieutenant Steel, reporting for duty, sir!"

"And what duty is that?" Logan asked him. He circled Kowalski as if he was a raw recruit, scanning him. "You're dressed like you just tumbled out of bed."

"Sir! I didn't have a chance to dress properly, sir!" Kowalski responded.

"At ease, son," Logan told him, chuckling. "Just like a jarhead."

Kowalski crossed his arms behind his back, feet

spreading apart. "I was taught to respect a superior officer, Colonel Logan."

"You learned well." Sahleen spoke up, sitting on the corner of the desk. He crossed his arms, big brown eyes scanning Kowalski as if he were trying to pick forensic clues off his skin and clothes. "Do you have any idea what this is about?"

"I assumed this was about the Army of the Hand of Christ," Kowalski said.

Logan looked at Watson, whose eyes bulged like hard-boiled eyes. "Is that so?"

"You told us that you needed to recruit some new members...." Watson blubbered, lips sticking together between words.

"As you were!" Logan ordered. "I gave Steel permission to stand down. Not you, sack of no-loads! He isn't even part of this operation and he was ramrod straight and pecker-hard!"

Watson and the others suddenly lurched to life, as if the puppeteers controlling their movements had grabbed their strings and pulled them straight.

"Sir! Sorry!" Blood continued to trickle over Watson's chin and all over his shirt. He was trembling now with the fear of God.

"Better," Logan growled. He looked over to Kowalski again. "Lucky for Watson, he was smart enough to mail us some information about you before he fumbled picking you up."

"Then you've read my file, sir?" Kowalski answered.

"Lieutenant Peter Steel. Instructor in Close Quarters Combat, Mobile Operations Urban Training, and Long Range Reconnaissance," Logan rattled off. "Our computer people are running a few checks trying to get through the Department of Defense to verify a few holes in your record with the Twenty-Six."

"Black bag stuff," Kowalski admitted. "I'd tell you more, but…"

He looked over to Sahleen, eyes widening and wary.

"Colonel Sahleen is on our side, son," Logan explained.

"A wise man once said, the enemy of my enemy is my friend," Sahleen explained. "If you know what I mean."

"The United States' government?" Kowalski asked. "It makes sense. But still…"

"I can understand your skepticism, Lieutenant," Sahleen cut him off, "but I have earned a position of respect with Colonel Logan and his men."

Sahleen glanced over to Watson and his three stooges. "Most of them, that is."

Watson glowered back.

Kowalski grinned. "Then you might actually be a pretty good friend of mine, Colonel Sahleen, sir."

Sahleen glanced back at Kowalski, then broke into a chuckle.

"I have four injured men here, thanks to you," Logan cut in, continuing in an effort to keep Kowalski from finding a balance.

"They didn't have to kick in the door while I was naked," Kowalski replied. "I was just doing what any American should have the right to do, defending my residence from attack. I only wish I'd had a gun, but then I wouldn't be here and your men would be in a morgue."

Logan bristled at the description of events and glared back at Watson. "Is this true?"

"Sir, we…"

"Is this true?" Logan demanded. Veins rippled along

his neck, his freckles disappearing as blood flushed his features.

Watson nodded.

Logan looked back at Kowalski. "And you're armed."

"Watson gave me the gun in the car. He wouldn't give me any explanation of what was going on, but he was stupid enough to give me a side arm," Kowalski told him. "I got the ammo off him myself."

"Why did you think that was a good idea?" Sahleen asked, sounding clinical and distant, voice soft and soothing.

"I was surrounded by four men who attacked me and one of whom who held me at gunpoint. I just figured I'd need some extra insurance against these morons in case they got upset. I don't even know why you're in such a rush to haul me out of my hotel room and bring me here. Don't you guys have e-mail? Even money for a stamp? You have my address."

"Perhaps we were less than clear with our instructions to Mr. Watson," Sahleen said. "There's still the possibility that you're someone planted. An undercover cop."

"You'd be idiots not to worry about that," Kowalski responded. "I don't see but four idiots in this room and they all are covered with owies."

"You son of a bitch!" Watson bellowed. He broke into a lunge, and Kowalski was already bracing for his attack when Logan grabbed the little guy by the arm and hurled him to the floor. The sound of breaking bone filled the air like cracking eggshells and the floored militiaman wailed in agony.

"That was your elbow joint popping," Logan informed him through the curtain of screams Watson was putting out. "It can be fixed if I don't do something stupid like lift you by this arm."

Watson swallowed hard and tried to keep his swollen, bloody lips clenched tight. Tears were flowing from the corners of his eyes.

"Lieutenant Steel, it's not nice to taunt my men," Logan explained. "No matter how incompetent they appear, they are good and brave men devoted to the cause."

"I apologize, Colonel," Kowalski answered with reverence.

"I believe you are sorry," Logan replied. "What would you have me do with Watson here?"

"Nothing, sir," Kowalski said. He walked over and took Watson by his uninjured hand, lifting him to his feet. "Rank hath its privileges. Colonels don't do the heavy lifting."

Logan smirked. "I like your attitude, son."

"No attitude. Just duty."

"Come on. Let's have a seat and talk about your new job. Watson, you and your men are dismissed."

CHAPTER SIXTEEN

Adonis thought he was hearing things at first. Then the twinkling ring of Sable Burton's cell phone chirped through his hearing protection in the back of the Black Hawk helicopter. The blond giant frisked the unconscious woman and pulled the little phone from her breast pocket, then flipped it open. He didn't speak, however.

There was silence on the other end. Adonis waited for a response.

"Are we going to wait all night and use up our batteries?" Mack Bolan asked.

"I figured it was you, Stone," Adonis answered.

"I guessed something was wrong when I heard a helicopter on the other end."

Adonis chuckled. "You know we have the woman and your bush pilot by now."

"Yeah."

Adonis had to admire the man. He was inflappable. "No curses? No threats? No warnings?"

"You're professionals. You'll keep them alive as bait or as insurance. I'll try to figure out a way to get them back, or failing that, avenge them. Bullets will fly. People will die. It all ends up the same," Bolan answered. "The only difference is which side is still standing at the end."

"Pretty mellow," Adonis answered.

"No point in getting hysterical," the Executioner returned. "I'll do my best to kill you and Dark and Harpy and whoever else is with you there."

"You're welcome to try, Stone. It'll be an enjoyable diversion," Adonis stated.

"That's all life-and-death struggle is worth to you? A pastime?"

"Got nothin' else to do with my time and skills," Adonis answered. "You?"

"I was born to put people like you in the ground."

"Looks like you'll fail that destiny, Stone," the blond giant proclaimed.

"I'd love to chat all day with you, but I have to get ready to shut you down," Bolan answered.

Adonis simply smiled on the other end of the phone. "It was a pleasure to hear your voice, at least. Hope to see you soon."

"Not if I see you first," Bolan promised.

The Executioner hung up and Adonis tucked the phone back into Burton's pocket.

The Nordic titan shivered, excitement tingling up and down his spine faster than a speeding bullet.

MACK BOLAN HAD BEEN behind this eight ball before, but this time, the pool table was more of a dangerous minefield. He couldn't so easily strike and retrieve against Dark and Adonis. They knew he was coming, and usually, that was something that worked in his favor. Against mobsters and terrorists and drug dealers, the Executioner's rampage of intimidation, shock and terror would unnerve the enemy.

Dark and Adonis were professionals, however.

Cold-blooded.

Dedicated.

The Wisconsin State Police were on hand at Sparta Municipal, working with the local sheriff's department to investigate the earlier shooting and abduction. Bolan flashed his Justice Department credentials to learn more of what was going on.

The descriptions weren't pretty. They told of a man dropping from a military helicopter and wading through a hail of bullets, unaffected, and knocking out two people before making off with them. A few of the witnesses said that the tiny woman with the man was strangled to death, but she was hauled out over his shoulder, as well. The authorities were discounting her death, because dead people make poor kidnap victims.

Bolan agreed, but declined to inform them of how he was so certain of Sable's survival. So far, the police knew nothing about the names and identities of the missing pair, which was good news for the Executioner. Nobody had placed Grimaldi's aircraft, which gave him the opportunity to raid the lockers aboard the Learjet.

Bolan slipped unseen aboard the Bombardier Aerojet Learjet 60. The equipment lockers opened to his fingerprint ID and he took a few moments to evaluate the combat kit he needed to go to war with Adonis and Dark. So far, he'd seen them wearing body armor. The description of Grimaldi emptying his pistol into Adonis was proof that they weren't going to be taken off guard, which meant Bolan would need some deep-penetrating firepower for them. Armor-piercing ammo would work, but it was like an ice pick on human flesh, having a minimum of stopping power.

That left the Olympic Arms OA-93 machine pistol. The OA-93 was essentially just an M-16, its barrel chopped from 20 to 6.5 inches, its rear stock removed and its carrying handle replaced by a sight rail. It still fired the high-velocity, hard-hitting .223 Remington rounds of the M-16, capable of punching through layers of Kevlar body armor as if they were foam.

The Olympic Arms had been customized by John Kissinger of Stony Man Farm only by the addition of a forward T-grip. Bolan wouldn't be using a stock on the short-framed M-16 variant, instead using the British Special Air Service method of resistance against the sling and a firm hold on the weapon to control it in full-auto. Bolan had worked with the little chopper and was satisfied with its control and accuracy in combat.

Bolan snatched up the trio of magazines already loaded with M-955 armor-piercing ammunition. He took several empties and filled them up with the hard-hitting AP rounds, then loaded all the magazines into his war bag. The OA-93 went in, too.

Spare magazines for the Desert Eagle and the Beretta also dropped inside, and Bolan grabbed the tiny Beretta 9000 in case Grimaldi needed something.

He was sure that Adonis or Dark wouldn't torture the pilot. It was a hostage situation, not an interrogation.

He got on the phone to Stony Man Farm.

"Am I clean?" Bolan asked.

"Signal's coming through strong. Nobody's got a tap on it," Price answered. "What's wrong, Striker?"

"They took Jack and Professor Burton," Bolan told her.

"Do you need assistance?" Price asked.

"There's really nobody in the area."

"We have Buck and a team of blacksuits at O'Hare. They moved in just after you took off for Sparta," Price replied. "Hal thought it would be a good idea to have a ready-reaction force on the site."

"Good plan. David and Phoenix?"

"Still in the Philippines."

Bolan chewed on the information for a moment. Hal Brognola had to have gotten some bad vibes from the discovery of the maps in Chicago. Without a solid lead, however, all Brognola could do was to station Buck Greene and some of the Stony Man security force on hand. Just in case. With the losses in the blacksuit force at Dulles, the Farm would be spreading themselves thin in this instance.

"Any joy from Able?" Bolan asked.

"They're still working in Northern California. The new kid is in with the AHC."

"So one of their leads worked out," Bolan mused.

"Striker, we can pull everybody back…"

"Just how much do we have at O'Hare?"

"Ten. And Buck. And Charlie Moss."

"Charlie? Did he happen to bring along *Dragon Slayer?*"

"Hal didn't want another Dulles incident. We got caught asleep at the wheel with that one, and even with some of our best people…"

"Considering the opposition, you're not going for overkill," Bolan explained. "I hope if my plan works, you won't run into any trouble."

"And if it doesn't?" Price asked.

The Executioner took a deep breath.

"Stay hard, Barb."

Bolan hung up the phone.

By 0100, Kowalski had a stomach full of coffee and the better part of a roast-beef-and-cheddar sandwich on a torpedo roll. Sahleen and Logan made the whole scene much more amenable.

"Thanks. I missed dinner thanks to the drive over," Kowalski stated. He dabbed his lips with a napkin, then sailed it into a wastebasket. "Now do we retire to the library for brandy and cigars?"

Sahleen laughed at the joke, though Logan stiffened, a little more discomfitted than usual. "I noticed one thing…"

Kowalski raised an eyebrow.

"You eat with your left hand," Sahleen mentioned.

"It's my dominant hand," Kowalski answered. "It was hard when I was stationed overseas. I just forgot myself now."

Logan looked between the two. "What?"

"The left hand is the unclean hand," Kowalski explained. "It's the hand which people 'wipe themselves with' and it is also referred to as the sinister hand."

"You've learned well from your time in the Mediterranean," Sahleen answered.

"Frankly, I never concentrated on what hand I wiped my crack with until you guys brought it up. And it's called soap and water."

"A rare commodity in the desert, Lieutenant," Sahleen returned.

Kowalski took a breath, then put his fingers to his forehead and bowed. "My apologies, Colonel."

"Enough meeting of minds," Logan rumbled. "We're here to tell you about the job that Watson was trying to recruit you for."

"What is it?" Kowalski asked.

"We need you to work security for us," Logan answered. "Someone's been shadowing our operations, and they're just getting way too close."

"Defensive posture or something more proactive?" Kowalski asked.

"Like making a hit on the men coming after us?" Sahleen clarified.

Kowalski nodded. "Like that."

"Once we get some information, maybe," Logan explained. "But for now, I want to look for possible holes in our own setup."

"This base seems more secure than I expected after Watson."

"Our men are dedicated," Logan stated. "I just want to have one particular area secured, and didn't like the idea of drawing too much attention with too many men on hand."

"So you decided to recruit someone with special operations skills," Kowalski spoke, to let Logan know he was on the same page. "Though I suspect you and a good portion of your men are former Special Forces."

"You wouldn't be wrong in that," Logan admitted. "But we don't have that many people to go around. Not when we're under full operational mode."

Kowalski nodded. "Where's this place I'm supposed to stake out?"

"San Francisco."

"Narrow it down for me a smidge."

Sahleen chuckled. "We'll take you there. It's just off the Bay. The most important problem is that it's a storefront location."

"And you're hanging your people out in the middle of San Francisco for what reason?"

"Well, the locals might be a little perturbed by

Logan's good old boys. But we have a hidden edge," Sahleen answered.

"Arabs?" Kowalski asked.

"Even better than that," someone said from behind Kowalski. He turned in his chair and spotted a new-comer, his face round and dark-skinned, straight black hair combed neatly on his skull. Almond-shaped eyes looked him over. "Who'd notice Asians in Frisco?"

"Good English accent," Kowalski said. "Filipino?"

The man looked surprised. "How'd you guess?"

"The Abu Sayyaf group. They had ties to al-Qaeda, but they also received demolitions training from American Christian Identity group members Timothy McVeigh and Terry Nichols," Kowalski answered. "I bone up on my history."

"I'm Suarez," the man introduced himself. "Not a bad guesstimate. Abu Sayyaf is old news, however."

"Really?"

"Why else do you think the three of us are able to coexist so easily, son?" Logan asked the question.

Kowalski shrugged.

"There is going to be a war, Lieutenant," Sahleen began. "A war where purity and virtue will once again rule the planet. Too long have the forces of corruption soiled the governments of the world."

"Secular governments have, for too long, dictated what the good and righteous people can do," Suarez continued. "And all that has happened is for the world to slip further into anarchy. Have you ever spent time in the Philippines?"

"No, sir," Kowalski answered.

Suarez shook his head. "Have you at least heard of the scandal of American servicemen avoiding prosecution for engaging in sex with child prostitutes, immoral even by the most radical of religious beliefs?"

"I heard that. They avoided prosecution by authorities in Manila," Kowalski replied. "Frankly, they also managed to avoid prosecution at home."

He didn't have to act to disguise his disgust at that. Given a shotgun, a crowbar and a blowtorch, he'd easily plow through the ranks of cold-blooded bastards who'd helped propagate the raping of innocent children. There was no excuse for a man to touch a child sexually, and be allowed to continue life with his arms, legs and genitals.

"Simmer down, son," Logan said. "No need to get riled up."

"I thought you were for cleaning up the government," Kowalski asked.

Logan nodded. "We'll take care of all of them. The pedophiles, the drug dealers, the abortionists, the homosexuals…"

Kowalski was glad that his anger was already being recognized in conjunction with the pedophiles. As soon as Logan began his bigoted diatribe, it was everything the young blacksuit could do to keep the fibers of his being from exploding with rage against the three soulless terrorists surrounding him.

But he needed to find out about the San Francisco HQ first.

Once he found out about that, then he could come back with Able Team and start laying these animals to waste. He swallowed his fury, saving it for the long stretch he knew was ahead.

THE EXECUTIONER SWEPT the mill with the 85 mm Zeiss Diascope. The spotting scope was a poor substitute for a map, but because Sable Burton hadn't had the opportunity to draw a map for Bolan, he had to make do with old-fashioned scouting. Even in the darkness, however, the Diascope showed details of the facility. The snap-on night-vision lens cast the area in a fuzzy green glow, but the Zeiss eyepiece was still powerful enough to give the soldier sufficient detail to plan an assault.

Bolan returned the Diascope to its place in the war bag. It was bigger than most binoculars, but its capacity to use a night-vision filter and the raw power of the spotting scope enabled him to keep distance from his enemies while learning about them. Even at one-thousand meters, it was as though he was watching right over their shoulders.

Something was missing from this scenario, Bolan could tell right away. The Black Hawk was still sitting, covered by a tarpaulin, and there were men patrolling the grounds. They were alert and intense. No cigarettes, no stopping to chat, no leaning against a wall.

Body armor was worn over their torsos, too, and they had probably emptied their armory, because the full-auto firepower was both state-of-the-art and in abundance.

It could have been the late hour, but Adonis had sounded plenty awake, and he didn't strike Bolan as the kind to snooze while an enemy was out stalking. No, the absence of the two RING members put the Executioner on the knife edge as he glided through the darkened woods. The OA-93 was leading the way, ready to rip the night apart in violent action, but if he could avoid a firefight, then so much the better.

He reached the edge of the mill, chain-link fence surrounding it. Bolan didn't touch it. Burton had told him security around the facility was tight, including an electrified fence. No signs were up to warn people strolling through the forest, but after Terintec left, it wouldn't be much of a problem to occasionally sweep up the remains of a body fried by thousands of volts and bury it, never to be found again.

Bolan planned to avoid such a fate. He plucked a canister from his war bag and held it up to the fence. Spraying in an arc, the links of the fence snapped almost musically, metal popping and twanging apart as freon froze it until it was too brittle to maintain its own weight. With a jingle, the fence began to topple, but the Executioner grabbed the section, now free from the rest of the fence, no longer holding current, and lowered it stealthily to the ground. The empty freon canister was stuffed back into his satchel, and Bolan tossed it through the opening.

One bag handle brushed against the chain links, a metal button raising a brilliant spark as it went through and the Executioner stayed still for several long, nerve-racking moments.

Nobody was reacting to the little flash.

Bolan hunched his shoulders tight together and slipped through the hole, snaking along. Once he was past the fence, he pulled himself up into a crouch and scooped the war bag, surveying the mill compound. Guards were still on patrol, in pairs.

No voices were carrying to him, which meant that they were keeping alert. Bolan wondered why they hadn't heard even the modicum of noise he'd produced, when he spotted something out of the corner of his eye. Two shadows were barely perceptible, but moving, behind a stack of fifty-five-gallon drums.

Bolan didn't look directly at them. He kept going forward. If he continued in a straight line, he'd be in the shadow of a warehouse. Finally, ears straining, he heard the faint crackle of a communicator. The Executioner whirled, bringing up the OA-93 with one hand, the other plunging into his war bag for a stun-shock grenade.

The men behind the oil drum rose as one. The guy with the radio was still calling out, leveling his auto-weapon single-handedly while his partner had two hands on his.

The Executioner dived to the ground, squeezing the trigger, letting the Olympic Arms machine pistol rip apart the night.

CHAPTER SEVENTEEN

The AHC gunners were still aiming at where the Executioner's position of a heartbeat earlier, filling the air at waist-level with a scythe of blistering lead. The warehouse's aluminum walls clanged as bullets peppered its side. The OA-93 in Bolan's right fist bucked and kicked, his salvo of .223 Remington flesh-rippers meeting his enemy at close range.

The M-955 armor-piercing ammunition, with its nondeforming hard core, punched right through the Kevlar the two militiamen wore, before striking fluid mass and tumbling like a series of buzz saws through lung and heart tissue. Bone fragments from violent breeches by some of the tungsten-cored slugs created further shrapnel, which left the industrious ambushers laying in a heap of twisted, mangled flesh.

Bolan's grenade sailed back toward the warehouse, pin and spoon flying free as it arced with the force of his throw. As two guards appeared from the other side of the warehouse, weapons leading the way, the XM84 stun grenade bounced off the ground in front of them and detonated. A wave of pressure slammed the duo,

knocking them off their feet. They wouldn't be getting
up any time soon, not deafened and blinded by the 4.5
grams of magnesium and ammonium in the grenade's
payload.

More gunners were coming now and Bolan got to his
feet, swinging the OA-93 around, ripping off bursts from
the 6.5 inch barrel. If it hadn't been for the flash hider,
the subgun would have produced a basketball size muzzle-flash that would have made him an easy target, not to
mention that the heat would have seared off his eyebrows.
The OA-93 swept a gunman from groin to throat, armor-
piercing slugs shredding him like so much coleslaw.

Bolan reached the warehouse as gunfire chased him.
The two stunned gunners were fumbling for weaponry,
one clearly giving up and holding both ears as glistening blood poured down his neck. The Executioner targeted the one with more fight in him and nailed him to
the earth with a crucifying burst of gunfire.

The soldier dumped his almost-empty magazine and
reloaded.

Five down, and by Bolan's count, nine more to go
on the grounds. He'd faced worse odds before, though
he still worried about the absence of Dark and Adonis.
Those two might be stalking him, waiting for his action
to move in. Judging by Dark's battle with Carl Lyons,
the man preferred a close-up battle. Adonis's pure skill
at hand-to-hand combat also weighed against the like-
lihood of the blond giant trying a sniper kill.

The rattle of a submachine gun threw Bolan into a
crouch. Bullets chewed their way at head and chest
height, and the soldier's sudden duck saved him from
a face full of shrapnel and splinters. He coaxed a burst
of autofire from the muzzle of the OA-93, ripping apart
the gunner who was pumping out the fire.

A quartet of men broke from cover, moving laterally toward a building that resembled a log cabin on short stilts. The quartet was sidestepping and firing on the move, keeping low and in motion to make themselves harder to hit. The ground near the Executioner exploded in clouds of dust as sweeps of 5.56 mm and 9 mm slugs punched divots of dirt into the sky. Bolan stepped back behind the cover of the warehouse to avoid catching anything larger than a grain of soil.

He reached into his war bag and plucked another XM-84 grenade and tossed it hard, sidearm style, and ducked back after his thunderbolt-quick throw. More bullets chased his sudden movement, but they collided only with empty air or quiet ground. Bolan's grenade detonated with sky-shattering force and he swept back around, OA-93 tracking for targets.

The four men were strewed about, stunned, but to varying degrees. The man closest to the door of the cabin was already shaking off the effects of the grenade. He clawed at the doorknob, struggling to get it open, when Bolan ripped into him with a burst of 5.56 mm, tungsten-cored manstoppers. Slammed against the door, he clawed desperately to stay on his feet, as if realizing that the moment his knees touched the ground the life would pour out of him. His strength wasn't enough, though, not with his internal organs whipped into an organic mess of pulped flesh and blood. Gore burst from his lips and he shuddered, collapsing in a boneless heap.

The other three were still not too quick on the uptake, but there were still four men firing from cover, their weapons chattering in response to the Executioner's own fire. Bolan dived toward the entrance to the warehouse, tumbling under the loading dock doors and barely avoiding a barrage of slugs that detonated in a precision line to where he'd been a moment ago. Plunging into the depths of shadow, he banged his shoulder hard against a stack of wood.

The Olympic Arms subgun bounced free from his hands, but he knew the weapon was secured to him by its nylon straps. Instead of grabbing the weapon, Bolan slipped into the darkness deeper, his hands feeling through the impenetrable blackness to guide him as he worked the maze of stacked planks. Behind him, gunfire ripped at the rolling door, bullets punching through corrugated metal with ease, spilling more dim light into the scene. It was still impossible to see, but the Executioner could tell that his enemies were charging after him.

He spun, pulling out his Beretta and Desert Eagle, guns filling both hands and speaking almost as one. Screams filled the air as the rounds found flesh on at least one target. The soldier in black then dived behind a column of stacked two-by-fours, gaining cover only moments before a hail of return fire chewed after him. Old wood splintered and exploded under the hail of bullets. The cover he found wasn't much, but it granted him an extra ten seconds to dart toward the back exit, the doorway illuminated by the small square of reinforced glass high in its center.

A head appeared in the little window and Bolan snap-aimed his Desert Eagle, thundering the last .44 Magnum shell through the glass. It broke, 240 grains of lead pounding like a freight train through the skull of the man at the door. The Executioner hit the doorway at full speed. Not even breaking stride, he went from step to full-force kick, slamming his two-hundred-plus pounds right under the doorknob. The lock frame exploded under the impact and he could feel the door only stop when it struck the inert, lifeless corpse slumped behind it.

Bolan dived to the right, out of the crack he had opened the door by, striking the ground in a skid before a burst of gunfire chewed along the wall. Rolling, he brought up his Beretta, flicking the selector switch to burst mode and hammered a trio of rounds into the belly and chest of the gunman trying to track him. The guy did his dance of death, twisting and tumbling to the ground, emptying the last of his SMG's ammo into the dirt at his feet before falling facedown.

Bolan got up to one knee, popping the empty magazine out of his Desert Eagle and feeding it a fresh one before returning it to its holster. The Beretta also got a fresh stack of Parabellum rounds before returning to its resting place under his left arm. He checked the load on the OA-93 and topped that off, too.

He finished just in time to spot a pair of men coming around from the front of the warehouse. One was limping, blood soaking his light-colored windbreaker from chest to waist. The other was a man that the Executioner recognized from the group looking to secure the office.

Bolan took the uninjured man first, cutting him off at the knees at 800 rounds per minute, hyper-velocity 5.56 mm bullets smashing through his legs and sending him flying. The soldier shifted, sidestepping as the injured man cut loose, trying to control his MP-5 with one hand. The gunfire went wild, missing the Executioner by a good foot. The soldier's return fire didn't miss. This time, the gunman flopped backward under an invisible baseball bat of force, multiple rounds punching through him in a deadly rainstorm of fire and lead.

The man on the ground continued to scream, holding both hands desperately over his severed leg. Tears were pouring down his face, and Bolan ended his suffering, tapping out a controlled, short burst that smashed open the side of his skull.

A gunner shouldered the door that Bolan had just come through, firing on the move. The impact threw off the shooter's aim, but the bullet sliced the top of his thigh. Ignoring the pain, the Executioner whipped around, holding down the trigger on the OA-93 and ripping a storm of 5.56 mm armor piercing rounds through the enemy gunman and the door. Bullets sliced through flesh and sheet metal with equal ease, the tungsten-cored slugs being undefeated by any surface encountered in the savage salvo. The gunman in the door vomited his lifeblood and slumped, held up by the squeeze of the door and the jamb, his shoulders wedged between them as he slid down.

Bolan fed the OA-93 a fresh magazine and continued on, scanning for more targets. By now, the gun battle should have drawn the attention of Adonis, Dark or Harpy. Nobody was racing for the Black Hawk, and the office itself was lit well enough that Bolan could tell nobody was moving around inside it. As much as the soldier wanted to rush the office, he had to make sure all the opposition was down. Being gunned down because he assumed the battle was over was the mistake of too many good soldiers.

Instead, Bolan moved slowly around the corner. Enemy gunners were still scrambling for cover. There were three of them, but they were already inaccessible before the Executioner could bring his weapon to bear on them. Ducking back, he avoided a snarling swarm of lead hornets searching for his flesh. His leg started to throb from the gunshot wound and he scrambled back behind more hard cover to take a look. The bullet had only creased his skin, creating a furrow four inches long and a quarter-inch deep. Blood still glistened and ran stickily down his leg. From the war bag, Bolan pulled out a square of gauze and pressed it onto the wound, taping it down and securing it with a strip of duct tape. Stashing his roll of tape, he fisted the OA-93 again and filled his other hand with an M-18 smoke grenade.

Popping the pin, Bolan rolled the grenade toward the trio of gunners. Plumes of white smoke billowed out and would continue to gout from the nozzle on the canister for the next fifty to ninety seconds. As soon as the cloud bank appeared, gunfire ripped into it and the Executioner waited the few seconds it would take for them to empty out their weapons. All three went silent at once, and Bolan rose, charging through the purple haze he'd tossed into the battleground.

A shout alerted Bolan to one gunner spotting him, and gave away the shooter's position. The gunman was frantically trying to stuff a fresh magazine into his weapon, but the Executioner denied him that chance, raking him with a burst of heartstoppers that crucified him against the porch of the cabin. The other two gunmen shouted curses and a pistol exploded at the Executioner off to his right.

Diving onto the porch, and having the high ground, Bolan targeted the remaining two AHC gunfighters, hosing them down with the Olympic Arms subgun.

Neither man rose, and Bolan crouched on the porch for several moments, recovering his hearing and scanning the smoky darkness for any further signs of life.

Nothing.

Bolan kicked aside the corpse slumped at the entrance to the office, testing the doorknob. It was unlocked and he opened the door, stuffing the muzzle of the OA-93 through it. Turning the corner slowly to keep as much cover as possible, the Executioner slipped into the office. It was silent.

A hallway just off the door lead down a deathtrap gauntlet of open doors, each spilling moonlight onto the floor. He grit his teeth and pressed into the building. A breeze through the open window of the reception area rustled a piece of paper taped to the wall. He turned and immediately was upon it, gun trained on the hallway.

"You might want to check the helicopter, Colonel Stone," it read.

Bolan grimaced, then turned out of the office, keeping his gun trained on the door to the cabin. The tarp-covered Black Hawk was sitting only twenty yards away. He reached it in no time.

Adonis, Dark and Harpy were gone. That much was obvious. He scanned some more, but nobody was moving except one half-blind, completely deafened AHC militiaman, his hands filled with his bleeding ears. Bolan ignored him and drew his knife, slashing open the tarp.

Sitting at the controls of the Black Hawk was Jack Grimaldi, blindfolded, ropes binding his arms to his torso. Jack's head jerked up.

"Sarge?"

Bolan didn't say a word, because packed around Grimaldi's seat were dozens of quarter-pound cakes of C-4 explosives, enough to launch the Black Hawk into orbit.

JACK GRIMALDI DIDN'T LIKE waking up a captive, but as Mack Bolan's pilot and fellow warrior, he'd done it often enough. This time, his eyes were taped shut, his skin peeling and burning as his facial muscles squeezed together in agony. His head hurt like hell, but other than that, he couldn't find anything wrong with him that getting out of his ropes and this seat couldn't fix.

He didn't know how long he'd been awake, but the rattle of gunfire through the blindfold-induced darkness had alerted him to the coming of the Executioner. The one-man cavalry was once more busting heads to save the Stony Man pilot's bacon, so he set about evaluating his current situation.

Grimaldi immediately recognized his surroundings by feel. He was in the bucket pilot's seat of a UH-60 Black Hawk, probably the same helicopter that Adonis used to swoop down and capture him. The bruise on Grimaldi's temple throbbed as he remembered the sledgehammer shot to the skull that had knocked him out. He winced and tried shifting his weight when a familiar odor filled his nostrils. His heart slumped.

Plastic explosives.

It was faint, but with his eyes covered and silence filling the cockpit, the familiar old nitrate smell was there. He opened his mouth and the scent disappeared some as he started breathing through his mouth. Plastic explosives had a slight odor, more easily picked up by the sensitive nose of a dog than a human, but Grimaldi and the other warriors of Stony Man Farm had been exposed to the stuff for the length of their careers. He wondered at the strength of the initial smell, especially since C-4 didn't vaporize that quickly. He had to have been surrounded by pounds of the stuff.

Neck stiff, he tested the limits of his movement, tendons popping along his spine. For all he knew, he was on a pressure plate and shifting his weight more than an inch would send him to his final reward.

Of course, that meant only one thing.

He was live bait for Mack Bolan.

If he could get any leverage with his feet, he'd do his damnedest to stand up right now, depriving Adonis and Dark of their cruel taunt. Better that he give his life so that the Executioner could continue his crusade to defend the helpless against Animal Man than—

Fabric ripped with the razor zip sound of a knife slashing nylon.

It was too late. If he moved now, he'd take out Bolan with him.

"Sarge?"

There was silence. He had to have been sitting on half the C-4 in Wisconsin to shock Bolan into silence.

"Sarge, just turn the hell around and head back home," Grimaldi said.

"You know I don't leave friends behind."

Grimaldi shook his head. "How bad is it? I mean, the smell—"

"Looks like ten, twelve kilos packed under your seat," Bolan told him.

Grimaldi felt the sweat break out on his hairline. He swallowed hard. "Just go. Call a bomb squad or something and they'll take care of it. You have to stop Adonis and Dark."

"Don't worry about them. O'Hare is wrapped up tight," Bolan told him. "I'll take care of this."

"There's probably a million booby traps."

"The biggest one being the boob sitting on top of it. Now be quiet," Bolan quipped. "I need to concentrate."

Grimaldi frowned. "All right, Sarge."

"Anything wrong?"

"Just kind of wishing I hadn't bought the extra-large coffee at the airport, that's all," Grimaldi replied.

"We'll be hitting the head in a few minutes," Bolan told him.

Grimaldi chuckled. "Yeah, but at what speed?"

Bolan grunted. He was probably doing some fine cutting. "How fast can you run?"

Grimaldi started to shrug, but didn't. "Not fast enough. I'm here, ain't I?"

"Well, hang on. I've got a couple more leads and wires to snip."

Grimaldi nodded, but couldn't be sure if Bolan was paying attention. There was a sharp intake of breath from the soldier, and the pilot clenched up.

"Relax, Jack."

Grimaldi tried to smile, but it ended up looking like a twitch. "Sure. Easy for you to say."

"Actually…" Bolan said. He paused, making a sucking sound, then continued, "No it's not easy for me to say."

"Cut yourself?" Grimaldi asked.

"Got shocked by a bare lead," Bolan answered.

"It'd be a lot easier if I could see what you were doing," Grimaldi admitted.

He heard Bolan chuckle. "After all these years, now you're doubting me?"

"Just worrying like hell about your safety, Sarge." The pilot knew, though, that Bolan was working on the bomb first, just in case it was on a countdown timer. If he was only having a few moments to work with, wasting time on peeling tape off Grimaldi's face would only slow things down.

Duct tape tore off its roll with the familiar quacking sound that gave it the nickname "duck" tape. Strips were ripping and Grimaldi felt Bolan's hands tuck something under his thighs.

"Just hang on," Bolan told his old friend. The side door of the Black Hawk rolled open slowly. The chopper shifted slightly as the weight of the big soldier was added to the vehicle and he padded around, duct tape quacking some more.

"Taping down the pressure plate I'm on?" Grimaldi asked.

"It's a stopgap. I took care of the bubble gauge that acted like a motion sensor," Bolan answered. "That's why I felt safe coming on board."

"Now if you mess up, there'll be two dead men flying."

Grimaldi felt his wrists suddenly freed with the soft hiss of steel parting the ropes around him. Blood rushed back into his fingertips and he reached up, tearing away the tape over his eyes. He winced at the tiny amount of light creeping through the slit tarpaulin.

"What's the plan, Sarge?" Grimaldi asked, letting his eyes adjust to being able to see again. His vision focused and his head stopped hurting within a few moments.

"We get out of the helicopter, go through the hole in the tarp and run like hell," Bolan said. "This isn't going to last long."

Grimaldi nodded.

"Go!" Bolan shouted.

The Stony Man pilot didn't have to be told twice, leaping down from the seat. He could already hear the beginning tearing of one tape strip from the metal seat. Grimaldi didn't even bother to look back, plunging through the knife-rent in the tarpaulin, legs pumping hard as he reached open air. The graying of dawn produced enough light to make his eyes ache. Footsteps pounded behind him.

He looked back to see Mack Bolan hot on his heels.

"Keep going!" the Executioner yelled.

The Black Hawk detonated a heartbeat later, and the two men found themselves tossed like leaves in a tornado.

CHAPTER EIGHTEEN

David Kowalski stirred from his quick catnap, feeling the car roll to a complete stop. His eyes opened and he looked at the young Filipino man behind the steering wheel. Glancing over to the mall as they pulled up, he noticed that except for a big department store on one end, and a restaurant just off the middle, everything on the roster was a branch of a Christian missionary center. Kowalski smirked at the sight of it.

"And this amuses you how?" Artemio asked.

Kowalski poked his thumb at the mall. "Hide in plain sight."

Artemio nodded. "That's the plan. See, nobody is going to give a shit about a bunch of Asians hanging around a Christian reading room."

"Does Suarez know you use such language?" Kowalski asked.

"Suarez doesn't care. He's too busy kissing up to Sahleen and Logan. We're the weak partners here," Artemio explained. "And the other two sides show it every time they look at us."

"Shame," Kowalski said.

"Yeah?"

"Well, the Filipino segment…they're a mixed religion contingent?"

"Muslim and Christian. Yeah."

Kowalski nodded and the two men got out of the car. "Way I see it, you're the bridge. After all, you show that true men of faith on both sides can coexist."

"That's true," Artemio answered. "But how come you see this and they don't?"

"I'm a Marine. Blacks. Filipinos. Japs. Arabs. All of them show they have the sacks to be the few, the proud," Kowalski told him. "I've been in the field and I don't base my trust on eye shape or skin color. If I did, I'd be insulting a lot of good men."

Artemio snorted. "Are you sure you're one of Logan's men?"

"I'm my own man. They recruited me because they thought I was exactly like them. Judging by your description, though, they're dead wrong."

"So why are you still hanging around?" Artemio asked.

Kowalski shrugged. "You're fighting a corrupt government. The system's broken, and someone has to sweep away the pieces so that the world can be a better place."

Artemio regarded him for a long moment.

"Course, you try to tell Logan that, I'll kill you. Can't have him busting a cap in my ass."

Artemio laughed. "All right, Pete."

They entered the mall, Kowalski holding the door for Artemio.

The U.S. Marshall settled back down into himself, mind racing as he took in the details of the mall. It was scarily empty, entire storefronts voided of their original wares and replaced with stacks of religious books that bordered on propaganda. He wondered if the mall itself didn't just implode, the religious fanatics at the missionary center driving out the jewelers and clothiers with their zealous presence. The whole building put his skin to a tingle, as if there were something dark and corrupt underneath the surface.

The mall, only a quarter-mile long, and one level, was completely empty. He stopped, looking at furniture from a previous store being used as display pedestals for books. Kowalski recognized the books by their covers, having had to read through countless such volumes as he'd researched Christian Identity groups. As a faithful man, these books filled him with a bottomless sense of hollowness; their contents didn't preach love and understanding, but appealed to fear and estrangement. They were barnacles that had spread out from a single source to cling to the wreckage of crushed businesses driven out.

"Peter." Artemio spoke up. "This way."

Kowalski turned to see the Filipino heading for a doorway. "Meeting Rooms 1-3" read a sign above the glass door. He followed, shuffling through the door that Artemio held open for him.

"This is where I'm going to be on guard duty?" Kowalski asked.

Artemio nodded. "It doesn't look like much, but this mall's got some impressive basement space. We've modified it."

The young man lead his comrade through a stairwell door and they took the steps down a level, exiting into a well-lit area. The walls were cinder block and fluorescent light fixtures hung from the ceiling. It smelled clean, and there was a row of cubicles just off the doorway. He spotted a frosted-glass-enclosed section down the hall.

"What's that?" he asked.

"The nerve center," Artemio answered.

Kowalski raised an eyebrow.

"We'll get you set up. Your office and guard station is down here, so we don't attract attention," Artemio told him.

Kowalski entered the office, and the young Filipino spent the next hour telling him about the setup. By the time Artemio finished, the U.S. Marshall looked at his watch. It was 9:00 a.m. The stocky ex-Marine gave a yawn.

"Come on. We'll get some coffee into you. Since you're now a mall employee," Artemio said, handing him a badge, "you get a discount at the buffet."

"Woo-woo!"

They had gone back up the stairs and were headed toward the restaurant when Kowalski's skin turned to brittle ice, cold water flushing through every blood vessel in his body. He looked at a titan stepping through the entrance to the mall. One of the giant's massive fists was raised to cover a gaping yawn, his other fist raised to nearly eight feet off the ground. The body of the pillar of muscle stretched out, another young Filipino directing him along, holding the door for the rippling man-god.

Kowalski's feet couldn't move, his eyes widened with horror as the massive blonde finished his loosening up and turned his cold, blue gaze toward him.

"Why, hello, little man. I was wondering when I'd see you again," Adonis boomed in the confines of the almost-empty mall.

"THERE'S NO SIGN of Sable," Bolan pronounced as he finished going over the mill with a fine-tooth comb. Jack Grimaldi was still a little dazed by the explosive shock wave that hit them earlier, but except for a knot on the side of his head and cramped arms and legs, the pilot was in relatively good health.

"In fact," Bolan continued, looking around, "there's absolutely no sign of anything resembling missile or laser manufacturing here on the grounds."

"So what was with the hardforce on this site? And Adonis and Dark?" Grimaldi asked.

Bolan frowned. "Terintec had this business aboveground, but they tested their weapons in the quarry for improved secrecy."

Grimaldi raised an eyebrow. "They moved the stuff to the quarry?"

"Nobody would have thought twice about looking at the bottom of a pit. And they had plenty of explosives and digging equipment," Bolan explained. "Enough to make a cave."

He thought about it for a moment and told Grimaldi his plans. "Take a car back to the airport. I'll check out the quarry. If there's trouble, I'll just pull back and stay quiet. I want the Learjet ready to go, though."

"I don't like the idea of letting you go there alone, Sarge," Grimaldi told him. "You do it all the time, but—"

"Yeah. I know. But if Barbara calls us back to Chicago, I want to be there as fast as possible. That means the Learjet better be prepped to go," Bolan replied.

Grimaldi nodded.

"And try for a head shot the next time you go up against Adonis," Bolan told him.

"You didn't," the Stony Man pilot quipped.

"I didn't even put a bullet in his chest," Bolan answered. "Get moving, and be careful."

Grimaldi nodded and found a car with the keys in it. Bolan decided not to bother hiking back to his borrowed wheels and did like his friend.

The cars swung out and the two men gave each other a wave before parting ways. It didn't take the Executioner long to reach the quarry, and he pulled in, past corpses of men he'd killed hours earlier. The battle scene had an eerie silence and carrion birds pecked at the dead. Bolan looked away from the scene, realizing it was just nature taking its course. Those who fell would feed the earth and her creatures, returning to the ecosystem what nutrients they contained.

Still, it was unnerving to see a raven tugging a string of flesh out of the throat of a corpse, even for a hardened warrior like Bolan. He considered beeping the horn to shoo off the carrion eaters, but in case there was anyone still alive in the quarry, he didn't want to announce his presence so soon. Bolan went EVA, keeping the OA-93 machine pistol strapped to his chest, just in case he ran into heavy opposition.

On his earlier run-through of the buildings in the quarry, while he'd been setting them up to blow, Bolan hadn't found anything out of the ordinary.

That only left heading down the staircase and into the depths of the mined-out quarry. He checked to see if there were any booby traps or security devices, and even though none was apparent, he gripped the OA-93 tightly with both hands and descended slowly. The muzzle pointed ahead of Bolan as he moved down the metal stairs, his boots making achingly loud clanks as he took each step as stealthily as he could. Continuing along the zigzagging stairs, the soldier finally reached a platform where a gaping cavern was formed along the slope of the cliff. Bundles of cables and PVC pipe snaked into the upper-right corner of the cave's mouth like a writhing mass of red, green and black tentacles.

One crimson tendril descended to a light switch and Bolan reached carefully for it, keeping himself tight against the mouth of the cave. He was already backlit, and if anyone was inside, they could have burned him down a thousand times over. His finger hit the button and slowly, one by one, amber lights popped on, trailing off into the tunnel. The floor was covered by grating and the golden light revealed no telltale signs of a tripwire or pressure plate attached to cakes of plastic explosives.

Bolan stepped into the mouth of the cave, OA-93 out front. He proceeded deeper, and nothing greeted his probing feet. He continued down the tunnel another 150 feet before it opened into a cleared-out area. Lights hung from the ceiling twenty feet above, and the Executioner could see that whoever had been down this tunnel had found a natural fissure in the mountainside where they were excavating stone. The formation he was in was old, but many of the fresh wires and pipes seemed only a year or two at most.

Moisture filled the air and Bolan looked up, seeing cracks in the ceiling where sunlight came through. Water had to have collected in the soil and dripped down. Walkways kept people from stepping in the accumulation. He could see drainage tunnels leading off into the darkness.

The catwalks formed a web, connecting several prefabricated buildings set on stone blocks. Bolan checked inside one and spotted a worktable full of electronics gear. He wasn't sure if it was for the laser or the missile guidance system, but the sheer level of technology convinced him that it wasn't someone's disassembled microwave oven. He checked a circuit board, looking at a sophisticated grid of transistors and microchips. Again, it could have been anything from the central processor of a missile guidance system or the control mechanism of a laser beam.

Either way, there were more components in plastic storage tubs behind him. Enough to build dozens of whatever he was looking at. It was enough evidence for the Executioner to realize that the RING and its minions were hard at work down here. And they were mass-producing weaponry.

One laboratory. He recognized the ionizing filters at the doorway, capturing errant air particles to keep the circuit boards and microchips from becoming contaminated. A single speck of dust could be the difference between proper function and a spectacular flame-out. Bolan had seen tests where a laser lens with the grease from a fingerprint caused the projector to overheat and turn into a flaming fireplace log, burning out of control.

The Executioner clicked off the ionizer. The low-powered magnet would no longer keep the RING's precious high technology safe.

Sometimes the flicking of a switch was more satisfying than putting a bullet through the enemy's systems.

Bolan stepped out of the prefab and onto the walkway.

In one corner of the dome, from this vantage point, he could see a concrete pallet, loaded with fifty-five-gallon drums. On the side was the international symbol for a biohazard. They were behind orange plastic netting and sheltered by a heavy tarp over a corrugated aluminum roof, to keep the dripping moisture from touching the drums. Bolan took a tentative step toward them, then closed to inspection range. The canisters were empty.

Bolan wasn't a man given to panic, but neither was he a man without a healthy sense of fearful respect for the horrors that man unleashed through chemical and biological experimentation. He saw that the drums were designed for hydrochloric acid, for etching circuit boards, or for storage of rocket fuel. What truly set the soldier's nerves on edge, though, was a square container, as tall as he was, nine feet wide and fifteen feet long.

Bolan recognized it as a transport trailer for bio-warfare weaponry. The door was cracked ajar and he pried it open farther, heart hammering, instinct telling him to drop everything and tell Hal Brognola to call in a napalm strike on this hellhole. The professional in him had to know what was inside. He was already exposed as the broken seal on the container allowed air in and out. He was breathing death or he was in the clear.

Silvered globes were suspended in parallel rows along the sides of the container, hanging free. About half of the spheres had glass capsules built into the sides, golden-brown fluid inside. Others had been stripped of their liquid prizes. Bolan wasn't a bio-chemist, but he knew the contents weren't Pilsner beer.

Grim realization swept the Executioner.

The O'Hare attack was intended to spread a biological agent across the globe.

Mack Bolan wasted no time, racing back to Sparta Municipal Airport.

KOWALSKI FOUGHT to stay loose as Adonis approached him. The giant was smiling and jovial. He even slid an arm around the man's shoulders.

"I was hoping we'd meet again," Adonis said. "What name are you going by today?"

"Peter Steel."

"You mean, this guy has another identity?" Artemio asked. His hand drifted toward a gun on his hip.

"Mr. Steel is a dweller in shadows, a mystery wrapped in an enigma. He's joined your numbers, though. He's no threat to you," Adonis said. "He is a man of courage and conviction. I can vouch for him."

"But…" Adonis's companion began.

"But nothing. Come. Let's grab some breakfast. I'm starving after my flight," Adonis stated.

Not one to pass up a last meal before his own execution, Kowalski joined the men. He ate well, answering when spoken to, smiling and shoveling hash browns and forkfuls of cheese omelets doused in ketchup into his mouth. A side order of sausage links soaking in maple syrup added to his idea of a perfect last breakfast, cold milk washing down the mixture. Adonis locked eyes with his.

"Enjoying yourself?" the giant asked.

Kowalski nodded. "How about you?"

"I've been better," Adonis answered. "But the food and company are good. I just got back from Wisconsin. I met our mutual friend yesterday."

"Colonel Stone?"

Artemio chuckled. "Lieutenant Steel. Colonel Stone? What next, General Diamond?"

"Quiet," Adonis admonished. His glare cut through the Filipino militiaman's confidence like lasers through tissue paper. "Just the man I was talking about."

"Did you get to talk much?"

"Not really. I had to leave to help work on the West Coast end of the project," he explained.

"Artemio, did you explain to him what's going on at the mission?"

"He's in security," the youth responded. "I didn't think—"

"The man is charged with protecting you. It would be good to provide him with everything he needs to know," Adonis once more scolded. "See, the mission itself is our cyberhub. The center of all our communications through Internet, broadcast and snail mail."

Kowalski nodded, impressed. "I haven't been in the nerve center yet."

"There's always time for that," Adonis said. "I'm going to go there after my nap. My charter flight took off well after midnight, and I didn't get much time to sleep. If you're still on duty when I wake up, maybe I'll give you the cook's tour."

Kowalski nodded numbly. "Sounds like fun."

Adonis smiled. "You look like you could use some sleep, too."

"The thought crossed my mind," Kowalski answered. He kept waiting for whatever bombshell Adonis had on hand to go off. The blond giant simply rose from his table.

"I love prepaying for a buffet!" Adonis exclaimed. "Walk with me a bit, Peter."

Kowalski got up and joined him, Artemio close behind.

"Is your name Peter, Artemio?" Adonis asked.

The Filipino halted, not wanting to press his luck. He stepped away and allowed the two to walk off into the nearly abandoned mall.

"I bet you nearly shit yourself when you saw me come in," Adonis said, plopping a tree-trunk of an arm around Kowalski's shoulders.

"Nearly?"

Adonis chuckled. "I'm not going to blow your cover. It really doesn't matter what you learn now. The countdown is ticking, the doomsday numbers are falling, and you can't fight your way out of this place as long as I'm here."

"So I just roll over and die, not even make an effort to keep you from slaughtering thousands?" Kowalski asked. "I'll fight."

"And you'll die," Adonis answered. "So just keep quiet. Get swallowed up by the organization. This place is due to be blown out any time soon. Survive that long, and you can scamper away while this joint is thrown to the wolves."

Kowalski tested the grip of the arm across his shoulders. It was like a yoke of iron. He couldn't pull free.

"Please, Peter, don't make a scene," Adonis warned.

"'Do not go gentle into that dark night.'"

Adonis sighed. "Is that your final answer?"

Kowalski looked up. He thought of the soldiers of Stony Man Farm who'd adopted him as one of their own, if only for a few days.

"Can I phone a friend, Regis?"

Adonis laughed.

That's when Able Team's van burst thunderously through the mall entrance, glass shattering and metal twisting in its path.

"THE U.S. ARMY IS SENDING a biological warfare team out to recover the container," Barbara Price explained over the phone link as Bolan and Grimaldi's Bombardier Aerojet Learjet 60 tore through the skies across the Wisconsin-Illinois border. "We're still trying to figure out the point of origin of the stuff, or even what it is."

Clouds whipped past the windows of the cockpit, Bolan was keyed in to Stony Man Farm via a secure SATCOM uplink, the headset snug around his skull, its boom mike hovering before his lips as he spoke. "Barbara, the exact what isn't as important as the fact that the RING is going to use the next airport accident as cover to spread an airborne virus at O'Hare. The disease could spread around the planet in the space of a day if they manage to pull this off."

"We're not even sure what kind of CB weapon it is," Price said. "If we shut down O'Hare, that'll spook our boys to try somewhere else. We don't even know what countermeasures to get ready in case something happens."

Bolan grimaced. "I know. I'm just thinking, at any time, there are thousands of people at that airport. A good delivery system could infect easily a third of them."

"The worst-case scenario would be that passengers would be exposed and sent off before we could shut down the runways," Price said. "If we could contain the infected passengers and flights, if it's a fast-acting bioweapon like Botox, we're talking three to six thousand dead and passenger jets being turned into mass coffins."

Bolan clenched his eyes shut, a tingle of anxiety rippling along him like a surge of electrical current. His teeth grit against each other. "Jack and I should reach O'Hare in about twenty minutes. What do we have on hand?"

"Buck and ten blacksuits," Price responded. "Automatic weapons, atropine injectors against nerve gas, but nobody's been inoculated against anthrax, Botox or smallpox."

"That's because the inoculation is sometimes as bad as the disease," Bolan responded. "Anyone I'm familiar with?"

"Toro Martinez. Anyone else who's worked with you is either on alert in their ordinary jobs or reinforcing us here at the Farm," Price told him.

"Able Team?"

"San Francisco. They've been trailing Kowalski all around."

The Executioner frowned, looking out the window. "I counted forty ampules missing from their containment spheres."

"Each one is supposed to hold enough to wipe out a city," Price said.

"We're looking at a big hardforce coming in," Bolan surmised. "Dark and Adonis aren't going in alone on O'Hare this time."

"You think that the RING has convinced our group of militiamen that those ampules are full of something other than bio-weapons?"

Bolan nodded. "I should have stuck around to look, but I'm betting that they're handing off atropine injectors to their cannon fodder. They throw what they think is nerve gas, pump atropine into themselves to fight off a neurotoxin that doesn't exist, and then they shoot their way out of the airport. If they don't escape, no biggie. If they do escape, they're infected with a killer bug and parading it throughout Chicago."

"God, you think they'd throw their allies away like that?" Price asked.

"Chicago will be under such mayhem, reliable news won't get out. If people do get out of the airport and to other parts of the country or other countries, the plague will spread, and raise even more noise-to-information so that the RING's cannon fodder won't know what the hell is happening. And even if they do find out, what is a single militia group or an al-Qaeda splinter cell in comparison who other pawn organizations we know nothing about?" Bolan asked. "Three heads lopped off, six more to take their place."

"But how are you sure what kind of distribution these guys have?" Price asked.

Bolan's lips drew tight. "Gut instinct. It's the simplest thing possible. The RING needs to do something massive. They're going to dump a load of highly communicable disease into the middle of one of the country's largest airports, and they have a large number of people to do it with. We have no possible way of cordoning off O'Hare short of having the Army clamp down, and when we do that, the RING has suddenly put the fear of God into the whole country anyway."

"Another battle at another airport isn't going to do much to alleviate the terror the country is in right now," Price said. "We're already trying to get O'Hare Security, the FAA and the Chicago police coordinated in response to the RING's follow-up. Hal's in Chicago, too, with a whole contingent of Justice Department personnel trying to get the entire city ready for Armageddon."

Bolan could see O'Hare International Airport. Grimaldi was already calling ahead to arrange a landing at the old National Guard refueling base airstrip. Buck Greene and his blacksuits had set up shop there after Bolan and Grimaldi had taken off only the day before.

The world was a blur around the Executioner. "We're at O'Hare now, Barb. Just about to land."

"Striker, just be careful."

A little part of the Executioner died as he heard the cracking pain in her voice. "It's too late for careful."

CHAPTER NINETEEN

As soon as they saw Adonis enter the mall, Rosario Blancanales and Hermann Schwarz shrugged into their load bearing vests and pulled weapons up from under the floorboards of the passenger section. The entire mission had gone south because of the blond giant's presence.

Jackie Sorenson looked back at her comrades. "I'll drive."

Blancanales and Schwarz paused.

"We're sorry we dragged you into this," Schwarz told her.

"I'm not," Sorenson answered. "Hand me a mini-Uzi and a pistol. They might try to take shots at me through the windshield and I want to be able to return fire."

Blancanales put a Colt .45 and a mini-Uzi in her small, dainty hands. "You know how to fire these?"

"I spend every other weekend at a range," Sorenson responded. "It's a hobby." She cleared and checked the Colt, then stuffed it between her thigh and the seat. She did the same with the mini-Uzi and hung it on its sling around her neck. "I know a few friends who get me range time every month with full-auto weapons, too."

Blancanales pointed to the entrance away from the department store and the restaurant. "Nobody is going through that entrance. We'll keep the fighting away from the restaurant. Chances are that the mission itself is keeping its offices out of sight of prying eyes, so if we do run into trouble, bystanders will be running like hell out the other way."

"I don't even think the 'Mart is connected to the main mall," Schwarz replied. He checked the Reflex scope atop his M-4 assault rifle. Accuracy was going to be the number-one rule in a potentially bystander-rich environment.

Blancanales looked, then gave a grim nod of agreement, clicking an M-203 grenade launcher sleeve over the barrel of his M-4. "Cuts down on potential trouble with the bystanders. Course, you never know. We might not have to do anything."

Sorenson pursed her lips. "I'll scout."

"We can't risk your life."

"Dammit, guys. Ski is in there, and he could need help."

She peeled herself out of her jacket, attaching a communicator with a throat microphone. The earpiece and its wire disappeared under her silken hair. Schwarz gave her an adjustable shoulder holster for the mini-Uzi and the Colt .45. Her lumpy windbreaker hid both guns and the radio admirably.

Sorenson slipped out of the driver's seat.

"And then there's Adonis, nature's proof that Godzilla wasn't the baddest cat humankind could imagine," Schwarz continued.

"He scares the Japanese. We Americans are tougher than that," Sorenson answered, racking the bolt on her Uzi for emphasis. She winked at Schwarz.

Sorenson smiled and closed the van door. "Be careful, Jackie," Schwarz called.

"I will," she answered.

She took the second entrance, seeing that it was unlocked, and walked in, stopping to peruse the Christian bookstore just off the entrance. From that corner, she could see down the center court of the mall. It wasn't much, just a single-story strip with storefronts on both sides, most of them abandoned or turned into missionary office space.

She spotted Adonis and Kowalski walking toward her, away from the Filipino men who had accompanied them into the restaurant. Sorenson keyed her throat mike.

"They separated from the Filipinos," she whispered.

"Roger," Blancanales answered.

"Peter, please don't make a scene," she heard the big man say.

Kowalski looked up at Adonis, and she heard the replacement Stony Man warrior quote a piece of verse.

He was preparing to fight to the death against a giant who could break him in two like a twig. Her heart went out to the blacksuit.

"Pol. Gadgets...now!"

The Able Team van blasted noisily through the glass behind Sorenson. She was already taking cover in the bookstore's entrance, but still, flying glass pelted her jacket and a chunk with a particularly sharp corner cut across her eyebrow. The sudden dodge for cover made her back hurt, but she dropped to a combat crouch anyway, flipping the mini-Uzi from its hiding spot under her coat.

"Ski!" Sorenson shouted, firing off a burst into Adonis. The big man took a 3-round burst, center of mass, and looked down at himself, then incredulously at Sorenson.

"That's the second time today someone's shot me!" Adonis growled, hand lunging for a gun under his own coat.

Kowalski exploded into action as the giant shifted his balance. He grabbed onto Adonis's shoulder and kicked off of the floor with all his strength, legs snapping up and wrapping around the titan's neck. With a twist of his stout body, he was yanking the golden-maned murderer off his feet and driving him forward.

Behind Sorenson, Blancanales and Schwarz were exiting the van, M-4s up and tracking. Doors burst open from the missionary offices, but it wasn't bibles and medical supplies these men were carrying. Not unless they fired 9 mm Parabellum rounds at a rate of 800 rpm.

Sorenson couldn't open fire on the monster known as Adonis without peppering Kowalski with a hail of lead, so she turned her aim toward the Filipino gunmen.

All hell broke loose when Blancanales sailed a 40 mm M 651 CS gas canister from his M-203. A white cloud filled the air, inflaming the mucus membranes and tear ducts of everyone within range.

Kowalski and Adonis struck the ground with a thump that masked the sound of the grenade launcher going off, but the swirling storm of stringing mist caught the U.S. Marshall's attention long enough for him to be grabbed by the six-and-a-half-foot-tall monstrosity he was in desperate combat with. Cursing himself as he felt those enormous fingers dig into his thigh, he let loose with a growl and punched the big man in the temple.

Adonis grunted and thrashed his head, as if to throw off the effects of the blow, and shrugged one shoulder, tossing off his adversary. The ex-Marine rolled to his feet, staring at the still-prone titan. Kowalski lunged forward, hands clasped in a hammer punch that chopped down onto his enemy's massive chest. The impact felt like slamming a drum and sounded half as loud. Adonis's breath exploded from his lips, but he reacted by slamming an elbow across Kowalski's jaw, throwing him aside like a rag doll.

The blonde reached for his gun again and Kowalski did a baseball slide that rammed into his hip and kidney. The impact felt like skidding into a brick wall, but the towering terrorist's grip on his gun wasn't complete. With a desperate twist, he brought his boot around and hammered it into Adonis's forearm. The Desert Eagle sailed from numbed fingers, clattering on the imitation brick floor.

Kowalski tried to push his luck for all it was worth, bringing his heel up into Adonis's clean-shaved, lantern jaw. Blood exploded from a broken nose and upper lip all across the blacksuit's sneaker, but his ankle was trapped in a cast-iron grip. Adonis cast his cold, blue eyes down on the smaller man.

"That was your last free shot," he growled.

Kowalski smiled.

"What are you smiling about?"

Kowalski lifted himself up hard and kicked the giant under his armpit. "You're bleeding! You bleed. I can kill you."

"Peter…"

"The name's Ski," Kowalski answered, getting up.

"Ski. Good. I like to know the names of men I rip in two with my bare hands."

Kowalski wasn't hearing much now. Crimson tainted his vision. His ears filled with the freight-train roar of racing, hot, adrenaline-charged blood. A split second seizure of muscles swept over him.

With a savage roar, the two men charged each other, ignoring the raging gun battle surrounding them.

"JACKIE, STAY THERE!" Schwarz called. He shouldered his rifle and pumped a couple rounds into a pistol-toting Filipino, the 5.56 mm hollowpoints leaping through the target's chest at nearly four times the speed of sound. The impacts reduced his vital organs to soup as the hypervelocity slugs peeled open from their cup tips and disintegrated in fluid mass.

The Abu Sayyaf gunman crashed back through the doorway, others tripping over him as a second M-651 tear gas round punched farther down the line of the mall's court. Blancanales was laying out the choking smoke to keep bystanders down and away from the gunfight.

Schwarz dived to the ground as the van's windshield and grille were lit up by a spray of sparks. Return fire impacted, tearing up steel and shattering glass. He was glad that the van's engine was protected by a sheet of armor plate, because after a blowout like this, they'd need to extract like lightning.

Out of the corner of his eye, the Able Team commando was certain that he spotted two sinewy animals lunging at each other, an inhuman set of roars splitting the air above the sound of staccato muzzle-blasts. Kowalski and Adonis were stopped against each other, whatever semblance of humanity that their companion bore stripped away as he engaged in savage combat with the golden-maned terrorist. Schwarz was drawn away from the battle by men coming up a stairwell in the open hub of this end of the mall. Railing surrounded a thirty-foot gap in the floor, winding staircases twisting a level down.

The gunmen were opening up, bullets ripping too high to catch the floored Able Team electronics genius, but that didn't mean Schwarz was going to let their assault go unanswered. He rolled and swung down on them. From behind him, he heard Sorenson's mini-Uzi ripping out its unique message, the two Able Team partners united once more in laying down a hail of vengeance against a heavily armed menace. Bodies crashed and tumbled back down the stairs, not even making it to the main floor.

"Pol! Jackie! I'm going down!" Schwarz called.

"Got you covered," Blancanales answered.

Schwarz burst to his feet and raced to the steps. A couple gunners were waiting for him on a landing just out of sight of the van, but from the top of the stairs, they were in open view to their judgment. The Able Team warrior triggered his M-4, ripping bursts into the two shooters, hammering them against the railing with a volley of 5.56 mm nails before they tumbled twelve feet to the sublevel below. Schwarz tore down the steps and was well below before the corpses stopped moving on the floor.

Making the turn, he spotted more men bursting out from behind a heavy fire door, weapons filling their hands and grim resolve etched upon their faces. Schwarz brought up his M-4, sidestepping behind the cover of the stairs, and triggered three long bursts that swept the Filipinos at chest level. Bodies gyrated under the slaughtering impacts.

Schwarz found himself driven back under cover by a hail of return fire that sent chips of concrete and tufts of carpeting flying in a cloud of debris from the staircase. He let the rifle drop on its sling, pulling one of his special flying disk grenades from his pocket. Setting the timer to four seconds, he flicked the disk-bomb out in an arc, then crouched low, letting out a yell to equalize the pressure in his ears.

Moments later, thunder ripped through the underground section as the remaining gunners were torn apart by the shock wave of the lethal disk-bomb, a small disk formed entirely from plastic explosives, with a ring of porcelain baked into the rim to make shrapnel. Add a low weight, low-profile timer and detonator, and the little hellbomb was perfect for launching into a crowd of malcontents, yet discreet enough to keep in a pocket.

Schwarz swung around, assault rifle in hand again, searching for more enemy targets. One gunman had escaped most of the blast, and even though he was covered in blood, he was still struggling for a backup pistol. The Able Team commando's rifle stuttered, making short work of the Filipino would-be champion. Blood and gore sprayed out of his back as the point-blank fusillade ripped through him.

Schwarz raced to the door. Above, the gun battle raged on, but the fire door drew the warrior. Dozens of heavily armed guards didn't spring out of offices without something going on. The basement was going to be ground zero.

Throwing open the door, the Able Team commando saw the muzzle-flashes of four guns. Hot blood exploded down his side as he spun to the ground.

KOWALSKI DIDN'T HAVE much of an advantage against Adonis, but what he did have was leverage. The giant's long, powerful arms left him vulnerable at close range. Kowalski had that much of a battle strategy, and he lunged in close, fists hammering at the pillar of muscle, swinging around the larger man's sides to strike him in the kidneys. A grunt escaped the taller man's lips and he brought his big arms down, trying to claw at the man latching on to him.

Instead, Kowalski wrapped his arms under Adonis's thighs and heaved. The three-hundred pounds of writhing flesh that made up the terrifying fighting machine was suddenly upended by the blacksuit who spun him. Both bodies whirled in a tornado of muscle, bone and sinew until finally the smaller man let go. The blond titan's hair flowed like molten gold as he soared through another storefront display, glass shattering.

Kowalski lunged, shrieking in raw fury, only to be swatted aside by a Victorian-style chair, bowed wooden legs shattering on his stocky body. Stunned for a moment, he gave Adonis an opening that wasn't to be missed. Massive fists rained down into him, shocking hammers of flesh and bone crushing into him with relentless persistence. Kowalski buckled and dropped back.

Adonis moved in too quick, sensing victory, then suddenly sidestepped. It was too late to avoid Kowalski's kick, but most of the force only glanced off the bigger man's knee. Instead of cracking the limb, the kick merely unbalanced the six-and-a-half-foot monster, dropping him into range of Kowalski's lashing fists.

A thunderbolt of a fist crashed against the U.S. Marshall's head and the world alternated between blackness and lightning for a few moments. He staggered away from his adversary. He had raised his hands to ward off the next in a rain of dooming punches when an Uzi ripped off to his right. He glanced and saw Sorenson racing to his side, her weapon fanning at the big man.

Adonis twisted, bringing up a table to block the bullets from crashing into his head.

Perceptions hyped by adrenaline, Kowalski watched as 9 mm slugs struck Adonis's jacket and bulletproof vest, bullets raising puffs of dust from shattered drywall and powdered glass clinging to his clothes. He didn't even react to the onslaught of automatic fire hammering into his chest, and Sorenson growled in frustration as her mini-Uzi locked empty.

She swung the frame of her Uzi, steel meeting flesh in an ugly sounding collision. The giant's head whipped around and he swung back, glaring at the tiny woman.

"I'm sick of you, bitch!" Adonis growled. He reached out for Sorenson, but the woman was a trained martial artist. She deflected the hand and snapped a knife-strike hard into a nerve juncture in the giant's biceps. The big man growled and grabbed at Sorenson's belt, hefting her in the air, ready to smash her spine to powder with a single body slam.

Kowalski came out of nowhere, both fists crushing themselves against the side of his opponent's head in an explosion of flying blond hair and blood. All three bodies tumbled to the ground, and it was all that Sorenson could do to bring her legs under her, cushion her fall and back from the pair.

She reached for her 1911 pistol, but a spray of bullets chopped the wall behind her.

Sorenson didn't even have to stop to make a choice. She turned and engaged the gunmen, leaving Kowalski to continue containing the escapee from a horror movie.

Kowalski whipped down fists, banging on Adonis like a bongo drum, his eyes wild, grunts escaping his mouth. He was reduced to inarticulate fury, lashing out at his dreaded enemy. This was the man responsible for the deaths of hundreds of innocent people at Dulles International Airport.

And the murderer had done it over David Kowalski's helpless body.

The bastard was going to pay with every ounce of furious impact that the rampaging ex-blacksuit could muster.

"Ski!" Sorenson shouted.

Kowalski awakened from his fury to look at the face of Adonis, reduced to a gory field of craters and mountainous swelling. Both of the big man's eyes were puffed shut and blood poured from his lips. Chilling horror filled the young blacksuit as he realized the sheer havoc he'd released onto the murderer. He recoiled, crawling off the downed murderer suddenly in fear that he'd become a similar monster. He whirled to see Sorenson being targeted by a trio of gunmen.

He tackled her, his stocky, short frame heaving her aside just before a firestorm of slugs tore into both of them. They landed near Adonis's massive Desert Eagle, and he grabbed it, Sorenson reloading her pistol.

"Gadgets went down there," Blancanales said, loading a fresh magazine and slipping the unmistakable stubby M-576 buckshot grenade into his rifle-grenade launcher combo.

"There's a stairwell into the basement through that door," Kowalski told Blancanales.

"Okay. Ski and Jackie, you two take that," the Able Team commando ordered. "I'll follow Gadgets's route. Be careful."

Kowalski looked back at the prone form of Adonis. Sorenson got her mini-Uzi and together they took the doorway.

BLANCANALES ADVANCED, poking the muzzle of his M-4 over the top of the stairwell. He saw Gadgets Schwarz on the ground, hand covered with blood as he clutched his side. Panic filled the Able Team warrior. A couple of Filipino hardmen were pushing through an open doorway, their weapons tracking for targets.

Blancanales knew his downed partner would have only a moment's respite, thanks to the concrete steps he was behind, but that respite would end in bloody murder if he didn't act. Stroking the trigger of the M-203 grenade launcher, he unleashed a hail of twenty, .24-caliber pellets from the M-576 buckshot round. The effect was similar to a sawed-off shotgun, except the cone of devastation was wider and more savage. The pair of Filipino gunmen were smashed instantly to the ground by the massive discharge of shotgun pellets.

Blancanales reloaded the M-203 as he descended the stairs, three at a time, racing down to his partner's side.

"Gadgets?"

"Get behind some cover, Pol," Schwarz called.

"How bad are you hit?" Blancanales kept his M-4 trained on the doorway. In the distance, the rattle of an Uzi and the booming of a Desert Eagle were met by automatic fire.

"I got clipped by a round that deflected off my body armor," Schwarz answered. "It's a flesh wound and it bleeds a lot."

"You sure?" Blancanales asked.

Schwarz scrambled to his feet. "Yeah. Sure, the stuff that hit the armor felt as though they would break my ribs, but my breathing isn't labored. I'll live."

"Jackie and Ski are in there," Blancanales said.

"Upstairs?"

"Cleared. Even Adonis is down."

Schwarz was about to say something when a huge shadow fell across Blancanales's back. Seeing the shock on his partner's face, Blancanales whirled and saw all six-and-a-half-feet of towering muscle looming at the top of the staircase, a massive potted plant held over his head.

"Die," Adonis growled through mashed lips.

Blancanales hurled himself over the railing as the plant, which had to have weighed more than two-hundred pounds, shattered the wood and bent the wrought-iron rodding of the staircase handrail. Plummeting to the floor, he hit hard and scrambled to avoid an avalanche of dirt and broken stone from the plant's pot. Blinking the dust from his eyes, he looked up to see Schwarz target him and empty a burst into Adonis's chest.

Able Team locked on to the giant and opened fire even as he leaped. Adonis's body sailed down the steps, knifing through the air. Landing on his hands, the titan somersaulted with far more agility than a man of his size should have shown, lunging for the fallen weapons of the Abu Sayyaff militiamen Schwarz had slain.

Schwartz locked on target first, his M-4 slamming rounds into Adonis's back, jerking him erect with the painful impacts. The giant still managed to turn, an M-16 in each fist, triggering both weapons, their muzzle-blasts thunderously deafening in such tight quarters. As Blancanales dived for cover, he triggered his M-203.

The buckshot grenade bellowed in counterpoint. It was like the fist of an invisible god, finally smashing into the chest of Thor reincarnated. Blond hair flew and the Nordic giant was smashed hard through drywall over cinder block. The crater created by the big man was enormous, and even after a point-blank impact, he was still on his feet, trying to fight, triggering his M-16 at a madly scrambling Blancanales.

Schwarz let his empty M-4 drop and brought up his Beretta 93-R, on 3-round bursts, firing to hit Adonis in the head, but the giant was moving too quickly, scuttling along. All he did was attract return fire, one 5.56 mm round striking the Able Team commando's body armor and driving the breath from his lungs.

Blancanales was in melee distance now. He drove the steel stock of his weapon into Adonis's jaw. Bone cracked, but the giant grinned and swatted the Able Team commando in the head with the frame of one M-16, sending him skittering across the floor. Pol rolled to put a stop to his out of control slide, only just barely twisting out of the way of an M-16 burst that was tearing up the floor tiles.

Blancanales triggered his M-4, sweeping Adonis across his legs. Flesh burst apart and bone shattered with the multiple impacts. Schwarz opened up from behind, bullets hammering into Adonis's right arm, 9 mm slugs tearing up into the shoulder, and one bullet striking the big man in his head. Golden hair suddenly stained with crimson, blood bursting in a cloud as Schwarz's Beretta round clipped the giant's head and tore open a flap of scalp on the other side.

Adonis crumpled, blue eyes glazing over, then finally closing.

"Is he dead?" Blancanales asked. He was busy reloading his M-4.

Schwarz walked slowly up to the bloodied monster, racking a fresh magazine into his own assault rifle. "His chest is still rising and falling. He's still breathing."

Blancanales aimed at the downed man. "Good God. What does it take to kill him?"

Schwarz glanced over. "I don't know, but are we really going to give up our only link to the heart of the RING to find out?"

Blancanales shook his head. "This is a monster. He's killed…"

"Hundreds. Thousands. But he'll be imprisoned. You blew his legs to hell. I took out one of his arms. He probably has brain damage anyway," Schwarz responded, pointing to the puddle of blood from where Adonis's torn scalp leaked. "You want to tell Striker we lost our best lead to take apart the RING?"

The gunfire had died down. Blancanales was hurting all over and Schwarz was still bleeding. Both Kowalski and Sorenson limped through the door.

"How did…" Kowalski began. "Is he still alive?"

"Tie him up before we do anything else," Sorenson ordered.

Schwarz tilted his head. "Anything else?"

"We're calling Brognola for backup on this," Kowalski explained. "Dr. Sorenson and I just discovered some new aspects of this nightmare."

CHAPTER TWENTY

The Learjet taxied up to the old Air Reserve Station hangar. Two blacksuits Bolan didn't recognize trotted up to the aircraft, their MP-5s kept low to their sides. They pushed up a rolling staircase and opened the jet's door.

Bolan handed one of them a brooding, gaunt little man and his war bag. Dark eyes looked the Executioner over.

"You must be Striker," the man said. He had a faint Scottish lilt to his voice. "Er, Colonel Brandon Stone, I mean, sir."

"That's right," Bolan answered. "And you?"

"My name's Ryker." The blacksuit jerked his thumb at a six-foot, powerfully built man with piercing blue eyes. "That's Priest."

Bolan nodded and offered his hand. Surprised, the two soldiers took the handshake. "I'm not going to butter this up for you. We're going to have a hell of a ride ahead of us."

"I signed up for Farm duty to do the best I could for my country," Priest answered in a deep, reverent tone. "If that means getting in harm's way to protect this airport, then so be it."

"And you?" Bolan asked Ryker.

"Making up for past mistakes," the Scottish-accented blacksuit answered. "I'm not worth half of what citizens are worth."

Bolan pursed his lips. "I'd say that kind of attitude makes you worth your weight in gold, Ryker."

The Scotsman regarded Bolan for a moment, then his brooding dark eyes flickered with a moment of warmth, a smile on his lips, before he helped the Executioner carry his war bag into the hangar.

Buck Greene awaited him. "Striker," he acknowledged. "We were just working out how we'd be protecting the airport. I already have a man stationed at the top of the O'Hare Hilton. He's been joined by the local FBI office's SWAT team snipers."

Bolan knew the tall, black hotel. Its concave shape and great height made it a perfect overwatch for the entire airport. Even though the Executioner was going to try to stay up close and personal to engage in the fight to protect the facility at close range, were he a sniper, he'd set up shop atop the curved wall of obsidian glass.

"They have enough range?" Bolan asked.

Greene nodded. "Three-thirty-eight Lapua Magnums. Reach out and touch you with power from a full mile away."

Bolan nodded. "They'll stay close to the terminals if they want to get the maximum disease spread."

"So they really are going to release something like anthrax or Botox?" Another person spoke up. Bolan turned and saw a bearded man approach. He had tired eyes and his forehead was wrinkled from frowning.

"That's Rutherford. USAMRIID," Greene introduced. "U.S. Army's version of the CDC."

"Yeah. The Medical Research Institute of Infectious

Diseases," Bolan recalled. "You have any counterterrorism training?"

"I was the medic in my Delta Force unit before transferring to the institute," Rutherford said. He sounded less tired and sad than he looked.

Bolan produced a silver sphere that he had taken from the quarry cave in Wisconsin. "Would you recognize what this is?"

"It's a biological munitions container. Right now, it has neither ampules with virus in suspension, nor a central detonation core," Rutherford explained as he opened the top of the sphere. "As for what virus would have been put in this, I don't know."

Bolan frowned. "If it's any help, the fluid was amber in color."

Rutherford pursed his lips and shook his head. "Did you pick up one of the ampules? There would have been an identification code on it. Nothing you'd have known if you weren't studying it."

Bolan frowned. "I didn't pull out a live ampule, but I do remember an eight-digit mix of numbers and letters."

Rutherford leaned closer to make out the code that the Executioner rattled off, then nodded thoughtfully as he listened. He didn't react except to say the name of the concoction, and Bolan congratulated him on his poker face. "Botulinum toxin."

"Botox for short," Greene muttered.

Bolan shook his head. "Almost always fatal. No countermeasures. It gets ingested or inhaled, and then the toxin kills by paralyzing the part of the nervous system that controls breathing."

"The good news is that there are antisera to counteract Botox," Rutherford noted. "But getting it here would take a miracle. And we'd have to administer it immediately to everyone. Waiting until clinical symptoms appeared would be too late."

"And doesn't inoculation against it take around a year's worth of shots?" Greene asked.

"Over the course of several months, at least," Rutherford confirmed.

Ryker rolled his eyes. "Maybe we could ask the terrorists to wait until next year."

Bolan grimaced. "We'll just have to stop them before they can release the toxin. Failure isn't an option anymore."

"Buck, we've got a message from the Farm," a newcomer answered.

The blacksuit paused. "Striker. They were just asking about you, sir."

"Let's go see what's up," Bolan said, nodding toward the radio center.

Sitting at the radio was one of the biggest men that the Executioner had ever seen, easily as tall and powerful as Adonis. He turned and recognized Toro Martinez, a DEA agent who had assisted Leo Turrin and Phoenix Force in breaking part of a ring trying to destabilize the Mexican presidency during a border fire war that flared up a couple of years earlier. He was still young and boyish, his dark complexion hiding wrinkles well.

"Yes, ma'am. Striker just showed up here," Martinez stated. He smiled at the Executioner and let him take a seat in front of a laptop set up with a miniature Web cam.

Barbara Price's face appeared on the screen. "Striker, we've got a new development. Able Team just discovered a communications center on the West Coast."

Bolan frowned. "So they're more widespread than we thought."

"I'm transmitting the image they found on one computer console," Price said.

At that moment Bolan found himself looking at a small radar circle in the upper corner of the laptop screen. Data windows surrounding it bore all the information for O'Hare International Airport. He felt a chill race through him. "They have control of O'Hare's computer network?"

"Bear's burning up the lines trying to cover that. We think that this is feeding to a SATCOM system," Price said. "But then it could be retransmitted to aircraft once the airport's transmitters are knocked out. If they time it right, nobody would know the difference."

"It's time-looped for 8:00 p.m. tonight," Bolan pointed out.

"Yeah, and it's allowing several flights to take off," Price responded.

Bolan ran his fingers through his hair. "The ampules have no metal in them. They're just glass."

"Excuse me?" Price asked.

"They're not going to try to perform a mass release of Botulinum toxin here. They might scatter one or two ampules, enough to cause a panic, especially with a couple explosions going on. But by now, Dark and Adonis are counting on us to have counterterrorism forces on hand to contain the threat," the Executioner surmised. "We respond to some sacrificial lambs and in the meantime, we have a bunch of unarmed thugs spreading out and delivering a deadly bio-weapon to dozens of cities."

"Not Adonis, Striker." Schwarz's voice came over the link. "He's here in San Fran."

"Dead?" Bolan asked.

"Alive, but comatose. We're keeping him alive. Hal's got us a team of Justice Department agents to secure the mall so the cops don't take away bodies, prisoners or evidence," Schwarz explained. "We want Adonis in custody, don't we?"

"If he wakes up, we'll be able to get what information we want out of him. Then he gets his sentence served," the Executioner answered. "Did you find anything else?"

"Twenty to thirty heavily armed Filipinos. In a Christian missionary center," Schwarz replied.

"A Christian missionary center?" Bolan asked for clarification.

"Striker, you don't think that they'd be..." Price began.

"What did you guys find over there?" Schwarz asked.

"I'm guessing that the RING intends to spread Botulinum toxin ampules to various airports around the country and to other countries," Bolan said. "Christian missionaries. That would provide plenty of cover for a large group of people to come into an airport at once, and then just split up."

"I'm having Jackie Sorenson check it on their computers. She's found their financial records," Schwarz replied.

Minutes ticked away while Bolan waited for a response. In the meantime, the Executioner conferred with Greene.

"We'll need security and our spotters to look out for buses that could be carrying in fake missionaries," the Executioner said.

"Local security and the cops have been working with

us. Toro here has been running back and forth between their HQ and ours to keep things secure," Greene replied.

"Oh?" Bolan asked.

"We ran a check. The whole phone system is tapped," Greene said. "And the thing is, it's all done through official channels. NSA, DEA, FBI—everything from office phones to pay phones. But the taps have a shadow signature on them, someone other than the real authorities is listening in."

"The RING," Bolan surmised.

Greene nodded. "In fact, according to our computer people, our own firewall is under attack constantly. He's shifting encryptions constantly to fight off unauthorized listeners."

Bolan looked at the comm center. "Probably other members of the RING's core group. I just can't see a terrorist organization having hackers who could match us."

"Sir." Martinez spoke up. The great bull of a man looked grim. "Able Team reports that the fake missionaries have bought thirty tickets to twenty-five different cities."

Bolan grimaced. "All right. We'll do what we can on this end. Have Able try to get here as fast as possible. I know they're tired, but we'll need all the muscle and firepower we can get."

"Yes, sir," Martinez answered, turning back to the comm center.

Bolan stepped to the door of the hangar, looking out over the airfield. Thoughts whirled in his mind as he balanced the news of potential apocalypse to the lost Sable Burton. At that moment, his cell phone vibrated.

"Stone," he answered, pulling the phone from his pocket.

Even though Bolan had heard the voice only once, he knew it was Dark. "Hello, Colonel. How's this afternoon treating you?"

"Why don't you come see me and I'll tell you in detail?"

"Thanks for the invitation, Colonel," Dark answered, "but I don't have to be there for a while. On the other hand, there is a lady who is dying to see you again."

"I told Adonis, if she got hurt, I'd bring the sky down on you and yours," the Executioner said, restraining his rage. He took a deep breath. "Oh, wait. I don't think Adonis is in a position to tell you that."

There was a grunt on the other end. "What do you mean?"

"Well, he ran into some of my people in San Francisco," Bolan told him. "You might not have heard yet."

"You're trying to tell me you've taken down Adonis?"

"He'll be in custody. Granted, we're not sure there's enough to testify, but—"

"Nice trick. I try to draw you out, then you try to get me to run to my friend," Dark replied. "He wouldn't be taken alive."

"We have him. And he's alive." It was Bolan's turn to taunt, but he kept it subtle. He didn't want to provoke Dark into hurting Sable.

Dark sighed. "You're not going to trade him for this girly girl here. Even though I know you fancy her."

"That's straight."

"Well, he must be in good shape, if you're still referring him in the present tense."

"I'm not guaranteeing he'll survive. He took a bullet to the head," Bolan replied.

As callous as Dark tried to make himself sound,

Bolan could feel the man seething on the other end. The brutal mercenary was loyal to his giant friend, and Adonis was the one thing the Executioner knew he cared about.

"Which is more important to you, Dark? Your mission or your partner?" Bolan asked.

"Once I finish with you here in Chicago, I'll go pick up my friend, and the RING will take care of their own," Dark answered. "You're living in your final hours, Stone."

"I've been living my entire adult life as if it were my final hours. If the secondhand reaches zero when I'm facing off with you, so be it. You're not going to murder any more innocents," Bolan informed him.

Dark chuckled. "And you're not going to murder any more guilty."

"This isn't fun and games, Dark. Your partner thought it was, and now he's half dead."

"You think I'm joking, Tall, Dark and Spooky? Watching you operate is like looking in the mirror. I'm ready for anything you can throw at me. Fun and games? No, I know you. I almost was like you once, but I just got tired of all the bullshit, Stone."

"The only bullshit I smell is your grasping for justification."

Dark sighed. "Well, if you can do your job in good conscience, I envy you. For me, murdering an airport full of useless eaters is the same as putting a bullet in the head of a sovereign government official who doesn't agree with our President. A few thousand people die? So what. Millions will wake up to the fact that they're no longer safe and that their so-called elected leaders only need them as votes and sheep for the slaughter. You mean to tell me you believe in a system you have to work outside of?"

"I believe."

"It'll be a shame to kill you, Stone."

"It's a shame you took the path you did," Bolan answered. "But there's no such thing as a 'useless eater.'"

"It's been a nice chat, Stone, but I must go. You'll know where to find me."

Dark disconnected and Bolan looked at the cell phone. He checked the Caller ID readout and realized that the mercenary hadn't called from Sable's cell phone. Bolan went back to the communications center.

"Barb, I need a quick rundown on a phone number," Bolan said. "It's 312-555-1326."

"Bear's got tracking software for that. We'll narrow it down in…we got it," Price answered. "It's the same neighborhood where you encountered the AHC and Fist of God soldiers."

"Figures," Bolan said. "Dark wants me to come visit."

"And leave our defenses of O'Hare that much weaker," Price returned. "Striker—"

"There's an innocent life at stake. And there's a chance I can head off those mercs. We already have O'Hare Security, FBI SWAT, the National Guard and the Chicago Police Department on full alert. You have the cyberteam working on a way to kill the enemy's taps?"

"Yeah, they're good. Dammit, you know how much of a difference one man can make."

"I'll make it back as fast as I can," Bolan replied. "In fact, I have an idea."

Jack Grimaldi came out of the locker room, freshly showered, his hair still wet, a mug of coffee in his hands. "Sarge?"

"Jack, feel up to taking the Lady for a spin downtown?" the Executioner asked him.

Grimaldi raised an eyebrow. "*Dragon Slayer?* Over Chicago?"

"A quick chopper insertion."

Grimaldi grinned. "Charlie, wanna come with? Just in case?"

Charlie Mott looked over from the back of the borrowed C-130. "Ready, willing and able…or do only Lyons and the gang get to say that last part."

"Come on, smart-ass. We're going to make some bad guys sweat," Grimaldi called.

The Lady, *Dragon Slayer,* was an impressive piece of machinery. Weighing a shade over three tons when fully mission equipped, it was a powerful, sleek machine. Thirty-eight feet from its sharklike tail to its graceful nose, with a rotor diameter of thirty-nine feet, it was as compact as possible, yet still capable of great speed and offensive capability. Grimaldi had taken the helicopter up past 200 miles an hour, skimming along at high speed. All that power stemmed from twin 742-horsepower Lycoming engines, providing nearly twice the combat range of an AH-64 Apache, and almost twenty miles an hour faster and more agile than the tank busting gunship.

The shell was designed out of state-of-the-art corrosion-resistant, composite-structure materials that allowed for maximum strength and maximum weight savings. Thanks to the efficient engines and lightweight structure, the *Dragon Slayer* was able to cruise for three hours at 138 miles per hour, or go tearing across the sky at a blistering pace.

The helicopter had weapons pods that recessed into the side of its sleek frame. A .50-caliber GECAL machine gun was one of Grimaldi's favorite weapons mounts on the deadly bird, a beast of a cannon capable of spitting out 2000 rounds of ammunition per minute. And considering that each of those rounds weighed nearly two ounces and traveled at nearly three times the speed of sound, the GECAL could destroy anything less than a five-foot-thick concrete bunker. The missile pods were a mix of two 2.75-inch artillery rocket pods and four TOW missiles, for those ten-foot-thick concrete bunker walls. For backup and pesky lighter targets such as riflemen and terrorists, an XM-134 minigun was mounted on each side, each capable of spitting out an almost literal death ray of 7.62 mm bullets at the astonishing rate of 3000 rpm, more than enough to sweep all but the most determined ground forces off the face of the planet with one long pull of the trigger.

Avionics were nothing short of amazing, too. The helicopter possessed a computerized flight management system that allowed Grimaldi or Mott the ability to set the aircraft into a stable hover fifty feet above a selected target, leaving the pilots free to take command of the weapons systems, operate the sling winch or concentrate on search and rescue with the helicopter's Foreward Looking InfraRed cameras and ground effect radar, which would allow the Stony Man pilots the capability to operate in near complete darkness without exposing themselves to gunfire by turning on lights. To cut the sound signature, speakers mounted around the rotorshaft projected the sound of the helicopter's rotorslap at right angles, the countervibration deflecting and flattening the sound waves. The muted helicopter wasn't totally invisible and silent, and it still would kick up a whirlwind at lower altitudes, but it would keep the chopper from being as easily noticed as possible. In fact, Bolan was counting on the "stealth" rotor system to drop him right on top of Dark's inner-city headquarters before he even realized what was going on.

"I'll keep in radio contact with you guys," Bolan explained. "Once you drop me off, get the hell out before they notice the winds you're kicking up. If I need close support, swing in and provide it, but O'Hare has top priority."

Grimaldi looked at Bolan, then out over the airport. "You think *Dragon Slayer*'s going to be needed here?"

"I know it. Harpy's alive and kicking. If anything, she might be trying to use the systems they ripped out of the SmarTruck," Bolan said. "We didn't see the Skycrane back at the mill, or any of the electronic warfare systems from Terintec."

"It would have a pizza rack." Mott spoke up. His mirrored sunglasses flashed under his green-and-yellow baseball cap as Grimaldi and Bolan looked confused for a moment. "Harpy's helicopter. It would have a pizza rack."

"Like on the Air Force PAVE Lows and PAVE Hawks," Grimaldi stated. "An electronics cabinet with a series of slots, like on a pizza oven, where you could slap a motherboard into it."

Bolan nodded. "Modular electronics systems racks. Of course. The SmarTruck was designed for battlefield use. A modular pizza-rack system would only make sense for the truck's components. If one gets damaged, plug in a fresh one. And if you have a second truck, just take a redundant board from the first."

"Only in this case, the SmarTruck's electronics boards can be popped out and put in a helicopter. No heavy sawing. They just wanted us to think it would take that kind of effort so that we'd be expecting them to be armed with a helicopter that could sneak up on the airport and usurp the communications and navigation systems," Grimaldi concluded.

Moss lowered his mirrored shades and winked. "Elementary."

"Don't go trading your baseball cap in for a deerstalker yet, Sherlock," Bolan replied. "I still need my top pilots to get me on target."

"Done," Grimaldi said.

The Executioner grabbed his OA-93, then looked at Buck Greene. "Buck, I'm going to need a full load of hollowpoints. I'm going urban, and all I had for this thing was armor-piercing."

"Right. Toro?" Greene probed.

The gigantic DEA agent unstrapped the pouched 5.56 mm ammunition from his vest, tossing them to Bolan. The Executioner replaced his pouches with the fresh loads. "You'll be able to refit?"

Martinez nodded. "I can get spare mags loaded for myself. You're in a hurry."

Bolan gave the big man a salute.

"Buck, make sure you call these two in case hell busts loose while I'm gone," Bolan told Greene.

"And what happens if you need air support?" Greene asked.

Bolan set his jaw firmly. "Then hell's already on the loose in Chicago."

CHAPTER TWENTY-ONE

Sable Burton's eyelids felt like sandpaper. She opened them to the harsh light of day and her head hammered. She was lying on a couch just under a window. She remembered being held in the sky by a blond giant, then darkness.

Now she looked up to see Dark walking around, using a cordless phone. He killed the phone link after seeing her awaken, and walked over to her, black trench coat swishing behind him.

"Good afternoon, sleepyhead," Dark greeted, sitting beside her on the sofa.

"Mr. Dark," Burton muttered, mouth dry and sticky.

"Please, Professor. I'm just Dark," the tall, lean mercenary said. He tilted his head, his black hair spilling off his shoulder as he grinned warmly at her. "Can I call you Sable?"

"How about calling me a cab?" Burton asked.

Dark laughed. "You get points for spunk right there, babe."

"Gee thanks." She looked around and saw crime scene tape on the floor in the shape of a body outline.

Stained floorboards told her that there had been a battle here, and she remembered her conversation with Brandon Stone the day of the SmarTruck hijacking. Her head throbbed and she realized that conversation was only yesterday.

The men responsible for killing him are dead or in custody.

This was the place where Stone had come through and slaughtered a group of murderers, meeting violence with violence, spilling blood to avenge blood and prevent further bloodshed. The whole room took on an odd new chill at that realization. Burton winced.

"Figure out that the mess was your boyfriend's handiwork?" Dark asked. "He's quite an efficient killer. Three dead. Three wounded. Hardly a scratch on him by the time I ran into him. One might think he's almost as dangerous as I am."

Burton's eyes narrowed. "He's not a murderer."

"That depends on who you ask. These men had mothers, fathers, families. You think that everyone Colonel Stone has ever killed grew up in a void?"

"Nobody asked them to be murderers. If they weren't guilty, they wouldn't be in his way. He wouldn't have to fight."

Dark snorted. "You're suffering from the same romantic delusions he is."

"That, or you're denying what you are," Burton retorted.

Dark grabbed her by the jaw, squeezing her cheeks together, making her green eyes bulge. The black-haired murderer's clear blue eyes flashed like lightning, his lips parted in a rictus, showing a mouthful of white, straight teeth. "Denying? Denying what, bitch?"

Burton felt herself shake from top to bottom, but

swallowed hard and shook her head free. "Denying that you're a weakling."

"You've seen what I can do."

"To helpless people."

"Armed professionals," Dark said.

Burton's eyes narrowed. "And all for what? The men and women who protect people for a living all die, and so do a bunch of innocent bystanders. All for what?"

"To wake up the world."

"Why not make a real change on your own? You want to eliminate governments? You're a one-man army. You could leave half the world without its leadership inside of a month," Burton stated. "You're just too lazy and queasy to do the work yourself."

"Professor, you think that killing figureheads would make the real powers pulling the puppet strings even flinch?" Dark asked, rising.

She shook her head. "But you know those puppeteers, don't you? You could destroy them. Leave them limping at least."

Dark smirked, then looked at her, as if lost in thought.

"Do I have a point?"

"Quiet."

"Do I have a point?"

Dark leaned in close to her. "You'll get a point between your pretty little tits, bitch, if you don't back off."

Burton only smiled, Dark's nostrils flaring as he exhaled and stomped off.

As soon as he turned away, she allowed herself a shudder of terror. Dark stalked into the dining room, leaving her alone on the sofa, looking at the outline where a dead man had fallen. She wondered who the man was and began asking herself questions that Dark had asked. Who died? Whose family did he belong to? Who once or still loved him?

The outline of a fallen pistol, also marked in tape, pulled her out of those thoughts. The man who died on that spot was a pistol-wielding killer, who had probably driven from Hector Terin's house with Shep's corpse in the back seat. The killer might even have been Shep's murderer himself.

Burton latched on to the anger. Surrender wasn't going to drag her soul under. She'd claw her way out of despair, and the first chance she got, she'd make a break for it. Even if she died, the noise would bring the police, or even Stone himself.

She looked around the living room, then to the window. She wasn't sure if she had enough strength to punch through the glass to raise enough of a racket that could be heard on the street. That was when she saw the shadow flicker overhead momentarily, blocking out the typical gray-white sky of a gloomy, late fall Chicago day. A tingle ran straight up and down her spine and she could feel the coming of Brandon Stone, almost as if he had triggered a long-dormant sixth sense inside her. Outside, the trees, with what few leaves were still on them, bent and swayed in a sudden wind.

She forced herself not to react to the dramatic increase in the breeze. While she was basically involved in lasers and quantum electronics, she wasn't completely in the dark about other pieces of applied military technology. She remembered being assigned to a program with a stealth helicopter that used lasers instead of radio beams to cut down the radar signature of the aircraft. She'd seen the thing hover, almost silent, despite a whipping wind, something no other fighting machine she'd ever seen had done.

If anyone had access to such technology, it was Colonel Brandon Stone.

Burton lowered her head.

That still didn't mean his job would be any easier.

DARK HEARD THE THUMP on the roof and froze in mid-stride. The other AHC and Fist of God soldiers in the dining room were still busy loading their weapons. He raised his fist and the men all stopped what they were doing.

"What?" one of the Arabs asked.

Dark grit his teeth, sneering at them. "Someone just landed on the roof."

"But we'd hear a helicopter," an AHC man said. He kept his voice low, though, to listen for anything further.

"Only one person landed," Dark whispered.

"If it's one man…" the first Arab started.

"He'll wipe the floor with you lot," Dark snapped back. "Evac now! Down the stairs!"

The terrorists paused for a moment, and the black-hearted mercenary shook his head, then swatted one in the skull with one of his Calicos. That got them moving as they hastily grabbed their weapons and scrambled for the stairwell. Dark spun, trench coat fluttering behind him as he walked quickly to get Burton. She was sitting on the sofa and her gaze met his as he was in the doorway. Defiance was hard-etched into her face. The merc paused.

"You're going to fight me for as long as you can so your boyfriend can get in here," Dark concluded.

Burton nodded.

The mercenary took a deep breath and pulled one of his machine guns. "I'm not that stupid. By the way, this is for cutting me with a fucking car antenna."

Burton's face flashed momentarily with fear.

The ceiling suddenly imploded and a figure in sleek black dropped with the grace of a panther out of the sky, weapon blazing.

THE EXECUTIONER FINISHED laying the net of detonation cord over where he figured the center of the living room ceiling was. He needed to interpose himself between Sable and the enemy as quickly as possible. Grimaldi, using the powerful infrared optics on *Dragon Slayer,* managed to peer through the ceiling to detect one heat source in the front and several more in the dining room. The det cord web was normally stuck to a door. Being composed of CV-38 low-velocity plastic explosives, it didn't make a sound, but still provided a powerful cutting power against doors and reinforced windows. The roof of a two-story residential building proved to be no greater an opposition to it than simple wood or glass.

The hole also was just perfectly sized for Mack Bolan to leap through. As he sailed down the ragged gap, he triggered the OA-93 before his boots even struck the floor, Dark whipping away and firing a wild burst as his aim was thrown off. Burton gave a defiant shout at his back, but the Executioner was in full-blitz mode. He'd brought up his subgun to rip open the trench-coat-clad mercenary when a powerful kick booted the weapon from his hands.

Bolan stepped back, barely dodging the followup kick that brought Dark's boot heel within inches of smashing his jaw. The breeze lifted Bolan's short hair, but he reached up, forearm blocking the forward momentum of the shin. He snapped his fist into the back of Dark's knee and thrust down hard, unbalancing the mass murderer and twisting him to the floor.

Dark's hands hit the floor, preventing him from smashing face-first into the ground, and Bolan felt the tall man's leg rip from between the trap of the soldier's forearm and fist. The Executioner took a quick half step back, his momentum increased as the mercenary's boot struck him just above his navel.

The blow, had Bolan stood fast, would have folded him over in crippling pain, maybe even damaged an internal organ. Again, the soldier reacted to an attack with an attack on the limb striking at him. He grabbed the booted foot and brought a knife-hand chop on the attacker's knee.

Flame stung the Executioner's hand as it struck a knee guard hidden under the BDU pant leg, and he recoiled from the stroke. Dark somersaulted away from Bolan, and the pair faced off, both breathing deep and fast as they locked furious, hate-filled gazes.

The two men lunged at the same time, fists flashing against ribs and abdominal muscles and backs as they hammered, armored chest to armored chest. The impact stopped them both, punches to kidneys and backs blunted by ammo pouches and Kevlar and trauma plate wrapping vulnerable torsos. Both warriors growled, bouncing a step back. It was Dark who acted first, forehead lashing toward Bolan's nose, but the Executioner braced his neck and turned his head, catching skullbone on his cheek. Had the original Stony Man not been spiking into adrenaline levels he'd rarely reached before, he'd have felt the skin under his right eye swell to three times its normal thickness, thousands of capillaries ruptured by the savage head butt.

Instead, with a snarl, the Executioner sliced both hands up into Dark's armpits, thumbs driving into the soft tissue. The RING killer gagged at the hit right beneath the major arteries that fed his arms. Despite the pain that washed across his face like a storm front, he clamped down tight on Bolan's hands. Before the soldier could pop his hands free, Dark grabbed his adversary's upper arms, fingers digging in like claws. The Executioner glanced down to see the trench-coat-wearing murderer's foot snake between his own, looking to hook an ankle for leverage.

Bolan denied Dark the advantage of his leverage, dropping to his knees and yanking the man off balance. After hitting the floor, he sprung up again, head and shoulders stabbing under the terrorist's breastbone, lifting him off his feet. The Executioner had his hands free, once more, and he grabbed his adversary, adding extra thrust to hurling away Dark. He was aiming to dash the man's skull against the doorjamb behind him, but with seemingly impossible catlike grace, the black-clad killer twisted, landing in a three-point crouch, balanced on his feet and one hand, the other clutched tight to his hip, fist clenched.

Dark snapped his head up, glaring at Bolan, then the two men dropped back out of their wild phase. With a flash of crackling black fabric, the RING warrior faded through the door just as the Executioner pulled up his OA-93 from where it hung on his sling and ripped off a sustained burst. Splinters flew as wood and drywall exploded under the Executioner's assault.

He was torn between charging to the top of the steps and possibly getting caught in an ambush, and checking on Sable Burton. Bolan pulled a flash-bang grenade from his war bag, bounced it off the far wall and down the steps, then turned to Burton.

"Are you okay? Can you walk?" The stun grenade detonated in punctuation to his statement, and he caught

a flash of surprise in the professor's eyes. He stuffed a
fresh magazine into his weapon.

"I can run," Burton answered, getting unsteadily to
her feet. "Brandon, you shouldn't have—"

"Shut up and follow me," Bolan cut her off, taking
her tiny hand in his. He pulled her along, passing the
top of the stairs. He interposed his Kevlar-protected
body between her and anyone still capable of fighting
in the stairwell. Burton rushed past and out of sight,
and Bolan caught movement below. He fired a burst of
5.56 mm hollowpoints at the shifting shadow, then spun,
racing for the back porch.

Burton was about to pull the door open when Bolan
slammed his palm against it, blocking her. He tugged
her back and away as the window exploded, the wood
shaking as bullets knocked on it.

"Well, that's out as an out." Burton laughed nervously.

"Keep it together, Professor," Bolan said gently. He
realized that he hadn't let her go, and the softness of her
body against his was cutting through the adrenalized
hyper-numbness of combat to awaken stirrings beneath
the ceramic trauma plate over his chest. She glanced up
at him, green eyes wide and swirling in a cascade of
emotions. He broke eye contact with her out of sheer
will and keyed his throat mike.

"Jack, we've got gunners outside and blocking our
exit," Bolan called.

"I've spotted them. Just waiting for your orders,"
Grimaldi answered.

"Burn 'em," Bolan ordered.

He glanced out through the window, spotting a flash
of aged orange-yellow on the side street the alley fed
into. His mind processed the image even as he heard the
sudden thunder from above.

Dragon Slayer dropped stealth mode in spectacular fashion, the sudden roar of spinning rotors drowned out only by the furious hellstorm of .50-caliber GECAL rounds. A porch across the way used to have a pair of armed riflemen. Now only two greasy smears remained. They made the error of trying to close the door on Bolan and his companion with their own weapons when they came under the gaze of Grimaldi and the helicopter's gun camera targeting system. As soon as the crosshairs came on target, the multibarreled machine guns ripped to life, and the two riflemen simply detonated in an explosive spray of pulpy chunks and blood. The wood around them also disintegrated, chewed to pieces by the impact of thirty rounds of 750-grain slugs.

The effect was like smashing two tomatoes against a wall with a sledgehammer. Bolan would leave it to the Chicago Police Department to sponge off the remains of the militiamen to determine if they were Arab or American. He threw open the door and exited to the porch.

The dead were all going into the same metaphysical hole.

"Jack, just before you opened up, I saw a vehicle heading off. It looked like a school bus, at least it looked that color," Bolan stated.

"I spotted two of them taking off," Charlie Mott replied. "They were parked the next block over, in the shade of some trees, which is how we probably missed them."

"Two busloads," Bolan repeated. Looking up, he saw a hatch to the roof. He climbed up onto the railing at the top of the porch steps and punched hard, knocking the door open. "Pick me up, we're going after those buses."

"What about me?" Burton asked.

Bolan reached down and took her hand. "You'll be safe on the helicopter. Come on."

He hoisted her up, bracing himself in the trapdoor's open mouth. It took her a moment to get her feet under her, and using his knee as a step, she scurried quickly up and through the opening. The Executioner slithered up like a mighty black python, hot on her heels. He was just in time to see the sling lowering from the side of *Dragon Slayer.*

"Slip the strap around you and sit in it like a swing," Bolan instructed the professor. She did so, holding on tight. The soldier grabbed the cable with both hands and as soon as he got his grip, the winch started pulling them both up.

"Is this safe?" Burton shouted over the roar of the helicopter's turbines.

"The winch is rated for six hundred pounds." He glanced down, then smiled at her. "And we're not gonna get dropped by Jack."

DARK EXECUTED a baseball slide down the stairs moments before the first 5.56 mm tumblers crashed and smashed into the wall. Looking back, he saw that the burst was perfectly centered on where he had been moments ago, a blistering hailstorm of death that had almost punched him out of the world, body armor or no, with a scything slash that would have cut through his exposed head.

Gunmen were racing back up the stairs, only a couple of them, though; the others had had enough sense to follow orders. Dark didn't care about fools who ignored him, and waved them on past, squeezed by and leaped down to the next landing. Something thumped down the steps to meet the rushing Fists of God. The mercenary grabbed the railing and yanked himself hard around the corner one more time. Even so, spilling out onto the bottom landing of the stairwell, he was hit by the shock wave from Stone's grenade. The thunderclap wasn't deafening, but Dark had to grab the wall to maintain his balance. Concussive force in the space of the landings would have proven all but crippling to the terrorists as they charged after Bolan.

Business was picking up, and the murderer in black wasn't going to be around to take the fallout from Stone's blitz. He was in the middle of a storm, and even though he'd managed to blunt most of his enemy's attacks, his knee was stiff and his head and back both ached. Stone proved himself, with their second confrontation, to be a man not to be fucked around with. Now he understood Adonis's giddy reaction to his conversation with the big mystery soldier. A jolt of adrenaline charged through him at the thought of facing an equal, a superior warrior with the skills to make his life a challenge.

Shooting fish in a barrel made for petty amusement, but wrestling with a shark, now that was the thing that got the blood pumping and promised you an opportunity to see the face of God and meet your judgment head-on. Dark burst out the front door, hearing the chatter of gunfire behind him. He pulled his radio and brought it to his lips. "Perimeter, contain the building!"

Answers in English and Arabic came to his ears and Dark stuffed the radio back into his coat pocket, racing for the school buses that were already crawling to the corner, men boarding while they were on the move. As soon as he cleared out from under the shadow of the building, he glanced back, spying a sleek, knife-tailed helicopter hovering silently, but only for a moment. In a heartbeat, the full roar of the engines and rotors washed down over him like an avalanche of sound. A heartbeat later, an even louder portent of doom filled the air as a turret on the belly of the flying beast opened up, spraying a short burst of heavy-metal thunder toward the alleyway.

Dark knew his snipers were dead meat and finished his mad dash to the school buses, legs burning as he cross the final few yards in three ground-eating strides, hand gripping the rails. He yanked himself through the door even as the ground beneath him started flashing past at greater and greater speed. Stuffing himself inside the bus, he looked back and saw the doom-spitting stealth copter hanging over his former headquarters. A sling was descending out the side door. He watched it lower to the roof as the bus retreated.

Dark snapped his gloved fingers, smiling at the man he knew the winch line was intended for. "Catch you later, Colonel Stone."

The buses drove hard toward the L-line and Dark smiled with the beginning tingles of victory. That's when the giant dragonship swerved from the roof, spinning and diving toward the street behind them, its rotorspan fitting easily between the rows of two-story brick homes.

Dark's eyes narrowed but sparkled with a glimmer of glee.

He admired a guy who wouldn't give up.

CHAPTER TWENTY-TWO

"Get closer to them. I don't want to risk hitting any bystanders, but we're not going to lose them," the Executioner ordered Jack Grimaldi from within the cabin of *Dragon Slayer.*

The sleek war machine continued on the tails of the pair of buses, keeping deftly between the buildings and within sight of its prey.

"I've got an image of both buses on infrared," Mott confirmed. "Switching it to your display panel in the back."

Bolan looked, seeing the shapes of the two vehicles as dull blue outlines with hearts of bright yellow, and seething with humanoid-blob shapes colored in red. Between both buses, he counted approximately four dozen men on board. "All right. Hold off on firing on them. This is a residential neighborhood and I don't need a .50-caliber round bouncing off asphalt and plowing through three living rooms and a baby's bedroom."

"We know, Sarge," Grimaldi answered. "Are you going EVA?"

Bolan started strapping himself into the harness

again. "With a vengeance. Swing over the first bus. We stop that, given the kind of parking on these streets, we've got the second one pinned."

He threw open the door and glanced at Burton. She was clutching her seat, green eyes wide as she looked at the buildings whipping past the windows. Giving him a look, she took a deep, desperate breath.

Bolan winked, then kicked out the door. He heard her yelp in surprise at his sudden drop, and then he only heard the sizzling whine of the winch decelerating his rapid drop. His boots slammed the yellow roof of the first bus and he hit the release latch on his harness. The bus accelerated with the sound of the Executioner's arrival.

Gunfire ripped through the roof of the bus. Bolan scrambled, racing ahead of the sudden rattle of bullets piercing metal, holes chasing his heels as he ran to the back of the bus.

The other driver accelerated, bringing his vehicle up hard and fast. Dark and a couple of other gunners leaned out the windows, aiming weapons at him. Bolan took the last strikes off the end of the roof at full speed, leaping with all his might, aiming his OA-93 ahead of him, holding down the trigger. The windshield detonated as thirty rounds of 5.56 mm NATO smashed through, turning glass to diamond-like chunks. The driver jerked and the school bus swerved hard into a row of parked cars. Behind him, the Executioner could already hear the strained shriek of brakes as his booted feet crashed onto the hood of the chase vehicle.

Letting the subgun flop freely on its sling, Bolan grabbed the roof of the bus and swung his feet through the shattered windshield. Bodies were already pouring out the windows, and he caught a flash of Dark, one of the first on the ground. Still, there were plenty of blood-thirsty souls waiting in the bus, bringing their guns to bear on the wraith in the blacksuit that had just barreled into their midst.

The Executioner threw himself to the ground, filling his fists with the Desert Eagle and the Beretta 93-R. He held the mighty Magnum in reserve, but the 9 mm machine pistol chattered out 3-round bursts that tore through knees and thighs of the half-concealed gunmen. They shrieked and desperately tried to retreat, several charging for the rear exit when Bolan let the powerful .44 Magnum Desert Eagle thunder and shatter the air inside the bus-turned-charnal-house, bodies jerking as 240-grain, torso-smashing hammers punched through exposed backs and out chests, tearing into men in front of them. After the initial exodus, nobody escaped the bus and the center aisle was heaped with torn, ruptured bodies, dead and wounded, all leaking their lifeblood.

Springing back to his feet, Bolan turned to cut off the rest of the terrorists as they caught up to the first bus. He holstered his empty handguns and grabbed up the OA-93 again, ramming home a fresh magazine. Dark paused, looking back, and swung up both of his Calico subguns, peppering the empty front windows with a salvo of Parabellum rounds. The Executioner dived beneath the dashboard. He lost sight of the enemy force for a moment.

"Jack? What are they doing?" he called through his throat mike.

"They're pulling out and heading for the next intersection. I think they're going to try to get under the next viaduct," Grimaldi answered.

"Do we burn it?" Mott asked.

Bolan heard *Dragon Slayer* thunder overhead and he

poked his head up, looking toward the fleeing bus. His eyes scanned the viaduct and he noticed an elevated train station, the fabled Chicago "El." His brow furrowed. "Dammit!"

"Striker?"

"Hold your fire! That's a crowded train platform they're heading for!" Bolan said. He leaped out the open side door and raced through the intersection. Cars beeped and honked at the passage of the tall man in black toting the fearsome subgun. Pedestrians on the sidewalk were already shell-shocked by the previous crowd of armed men swarming past and into the school bus, but some pointed in fear at him.

Gunfire broke out up ahead, and Bolan could see that the bus had ground to a halt. A Chicago Transit Authority ticket booth had been chewed to ribbons by a merciless cloud of lead, and the Executioner grit his teeth in impotent rage. More helpless innocents were dying, and there was nothing Bolan could do about it.

"Jack! Tell Buck that Dark's bringing his gunners in through the subway system! The train leads right underneath the major terminals at O'Hare!" Bolan shouted as he charged up the staircase. A militiaman sidestepped out at the top of the stairs and the Executioner didn't blink, triggering the Olympic Arms subgun, a 3-round burst that blew out the AHC murderer's intestines and severed his spine. Bolan vaulted over him before he even hit the ground, watching the last few terrorists charging on board the train as the doors shut.

Dropping the OA-93 on its sling, Bolan put on a burst of speed. Leaping from the platform, he grabbed one of the El car's rails as it pulled out from the station.

"We've got Buck apprised. But those are gunmen.

They're not going to be able to get on an airplane. What about the guys carrying the Botox?" Grimaldi asked.

Bolan pulled himself tight against the side of the silvered train, watching the city flash by his back. "The guys carrying the Botox would be with the ones disguised as the Filipino missionaries. That's who had the tickets. Dark's leading a diversionary force!"

"It's a hell of a diversion, Sarge," Grimaldi admitted.

"We've got a dozen squad cars pulling alongside the train," Mott added.

Bolan looked down at the hurtling Chicago police cars on the street below, their light racks strobing out red, white and blue, sirens howling above the rush of wind over his ears. He clenched tighter against the side of the train. "It's a hostage situation here. Dark's got a solid-gold advantage with the people already on this train. Someone get in touch with CTA central control. Clear the tracks. And tell Buck that I need a reaction force at the O'Hare train terminal as soon as possible."

"Relaying this back to Buck and the Farm, Sarge," Grimaldi answered, frustration making his voice as tight as a piano wire garrote across yielding flesh. "We might have to take the train out to save lives."

"If that happens, I'll still be on the train," Bolan answered. He reached up, found another handrail and climbed up and over the trio of chains forming one side of a corridor between cars. His foot rested on the top one for a moment as he crouched, seeing the city ahead of him. They were still going to have to go through the underground deep under the heart of the Loop, and Bolan might have a chance at stopping the killers that way.

He wasn't going to bank too much on it, though. The odds were long, and there were too many innocent lives at stake. He dropped back down and entered the train, people screaming as they spotted him. He put his fingers to his lips, pulling out his Justice Department badge. It seemed to keep most of the screaming down, but they clearly were unsettled at the sight of a six-foot-three man, bristling with all manner of high-tech weaponry.

"Everyone, get to the rear of the train, now!" Bolan ordered. He stalked down the center aisle. "Move it, people!"

He gave the OA-93 a shake and that motivated the startled Chicagoans. They moved en masse to the back. Bolan paused, watching them scramble to get through the tiny doorway. He glanced to the next car down, tension scraping at his nerves like the edge of a knife on raw skin. Dark's flunkies were in the next compartment, and frightened people were huddled on the floor. Their weapons were aimed at the prone and helpless hostages, and one AHC murderer even walked right up to the door, arms spread, taunting the Executioner to take a shot. He blew a kiss to Bolan, laughed and flipped him off.

The Executioner held his cool. His ego was strong enough to take the insults, but it wouldn't be enough to help him get over the trauma of watching this group of jackals open fire on helpless hostages.

Bolan backed off, looking at the empty passenger car he was in. He remembered where he'd jumped on. It was three cars from the end. He'd got the civilians into the last two cars, and he had a buffer zone between them and Dark's forces. There were still three carloads up ahead. He didn't take a head count, but considering twenty or twenty-five per car, it just wasn't a sacrifice he wanted to make.

"Jack, I've got the last two cars isolated. Anyone puts me down, you light this car up to keep those people safe. Got it?"

"That's not going to happen," Grimaldi answered.

"I'm not kidding, Jack. I don't care if you have to put a missile right through me. You do it if it'll save the hostages."

"Dammit, Sarge—" Grimaldi answered.

"Striker, I just got off the horn with Buck. He says that the C.P.D. is getting the CTA to route trains off the tracks, so that you can continue on without stopping. Nobody else is going to get on that train," Mott interrupted.

"Good. I noticed we sailed through that last stop," Bolan said.

The train rolled through Chicago, tilting down as it aimed for the dark safety under the city. Already Bolan heard the hiss of static cutting his radio contact with Grimaldi and Mott.

DARK PACED UP and down the length of the compartment, soothing his nerves with a cigarette.

"That guy's in the fourth car," one of his men told him. "He's got some kind of throat mike and radio setup, so that must be how we're getting a free pass."

Dark glanced over to the trembling engineer, his bald head glistening with a sheen of cold terror sweat. He offered him a cigarette, seemingly ignoring his subordinate. When the engineer refused, Dark shrugged and took another drag, turning to the AHC militiaman.

"Want a smoke?" Dark asked him.

"That Stone guy. He's on—"

"I know he's on the train. As long as we have men pointing these things at the people huddling in terror on the ground, he won't act. You know, the guns. The hostages. That crazy concept."

The AHC man trembled at the slight. "You've got a mouth on you."

Dark tucked the cigarette in the corner of his lips. "Most people do. It's how they eat and talk."

"You're a flip bastard—"

Dark cut him off with a grab to the throat, and he leaned in close, blowing smoke into the militiaman's eyes. "That's the nice thing about you sorry rotten bastards. I can abuse you as much as I like, but because you're a racist piece of shit, nobody will think the less of me."

Dark squeezed harder, lifting him off the ground. "Then again, a lot of people don't like me for being part of a massacre that killed hundreds of Americans. But hey, it's not a perfect world."

The others looked at Dark, terror filling their faces.

"Now, anyone wants to give me lip, there's the exit," Dark snarled. "I won't have the train slow down for you."

The AHC man in his grip whimpered, standing on tiptoes, sputtering through his lips and nose, trying to get fresh air into his lungs.

Dark let go and the man collapsed at his feet. "Just remember who taught you everything you know…but not everything I know."

He glowered at his men, and they each took a step back. He allowed a grin to cross his face and shrugged his trench coat, brushing off an imaginary fleck of dust. "What do you think? After this, should I get a nice leather one, red silk lining?"

The engineer looked him over. "You already look totally badass, sir."

Dark smiled and rubbed his bald pate. "Now this is someone who knows how to speak to a superior being."

He spun away, the tails of his trench coat flying like wings. He strode with purpose toward the next car and cut through to the third car, seeing his man taunting Colonel Stone at the juncture between the third and fourth compartments. He reached up, grabbing a handful of hair and yanking the man out of the way, pushing him face-first into the engineer's compartment window, cracking glass and spraying blood down the shiny, silvery metal door.

"Behave, asshole," Dark snarled.

He stood at the window, looking at Bolan, their eyes meeting. He was right, they could have easily been brothers, especially if Dark had trimmed his hair to a neat, semishort military cut. He smirked and ran his hand through his long mane.

"What's so funny?" Bolan asked.

"Us. Mirror images."

"We've talked philosophy before. I'm here to talk about those people you have on the floor."

"Yeah. But you know, the villain and the hero have to talk face-to-face. They have to define their worlds, before one kills the other."

Bolan's eyes narrowed. "What makes you think I won't put a slug right through your gut?"

Dark rolled his head back over his shoulder. He was pleased that only one of his men took the cue to dramatically rack the bolt of his submachine gun.

"Sixty hostages, Captain Whitebread."

Bolan took a deep breath. "What are your conditions?"

"I don't really have any, but I am going to tie up your precious airport. There's no way you could block everything we have planned for O'Hare."

"Well, slipping the Filipinos through as missionaries was a clever idea. Did you convince them the Botox was nerve gas and that they had atropine to protect themselves? Or are they suicidal fanatics?" Bolan asked.

"We told them that the ampules were Tabur. They have atropine injectors hidden in their toiletry kits disguised as insulin syringes or asthma medicine," Dark replied. "Totally useless against a good virus."

"The RING won't be trusted again," Bolan said.

Dark chuckled and watched the soldier's face harden.

"Don't tell me you've never sent men into action as cannon fodder, Colonel."

"No. But there's that difference again."

"So your real name is Light?" Dark asked.

"My name is pain. And it's people like you who made me. I'm every ounce of pain from every victim, dead or alive, everyone touched by the fear and terror your kind have inflicted on the world. My name is pain, and I'm here to give judgment."

Dark leaned close to the glass, his brain whirling. Something about that statement, it was triggering a memory, deep and dark in the depths of time.

Bolan stood there before him, surfing the El cars as Dark did. The jostling train did its best to unbalance them, to break their staring contest. Finally, he felt the floor beneath his feet starting to shift itself, rising back up out from underneath the Loop. He glanced out one window and saw the expressway. Ribbons of road surrounded the train tracks and he knew they were in the final stretch toward O'Hare International Airport.

"If a sniper tries to take any of us out, I'm going to

have my boys kill everybody," Dark told Bolan. "Give that message to your boys."

Bolan keyed his throat mike, talking softly, and not mentioning any names except Dark's. The mercenary kept his eye on the Executioner, counting the stations as they passed them, a countdown to the big finale. Dark was wired on adrenaline, but instead of growing more antsy, it calmed him, making him sleeker, harder, meaner. His face twisted into a grin.

Dark admitted it reluctantly. He was a man who loved his job.

Bolan turned back from talking on his throat mike. "You've got your free pass. Nobody's going to take a shot at you."

Dark nodded. The AHC man he'd slammed into the window was just recovering his senses, mopping a torrent of blood from his broken nose and lips, staring at the RING leader.

"What the hell did you do that to me for?" he asked thickly.

"You were playing games with him, and not paying attention to your job," Dark said, not looking at him. "That could have been a sniper bullet and you could be dead. At least now you look prettier than before I rammed that ugly gob of yours through reinforced safety glass."

He turned and glanced at the AHC militiaman over his shoulder. "Thank me for saving your life."

The man shifted through a phase of anger, then fear, then confusion. "What's that?"

Dark tilted his head, eyes darting both ways before he turned around, looking for what the terrorist was talking about when he saw Bolan holding his throat mike to a small, handheld unit. Squinting, he tried to make out what it was.

"MP3 recorder," Bolan said, "with external microphone pickup and minispeaker playback. Perfect for gathering intelligence."

Dark's mouth went dry, hot blood flushing his face.

"I'm sorry, but it looks like your mouth finally wrote a check your ass couldn't cash," Bolan continued. The MP3 recorder stopped, and the Executioner slipped the tiny piece of electronics back into the pocket of his harness.

Dark spun away. "We have layers upon layers of backup plans."

"Oh, yeah. Like the improvised gunship loaded with MARS missiles?" Bolan asked.

Dark halted, looking back over his shoulder. He watched the Executioner's thumb jerking towards *Dragon Slayer,* skimming over oncoming traffic, visible to both men. "Harpy could take that bird any day of the week."

"You willing to risk another partner?"

Dark smirked. "She's an associate. Associates are expendable, and there's no way you can blackmail that information to *her.* She knows how I feel about her."

"We have your gunmen in our sights. We'll convince your Filipinos that they're on a suicide mission, and your gunship will be blasted out of the sky by ours," Bolan told him. "Your mission is over. You don't stand a chance."

Dark shrugged and tugged down his lapels, the tails of his trench coat rustling behind him like a living thing. "You ever let the odds force you to surrender?"

Bolan's lips pursed.

"I didn't think so, Stone. We're at a stalemate, be-

CHAPTER TWENTY-THREE

The Executioner stepped back, giving the terrorists some space. His earphone was already feeding him a mixture of news.

"We can't spare Able for O'Hare. There's a stack of militiamen and Fist of God terrorists in Northern California, and Rosario decided to try to clean them out before we lost track of them," Price told him. "That's the bad news."

"I don't know," Bolan answered. "Pest control is always good news. Give the guys my best wishes."

"Then you might feel even better about this news. We've got the visuals on a pair of motorcoaches with missionary banners coming to the entrance to O'Hare. Our sniper spotted them and gave us a radio call," Price replied.

"All right. Has Buck got a plan for separating them?" Bolan asked.

"It's in effect."

Bolan took a deep breath. "Buck and the blacksuits have the recording, right?"

"Definitely," Price answered. "He's sending Rutherford and a couple others to meet the motorcoaches since we have the MOPP gear and antisera for them."

"And who's meeting us at the station?"

"Buck, Carmichael, DeForest, Jager and Priest," Price answered. "We've cleared the station and Chicago P.D. is hanging back, providing crowd control."

"Right. I have Jack and Charlie disengaging from the train to keep an eye out for Harpy and her helicopter," Bolan said.

"We've got *Dragon Slayer* on our screens, but Harpy must have been a no-show."

Bolan squinted, looking as the train passed the Rosemont convention center, still keeping up its charge toward destiny. "No. Harpy didn't skip out. We just can't see her."

CHARLES ROCHENOIRE was nestled behind the length of the SIG R-93 LRS2 sniper rifle, it's Leupold scope allowing him to follow the path of the two motorcoaches as they crawled up the driveway toward the terminals. The fully adjustable matte-black synthetic stock was tight to his cheek, which was nearly as dark as the polymer weapon he was pressed against. In his left ear, his Motorolla-encrypted radio relayed messages through an ear-clipped headphone, small and unobtrusive, on a wire with enough slack not to restrict his head movement, but not too loose as to snag on anything. Though, at six-foot-four, Rochenoire was kind of tall to snag himself on any low-lying shrubbery.

The rifle was chambered for the awesome .338 Lapua Magnum round, and he knew it was more than a match for any bus, fancy name or not. As a former SEAL, top marksman in his class, Rochenoire had used similar rifles in operations from Bosnia through Africa.

"Go!" came the hurried order.

Rochenoire touched off the first Lapua Magnum round. Even being two hundred and sixty pounds of muscle, and with the use of a cushioning stock, the rifle still spiked painfully into his shoulder. He didn't mind, though. It was feel-good pain. Every time he felt the sting, innocent people and fellow soldiers were being protected by his marksman's skills.

The grille of the first bus blew out dramatically, and Rochenoire mentally figured on the effect of the pile-driving bullet, tearing through relatively soft aluminum and plastic to punch deeply into the steel of the engine block, smashing the radiator on its journey through. The motorcoach's windshield was suddenly bathed in smoke and steam, brakes pouring out wedges of mist and obviously squealing despite their sound being dampened by distance. The driver skillfully brought the vehicle to a stop, keeping it from flipping over.

The Cherokee whirled and spun out, blocking the path of the other bus on the road. Rochenoire made sure that the second motorcoach couldn't pull any tricks such as backing up and ramming the Jeep. Chambering the second round, he punched a second .338 sizzler across the distance. The Finnish-designed bullet was meant to be the bridge between conventional caliber sniper rifles and the big, booming .50-caliber weapons designed to knock out armored personnel carriers. Against a standard eight-cylinder Detroit engine protected by the front end of an ordinary bus, it was like a head-butting contest between a Chihuahua and a moose. The hood of the vehicle burst open, engine cracked down the center and knocked off the drivetrain.

"Buses down. All yours," Rochenoire called to Rutherford, Ryker and Martinez.

RUTHERFORD SKIDDED the Jeep to a halt and watched the impressive detonation of the engine compartment of the second motorcoach. Because he was driving, Martinez and Ryker went EVA, Heckler & Koch G-36 assault rifles up and tracking. The rifles were sleek, space-age-looking weapons with efficient combat optics built into their carrying handles, and side-swinging folding stocks that the two blacksuits popped open as soon as they left the vehicle.

"Federal officers!" Martinez thundered in his best DEA raid voice. The lungs of the gigantic Hispanic were like bellows, amplifying his voice into a leonine roar.

Ryker poked the muzzle of his G-36 into the face of the driver of the first bus, locking eyes with him. "Keep your hands on the wheel!"

Rutherford was the last one out of the Jeep. Since he was going into the motorcoaches by himself, he wasn't carrying even the compact HK assault rifles; instead he carried the old tried-and-true MP-5K subgun. He swung around and up onto the stairs, bracketing the driver and keeping his weapon locked on the man, an American, while he looked into the coach. Twenty faces looked back at him, all grim and tight-lipped, dark, almond-shaped eyes staring hard, glaring daggers.

"The ampules," he ordered. "Surrender them now."

"Fuck you, Fed," the driver growled. He was reaching for a handgun when outside, a rifle blasted. The brains of the AHC hardman rocketed out a grapefruit-size exit wound in his skull, splashing spectacularly over the roof and the interior windshield. The Filipino men, who were starting to move with the driver's act of defiance, paused, half-risen.

Rutherford leveled his MP-5K at waist level, his features now as intense as theirs had been.

"The ampules! Where are they?" he repeated.

The Filipinos looked among themselves. Outside, more automatic fire filled the air, punctuated by the sonic crack of a heavy rifle.

"Doc, you better hustle it. They're starting to leave the second bus. Toro and I got two," Rochenoire's voice called over his tac radio.

One Filipino reached into his pocket and pulled it out, smiling. "Most everyone else packed theirs with their luggage, but we drew straws. I kept mine, in case someone tried to stop us."

"You'd kill all your people?" Rutherford asked, suddenly aiming the MP-5K at the man's face.

"We took one shot of atropine before we got on the bus," the Biotoxin wielding terrorist said with a grin. "We're protected from—"

"That's not nerve gas," Rutherford answered. "That's Botox. Botulinum toxin."

The man froze.

He turned up his radio. "Play Dark's speech."

"'Well, slipping the Filipinos through as missionaries was a clever idea. Did you convince them the Botox was nerve gas and that they had atropine to protect themselves? Or are they suicidal fanatics?'" one familiar voice, Striker's, asked.

"'We told them that the ampules were Tabur. They have atropine injectors hidden in their toiletry kits disguised as insulin syringes or asthma medicine,'" came the reply in a voice the Filipino man recognized. "'Totally useless against a good virus.'"

Rutherford nodded to the ampule-holding Filipino. "That is an extremely good virus. It'll kill within forty-eight hours, strangling you to death by attacking your body's breathing reflex. There's not enough antisera in this entire city to protect the people in this bus."

The Filipino looked at his glass globe of death, eyes wide, sweat making his bronzed skin glisten. He looked back to Rutherford.

"Put it down. Your fight is done," the blacksuit growled.

That's when Rutherford saw knives appear in a dozen hands, setting sunlight glinting off their polished sides. The dark eyes of the terrorists locked on him.

"No. It's not," the globe-armed Filipino said. He lunged at the blacksuit.

Rutherford ripped off two 3-round bursts, 9 mm slugs smashing the man in the chest and kicking him backward. The ampule fell from shocked fingers as the crowd of Filipino terrorists rose as one. Only the fact that the center aisle of the bus was so tight and the seats were too high to climb over gave the Stony Man blacksuit an opportunity to pull back toward the door, submachine gun ripping out withering bursts of fire. Men screamed as slugs slashed through yielding flesh, but strong hands grabbed Rutherford's gun arm, yanking him up and back into the bus. The sound of smashing glass filled the air and the bio-warfare expert looked to see the ampule, still rolling toward the driver's seat.

Instead, the breaking glass was the windshield, Ryker and his G-36 appearing at the hole. The brooding commando was holding the windowframe with one hand, his assault rifle was in the other, sling tight around his neck.

"Let him go!" Ryker ordered.

The Filipinos yanked harder, trying to drag up Rutherford as a human shield.

"Toro!" Ryker boomed.

Suddenly the entire bus was lit up, 5.56 mm slugs punching through glass and sheet metal, tearing on through human flesh, making the rioting busload of murderers jerk and dance as Martinez and Ryker cut loose. Rutherford pulled his Heckler & Koch with his off hand and brought it up and into the face of one Filipino, smashing a 9 mm skullbreaker between the eyes of one particularly strong man who had a death-grip on his arm. The fingers let go and Rutherford tumbled backward. He scrambled, grabbing a railing, and hauled himself up into the driver's well, hand grabbing the rolling globe of death before it fell to the next step.

A Filipino howled and lunged for the blacksuit and the deadly bio-weapon. Rutherford snapped up his weapon and fired, watching his 9 mm bullets strike the man at the same time his face and upper chest were blasted into chunks by Ryker's G-36.

"The second bus is compromised!" Rochenoire yelled across the tac net.

"Light it up! Light it up!" Rutherford ordered.

Outside, Martinez, whose G-36 was fitted with an HK-79 grenade launcher, cut loose with a single boom-ing round. The motorcoach lurched, a massive fireball spitting out of its side. The luggage compartment was the target of the big blacksuit's weapon, a thermite charge punching through the thin metal and detonating just inside. At thousands of degrees, it would crack glass and cook the viruses in their ampules. The jetting fireball to the outside through the entry hole was only indicative of the initial fury. Up through the floorboards, more flame roared.

"I've got two men running!" Rochenoire warned.

"Heading back to the entry gate! I see something reflecting in their hands!"

Rochenoire's rifle boomed loud enough to be heard over the tac-net radio.

"One runner!" he called.

"I've got the other!" Ryker yelled.

Rutherford slid out of the bus, watching the wiry form of the blacksuit racing down the ribbon of road, G-36 discarded on the ground.

Martinez was busy hammering out bursts, keeping burning terrorists from escaping with more of the deadly Botox. Rutherford started forward, pistol gripped tightly, to assist the big man when a pair of arms wrapped around his head and throat, crushing down on his windpipe. He tried sucking in a breath and found another pair of arms wrapping around the hand holding the glass ampule of death. He struggled hard, stars flashing across his vision as a punch slammed into his kidney. He coughed and snaked his gun hand around and under his armpit, pulling the trigger as he did. The body on his arm went limp, blood spraying and soaking his back and leg, weighing him down.

The vise grip on his neck was still unyielding, and he was feeling the blood hammering inside his skull, trying to escape and get back into his circulatory system. The pressure was crushing. Rutherford, however, wasn't going to play around trying to peel a headlock off him. This wasn't professional wrestling. Instead he brought the muzzle of the H&K to the Filipino's elbow and pulled the trigger. Bone and gore exploded as the joint disintegrated. The stranglehold on his throat was gone and fresh oxygen poured through his bloodstream back into his brain.

The ex-Green Beret spun, slamming his wrist, hand

and the butt of the pistol into the side of his wrestling partner's head. He stomped the Filipino's foot and pushed away and took a step back. He spotted the bloodied and wounded man, glaring hatefully at him, the only glint of hope showing in the eyes of one man watching the glass sphere full of Botox in his hand. Rutherford mentally ran over the number of shots he'd expended from the USP and knew that against six men, even when they were wounded, he wouldn't have enough, not in a mad rush.

"Ryker took down the runner!"

"Charles," Rutherford whispered, "I'm surrounded."

"Shit, Doc. Hang on."

"Where's Toro?" Rutherford asked.

"He went down. A secondary blast from the second bus," Rochenoire answered. "Dammit. Step back. I don't have a clear shot on any of the tangos."

"There's not enough time," Rutherford grated.

"What are you?" Rochenoire began, but Rutherford gave a hard shake of his head. His earpiece popped free. He let go of the pistol, letting it clatter to the ground.

The Filipinos charged him and Rutherford spun, clutching the ampule tight against him. Hands clawed at his chest. He felt the hot fire of a knife plunge into his side, carving his flesh even through his body armor. Wincing, he still managed to rip a soup-can-shaped object from his chest harness. Another blade slashed across the back of his exposed neck, clinking off the bone.

Reaching paws plucked the two orbs from his hands.

"What the fuck?" a Filipino holding Rutherford's canister said, looking at the almost-glowing glass sphere held by one of his partners.

"The Botox doesn't leave this stretch of road," Rutherford croaked as he released the pin on the insurance clause he'd strapped to his chest. The blacksuit closed his eyes peacefully. The fuse on the AN-M14 TH3 thermite grenade finally sizzled down to zero.

The 4000-degree Fahrenheit fireball didn't hurt at all. Especially knowing that the deadly germs wouldn't harm another soul.

THE EXECUTIONER HEARD Charles Rochenoire's shouted "Fuck!" over his tactical radio, and keyed his throat mike.

"What happened?"

"Dammit. Doc blew himself up!" Rochenoire answered, choked with tears.

Bolan felt a pang of regret as the train pulled into the station. "Rutherford?"

"Yeah. He said he was surrounded. He had one of the ampules. I think Toro's down, too."

The Executioner glared at Dark.

"Something wrong?" the madman called from the other car as it ground to a halt.

"You lost the Botox," Bolan told him. "And I lost one, maybe two men."

The doors opened and Bolan, the terrorists and their hostages stepped out onto the platform. Frightened people circled the gunmen, sobs filling the air.

"Go ahead. Open fire. Maybe I'll be dead before half these people die."

Bolan's eyes narrowed. "That's not my plan."

"Just how are you going to do it?" Dark asked.

"That would be telling," Bolan answered. He turned and made an arm motion, keeping the people in the last two cars in place. They took the signal and stayed put.

Dark turned back and pointed to the engineer. "Take them away."

"Not going to go through me to get more hostages?" Bolan asked as the driver raced into the first car.

"No. We can afford a couple extra bodies," Dark responded.

Bolan circled the group, watching the train back out of the station from the corner of his eye. The platform was parallel to three others, separated by four sets of train tracks. Slabs of walkway were along each wall, and the roof was amazingly high from the Executioner's perspective. If he measured it, he'd figure it to be seventy-five, eighty feet high above the tracks, with escalators leading to each platform swooping up to a walkway leading off into a cavernous tunnel to the right. The train had come through a half mile underground into the womb beneath O'Hare's terminals, and he knew that they were right beneath the complex of buildings where passengers were probably packed.

The tunnel, though, was empty of the enemy. All he could see were the black-clad figures with Heckler Y Koch G-36 assault rifles, aiming down from the choke points at the top of each set of escalators and stairs. Bolan knew that the men and woman behind those rifles could put a bullet through a target the size of a playing card at one hundred meters with the accurate, well-calibrated combat weapons. The only problem was that as good as they were, Buck Greene and his forces simply didn't have the ability to take out more than a handful of targets in a second. And after that second was up, the terrorists would react with their own gunfire, slaughtering hostages.

According to Greene, the National Guard and O'Hare security were keeping the crowds of civilians back from the entrance of the tunnels, themselves beneath the main concourses matriced above. Right now, they were at the very bottom of the airport, only utility tunnels conceivably running below his feet. He felt the empty glass sphere in his pocket and narrowed his eyes.

Bolan pulled it from his pocket, letting the reflection of the fluorescent lights high above flare dramatically. He looked down at it, then up at Dark.

"Funny thing, these. They take a particularly hard impact to break," Bolan said, rolling the ball designed to hold death between his fingers, keeping it hidden enough so that, watching from twenty feet away, they couldn't tell it was empty. "But they will eventually break."

Dark's eyes narrowed. "He's bluffing!"

Bolan glanced up, seeing doubt forming on some faces. Two men, one of whom Bolan recognized as the AHC terrorist Dark had slammed face-first through a window, was staring daggers at their leader. He returned his gaze impassively to the globe in his hand. "There's enough sera in these spheres to take out a small town, or a company of soldiers."

The hostages were terrified, but panic was sweeping across the group of gunmen. Bolan had an ace in his hand, to them, because you couldn't shoot a virus. Even if they blew away their human shields, eventually they would succumb to whatever horrors the Executioner gripped in his hand. The riflemen that were staring down at them were suddenly of no consequence.

He kept up the pressure. "And of course, these were designed for airburst. There's more than enough anti-sera being shipped in to protect the men aiming those nasty black rifles at you. However, I don't think we'd have enough to spare on a gunman hiding behind a hos-

SEASON OF SLAUGHTER 315

tage. I think saving the taxpayers' money on life-saving drugs for you *and* a trial would be all for the best."

The gunmen were shifting now. Instead of ringing themselves with hostages, they were shoving their captives to form a wall between them and Bolan, as if the human bodies they hid behind could somehow stop a sudden wave of death.

Dark was standing in front of that wall of humanity, glaring back at his troops as they cowered in retreat. "You're good, Stone. Very good. But my boys are still behind cover."

Bolan looked at the wall behind the terrorists. It was the middle of an arch over tunnels that lead a short way even deeper beyond the platform, though in each entrance a red and blue concrete divider with yellow and black stripes across the top prevented further progress of the trains. He looked back to Dark and shrugged, then lobbed the glass ampule up and over the group of people, sailing it to shatter against the concrete wall behind the terrorists.

Panicked hostages and militiamen alike dived to the ground or raced forward to escape Bolan's bluff.

CHAPTER TWENTY-FOUR

Buck Greene had known that the Executioner was a man of great battle savvy. He was one of the most blooded, experienced soldiers alive. He'd rarely seen the man in action, had only glimpses of his battlefield skills as he'd assisted in repelling assaults on Stony Man Farm from the forces of COMCON, or the hypnotized members of Able Team. It was only now, watching him coordinate Dark and his forces into a corner, and bluff them into blind panic, that he truly understood the skill of the soldier.

It was one thing just to go blazing insanely into action. But thinking with his guns wasn't what kept the warrior alive through countless battles with the forces of organized crime and the wet works sections of some of the most ruthless intelligence agencies in the world. Even the savage street cunning of terrorist organizations would have been enough to pin down and slaughter one man who wasn't a tactical genius. But the genius just wasn't in combat movement.

It also came in the form of psychology.

It was all about the bluff, being someone who was

either important and had purpose, or was just completely relaxed and part of the backdrop.

That bluff was also a weapon that the Executioner had used to slash apart alliances, a deadly cutting tool that wrecked faith and trust and set partners against each other, leaving them off balance for his own deadly Bolan blitz, a final knockout punch that smashed the remnants into useless garbage. Greene knew the after-action reports that detailed these things, reconstructions from law enforcement agencies and data picked up by the Farm's cybercrew.

Watching the man at work, though, was like seeing a master sorcerer work his spells. A determined, hostage-holding force was suddenly thrown into disarray by a single, empty glass ball.

"Take them!" Bolan's voice growled over the tac radio. "No survivors!"

The Executioner yelled again. "The third rail's off! Take cover!"

To his left, Jager was first on target with his G-36. A 3-round burst drilled into a Fist of God soldier just above his collarbone. From the angle, the slight rise of the high-tech rifle on recoil sent the second and third bullets sheering off the gunman's jaw and smashing his nose down and out the back of his neck in a volcanic blast of gore. It was as though he'd run into an invisible clothesline, his legs kicking out in front of him, his body flopping hard onto his back. The blacksuit on his immediate right fired a longer burst on full automatic, sweeping two targets with an extended blast of 5.56 mm NATO hollowpoints, catching them both in their chests, ripping them through and through.

The youngest of the blacksuits, John Carmichael, opened up, stepping out in the open and making himself a more attractive target to the killers below. It was a crazy, almost suicidal ploy, but the gunmen below were too frantic and terrified to aim well, especially with hostages jostling past them. Pulling the stock of his G-36 to his shoulder, he fired off three quick shots in rapid succession, semiauto all the one. One bullet, one target, and three of the terrorists crashed to the ground before the blacksuit took a dive to avoid a wave of gunfire flashing up toward him. The easy mark denied, the terrorists realized that they were too far separated for the civilians to make decent human shields.

Priest and Greene cut in with their HK autorifles, sweeping the gunners as they were disorganized and demoralized. Bodies twisted and jerked, coming under assault from two levels as Bolan had joined the party now, having held his fire until the hostages instinctively threw themselves off the platform and onto the tracks, seeking the safe shelter of the concrete slabs. The terrorists, certain that Bolan's warning was a trap, and seeing Dark take a flying leap from one walkway to another, were huddled out in the open.

Cover and concealment weren't their strong points, and Greene's rifle ripped out a staccato lesson to the doomed terrorists, bullets smashing and pulverizing flesh and bone. Impacts shattered the tile-covered concrete the Stony Man security chief was crouched behind, but he didn't allow himself to flinch. As long as enemy fire was hitting something solid and not him, he was going to keep pouring on the heat.

The last demoralized terrorist hit the ground, blood still pouring from his sieved torso, and Bolan was taking off on foot, reloading his OA-93 assault pistol as he raced along. Greene scanned around, looking for a trench-coat-wearing corpse, and realized that Dark had once again escaped. Greene rose slightly.

"Buck, take care of the hostages! Nobody else goes after Dark except me!" Bolan ordered.

"Don't get cowboy on me, Striker," Greene growled.

"I'm going to contain this conflict. You need to get the hostages to safety. Which is more important to you?"

"Dammit," Greene muttered.

"Make sure all the accesses to these tunnels are covered," Bolan shouted. "Anyone spots Dark making a break for it, blow the hole and don't worry about me getting caught in the backlash. He gets stopped here!"

THE EXECUTIONER EXPLODED full speed down the tunnel, only slowing to plant his hand on the top of the concrete divider and launch himself over the yellow-and-black banded top, sailing six feet past the blockage before his boots crashed to the ground. He picked up speed again and accelerated.

Dark's men were bleeding and dead behind him, cast to their universal judgment, whatever it would be. Only one man escaped, Dark himself, disappearing with the speed and slickness of a snake. If Bolan hadn't caught the flash of his trench coat slithering over the top of the divider that lead into the train tunnels during the firefight, the murderer would have been gone for good. As it was, the mercenary in black still had a head start, and Bolan heard the sound of boot soles scraping the sides of a ladder up ahead.

He raced to the hole, skidded to a stop just in front of it and plucked a flash-bang grenade from his harness. He dropped the stun bomb down the entrance to the access tunnel. Bolan barely pulled his hand back in time to avoid having it shot off by a spray of fire from a 9 mm Calico submachine gun. There was a muffled curse and the sound of stomping feet.

Bolan stepped forward and let himself drop, grabbing the ladder and skidding down the same way Dark had. As soon as he was about ten feet from the bottom of the ladder, he let go, twisting his body in middrop and coming down on one knee. The Olympic Arms chattergun was up and tracking down the tunnel where he saw a flash of Dark's trench coat, like a fleeing demon's wings. He triggered the OA-93, sending a short burst after his enemy, rounds sparking on concrete and pipe. A hand snaked out around the corner.

Bolan threw himself flat as the muzzle-flash of the Calico slashed the half shadows ahead. The burst of 9 mm hollowpoints rang out as they struck the tubed steel of the ladder, and he hissed as a single ricochet sliced along his calf.

The Executioner drove himself to his feet, ignoring the nick and holding down the trigger to send out a volley of six rounds, driving Dark farther behind cover. He charged the corner, free hand reaching into his war bag to pull another grenade. He spotted something skid around the corner, rebounding off a pipe. The bounce was exactly right to angle it toward the speeding soldier, and Bolan recognized the hockey puck, at least in principle.

The warrior ground to a halt, sweeping the ground in front of it with a volley of 5.56 mm NATO rounds. One round smacked into the black shell of the mini-bomb, kicking it back along the hallway. Bolan whirled and threw himself as far as he could, landing in a curled ball just before the detonation of the plastic explosive went off in a blast that shook him to the core.

After the blast faded, he saw the space beneath the pipes running along the left side of the tunnel and instinctively rolled for them. He had barely wedged underneath when a second volley of 9 mm autofire chased hungrily out around the corner, gouts of concrete dust puffing into the air as Dark held down the trigger. Bolan couldn't maneuver even the short OA-93 out from under the pipes, so he grabbed his Desert Eagle from its hip holster and took aim.

Three trigger pulls and a trio of 240-grain hollow-points screamed out of the barrel of the mighty Magnum pistol, ripping across the distance between the muzzle and Dark, and punching quarter-size holes in the wall of the T intersection the murderer had ducked into. The man spun out of the way and disappeared down the turnoff. Bolan yanked himself out from under the pipes and was on his feet in moments, the big Israeli Magnum autoloader still in his fist. Still tightly clenched in his other hand was the Olympic Arms subgun. He swung around the corner, bringing up both weapons.

Both guns were triggered as he entered the mouth of the new tunnel, .44 Magnum and 5.56 mm NATO slugs screaming in a maddened swarm toward any and all living flesh in the tunnel, but Dark was gone. The soldier bit off a curse and continued on, steam hissing from the damage he had caused to some minor pipes with his fusillade. Running at full throttle, he hit the corner and felt the impact of several pounds of steel and polymer bouncing hard off his chest.

The Desert Eagle flew from his fingers, the Olympic Arms bouncing on its sling around his neck as Dark's double pistol-whip with his Calico 950 SMGs struck Bolan in his ribs. He felt his feet slipping out from under him, body going into an out of control slide when he reached out, grabbed the heavy fabric of his enemy's trench coat and pulled hard.

He gained a small measure of his balance and snapped his head forward into Dark's breastbone, the impact causing him to see stars as he struck his enemy's trauma plate. The black-clad mercenary clawed down hard at the Executioner's face and only succeeded in getting one hand trapped by his iron-hard grip. Bolan shoved the Calico-filled fist back toward the pipes as Dark twisted the gun and fired.

Though no bullets came anywhere near the Executioner's head, the bottom-ejecting machine pistol sent a stream of hot 9 mm brass bouncing right off of the soldier's face, shocking him into letting go and finally dropping to the floor. Dark brought his guns back around, swinging them both to empty them into Bolan at point-blank range, but the soldier thrust his fist hard between his enemy's thighs, putting every ounce of force he could behind the punch. Dark let out a strangled gurgle, his body bouncing off the wall.

The long-maned killer spun away, gasping for breath as Bolan clawed to get into a seated position, leveling his weapon at his adversary's exposed back. With a sudden intake of breath, Dark recovered and whipped one leg up and around, smashing the OA-93 between boot heel and wall. The Executioner let go of the gun at the last moment, saving his hand from being crushed between concrete and the frame of his own weapon.

Dark took off again, dropping a pair of canisters behind him that spit out torrents of heavy fog. Bolan pulled his Beretta 93-R and launched a salvo of 9 mm bursts through the accumulating clouds. He recognized the quick work of a pair of M-18 smoke grenades. There was a muffled curse from beyond the smoke screen and the Executioner lurched back to his feet. He spun away and inspected the Olympic Arms subgun, feeling a massive dent in the magazine well. The gun was completely useless now, unless Bolan was going to feed single rounds through the exposed breech, a combat strategy even the desperate soldier considered nothing but pure folly at this point. He pulled the sling over his head, let the weapon clatter to the ground and looked around for the .44 Desert Eagle. The big pistol was on the ground not far from his foot and he scooped it up, holstering it after a quick check to see that the heavy frame and slide were undamaged.

Bolan cut through the smoke, Beretta leading the way.

JACK GRIMALDI SAW the detonation off in the distance and felt his stomach twist queasily as he heard Rochenoire's report of Rutherford's death. *Dragon Slayer,* though, was ordered by Bolan to continue a sweep for an invisible-to-radar helicopter that was stalking O'Hare, and the distance across the facility was too great, not to mention that crossing the paths of several runways would have caused accidents and harmed countless more innocents.

It still didn't make the sacrifice of a single brave man any better.

Grimaldi's jaw clenched tight and he continued looking. A short glance over to Charlie Mott told the Stony Man top gun that he wasn't the only one left seething over the loss of the brave blacksuit.

These bastards were going to pay.

Out of the corner of his eye, Grimaldi spotted two flashes and he swung around to see another helicopter rising from behind an overpass on the highway. The twin missiles soared, looping up and over the road and beelining toward the radar tower.

There wasn't even time for Grimaldi to shout, "Hold on!" He pushed the throttle for all it was worth, cranking *Dragon Slayer* around in a body-wrenching spin. His targeting optics tracked the first of the sizzling pair, and he let go of a burst with the GECAL. Instead of taking out the missile, he only ended up shattering a hole in the tarmac skirting one of the terminals.

Mott slammed a button on the console, hissing a curse as he did so. "Evasive!"

Grimaldi glanced at Mott, wondering if his partner had gone mad, then he noticed the console was lit up, the ground-effect radar screen glowing with the images of the two missiles. The deadly darts swerved off their course, turning in as tight a circle as they could. *Dragon Slayer* yanked into a power dive, the sleek craft knifing between the roaring weapons before they came out of their turn, but still long after they committed to charging after the Stony Man war machine.

Mott turned off the radar and checked the rear-looking camera. "The missiles are changing course."

"Picking up on O'Hare's radar again," Grimaldi cursed. "Buck! Barb! Anyone! Can we get that thing turned off?"

"Working on it," Price answered over the tac net. "But we have to get the airplanes up and into an orbit around the airport."

"Just get it done," Grimaldi hissed. He was flashing back to the 737 smashing into the ground at Dulles, the helpless moments when he was fighting an imaginary stick to keep the aircraft from crashing. "What about the data being piped in from San Fran?"

"That's shut down," Price answered.

"It'd take too long to program new routines into the ground control software they hacked," Grimaldi growled.

"That, and Gadgets and company are ripping the hell out of a militia base as we speak," Price responded. "I just wish you guys had a magic laser—"

"You have better than that," Professor Sable Burton interrupted. "You have a quantum electronics physicist. I'm not a rocket scientist, but I think I can take out the missiles."

Another pair of MARS rockets took flight and Mott activated the ground-effect radar again, sweeping the duo that had just launched. They snapped around, facing down *Dragon Slayer* head-on. Grimaldi, not having to aim ahead of the racing missiles, locked his GECAL onto one then the other, ripping out short taps of .50-caliber devastation that blew the deadly pair of missiles out of the sky.

"O'Hare's main radar down!" Mott called.

Something detonated on a rooftop on one of the terminal buildings, and Grimaldi's knuckles tightened on the stick.

"The MARS found a secondary target," Burton explained. "Weather radar!"

"That means we have aircraft in danger because they have their own radar systems!" Mott noted. "We're not the only things up here with radio signals pouring off them."

"It takes a few moments for the MARS to weasel in on a frequency, though," Burton answered. "And I'm working on something back here. You won't need these radios, right?"

Grimaldi looked back over his shoulder to see Burton fiddling with some tape and the AN/PRC-68 radios that were stored in a cabinet under the back seat. "What are you doing?"

"Radar is a radio transmission. The missiles lock on to that signal, be it from a weather radar or a communications center," the woman said, taping down the transmit button on the first radio after setting it to a certain frequency. "The MARS system was found in testing to be attracted also to communications signals as well as active radar."

Grimaldi watched as another missile flashed, locking on to *Dragon Slayer* and curving toward her flight path. He checked the console, but Mott hadn't activated the radar again.

"Get us over some clear ground!" Burton ordered.

Grimaldi swung *Dragon Slayer* over a grassy strip between runways and Burton pitched her radio out the window. The Stony Man pilot watched the distance between the missile and the helicopter shrink before it finally dipped and swung into a dive. Ground detonated, sending divots of earth vomiting into the sky.

"Barb! Was anyone hurt when that missile hit?"

"The National Guard and O'Hare security have been working on evacuations, so the top floors were empty. There's a hell of a hole in that roof, though!" Price answered.

"Another missile! It's homing in on us!" Mott shouted.

"Shit! Sorry, Barb!" Grimaldi killed the radio and swung the helicopter around. Instead the MARS speared skyward, seeking out a new concentration of radio signals.

A collection of squad cars that left their dispatch radios turned on.

"No!" Grimaldi shouted.

A couple of officers who had stayed back at the cars looked up, seeing doom sizzling in on them, and the Stony Man pilot had no clear shot.

"Light 'em up!" Grimaldi told Mott, who was already hammering the ground-effect radar controls. A pulse of invisible energy swept out of *Dragon Slayer* and washed over the MARS rocket. It suddenly rose, engines straining, swinging up and around to go after the Stony Man sky warriors.

"Get that next PRC working!" Grimaldi called back.

"Already doing it!" Burton answered.

"You know, this is a hell of a bug for a weapons system," Mott said over his shoulder.

Burton tore free the strip of electrical tape and launched the radio out the window. "Yeah, well we were deciding whether to fix it to a certain range, or just tell the military that they could target communications centers with it."

The tarmac exploded erupting chunks of concrete and asphalt as the MARS met the signal-spitting PRC to punctuate Burton's point.

Grimaldi laughed. "And you know, they'd probably pay you double for that bug."

HARPY SIGHED as the last of her missiles took out nothing more important than a stretch of clean tarmac. At least she'd made a couple of impressive potholes with the MARS weapons system that they'd spent so much time and energy to steal. Chicago's O'Hare airport was at least shut down, and airliners were circling high above, running low on fuel, passengers gripped in terror at the aerial fight going on below.

When it came down to it, Harpy didn't give a damn about high-tech weapons, and she shot the Bell JetRanger forward. Built on the same technology as the military-spec Kiowa OH-58 Warrior, the JetRanger was easily retrofitted by Fixx, the RING's mechanical genius and weapons engineer, to carry all the power, technology and firepower of its armed forces' counterpart. She had even managed to turn the 4-shot Hellfire modular pod designed for the Kiowa craft into a 6-shot MARS launcher. On the other side of the craft, an M-2 Browning .50-caliber heavy machine gun rode on its own.

The only thing missing on the JetRanger from the Kiowa was the mast-mounted sight containing a cluster of thermal imaging, television, laser targeting and boresight systems. Harpy didn't mind. That big gourd-shaped protrusion from the top of the helicopter's rotorstalk only made the ship slower and less agile. Harpy swung the JetRanger out and swooped toward the terminal concourse, activating the firing control on the M-2 hanging off her right side. It wouldn't provide the same kind of explosive force as the MARS missiles, but the .50-caliber machine gun was a destruction machine.

Her first burst targeted a fuel truck, sending a column of fire and smoke spitting up from the ground, not far from her enemy's gunship. The war machine whipped away from the sudden updraft of blazing flame, the turret underneath stuttering in response.

Harpy had watched the GECAL machine gun at work before, and knew that it was probably optically guided. She had just barely dipped the JetRanger behind the top level of a terminal building before an explosive line of impacts signaled the GECAL's assault on the roof of the building. Twisting her own craft around, she popped out at the far end and triggered her M-2, the machine gun releasing a spray of sparks across the side of the aircraft.

Dragon Slayer flinched under the multiple impacts, and a second burst from the GECAL missed Harpy's killer bird by several feet.

As soon as the GECAL started, it stopped, and Harpy felt a grin cross her hard face. The enemy pilots were afraid to use too much of their terrible and much more effective machine gun for fear of having their bursts hit homes miles away or penetrate into areas where civilians were huddling in fear.

"Fun at your expense," Harpy quipped as she kept her craft swinging low by the terminal buildings, sweeping her fire toward the big helicopter, which dodged, jinking straight up, forcing her almost to go climbing after the chopper. But she caught herself as the enemy pilot flipped his ship around, taking aim.

"C'mon, shoot me," Harpy said out loud, knowing her enemy couldn't hear her, but enjoying throwing the taunt anyway. She had control of the situation, and fired off a couple more bursts from the M-2, wanting to take down the defending helicopter, but also keeping enough in reserve to cut loose with a barrage of slaughter on the airport.

Tears were going to be shed by the gallon today, if she had her way.

"THAT BITCH, Harpy, is living up to her name," Burton commented as she looked out the window. *Dragon Slayer* was a mess inside. The pounding by the enemy machine gun had hammered across the insides of the helicopter. The cockpit windshields were cracked and starred, and all but impossible to see through, Grimaldi having to use the television cameras installed on the high-tech craft to steer by. Charlie Mott was squirming into the back of the cabin with her.

"Name or not, we can't use our big guns on her," Mott replied. "Not when we've got her using the civilians behind her."

Burton watched as he snapped down one of the XM-134 Gatling guns on its mount.

"That's not a heavy weapon?" Sable asked.

"It's 7.62 mm NATO. At this range, it won't punch through ordinary building materials," Mott answered, "even at 3000 rpm."

"Three thousand rounds per minute?" Burton asked. She watched him set up the gun, then reached up and brought the one on her side of the cabin down.

"What are you doing?" Mott asked.

"Repetition after observation," she answered. "It's how I learned to be a fencer, it's how I learned to drive like a demon. It'll be how I learn how to shoot one of these video-game chain guns."

"Gatling gun. Electric-motor powered," Grimaldi corrected. "No chain function involved. If we get through this, I'll show you a real chain gun."

"I guess this is your answer to rocket science," Burton replied.

"Strap into your harness!" Mott called to her.

The woman spotted the harness attachments in the ceiling. Heavy bolts, thick nylon webbing and strong steel links formed a suspension system that was quick to get into. She grabbed the pistol grip of the XM-134 and her other hand found a side-mounted handle that she gripped tightly. She glanced back to see if Mott was doing the same. In that instant, the helicopter swung around and momentum swung her out the side door.

Sheer panic hit her, and she immediately regretted

being stuck out on a suddenly flimsy-looking network of straps and buckles as O'Hare airport spun crazily beneath her.

"Sable!" Grimaldi shouted. "Are you okay?"

Gunfire thundered on the other side as Charlie Mott opened up with his own weapon. He was hanging out in the wind, too, and he wasn't looking much more comfortable than she was.

"Sable! She's coming around your side!" Mott called.

The woman looked out at the world sweeping past her and saw the ugly black shape of the Bell JetRanger in the distance. "I see her!"

Muzzle-flashes flickered on the side of Harpy's craft and Burton let out a scream as heavy slugs smashed into the side armor of the whirlybird. She pulled the trigger, letting off a tongue of flame three feet long, bullets arcing out. It was an unaimed burst, but the enemy helicopter banked and ducked.

"Use your sights!" Grimaldi recommended.

"No shit," Burton hissed as *Dragon Slayer* was still soaring, racing in a tight circle. She brought the JetRanger into the middle of the huge 3-inch-diameter crosshairs of her gun and held down the trigger. Sparks of fire danced along the skin of Harpy's warbird and the Bell aircraft swerved and ducked around the corner of the terminal.

"G-Force, this is Blacksuit 10," the voice of Charles Rochenoire called. "Enemy helicopter is now strafing Chicago police positions along the concourse!"

"Who was that?" Burton asked.

"The sniper we have atop the Hilton!" Mott answered.

"Chuck! You have a shot?" Grimaldi asked.

"I'm taking it!" the sniper answered.

Dragon Slayer zoomed around, hot on Harpy's tail, and watched as the JetRanger jerked in reaction to a heavy impact. From below, beleagured lawmen were firing their weapons into the sky, National Guardsmen pouring out of one terminal and emptying their M-16s into the air. Burton, hanging out the side of the Stony Man warcraft, watched all of this with breathless amazement.

Squad cars detonated as .50-caliber slugs smashed into them. Wounded police officers were being dragged aside by anyone who could still move, including civilians who were rushing out the doors to grab the brave Chicago lawmen. Harpy's helicopter spun around and was flying backward, spitting more hellfire toward the scattering National Guard troops. A couple fell, others diving behind parked vehicles that shook under the devil's storm that swept down onto them.

Burton pulled the trigger on her Gatling gun, feeling it shake violently against her. On the other side, Charlie Mott was shooting, too, but the combined fire once more proved only to be a nuisance to the armored Bell. That's when *Dragon Slayer* truly shook.

Grimaldi had a straight bead on her, and there was nothing but road behind Harpy. The GECAL .50 opened up, and now, being almost on top of the machine gun, Burton could truly feel the air vibrate, her own heart feeling the shock waves off the muzzle of the thundering cannon. The JetRanger banked, swerved and dodged as asphalt behind her was chewed up, chunks of stone turning to clouds of dust under Grimaldi's merciless jackhammer assault.

"Why won't she die?" Burton shouted.

Dragon Slayer slashed around the corner, hot on

Harpy's tail. The black helicopter was making a break for it, racing toward the expressway.

Burton triggered her gun, watching her rounds miss and create puffs of smoke on the ground just past the hurtling craft. She growled angrily when the GECAL exploded again.

This time, there was a hit. The tail boom, sticking out like the tail of some muscular shark, suddenly disintegrated under a hail of .50-caliber slugs. The JetRanger, crippled, began to spin out of control. A slash of gunfire from both Mott and Burton joined in with Grimaldi's .50, but it was just icing on the cake. The professor was getting in her licks, emptying out a belt of 7.62 mm shells into the tumbling enemy aircraft. It burst into flames as it continued its wild, out-of-control drop from the sky.

All that was left when it hit the ground was a brittle eggshell that smashed apart, vomiting red-gold flames in blossoms of ejecta.

Doomsday had finally come for Harpy as Jack Grimaldi whipped his aircraft over the churning remains of the downed mercenary.

CHAPTER TWENTY-FIVE

Spinning around one corner, Bolan saw Dark hurtling up a ladder. Bolan's Beretta chugged out a quick 3-round burst, the slugs sparking on steel and rebounding off the stone ceiling of the tunnel. A hissed curse reached his ears, and Bolan poured on the speed, in time with another dropping object.

Dark wasn't out of grenades yet, and he was throwing another hellbomb into the Executioner's path. Bolan launched himself in a desperate leap around the corner he'd come from just as a shock wave flashed past him. His head rang, but thanks to a loud yell that equalized the pressure inside and outside of his eardrums, he still retained the ability to hear, and possibly saved himself from even brain trauma. Bolan turned to head back for the ladder when a second object dropped down and he slipped back behind the corner again.

This time, the flash-blast swept by harmlessly, Bolan still pressurized against the shock wave.

Two grenades in five seconds, Bolan figured. Dark was heading for the surface and looking to keep his adversary at bay, not wanting to end his career shot in the back and dropping lifelessly down a tall ladder. The soldier counted a few more moments, then risked heading down the tunnel, racing full-speed for it. He skidded to a halt under the opening, aiming his Beretta up into the shaft, just catching sight of Dark's legs and the tails of his coat. A 3-round burst zipped up at 1200 feet per second, but there was no distant cry.

Bolan holstered the Beretta and grabbed the rungs, climbing for all he was worth. His arms and legs rippled as he pushed them, but he ignored their protests. He was bordering on exhaustion. He remembered the past twenty-four hours, and the catalog of conflict he'd torn through in that time was a frantic sweep of terror and mayhem that made his fatigued body yearn for the comfort of a bed for about a week.

Finally popping up through the opening, Bolan saw that it was a level of a parking garage. A blast of 9 mm Calico fire slashed at him and he ducked.

The Executioner went over his knowledge of the area and didn't come up with good news. The parking garage was a six-story structure in the V formed by Terminal Three, the bus and shuttle center, and Terminal One. There were too many variables for Dark to take now. If he got to the center of the structure, and Bolan wasn't even sure where they were in relation to it, he could drop back down and into the Airport Transit System. Operating as a free train system, it connected the three domestic and one international terminals, as well as the parking lot and, most importantly, the Metra train station.

Dark escaping by train would be another nightmare, especially since he'd have access to a whole new group of hostages, or could disappear into a crowd at almost any stop along the line.

Bolan climbed out of the hole and scanned the area for his enemy. He caught the shadow of a racing figure pounding up a ramp and took off in hot pursuit. Rounding to the entrance of the road, he was rewarded by a wild slash of autofire that he charged past, plunging forward and keeping ahead of Dark's ability to adjust his aim.

"Sarge? Is that you huffing and puffing?" Grimaldi asked over the tac radio.

"Yeah. I'm in pursuit of Dark. He's heading up the floors in the main parking garage. What kind of presence do I have in here with me?"

"Blacksuit Prime here. We've got Chicago P.D. at the entrances, but the structure was evacuated while the Filipinos were coming up from I-294," Greene's voice cut in. "In case we had a Botox escape."

Bolan turned another corner and spotted Dark at the top of the ramp, aiming both Calicos at him. With a leap, the Executioner took to the air, twisting his body in midflight as 9 mm slugs ripped below him. The soldier got off several shots; .44 Magnum rounds drilled toward the RING killer. Dark jerked under one impact, and he spun away, letting out a loud curse. Bolan came down, skidding on the hard concrete, but still maintaining his grip on the big cannon in his fist.

"Give it up! You're surrounded!" Bolan ordered.

Dark slithered out of sight, but there was no more sound of running. Only painful panting.

"You're offering to take me alive?" Dark asked.

The Executioner lifted himself from the ground, aiming at the concrete wall of the ramp, the corner of stone that Dark was hiding behind. He advanced slowly. "I'm offering you more mercy than you've ever given in your career."

"A bullet in the head instead of rotting in a hole?"

"Your call," Bolan answered, stepping closer. Fatigue weighed on him like a hundred pounds of wet blanket, but he still walked toward the turn.

"But you'd so rather prefer I tell you everything I know about the RING, wouldn't you?" Dark asked.

A lazy burst of 9 mm autofire came around the corner, but it was nowhere close to Bolan. The far wall was pocked with fresh bullet scars.

"Just drop the gun, Dark."

It clattered to the ground.

"Is there any reason why you have to be a right bastard?" Dark asked.

Bolan paused as he neared the corner. "Only because you're always wrong."

Turning the corner, he caught sight of Dark's boots and trench coat poking out around the corner. Something was wrong, though. He took a giant step back and spotted the coatless and barefoot Dark hanging from the lip of the road above the way.

The Executioner snapped up his Desert Eagle, but he knew in his heart he was too late. Naked soles crashed painfully down into his chest as a 240-grain hollowpoint only glanced off Dark's chest armor. The two bodies plowed into the railing and Bolan winced as his back barked against the sharp corner of concrete. Dark's legs snaked around Bolan's arm and the barefoot killer dropped back to his shoulders, gripping the Executioner's gun hand.

Incredible pain flared through the soldier's body as his joint was stressed. A heel pressed hard up against the corner of his jaw, and Dark's other leg was over the top of Bolan's bicep and across Dark's own shin. The Executioner knew he had only a few moments before his bones shattered and his enemy ripped his arm right out of the socket. His left hand flashed down to a pocket in his battle harness and pulled out an L-shaped piece of fiberglass with a ring-style wrench head at one end.

It was an Impact Kerambit, developed by Kelly Worden. Based on the hook-bladed knife of the same name, it was a replacement for the Executioner's brass knuckles. As soon as his left finger hooked through the wrench head at the top of the L, his fingers wrapped around the handle, leaving a jutting hook of fiberglass, able to amplify punching force dozens of times.

His first punch struck the muscle of Dark's thigh, eliciting a screech of pain as the striker plunged into vulnerable flesh. A muscle spasm shot up the murderer's leg and suddenly the agonizing pressure on Bolan's shoulder was halved. The Executioner threw himself bodily against the upended Dark, driving him harder into the ground and cutting the distance between his fist and the barefoot terrorist's more vital areas. A second fist pumped with jackhammer force into Dark's gut, and despite the heavy Kevlar protecting the man's vitals, there was a sickening, almost wretching noise.

Dark pulled his foot from Bolan's jaw, then stomped out hard, the kick holding enough force to daze the tall wraith in black. The Executioner didn't drop his Kerambit, though, punching his enemy in his other thigh, this time hitting right over the bone. The pressure on his joint disappeared suddenly, both legs falling from around his right arm.

There was still the deathgrip on Bolan's wrist, however, and with a savage twist, the Executioner felt his tendons overextending. The soldier hammered a merciless fist down into Dark's chest, trauma plate cracking under the savage impact of Bolan's desperate punch.

Bolan pulled back, free of Dark, wrist and shoulder throbbing until they were insensate.

With a frantic lunge, Dark was away from the Executioner. Bolan let the Kerambit drop off his hand and was reaching for his holstered Beretta 93-R when one of Dark's boots hurtled at him. The move took the soldier off guard as the thrown size 12 combat boot mashed hard into his nose and cheek. Flesh tore on Bolan's cheek and his draw was interrupted enough for the barefoot battler to move and take the offensive.

Fists pumped into the Executioner's sides and kidneys, only his Kevlar armor blunting the force of the blows enough to keep him on his feet. Bolan popped his left palm into Dark's jaw, his heel slipping over his enemy's chin and smashing up and into the pointed nose of the black-maned terrorist. Blood gushed into his hand and the murderer spun away from his assault, dazed by the sudden impact.

Bolan pressed his advantage, hammering the base of Dark's skull with a solid hit that made his hand sting. The Executioner stomped down hard on one bare foot, feeling bones crunch even through the sole of his boot. The double impact was answered with a piston-quick elbow that felt as though it cracked a rib, even through his body armor. Lungs on fire from exertion and the sudden spike of pain searing through his torso, Bolan snaked his right arm around Dark's throat and pulled back with all his weight.

The tall terrorist in black didn't bother trying to break the noose of Bolan's arm, instead hooking his fingers under the Stony Man warrior's forearm and wrenching him completely off the ground, flipping his back down mercilessly onto the concrete. The Executioner hit with a stunning impact, but snapped off a kick that cracked hard against Dark's shoulder. There was the sound of crunching bone, and the RING assassin recoiled.

Bolan rolled to his hands and knees, his right elbow giving out as he tried to keep himself somewhat upright. He looked up in time to see his barefoot foe leapfrog over him and scramble away, loping with impressive speed despite favoring one foot. The Executioner whirled to see his enemy race out of sight up the ramp.

Pulling his Beretta with his still throbbing left hand, he scrambled up the ramp.

An engine growled throatily to life.

Dark had stored a car on the third level of the main parking garage. He probably had his whole route mapped out, Bolan figured. He didn't doubt that the professional killer had scouted this path months before, and had an escape clause only he would know about. Something to get him away from both the law and possibly even his RING allies in case of a failure.

Bolan watched a pair of headlights turn the corner, blazing as they aimed at him. The Executioner stabbed the Beretta ahead of him, ripping off 3-round bursts as he frantically dived out of the way of the speeding car. It was coming around so suddenly that he didn't even have time to see the make of the car, just that it was big and fast and bearing down hard on him. He felt the rush of air as the four-wheeled missile continued on its suicidal charge.

Stone exploded and the front end of the car smashed inward, but sheer momentum plowed the vehicle out over the outdoor parking lots. Bolan whirled, watching in shock as Dark's car tumbled in midair, knifing through the sky as it sailed toward parked automobiles below.

The shock wave released on impact with the parking lot bowled the Executioner over even on the third level of the garage. Policemen below screamed in terror and awe as Dark's getaway car detonated with the force of a bomb.

Knowing Dark, it probably *was* a bomb.

Bolan dragged himself toward the ragged exit hole, swallowing hard as he slumped against what was left of the railing, looking at the funeral pyre, boiling smoke billowing from a white-hot field of melting metal and rubber. The crater formed by the impact was big enough to have taken out at least ten cars, several more being splashed with flames, hoods and roofs burning in a circle of devastation.

"Sarge!" Grimaldi called loud enough to be heard, even though the earpiece was dangling and bouncing on Bolan's shoulder.

He plucked up the bean-size speaker and tucked it back into place, gulping down fresh air, regaining his strength.

"I'm fine," he said through his throat mike.

"What the hell was that?" Grimaldi asked.

"That was Dark's getaway plan," the Executioner answered.

"Are you okay?"

"No way in hell," Bolan answered. "But nothing serious. I'll be fine."

The Executioner watched the circle of burning cars, his intellect telling him that no living human being could have survived that blast. In the ensuing investigation, it would be confirmed that the car had twenty kilograms of plastic explosives loaded into various compartments, presumably to erase all evidence of Dark's presence inside the vehicle. There were leftovers of a body found within, fragments of bone and teeth that somehow had survived an inferno that didn't even leave a piece of the original automobile larger than a corn flake. DNA testing was impossible, even with the swabs of blood from the site of Bolan's fight with him, and dental records were a joke. Even if they had records on the original madman, the fire was so hot it cracked teeth and the explosion splintered the jaw into a thousand shards.

The facts told him one thing.

His heart told him that the Dark never was so easily dispersed.

After all, in a former lifetime, Colonel John Phoenix rose from the ashes of an Executioner.

He turned, looking back up into the garage.

The Executioner had no fear of the dark. But from now on, he'd be a little extra aware of the dangers within it.

The RING.

The Army of the Hand of Christ.

The Abu Sayyaf Group.

The Fist of God.

Dark, risen from the grave.

He'd be ready for every single one of them.

EPILOGUE

The morning light was coming through the window, and after a night of healing lovemaking, Sable Burton was rested, even though she'd only dozed off for a half hour. The soldier's stamina was amazing, but he was also gentle, exploratory, and when he found a place where he could give her pleasure, he seized upon it as if it were a weak point, the target of a precision military raid giving her the most joy possible. Burton returned that passion and found herself rising to levels of lovemaking she hadn't realized she was capable of.

She looked over at Brandon Stone, his craggy face, handsome despite the bruising and the surgical tape on one cheek. Even then, that side of his face was resting on the pillow, his eyes closed in restful slumber. She felt the urge to bend over and kiss him again, but decided to let him sleep. He struck her as the type of man who easily awakened.

She crawled out of the bed and walked toward the bathroom.

There was a knock at the door.

She looked back to Stone, who hadn't moved in the

bed, then hustled to the bathroom, grabbed a robe and went to answer it, closing the bedroom door behind her.

It was Hector Terin, dressed in a suit. Behind him, the hulking form of one of his bodyguards loomed, glaring at her from behind mirrored sunglasses. Burton pulled her robe tighter around herself.

"Mr. Terin," she greeted.

"Hello, Professor. I hope I didn't wake you up," Terin said. His suit was all sharp creases and he was the ultimate in neatness, from his razor-thin mustache to his knife-pleated slacks. Burton wondered why her eyes weren't cut to ribbons looking upon such a hard-edged man.

"What did you want, sir?" Burton asked. She held out her hand, pointing to the sofa.

Terin sighed as he entered, closing the door on his bodyguard. "Just to tie up some loose ends."

"What?"

The door suddenly kicked in hard, the frame splintering as the handle and lock were booted through the wood. The ruined remains swung slowly inward, the hulking figure with the mirrored shades looking through the wreckage he'd created.

"Well, it seems that someone broke into your home this morning, raped and murdered you. Really a shame," Terin said. She noticed that he was tugging on black leather gloves.

Burton took a step back, forcing herself not to look at the bedroom door.

"Mr. Terin, Hector…what… Why?"

"Just in case Glen told you anything about my outside dealings."

He reached out and grabbed a handful of robe and

pulled the woman forward. She feinted with her fingers stabbing at Terin's face. When he caught her wrist, she brought up her knee. Instead of hitting his groin, the CEO blocked with his thigh and twisted her around, wincing at the force of her blow.

"Dammit. Get the door, Eugene," Terin growled.

The wall of human flesh in a black three-piece suit strode to the bedroom door. He bent to turn the handle when it flew open, a pair of rippling, bare arms reaching out and yanking Eugene face-first into the frame. The mirrored shades snapped in two on contact, a crunching collision that sent the huge thug stumbling backward.

Bolan burst through the door, swinging up his foot and catching the henchman right in the gut, folding him over. Grabbing both sides of his head, the Executioner snapped the goon face-first into his knee and gave a savage twist that ended in the sound of neckbones crackling.

Eugene slumped bonelessly to the carpeting, only moments after he tried to open the door.

"Hector," Bolan said.

"Colonel Stone," Terin replied, pulling Burton into him as a human shield.

"Let the professor go," he demanded, aiming the 93-R at the CEO.

"Or what? You'll kill me?" Terin asked. "It's your word against mine in a court of law."

"My job isn't to send people to jail. I don't testify against anyone," Bolan answered. "But for the record, tell Sable why you murdered Glen Shephard."

"I can figure that out, Brandon," Burton answered. "Glen found out what his boss was doing, found out enough about his dealings with the RING and its support groups...and he killed him."

Terin chuckled. "Almost, but not quite the whole story, cutie pie."

Burton felt herself being lifted farther off the carpeting.

Terin kissed her ear before continuing to speak. "See, I wasn't sure that Glen was all for really doing the right thing."

"The right thing?" Bolan asked. "Give me a break."

"How about her little neck?" Terin taunted.

"So that's why your home looked tossed," Bolan said. "Glen was getting evidence to take to the authorities."

"That's when I decided that he'd be perfect for a little trade. Seems the Army of the Hand of Christ needed the body of a man about six-two, six-three, two hundred pounds," Terin answered.

Bolan's eyes narrowed and Burton's heart skipped a beat.

Could it have been?

"Killing two birds with one stone," Bolan said, interrupting Burton's speculations.

"You could say that, Colonel *Stone*. Kindly point that thing in some other direction. You're making me nervous."

"I'll keep it aimed right where it is now. Why did you do it?" Bolan asked. "Can't be money, you've got pockets deeper than Bill Gates with your military contracts."

"I'm doing it to make sure that the world will be worth living in."

Something clicked beneath Burton's elbow, sharp metallic tics that made her spine shiver at the thought of a gun pressed to her kidney.

"And so you kill innocent people?" Bolan asked.

"Burton? This bitch is a sinner. Shephard? A traitor to Christ."

"Christ said to love thy neighbor."

Terin smirked. "He also said to sell thy cloak to buy a sword to defend thyself."

Bolan frowned. "Defend thyself. Not murder."

"Who are you to make that kind of distinction? God?"

"God would forgive," Burton said. "He doesn't."

"Not really," Bolan said. "I forgive small stuff."

"And the 'big stuff'?" Terin asked.

The sound-suppressed machine pistol chugged and hot, sticky gore splashed into her hair again. This time the woman barely flinched, only clenching her eyes tight against the gooey mess that was now dripping like raw pulp down her neck and into her ear.

"Fire and forget," Bolan answered, lowering his Beretta. He rushed forward to catch Burton, but she managed to keep standing as Hector Terin's decapitated body slumped to the floor like a sack of boneless meat.

She looked down over her shoulder. "This is why you don't stick around."

Bolan squeezed her tight. "Think of the cleaning bills you'd save without a fresh corpse on the carpet every month."

"And this is the second time in three days I'm covered with someone else's brains. Dammit, I don't know if I need therapy or a really good shampoo."

Bolan cupped the back of Burton's head and let her rest her cheek on his chest. "I'll call a friend. He'll take care of things here."

Bolan freed himself from her embrace for a moment and closed what was left of the door after checking to make sure nobody was in the hall snooping. The handle and lock were gone, and there was a split down the center, but with the umbrella stand acting as a doorstop, it would give them enough privacy.

Burton looked at the splattered corpse of Terin, then to the lump of insensate flesh of the bodyguard.

"Brandon..." She began. "I'm sorry. I'm just not cut out for all this."

"You don't have to be. Now you know."

THE CLEANUP CREW wasn't long. Her carpet was deep-cleaned, the door frame repaired, a swarm of activity to remove every ounce of evidence of a death in her living room.

With a queasy emptiness, she noticed that the biggest evidence of anyone being killed in her living room, Brandon Stone himself, was gone. She wiped away a tear as Hal Brognola's crew of irregulars finished their job.

The mystery man was gone again, no longer a mystery to her.

TAKE 'EM FREE

2 action-packed novels plus a mystery bonus

NO RISK
NO OBLIGATION TO BUY